"I wanted to be alone with you."

"We could have been alone walking down the pier."

"That did occur to me, but you're not dressed for the cold night." He lowered his gaze as if pondering the pattern his fingers were painting on her palm. He raised his eyes a moment later and she gasped. Gentleness and humor were gone, that grim god of the desert back. She shuddered with the fierceness of her response. "You know where I really want to be alone with you. In my place. In my bed."

Dear Reader,

When I wrote "The End" in my first Desire™ trilogy, THRONE OF JUDAR, I was already dreaming of a sequel in the neighboring allied kingdom of Zohayd. I am so excited to be realizing this dream and beginning my new trilogy, PRIDE OF ZOHAYD, starring princes Shaheen, Harres and Amjad.

The trilogy kicks off with the youngest brother, Shaheen, who is about to sacrifice his freedom for his kingdom in a marriage of state. Then he meets the woman of his dreams and everything changes. But like every profound love story, everything is against them, from his commitments to a brewing conspiracy that could topple the royal house of Zohayd and plunge the whole region into chaos. The worst part is that his beloved Johara and her father are the main suspects or at least seem to be pivotal instruments in his family's plotted downfall.

Will his love stand the test of shocking revelations and discoveries? Will he and his brothers succeed in uncovering the conspiracy and defending their throne and kingdom before it's too late?

I adored writing Shaheen and Johara's story, and I hope you enjoy reading it! I would love to hear from you at oliviagates@gmail.com. You can also visit me on the web at www.oliviagates.com.

Enjoy, and thanks for reading.

Olivia Gates

TO TAME A SHEIKH

BY
OLIVIA GATES

Published in Great Britain 2011
by Mills & Boon, an imprint of Harlequin (UK) Limited,
Eton House, 18-24 Paradise Road, Richmond, Surrey TW9 1SR

© Olivia Gates 2010

ISBN: 978 0 263 88326 8

51-1211

Harlequin (UK) policy is to use papers that are natural, renewable and recyclable products and made from wood grown in sustainable forests. The logging and manufacturing processes conform to the legal environmental regulations of the country of origin.

Printed and bound in Spain
by Blackprint CPI, Barcelona

Olivia Gates has always pursued creative passions—singing and many handicrafts. She still does, but only one of her passions grew gratifying enough, consuming enough, to become an ongoing career. Writing.

She is most fulfilled when she is creating worlds and conflicts for her characters, then exploring and untangling them bit by bit, sharing her protagonists' every heart-wrenching heartache and hope, their every heart-pounding doubt and trial, until she leads them to an indisputably earned and gloriously satisfying happy ending.

When she's not writing, she is a doctor, a wife to her own alpha male and a mother to one brilliant girl and one demanding Angora cat. Visit Olivia at www.oliviagates.com.

To Mom, my daughter and Maria.
I hope you know how much each of you helped me
in writing this book. Love you all.

One

Johara Nazaryan had come to see the only man she'd ever love.

Before he married someone else.

Her heart sputtered on a mixture of anticipation, dread and despondence as her eyes scanned the throngs of top-fashion, highest-class denizens of the party being thrown in his honor.

There was still no sign of Shaheen Aal Shalaan.

She drew in a choppy breath and pressed deeper into her corner, hoping to continue avoiding attention. She was thankful for the extra time to compose herself even as she cursed it for giving her more of a chance to work herself up.

She still couldn't believe she'd decided to see him after twelve years.

Oh, she'd drunk in every drop of news of him for all those years, had stolen glimpses of him whenever she was near where she'd heard he'd be from the time she'd started traveling on her own. But this time, she was determined to walk up to Shaheen and say, *Long time no see.*

Shaheen. To the world he was a prince of the wealthy desert kingdom of Zohayd, the youngest of King Atef Aal Shalaan's three sons from the deceased queen Salwa. He was also a businessman who'd risen in the past six years to become one of the most respected powers in the worlds of construction and transportation.

To Johara he'd always be the fourteen-year-old boy who'd saved her life twenty years ago.

She was six then, on her first day in Zohayd, where she'd come to live in the royal palace with her family. Her Armenian-American father had been appointed first assistant to the royal jeweler, Nazeeh Salah. It had been "Uncle" Nazeeh, her father's mentor, who'd suggested her name, *jewel* in Arabic.

During her father's interview with the king, she'd slipped onto the terrace and ended up falling off its balustrade and dangling from the ledge. At her screams, everyone had come running. Unable to reach her, her father had thrown her a rope noose to slip around her wrist. As she'd tried to put it on, someone below her had urged her to let go. With panic bursting in her heart, she'd looked down.

And she'd seen him.

He'd seemed too far away to be able to catch her. But as her parents had screamed for her to hang on, she'd let go of the ledge and plummeted down the thirty-foot drop, just knowing he would.

And as fast and precise and powerful as the hawk he was named for, he had. He'd swooped in, plucked her from midair and welcomed her into the haven of his arms.

She still dissected those fraught moments from time to time. She knew she would have been able to slip the rope on. But she'd chosen to trust her safety to that magnificent creature who'd looked up at her with strength and assurance radiating from his fiery-brown eyes.

From that day on, she'd known. She'd always be his. And not only because he'd saved her. With every day that passed, the knowledge that he was the most incredible person she'd ever met had solidified, as he became her older brother Aram's best friend and far more than that to her.

But as she'd grown older, she'd realized that her dream of being his one day was impossible.

Shaheen was a prince. She was the daughter of a servant. Even though her father had become the royal jeweler, who both designed new jewelry for the royal family and had the all-important responsibility of maintaining the nation's highest treasure, the Pride of Zohayd royal jewels, he was still an underling, a foreigner who came from a poor background and had worked his way to his current position through his extraordinary talent.

And then, Shaheen wouldn't have looked at her that way even if she were the daughter of the noblest family in Zohayd. He had always been incredibly nice to her, but when it came to romantic partners, he'd had the world's most beautiful, sophisticated women falling at his feet from the time he turned seventeen. Back then, she'd been certain she possessed no beauty and would never attain any sophistication. But she'd found it enough to be near him, to love him.

For eight blissful years, Shaheen had offered her indulgence and friendship. To stay near him, she'd chosen to remain with her father when her parents had separated when she was twelve and her French mother had left Zohayd to go back home and continue her career in fashion design.

Then, suddenly, it was over. Just before her fourteenth birthday, Shaheen had abruptly pulled away from both her brother and her. Aram had told her that Shaheen thought it time to stop fraternizing with the "help" to observe his role as a prince of Zohayd.

Though she couldn't believe it of Shaheen and thought Aram's bitterness had other origins she couldn't guess at, Shaheen's sudden distance was still a wake-up call.

For, really, what did she have to look forward to but to love him, unrequitedly, until he one day entered the marriage of state that was his destiny? He might even have turned away from her because he suspected her feelings for him and was being cruel to be kind. His withdrawal *had* influenced her decision to leave. A few weeks after her birthday, she'd left Zohayd to live in France with her mother. She'd never returned.

Ever since that day, Johara had found comfort from the sense of loss only when she found news of Shaheen, saw that he was doing phenomenally well on every front. She'd felt she was entitled to hold on to that secret, one-sided love.

But now, the blade was about to fall and she'd never again have the right to indulge her emotions, even in the privacy of her heart and mind. And she had to see him. *Really* see him. One last time…before he committed himself to another.

She'd slipped into the farewell party that one of his business partners, Aidan McCormick, was throwing for him in New York City. If anyone questioned her presence, she'd easily defend her right to be there. As a jewelry and fashion designer who'd been making a splash beyond France in the past couple of years, she was considered one of the glitterati who were expected to stud such a function.

But validating her presence wasn't the difficult part. That was still to come. Working up the nerve to approach Shaheen.

She was praying one thing would happen when she did. That she'd find out that she'd blown him all out of proportion in her mind, and her feelings for him, as well.

Suddenly, a wave of goose bumps swept her from toes to scalp.

She turned around, the rustle of her taffeta dress magnified in her ears.

Shaheen was here.

For a long moment, she couldn't see him. But the people-packed space receded into a void where his presence radiated like a beacon. Not from the entrance, where her gaze had been glued for the past two hours, but from the other side of the room. It made no sense, until she realized he must have used McCormick's private elevator.

His aura, his vibe, hit her like a gut punch.

Then she saw him. Only him.

Everything stilled inside her. In awe. In confusion.

He'd towered over her before, though she'd been five foot seven at fourteen. Now she stood six feet wearing two-inch heels, and he still outstripped her by what appeared to be half a foot. Had she never realized how imposing he was?

No. This wasn't the Shaheen she remembered. This was new.

He'd been twenty-two the last time she'd seen him up close. She'd seen him in the flesh half a dozen times since, most recently a year ago, across a ballroom in Cannes. But during those stolen sightings, she'd barely gotten more than an impression of vitality and virility, of class and power. She'd seen photographs and footage of him throughout the years, but it was clear that neither memory, nor sightings from afar nor photographic evidence had transmitted any measure of the truth.

Sure, he'd been like a god to her anyway, but it seemed there were levels of godhood. And his present rank was at the top of the scale. A desert god, forged from its heat and hardness and harshness, from its mystery and moodiness and magnificence.

His all-black formal silk suit and shirt clung to a breadth that was almost double his younger size. There wasn't an inch of padding to his shoulders, no boosting of the power of his chest, no accentuation to the hardness of his abdomen and thighs or the slimness of his waist and hips. If he'd had the lithe power of a young hawk before, he now packed the powerhouse majesty of a full-grown, seasoned one.

And that was before taking the changes to his face into account. He'd always been what the media had called spectacular, with that wavy mane of deepest tobacco hair, those unique fiery eyes a contrast to his natural tan. Now, with every trace of softness and youth chiseled away to leave a bone structure to tear heartstrings over, he was breathtaking.

But it was his expression—and what it betrayed of his inner state—that sent tremors radiating through her.

Shaheen wasn't happy. He was deeply dissatisfied,

disturbed. Distraught, even. It might not be apparent to anyone else, but she could sense it as deeply as she felt her own turmoil.

All hope of reprieve, of closure, vanished.

If she'd found him serene, content, she would have been able to move on. But now...

At least there was one thing to be thankful for here. He hadn't seen her. And he wouldn't, if she didn't go through with what she'd planned. And maybe she shouldn't.

No. No maybes about it. Approaching him now would have nothing but terrible consequences. If he had this devastating an effect on her while unaware of her presence and standing thirty feet away, what would he do to her face-to-face?

Infatuated, immature moron that she was, she'd achieved only one thing by seeing him again. She'd compounded her problem and added more heartache to deal with. She could now only curtail further damages.

Cursing herself for a fool, she stepped forward to leave. And felt as if she'd slammed into an impenetrable force field.

Shaheen's gaze.

The impact almost demolished her precarious balance as his eyes bored through her.

She'd always thought they resembled burning coals, even when he'd trained them on her with utmost kindness. But now, with the flare of recognition accompanied by a focus searing in intensity and devoid of gentleness, she felt their burn down to her bones. Her blood started to sizzle, her cheeks to steam.

She'd gravely underestimated the size of the mistake

she'd made coming here. She now had no doubt it was one she'd regret for the rest of her life.

She stood, rooted, mesmerized as he approached her, watching him with the same fatalism one would an out-of-control car on a collision course.

Regret had swamped Shaheen the moment he'd set foot in Aidan's sprawling penthouse. It intensified with every step deeper into the cacophony of forced gaiety.

He shouldn't have agreed to come. He should have told Aidan this wasn't a farewell party to him, but a funeral pyre.

And here was his friend and partner, coming to add to his misery with a blithe smile splitting his face.

"Hey, Sheen!" Aidan exclaimed over the skull-splitting techno music. "I thought you'd decided to let me look like a fool. Again."

Shaheen winced an attempt at a smile. He hated it when his friends abbreviated his name to Sheen. His western friends did so because it was a more familiar name to them, and those back home because that was the first letter of his name in Arabic. He didn't know why he put up with it. But then again, what was a nickname he disliked compared to what he would be forced to endure from now on?

Shaheen peered down into his friend's grinning face, his lips twisting on his barely leashed irritation. "If I'd known what kind of event you were planning, Aidan, I would have."

"You know what they say about all work and no play." Aidan hooked his arm high up around Shaheen's shoulder.

Shaheen almost flinched. He liked the man, and he did come from a culture where physical demonstrations of affection were the norm, contradictorily between members of the same gender. Apart from immediate family, he didn't appreciate being touched. Even in sexual situations, he didn't like women to paw him, as they seemed to unanimously wish to. His liaisons were about taking off an edge, not about intimacy. He'd made that clear, on a take-it-or-leave-it basis, to all the women he'd had such liaisons with.

He could barely remember his last sexual encounter. Such carnal couplings, devoid of any deeper connection, had lost their appeal and begun to grate, to defile. To be expected, he guessed, when the women he liked and respected didn't arouse any carnal inclinations in him.

He stepped away smoothly, severing his friend's embrace without letting him feel the distaste behind the move. "If being dull is the opposite of this…frenzy, I assure you, I prefer it."

A disconcerted expression seeped into Aidan's eyes, replacing the teasing. After six years of business partnership, the man had no idea what Shaheen appreciated. Probably because he kept Aidan, like everyone else, at arm's length. But Aidan had set this up with the best of intentions. And though those usually led to hell, it wasn't fair to show him how wasted his efforts truly were.

He gathered the remnants of his decorum. "But it's not every day I say goodbye to my freedom. So the… fanfare is…" he paused before he forced himself to add "…welcome."

Aidan's face cleared, and his words came out in the rush of the eager to please. "It's not like you'll really lose your freedom. I hear these royal arranged marriages are the epitome of…flexibility." Aidan added that last word with a huge wink and slap on the back.

Shaheen almost snapped his oblivious friend's head off. It was a good thing Aidan turned away from him, exclaiming at the top of his voice to the people who'd flocked over to shake Shaheen's hand.

Shaheen set himself on auto, performing as Aidan wished him to. No point in setting Aidan straight anyway. He wasn't really all there with a few drinks in him. Shaheen should let him wallow in his rare surrender to heedlessness without dragging him into the land of harsh reality where *he* now existed.

His whole existence was about to cave in.

Not on the professional level. There, he'd never stopped soaring from one success to another. But on the personal level, things had been unraveling for a long time. He could even pinpoint the day when it had all started to go downhill. His fight with Aram.

Before that point, he'd lived a carefree existence where he'd felt his future was limitless. But things had gone from bad to worse since then.

He'd long known that, as a prince, he was expected to make a marriage of state, but he'd always shoved that expectation to the back of his mind, hoping that one or both of his older brothers would make a terrific political match. Then Amjad, his oldest brother and crown prince, *had* made such a match. And it had ended in disaster.

Amjad's wife had come to the marriage already pregnant, had schemed to murder Amjad and pass the child as his, to remain forever a princess and the mother of the heir to the throne.

After Amjad had divorced her in a scandal that still resounded in the region, he'd torn through the world acquiring power until he'd become almost as powerful as all of Zohayd put together. No one dared ask him to make another political match. He'd said that, when it was time for him to become king, his brother Harres would be his heir. Failing that, Shaheen. Period.

As for Harres, he would never make a political match, either. It had been agreed that his marriage into any tribe in the region would compromise his position. He'd become the best minister of interior and head of central intelligence and homeland security that Zohayd had ever had, and no one wanted to see the belief in his impartiality tainted. So, if he ever decided to marry—which seemed unlikely, since he hadn't favored any particular woman of the reported hundreds he'd bedded in his thirty-six years—Harres would nevertheless be free to choose his own wife.

So it fell to Shaheen to make a blood-mixing marriage that would revitalize the wavering pacts between factions. He was the last of the king's "pure-blood" sons, born to a purely Zohaydan queen. Haidar and Jalal, Shaheen's half brothers from the current queen, Sondoss, who was Azmaharian, weren't considered pure enough for the unification the marriage was required to achieve.

For years now, he'd known there was no escape from his fate, but instead of becoming resigned to the idea, he'd hated it more daily. It felt like a death sentence hanging over his head.

Only days ago—the day following his thirty-fourth birthday, to be exact—he'd decided to get the suffocating suspense over with, turn himself in to the marriage pact. He'd announced his capitulation to his father, told him to start lining up the bridal candidates. The next day, the news that he was seeking a bride had been all over the media. As one of the most eligible royals in the world, his intention to marry—with the identity of the bride still undecided—was the stuff of the most sensational news.

And here he was, enduring the party his associate was throwing for him to celebrate his impending imprisonment.

He flicked a look at his watch, did a double take. It had been only *minutes*. And he'd shaken a hundred hands and grimaced at double that many artificially elated or intoxicated faces.

Enough. He'd make his excuses to Aidan and bolt from this nightmare. Aidan was probably too far gone to miss him, anyway.

Deciding to do just that, he turned around…and all air left his lungs. Across the room, he saw…*her*.

The jolt of recognition seemed to bring the world to a staggering halt. Everything held its breath as he met her incredible dark eyes across the vast, crowded space.

He stood there for a stretch that couldn't be calculated on a temporal scale, staring at her. Hooks of awareness snapped across the distance and sank into him, flesh and senses, causing animation to screech through him for the first time in over twelve years.

There was no conscious decision to what he did next. A compulsion far beyond his control propelled him in her direction, as if he were hypnotized, remote-controlled.

The crowd parted as if pushed away by the power of his urge. Even the music seemed to observe the significance of the moment as it came to an abrupt stop.

He finally stopped, too, just feet away. He kept that much distance between them so his gaze could sweep her from head to foot.

He devoured his first impressions of her. Gold and bronze locks that gleamed over creamy shoulders and lush breasts encased in deepest chocolate off-the-shoulder taffeta the color of her eyes, the dress nipping in at an impossibly small waist then flaring over softly curved hips into a layered skirt. A face sculpted from exquisiteness, eyes from intelligence and sensitivity, cheeks from inborn class, a nose from daintiness, and lips from passion.

And those were the broad brushstrokes. Then came the endless details. He'd need an hour, a day, to marvel at each.

"Say something." He heard the hunger in his rasp, saw its effect on her.

She shuddered, confusion rising to rival the searing heat in her eyes.

"I…"

Elation bubbled through him. "Yes. You. Say something so that I can believe you're really here."

"I'm… I don't…" She paused, consternation knotting her brow. It only enhanced her beauty.

But he'd heard enough of her rich, velvet voice to know it matched her uniqueness, echoed her perfection.

"You don't know what to say to me? Or you don't know where to start?"

"Shaheen, I…"

She stopped again, and his heart did, too. For at least three heartbeats. He felt almost dizzy, hearing her utter his name.

A finger below her chin tilted her face up to him, to pore into those eyes he felt he'd fallen into whole.

Then he whispered, "You know me?"

Two

He didn't recognize her?

Johara gaped at Shaheen as the realization sank through her, splashed like a rock into her gut.

She should have known that he wouldn't.

Why should he? He'd probably forgotten she existed.

Even if he hadn't, she looked nothing like the fourteen-year-old he'd known.

That was due in part to her own late blooming and in part to her mother's influence. In Zohayd, Jacqueline Nazaryan had always downplayed Johara's looks. Her mother had later told her she'd known that Johara, having inherited her height and luminescent coloring and her father's bone structure and eyes, would become a tall, curvaceous blonde who possessed a paradoxical brand of beauty. And in the brunette, petite-woman–dominated Zohayd, a woman like Johara would be both a prized jewel and a source of endless trouble. If she'd learned to emphasize her looks, she would have become the target of dangerous desires and illicit offers, heaping trouble on her and her father's head. Her mother had left her in Zohayd secure that Johara had no desire and no means of achieving her potential and would continue looking nondescript.

Once she'd joined her mother in France, Jacqueline had encouraged her to showcase her beauty and had done everything she and her fashion-industry colleagues could to help Johara blossom into a woman who knew how to wield what she was told were considerable assets.

As Johara became a successful designer and business-woman herself, she learned her mother had been right. Most men saw little beyond the face and body they coveted. Several rich and influential men had tried to acquire her as another trophy to bolster their image, another check on their status report. She'd been fully capable of turning them down, without incident so far. Without the repercussions her mother had feared would have accompanied the same rejections in Zohyad.

So yes. She'd been crazy to think Shaheen would recognize her when the lanky, reed-thin duckling he'd known had become a confident, elegant swan.

And here he was. Looking at her without the slightest flicker of recognition. That instant awareness, that flare of delight at the sight of her hadn't been that. It had been...

What had it been? What was that she saw playing on his lips, blazing in his eyes as he inclined his awesome head at her? What was it she felt electrocuting her from his fingers, still caressing her chin? Was it possible he...?

"Of course you know who I am." Shaheen cut through her feverish contemplations, shook his head in self-deprecation. The flashes from the mirror balls and revolving disco lights shot sparks of copper off the luxury of his mane and into the fathomless translucence of his eyes, zapping her into ever-deepening paralysis. "You're attending my farewell party, after all."

She remained mute. He thought she recognized him only because he was a celebrity in whose name he thought she was here having free drinks and an unrepeatable networking opportunity.

He relinquished her chin only to let the back of his fingers travel in a gossamer up-down stroke over her almost combusting cheek. "So to whom should I offer my unending thanks for inviting you here?"

Her heart constricted as the reality of the situation crystallized.

She hadn't even factored in that he might not know her on sight. But she'd conceded she shouldn't have expected it. But that there was nothing about her that jogged any sense of familiarity in him—that she couldn't rationalize. Or accept.

Her insides compacted in a tight tangle of disappointment.

His words and actions so far had had nothing to do with happiness at seeing her after all these years. There was only one reason he could have approached her, was talking to her, looking at her this way. It seemed absurd, unthinkable. But she could find no other explanation.

Shaheen was coming on to her.

As if he'd heard her thoughts, he seemed to tighten all of his virility and influence around her, dropping his voice an octave, sinking it right through to her core. "This will sound like the oldest line in the book, but even though you haven't said one complete sentence to me yet and we met just minutes ago, I feel like I've known you forever."

The music chose that second to blare again, as if accentuating his announcement, cutting off any possibility of her blurting out that he felt that way because he had.

At the deafening intrusion, he dropped his hand from her cheek, raised his head, his eyes releasing hers from their snare as he cast an annoyed look at the whole scene. He caught her again with the full force of his focus a moment later. "This place is incompatible with human sanity." His eyes forged another path of fire down her body to where her purse was hanging limply from her hand. "I see you've got your bag with you. Shall we go?"

She gasped as currents forked through her from where his hand curved around her upper arm in courteous yet compelling invitation. "B-but it's your party."

His eyes crinkled at her as his lips spread, revealing the even power of his teeth. "*Aih*, and I'll leave if I want to." His thumb swept the naked flesh of her arm, causing a firestorm to ripple through her as though through a wheat field in a storm. "And how I want to."

Her free fist came up, pressing against a heart that seemed to be trying to ram out of her chest cavity.

The world had always transformed into a wonderland when he smiled. But this was…ridiculous. There should be a law against his indulging in the practice in inhabited areas!

She blinked, her sluggish gaze drifting from his at the pull of something vague. And she blinked again. In disbelief.

She was no longer in the middle of the party. She was in a spacious marble hall, walking on jellified legs toward what she judged to be McCormick's private elevator.

Had she really walked here? Or had he teleported them?

Suddenly it was all too much. His every move and glance stripping her of basic coherence, his very nearness inching her to the verge of collapse as she and the situation spiraled out of control. He didn't have the slightest memory of her, was enacting this aggressive seduction based on her anonymity, confident of her availability.

Still, only when they stopped in front of the elevator did she manage to attempt to extract herself smoothly from his loose yet incapacitating grip. Her spinning senses made her stumble back instead, wrenching her arm away.

She could see astonishment reverberate through him as the spectacular wings of his eyebrows snapped together and his lips lost the fullness of intimacy, chiseling into harsher lines that accentuated their perfection. And showed her yet another side of him that she'd never been exposed to—the ruthless royal he could become when provoked or displeased.

So he couldn't comprehend that a female would have the temerity to not fall all over herself to obey his decrees? Maybe this encounter would end in closure, after all. Just in a different way than she'd imagined.

She glared her disillusion up into his eyes. "You're so certain I want to leave with you, aren't you?"

Bitterness hardened her voice. She knew he heard it loud and clear, too.

The last of the heat in his gaze drained as stillness descended. "Yes, I am. As certain of my desire to leave with you."

She huffed her fury. "You're right. You *are* spouting the oldest lines in the book."

His pupils expanded, almost engulfed his vivid irises. "I realize they sound like that, but they happen to be true."

Her lips twisted, mimicking a fiercer contortion of her heart. "Sure they are."

"You think I'm so lacking in imagination or finesse that I'd use something so hackneyed to express myself if it wasn't the simple truth, and no other words would do?"

"Maybe you're just too lazy, too jaded to think of something new. Or you can't even fathom the possibility that you might need a new line. Or maybe you didn't think I warranted the effort of coming up with something a tad more original, since you thought I'd fall flat on my back at the idea of your interest."

He seemed more taken aback at every word firing from her lips, his scowl dissolving into a flabbergasted look.

She was as shocked as he was. Where had all that come from? It was as if pressure had been building up inside her, and disappointment was a blade that had slashed across the thin membrane holding it in, her feelings bursting out of containment.

She'd just loved him for so long!

She'd fantasized about how it would be if they met again, and reality had demolished every comforting scenario. His indiscriminating carnal purpose made a mockery of the soul-deep connection she'd been convinced they'd resurrect on sight. A connection, it seemed, that existed only inside her lovesick mind.

The insupportable deduction squeezed more resentment from her depths. "And didn't it occur to you that the person you felt you owed unending thanks to for bringing me here might be my boyfriend, or even my fiancé or husband?"

All expression evaporated, leaving his face a hard mask. "No. It didn't."

"It didn't, or the possibility of my being committed to another man didn't seem relevant to you?"

"You *can't* be. I would have felt something, from you, a connection with someone else, a disconnection from me. But—"

He stopped abruptly. That limitless energy that had radiated from him from the moment he'd caught her eye flickered, wavered. Then it blinked out. The gloom she'd thought she'd seen tainting his aura before he'd noticed her descended on him again like a roiling thundercloud, seeming to slump his formidable shoulders under its weight.

He closed his eyes, swept a palm over his eyes and forehead. His other hand joined in, raking up through his hair before rubbing down his face.

Then he let his hands drop to his sides, leveled his eyes at hers. The bleakness there shriveled her insides.

"I don't know what came over me. I saw you across the room and I thought… No, I didn't think. I *knew*. I was certain you looked at me with the same…recognition. That sense I've heard people experience when they meet someone who's…right. It must have been a trick of the lights. Your recognition was of the literal variety, and I saw what I subconsciously wanted to see. I must be in worse shape than even I thought, imagining I'd found an undeniable connection at such a party. Or at all. I apologize. To you, and to your man. I should have known you'd be taken."

His fists clenched and unclenched as he spoke, as if

they itched with the same sick electricity discharging inside her limbs. Then with a shake of his head and an indecipherable imprecation, he turned away.

She stood feeling as if she'd been struck by lightning, watching his long strides take him away from her. All she could think was that he didn't seem callous or indiscriminating, only hurt, and that the last thing she'd ever see of him was that look of despondency on his face.

"It was a hypothetical question."

At her squeaking statement, he stopped. But didn't turn. He only inclined his face so that she saw his profile, eyes cast downward, tension emanating from him in shockwaves.

She forced the explanation he was waiting for between barely working lips. "When I mentioned a boyfriend or fiancé or husband, it was only in a 'what if' scenario. I don't have anyone."

"You're not taken." His hoarse whisper shuddered through her as he turned toward her, animation creeping back into his face. She shook her head, had locks snaring in her trembling mouth. "You objected to me sweeping you away because—" he accentuated every other word with a leisurely step back to her side, each hitting her like a seismic wave "—you mistook me for a lazy, jaded oaf who doesn't possess an original bone in his body to express his inability to wait to be alone with you, or a poetic cell with which to do justice to the wonder of our meeting."

She was panting as he fell silent. "Okay, I hereby revise my opinion. You have nothing but original bones and poetic cells."

The elation reclaiming his expression spiked on a guffaw. Her knees almost buckled. And that was before a hunger-laden step obliterated the last of the distance between them. Every hair on her body stood on end as if with a giant static charge.

Then he whispered, "Tell me you feel it, too. Tell me the almost tangible entity I sense between us exists, that I'm not having a breakdown and imagining things."

This was the second time he'd alluded to his condition. The idea of his suffering spread thorns in her chest. She bit her lip on the pain. "The...entity exists."

"I am going to touch you now. Will you shake me off again, or do you want me to?" She shook her head, nodded, groaned. Her teeth would start clattering any moment now with needing his touch.

He took both her arms in the warm gentleness of his hands. Then he pulled her to him. She stumbled forward, ended up with her head where she'd dreamed of having it since she'd been old enough to form memories. Where it had rested once before, during that moment that had changed her destiny. On the endlessness of his chest. He pressed it there with a hand that smoothed her hair, his rumbling purr of enjoyment echoing her own.

He finally sighed. "This is unprecedented. We've had our first fight and reconciliation before you've even told me your name."

"It wasn't really a fight," she whispered as she pulled back a bit, so she could breathe, so her heart wouldn't stop.

He smiled down at her, his eyes telling her she delighted him. "Not on my end, but you were about to claw my eyes out. And I would have gladly let you. But I'm not putting it off any longer. Your name, *ya ajaml makhloogah fel kone*. Bless me with its gift."

He'd just called her the most beautiful creature in the universe. He probably didn't realize he had spoken in his native tongue, or he would have tagged it with a translation.

"J…" Her voice vanished on a convulsive swallow as he drew nearer still, as if to inhale her name when she uttered it like the most pleasurable fragrance, like life-sustaining air.

And she realized she couldn't tell him who she was.

If she did, he'd pull back. There would be embarrassment, consternation followed by distance and decorum. And she couldn't bear to lose this moment of spontaneity with him.

It would be the last thing she had of him.

"Gemma."

She almost slapped herself upside the head. Gemma? Did she have to go for a literal translation? How obvious could she get?

But then, she'd started to say her name, and he would have thought it suspicious if she'd gone on to say Dana or Sara or something. Gemma had been the only name that had come to her that started with a *J* sound.

Before she made it worse, she had to tell him how nice it was to meet him and walk away. *Run* away. Without looking back. She had the rest of her life to look back on this magical encounter.

He thwarted her feverish plans, pressed her head closer as he sighed his contentment. "Gemma. Perfect, *ya joharti*." She lurched at hearing her real name. Before she could have a heart attack, he loosened his embrace, smiled his pleasure. "That's 'my jewel' in my mother tongue. So, my precious Gemma, will you come with me?"

"Where?" she choked.

"As long as you're with me, does it matter?"

* * *

It was clear by now that nothing mattered.

Not to Johara. Not when measured against wringing this opportunity to be with Shaheen of its last possible glance and smile, touch and comeback. Of the sheer unbridled joy of being the object of his interest, the target of his appreciation, the instigator of his desire.

Another breaker of pleasure frothed inside her as she beheld him, a vision made man, sitting across from her in the exclusive restaurant he'd made literally so for their dinner.

They'd been talking nonstop since they'd left McCormick's penthouse. She'd answered his questions about herself without specifying names or places, and nothing she told him had rung any bells. That still rankled, but her thankfulness for this time out of time his unawareness afforded her with him surpassed any disappointment.

"Do you want to know what the maitre d' told me after emptying the restaurant?" His eyes glittered at her as his hand covered her upturned palm with hypnotic strokes. "That such heavy-handed tactics wouldn't work on a lady of such refinement as you."

She giggled, surrendered her hand to his possession. "A very astute gentleman."

He gave an exaggerated sigh. "I wish you had told me that before *he* emptied half of my supposed no-limit credit card."

She giggled again at his mock woe. Even in her upheaval, the thrill rose. Her fantasies throughout the years had gotten it right. Their connection *was* there. And he was showering her with the delighted, delighting banter that had always textured and colored her life.

He remained the man she'd loved since she could

remember. No, he was better than that man. Much, much better.

She sighed at the bittersweetness of it all. "But seriously, you shouldn't have gone to any expense. I thought we'd agreed it didn't matter where we were."

"I wanted to be alone with you."

"We could have been alone walking down the pier."

"That did occur to me, but you're not dressed for the cold night." He lowered his gaze as if pondering the pattern he was painting with his fingers on her palm. He raised his eyes a moment later and she gasped. Gentleness and humor were gone, that grim god of the desert back. She shuddered with the fierceness of her response. "You know where I really want to be alone with you, Gemma. In my place. In my bed."

She squeezed her eyelids shut as emotion tore through her.

She couldn't handle this. She shouldn't have sought him out…

His tough rider's fingers smoothed over her eyes, making her open them, so that there was no escaping his fierceness, his intention. "I want you, Gemma. I never knew wanting like this existed, that I could feel anything of this intensity and purity."

"Purity?"

"Yes. It's unclouded, untainted, absolute. I want you, in every way. And you want me in the same way. I know I wouldn't be feeling like this if you didn't also. My desire surges from me as much as it stems from you. It flows to you and is reflected back at me exponentially, then back to you in a never-ending cycle. It's taking on a life of its own, growing too powerful to deny. With every breath its power heightens, sharpens. Will you let me fulfill our desire? Will you let me worship you?"

"Shaheen, please—"

He suddenly pushed his chair back, stood up. Before her heart could stumble on its next beat, he was bending to pluck her from her chair and into his arms. Her head lolled back over his arm with shock as he tightened his hold behind her back, beneath her knees and buried his lips in the neck she exposed to him. "This is all I want to do. Please you. I never want to stop pleasing you."

Voices yelled inside her head. *Tell him who you are. He'll stop this torment the moment he realizes your identity.*

And he'd be furious with her for hiding it. She couldn't let it end like that. With him feeling deceived. And hating her.

She had to say no. He'd abide by her refusal. She hadn't meant for any of this to happen. From the moment he'd caught her eyes and zapped her control across the room, she'd been reacting without volition.

Then she opened her mouth and without any trace of it she whispered, "Yes. Please."

Three

Johara hadn't known what to expect when she'd said yes to Shaheen.

It certainly hadn't been anything that had happened in the two hours since.

After he swept her into his arms and obtained her unconditional capitulation, he put her down, let her walk out of the restaurant and to his limo. He gave his driver an order in Arabic to take the most roundabout way home then sat beside her talking, about everything under the sun. All through the long drive to his penthouse, he didn't touch her at all, except for resuming his thorough fascination with her hand.

For a stretch, he showed her family photos on his phone. He had a few of his father and brothers. They looked much like she remembered, just older and harsher towering specimens of manhood. But the photos were mostly of his aunt Bahiyah, his half sister, Aliyah, and his cousin, Laylah, the only three females born in their family in five generations straight. Shaheen said they were the only ones worth taking and keeping photos of, the vivacious centerpieces of their all-male family, splashes of beauty and grace and exuberance among the range of darkness and drive of what the ladies called their testosterone-compromised relatives.

Aliyah, who was three years older than Johara and who'd seldom been around in the eight years Johara had lived in the palace, had been thought to be King Atef's niece. It was only two years ago that it had been revealed that Princess Bahiyah had adopted her and passed her off as hers from her American husband, when she was actually the king's daughter from an American lover. Instead of causing a scandal, the discovery had aborted the looming wars in the region when Aliyah entered a political marriage with the new king of Judar, Kamal Aal Masood.

Aliyah looked nothing like the sallow, spaced-out girl she remembered. In fact, she looked the epitome of femininity and elegance. And bliss. It was apparent her forced marriage to Kamal had become a love match. Like Shaheen's impending marriage would no doubt become. For what woman wouldn't worship him?

She blinked away the mist of dejection and concentrated on Laylah's photos. The twelve-year old girl she'd been when Johara had last seen her had fulfilled all the promise she'd shown of becoming a spectacular beauty. Johara had never had a chance to really know her, since Laylah's mother, Queen Sondoss's sister, had never let her mingle with the help, as Aram had put it.

Shaheen said Laylah was one of three reasons he forgave his stepmother for existing, since she'd married her sister to his uncle, the other two being his half brothers, Haidar and Jalal. He also said that the ladies reveled in giving their male family members—especially Shaheen and his brothers—a view of a life that didn't have to bend to their wishes. Because of that, along with many other things he could see they shared with Johara, he was certain they would set the palace on fire getting along.

Everything he said alluded to his taking it for granted that her presence in his life would continue beyond tonight. But he must know there was no chance of that.

Yet not only had he already secured her surrender, so he had no reason to say anything more to encourage it, he seemed to believe in what he was saying, to have forgotten the marriage of state he'd announced his intention to enter only four days ago.

She guessed that the marriage was what had been weighing so heavily on him when she'd first seen him. He was loathe to succumb to duty. But it seemed to have slipped his mind since he'd seen her.

She wouldn't remind him. They'd both remember harsh reality soon enough, live with it for the rest of their lives.

Tonight was theirs.

So here she was, standing in the middle of his extensive, austerely masculine foyer, watching him as he hung his jacket and her wrap with tranquil, precise movements.

Why was he wasting their precious time together?

She might not have known what to expect, but she'd thought he'd escalate the urgency he'd shown so far. She'd had visions of him carrying her to the limo, drowning her in kisses all the way here, pressing her against the door the moment they entered and showing her how eager for her he was.

Had he remembered his commitments and decided to cool things off, let her down easy?

She should spare him the discomfort, should leave. She shouldn't have come at all, shouldn't have said yes, shouldn't have gone to that party...

Something whirred, flashed. She blinked in surprise, her left eye riddled in blue spots.

He'd snapped a photo of her with his phone. Now he walked toward her, big and lithe, gloriously male and impossibly beautiful. But it was his expression that made her sway, sending her heart swinging in her chest like a pendulum.

The lightness of the trek here was gone, sizzling sensuality replacing it, setting his eyes deeper on fire and his charisma to a higher level.

He stopped a foot away, reached for the hands he seemed so enamored with. "You looked so...pensive. And if possible, even more breathtaking. This photo is the stuff of the immortal masterpieces the old masters would have begged to portray." He took her hands to his lips, giving each finger a knuckle-by-knuckle introduction to the cosseting of his lips, his eyes empty of all but seriousness. "Are you having second thoughts?"

"No." The denial shot out of her, its fierceness mortifying her as it rang around them. But she had to know. "A-are you?"

He huffed. "The only thoughts I'm having are where to begin worshipping you and how to stop from swallowing you whole."

So that was why he was holding back. He feared being too aggressive. She was being insecure again.

But who could blame her? All through the years, her love for him had been emotional, spiritual, with slight sensual overtones. She'd never imagined he could actually want her, and when she'd fantasized that he did, even in the freedom of her own imagination, he'd done no more than hold and kiss her. Yet she couldn't breathe with wanting all he was willing to give her, with needing to experience him to the fullest.

She swayed closer, her heartbeats merging like the wings of a hummingbird with the enormity of what she was feeling, what she was about to reveal. "B-begin any-where, Shaheen. J-just begin. And don't stop yourself. I don't want you to stop."

His eyes flared with her every faltering word. When she fell into embarrassed, panting silence, he entwined her hands in his, brought them to her face, twisting their embrace around so the backs of his hands stroked up and down her flaming cheeks.

"Then I'll begin here. Your skin. It's incredible, like every part of you. Lush, thick cream, free of paleness and fragility. It doesn't flush with your emotions, no matter how strong, only becomes more vital, more vivid. It's glowing now. Your eyes are gleaming like polished onyxes under spotlights, inundating me with an avalanche of expressions, each intoxicating in its clarity and beauty. And your lips. The way they mold to your every thought, the way they take the shape of your every emotion, the way they tremble to the frequency of each sensation…each tremor shudders through me until I am nothing but uncontainable hunger."

She almost choked with stimulation. "I was right. You are made up of nothing but original bones and poetic cells."

His lips twitched in a lethal mix of appreciation and

predation as he touched the pad of his thumb to hers, stilling those tremors that so affected him. "It seems you didn't hear my last words clearly."

Her lips trembled even more as humor warred with anticipation and agitation. He rubbed his thumbs against them, his breathing becoming harsher.

She closed her eyes to savor the long-dreamed-about sensations. Her wildest imaginings hadn't prepared her for reality. She moaned with the pleasure that cork-screwed through her, emanating from his breath, his nearness, his touch, to her every inch, her deepest reaches. Then her lips did what they'd been longing to do for most of her life—caressed the fragrant warmth and power pressed to them with a trembling kiss.

She heard his intake of breath. It sliced away more of the leashes of her inhibition. She opened her lips, grazed her teeth against his skin. Its texture, its scent, brought more moist heat surging from her core.

A fiercer inhalation expanded his chest until it pressed against her swelling breasts. She knew he could scent her arousal, felt the wildness it sent seething through him. It made her light-headed, the knowledge that she could do this to him, that he was doing this to her, that they had this to share.

Feeling bolder, she swept her tongue against his skin. Her knees did buckle at her first taste of him. He disentangled his other hand, caught her around the waist. She kept her eyes closed as she dove deeper into the sensations, her whole existence centering on his thumb against her tongue as he began to thrust it gently in and out of her mouth.

"This is extremely dangerous." His bass hiss made her eyes snap open. His bore into them before moving to her lips with burning intent as he fed them his thumb, as they suckled it with increasing greed and abandon. She knew what he meant. He still elaborated. "That you want me as fiercely as I want you."

She nodded, breath leaving her body under choppy pressure. She felt she was disintegrating with need for him.

He let go of her waist, grazed across her lower teeth as he slid his thumb lingeringly from between her lips, then dropped his forehead to hers, nuzzling her, inhaling her. "This is unparalleled. Agonizing but sublime."

"Yes," she whispered.

Though she had no experience to back up her belief, she knew the protracted inflammation of their senses was far more satisfying than any frenzied mindless coupling would be.

He eased her away only to glide both arms around her back, to her dress's zipper. He slid it down with torturous slowness, never letting go of her eyes as he went back up to unclasp her bra. She gasped as its constriction eased, and again at the spike of ferocity in his eyes as he monitored her reaction. He drew more gasps from her as he caressed her dress and bra loose, then in one silky sweep, freed her from their shackles.

Before she could snap her arms across her nakedness, he dragged her dress beyond her waist to her hips, dropping downward with it. He ended up on his knees before her.

Her mouth opened, closed, opened again. From unbearable stimulation. From the way he looked her up and down, as if he would truly gobble her up.

Then he pulled her to him, rumbling, "Now, I worship you."

She would have keeled over him if his shoulders hadn't stopped her forward pitch. He added to her imbalance, burying hot lips into her flesh. She whimpered at each press into her abdomen, every tongue thrust into her navel, each tooth drag across her breasts. Her moans sharpened as he gently clamped her nipples, until a cry rushed out at his first hard pull. "Shaheen...*please*."

In answer, he bunched her skirt in his hands, his thumbs hooking into the top of her panties. Then, in one magical move, every shred of covering was shed off of her.

Standing in nothing but her shoes with her clothes pooled at her feet, she felt the world recede. Shaheen looked up, the worshipping he'd promised her setting the hard nobility of his face ablaze.

This was beyond unprecedented. Beyond unparalleled. *She was with Shaheen.* Standing before him naked. She was about to be his in the flesh, just as she was already his in every other way.

She watched as he raised each leg to kiss and fondle from calf to thigh, her consciousness flickering like a bulb about to short out. She heard his magnificent voice as he raggedly lavished far better than poetry on her, spontaneous wonder pouring out in whatever language expressed it best.

She moaned constantly, becoming a literal puddle of arousal by the time he rose. She would have collapsed at his feet if he hadn't swept her up as he stood.

When she flopped in his arms like a ragdoll, he whispered into her ear, "Wrap yourself around me, my Gemma. Cling to me with all of your priceless flesh and desire."

That injected power into her limp muscles. She wanted to. *He* wanted her to. She only ever wished to give him what he wanted.

She clasped her arms around his shoulders, her thighs

around his hips. And it was indescribable. Feeling all of his heat and bulk and power and arousal encased within her limbs, being draped around all of that. She'd be forever empty and anchorless when she no longer had him to enfold, to hang on to like this.

But she had him now.

She rested her head against his shoulder as he strode across his penthouse with her clasped in his arms. Her eyes remained open, but she registered only impressions of his character, his taste and wealth imbuing the spaces, all the more impressive for being unpretentious. Then he crossed into a bedroom. His bedroom.

This was the last thing she'd expected would happen when she'd embarked upon her mission to see him one last time. That she'd end up in his bedroom. In his bed.

But she wanted to be here more than literally anything.

Her senses revved out of their stupor. This was where he slept, where he woke up, where he read and showered and shaved, where he dressed and undressed. Where he pleasured himself. And where she was convinced he'd never pleasured another.

This was his sanctum, when he lived in New York. And he was giving her the exclusive privilege of being here. It would be a one-time pass. She had to make all she could of it.

The huge, high-ceilinged room was lit with only a bedside lamp. Her gaze, avid to soak in more of his privacies and secrets, had just registered the slashes of bold décor, gradations of dark grays and greens with accents of hardwood the color of his eyes when her wandering ones came to a hiccupping halt.

He pressed her against the door as she'd vaguely

hoped he would before, held her there with only his bulk bearing down on her.

She shuddered at the sensory overload. The coolness of the polished wood against her back, the feel of him pressing against her, the heat and hardness of his erection against her intimate flesh with nothing but his clothes between them.

Until minutes ago she'd been too shy to inspect his arousal. Even now she couldn't make the leap of imagining anything beyond this. Her mind almost shut down at the thought of having him inside her. And he hadn't even kissed her on the lips yet....

He raised his head from razing his way down her throat. "And now, I pleasure you, *ya galbi*."

Hearing him call her "my heart" tore a sob from her depths.

He frowned at the sound. "Gemma, if you want me to stop, I will. If you're not totally sure..."

She dragged his head down to her, took the kiss she'd been starving for all of her life.

He stilled under her uncoordinated frenzy, let her smash her lips against his, imploring his reciprocation, his taking over, before he wrenched his lips away.

"What's wrong, my Gemma?" He swept her around, took her to the bed, laid her down on it, where the lighting afforded him the best view of her. And he jerked up in dismay. "You're crying!"

Her hands flailed over his shoulders, trying to drag him back to her. "I-I'm not...I just want you, too much. I can't wait anymore. Please take me, Shaheen. T-take me now."

The concern on his face dissipated, sheer ferocity slamming down in its place. "I want to take you. I want to invade you and ride you until you weep with pleasure this time. But I can't. I have to ready you for me first or I'll hurt you."

"You won't. I'm ready. Just…just…"

"*Galbi,* let me pace this. I need to make it perfect for you."

"It will be perfect. Anything with you is perfect."

He growled something as he dragged her onto his lap. "Don't say one more word, Gemma. If you don't want to have a raving lunatic all over you. I've never even imagined being out of control. But I am now."

She sobbed a giggle. "If this is you out of control, I'd hate to see you in it. You'd probably kill me with frustration."

This time it was his lips that stopped her words, in that kiss she'd imagined since she was old enough to know what kisses were. It turned out she'd never even come close to knowing.

This was a kiss. This tender ferociousness. This gentle devouring. Only this. Shaheen possessing her lips, each sweep and pull and thrust layering sensations, burying her in pleasure. His scent and taste and feel filling her, his hunger finishing her.

She undulated beneath him, until he subdued her, held her arms above her head as his other hand flowed down from her face to her shoulder, ending up cupping the aching heaviness of one breast. "You're only allowed to moan for more, and cry out with pleasure. That will be enough to drive me out of my mind."

"Let me see you," she moaned.

"Not yet. And you're already breaking the rules."

"You said I could moan for more. I am, for more of you."

"You'll have all of me, every way you like. Just not now."

"You're being unfair," she whimpered.

"It's you who's unfair. Nothing should be this magnificent."

She tried to free her hands. She needed them on him, any part of him, without the barrier of clothes.

He growled deep in his chest, spread her back and continued owning her body with his sensual torment. But it was only when he slid her hips to the edge of the bed and kneeled before her again that she realized his intention. Her heart stuttered.

It was stupid to feel embarrassed at having his mouth and hands on her intimate flesh when she was begging for far more. But there it was. She tried to close her legs.

He insisted, caressed them apart. "Open yourself to me, let me feast on you. Let me prepare you."

"I'm prepared," she cried out. "Please!"

"I don't want to hold back when I take you, and only a few climaxes will prepare you for my possession."

"A *few…?*" She choked on incredulity.

What was he going to do to her?

Anything. She'd take anything and everything he did to her.

She opened herself to him and those long, perfect fingers caressed her feminine lips apart, slid through her molten need. She keened, lurched with jolts of sensation almost too much to bear. And that was before he dipped one finger in. Each slow inch felt like pure pleasure. It made her realize how empty she'd felt. How only having him inside her would fill the void.

She tried to drag him up to her with her legs. He only opened her fully and burned her to the core in his ragged hunger.

She malfunctioned completely as his magnificent head settled between her thighs and his lips and tongue scorched the heart of her femininity. The sight, the concept of what he was doing to her, giving her, was almost more incapacitating than the physical sensations.

Through the delirium, she watched him cosset her, strum her, drink her, revel in her essence, in her need and taste and pleasure. He seemed to know when she couldn't take any more.

"Now, *ya roh galbi*, let me see and hear how much I pleasure you." Then his tongue swept her flesh again.

Her body unraveled in a chain-reaction of convulsions, in soul-racking ecstasy, as she held his eyes all through, letting him see what he was doing to her.

She subsided, unable even to beg him to come to her, and he began again, varying his method, renewing her desperation, deepening her surrender.

She'd lost count of how many times he'd wrung her pleasure when at one point he kept her on the brink, came up to straddle her.

He painted her with caresses, kneaded her breasts, gently squeezed her nipples. "I've never seen or tasted anything so beautiful."

Her hands shook on his belt, trying to undo it. "I want to see you—all of you. I want you, inside me, filling my body. Please, Shaheen, please *now*."

He surged up to stand over the bed, over her, stripping off his clothes with barely leashed violence and absolute economy.

Though she was dying for him, the one opportunity she'd have to see his exposed glory took precedence. She swayed to her knees, gaping at his proportionate perfection, the rippling power encased in polished bronze and accentuated with dark silk.

With a cry she surged forward, her hands and lips

seeking all she could reach of him, wanting them everywhere at once.

"Shaheen..." she moaned between kisses "...you're more beautiful than I imagined...I want to worship each inch of you, too."

He threaded his fingers through her hair. "Later, *ya hayati,* we'll worship each other inch for inch. Now I take you. And you take me."

"Yes." She fell to her back, held out her arms.

He surged to her, covered her. She cried out, reveling in how her softness cushioned his hardness.

Perfect. No, sublime. Like he'd said.

She opened her legs, as she'd always opened everything she was to him. He guided them over his waist, his eyes seeking hers, solicitous and tempestuous, his erection seeking her entrance.

Finding both hot and molten, he growled his surrender at last, sank into her in one forceful thrust.

She'd been certain it wouldn't hurt, that she was ready.

But she couldn't have been ready for this. For him.

And it wasn't only her untried body. She was sure experience wouldn't have helped her withstand the first invasion of his girth and length.

It was on the second thrust that he seemed to realize. Why the first had taken such force, found such resistance, why her cry had been so sharp, why her body was so tense and trembling.

He froze. Shock rippled over his face. At last he choked out, "You're a *virgin?*"

"It's okay...I'm okay. Don't stop...please, Shaheen, don't stop."

"B'Ellahi!" he rasped, tried to pull out of her.

She clamped her quaking legs over his hips, stopping him from exiting her body.

"Stop, Gemma!" he growled, resisting her. "I'm hurting you."

"*Yes.*" This made him heave up, his eyes horrified. She only clung harder to him, arms and legs and core. "And the pain is nothing compared to how you feel inside me, is making it all the more…intense. I feel you…branding me. Please…you said you wouldn't hold back."

"This was before I knew you were…!" He shook his head, his disbelief and bewilderment rising. "*Ya Ullah,* I'm your *first.*"

"Are you…disappointed?"

"Disappointed? Try flabbergasted, overwhelmed. *Ya Ullah.*"

Mortification flooded her. Her limbs relinquished their hold on him. "I should have told you. It wasn't a conscious decision not to…but you have no reason to believe that…" She swallowed the weeping jag that was building behind the barrier of her throat. "Let me up. I'll go and you'll never—"

He slid deeper into her, gentler, slower, his eyes heating again. "Does this feel like I'm sorry I'm your first? I already knew you were the biggest gift I'd ever received. But now you've bestowed this on me, and the gift is even bigger. I wish I could offer you something of the same magnitude."

"You *are* giving me the biggest gift, too." Tears were overtaking her. And that would spoil everything. Her lips trembled with what she hoped approximated teasing. "Figuratively *and* literally." He inhaled sharply, grew even bigger inside her. Even through the burning, she

thrust her hips upward, engulfing more of his erection.
"So if you really want to give me a gift, don't hold back.
Give me all of you."

"You do want a raving lunatic all over you, don't
you?"

"Oh, yes, please."

"You say, yes, please, and everything insides me
snaps," he growled as he rose, cupped her hips in his
hands, tilted her and thrust himself to the hilt inside her.
It was overwhelming, being stretched by him, being full
of him, beyond her capacity.

He withdrew, and she cried out at the loss, urged him
to sink back into her. He resisted her squirming pleas
for a moment, his shaft resting at her entrance before
he sank slowly back inside her.

She cried out a hot gust of passion, opening wider for
him. He watched her, gauging her reactions, adjusting
his movements to her every gasp and grimace, waiting
for the pleasure to submerge the pain before he let her
really have all of him, before he quickened his pace. All
through, he kept her at fever pitch, caressing her all over,
suckling her breasts, draining her lips, raining wonder
over her.

Then he groaned into her lips, "Glorious, *ya galbi,*
inside and out, literally and figuratively. Everything
about you, with you."

She keened as her depths started to ripple around
him. As if he knew, he tilted her, angled his thrusts,
and snapped the coil of tension inside her. Convulsion
after convulsion squeezed shrieks out of her, clamped
her tight around him, inside and out.

Only then did he let go, a moment she'd replay in
her memory forever. The sight and feel of him as he

surrendered inside her to the ecstasy that union with her brought him. She peaked again as he threw his head back on a roar of pleasure, as the heat of his release surged into her womb until she felt filled, never to be empty again.

Shaking with aftershocks, she whimpered as he moved, needing him to come down on top of her. He swept her around instead, took her over him, careful not to jar her, to remain inside her.

She lay on top of him, the biggest part of her soul, satiated in ways she couldn't have imagined, in perfect peace for the first time in her life.

As he encompassed her in caresses and murmurs of appreciation, awe overtook her at everything that had happened tonight.

Then he made it infinitely better.

He shifted, brought her to her side facing him, kissed her deeply, leisurely, then whispered into her lips, "This was, hands down, the best thing that has ever happened to me. *You* are."

She believed he meant it.

But he wasn't free to mean it.

The knowledge expanded inside her soaring heart, a ton of dejection bringing it crashing to the ground of reality.

But she still had the rest of tonight with him.

Shaking off despondence, she focused on the miracle in progress, in her arms.

She suckled the tongue rubbing against hers, caressed the muscled back rippling beneath her fingers, smiled into his kiss. "Your feelings, sir, are a mere reflection of mine."

He pulled back to look down at her, his own smile bliss and bedevilment at once as he pressed her buttocks closer, driving his intact arousal deeper into her. "Then it's up to me to prove to you how authentic my feelings are."

And for the rest of the night, he left her in no doubt.

Johara drank in the magnificent sight Shaheen made.

Sprawled on his back, the dark green cotton sheet twisted around one thigh and leaving the rest of him bare for her to devour, he had one muscled arm arced over his head, the other with its palm flat over his heart. He looked as if he were holding the kisses she'd planted there before she'd left his side, telling him she'd go to the bathroom and would be back in moments, in place.

Her heart constricted. Her vision blurred.

And she choked out her pledge. "I will always love you, *ya habibi*."

He sighed in his sleep, his lips curving in contentment.

Even though she was across the room, she thought he said, "I love you, too, my Gemma."

Tears poured thicker, as if they were flowing from her heart. She closed the door and walked away from his room and out of his penthouse. Out of his life.

She felt as if hers was over.

Four

The moment he opened his eyes, Shaheen knew something was wrong. Wonderfully wrong.

He was...serene.

He remained still, closed his eyes again, to savor the alien sensation of absolute contentment.

Yes. Alien. He'd never felt like this, even on his best days.

He'd always been aware of all he had to be thankful for, had never taken any of his privileges for granted. He'd accepted the prices he had to pay for them, had even considered the payments and the load they placed on his shoulders more privileges. He'd reveled in all the challenges and hardships that making use of those privileges had dictated.

What he'd never been as fond of were the constraints they placed on his choices, the frustration he encountered when bowing to their demands meant doing less than what he thought was right.

Usually he relegated those limitations to the back of his mind, but they were still there, a source of constant tension.

There was not a trace of that now. He felt something he'd only ever experienced partially, had never imagined feeling in full. Peace. Permeating. Absolute.

And it was because of her.

Gemma. Even her name was perfection. Everything he'd felt from her, seen of her, had with her had been that. And the wonder of it seemed to have wiped him clean of all that had come before her. That he had to exert conscious effort to remember anything but her was amazing. One night with her felt like the sum total of his experience in life.

He stretched, humming to the tune of satisfaction and elation that strummed through him.

So this was *passion*. He hadn't felt anything like it before. He'd known passion for commitment, for success, for details, he felt love for his family, had felt mild and ephemeral interest in some women. But he'd never imagined anything so encompassing, so consuming. From the moment he'd laid eyes on her, his feelings had engulfed him whole, had overwhelmed his reason and control. Not that what he felt went against either. She satisfied the first and he felt no need to employ the second. Being with her had emptied him of tension and inhibition, had freed him to focus his all on the wonder of being with her, experiencing her, savoring every moment with her.

He did feel he'd known her all his life.

And now he couldn't imagine his life without her. The life she'd derailed. And righted.

He sighed deeply as images and sensations of the previous night and early morning cascaded through his mind and body.

He *had* taken her as if he'd been craving her all his life. He hadn't even been able to stop when he'd found he'd been her first. Or later, when he'd told himself he wouldn't do it again that night. But she'd again hijacked his sense and control…

Suddenly unease slithered through him, unraveling his surreal state of bliss.

He'd approached her, taken her, as if he was free to make his own choices and pursue his own destiny. And he wasn't.

How had he forgotten that for a minute, let alone a night?

But he *had* forgotten. Totally. And he remembered now.

Dammit, no. It made no difference what was demanded—no, *needed*—of him. There was no way he could blindly point at a bride from the royal catalogue now.

He had no idea how he'd be able to avoid the arranged marriage, but he would. No matter the pressures or the exigencies. Everything in him demanded that he make Gemma his.

He foresaw an epic battle.

He wiped both hands over his face, bunched them in his hair, pulled with a steady, stinging tension as if that would counteract the pressure building inside him.

What a mess.

But what a delight, too.

On the heels of visualizing the upcoming strife, images of her, of them together, conversing, caressing, joined, filled his mind again. In a balance where all the troubles he had piling ahead were weighed against being with Gemma, there was absolutely no contest. Claiming her outweighed the whole world.

He sat up, swung his legs off the bed. He ran his hands over the place where she'd slept—or at least lain—in between their lovemaking sessions. They hadn't slept until morning, too busy talking and experiencing each other in every way, sensual, sexual, mental. His body, already hard, started to pound at him in demand for her.

He tried to convince it to subside. There was no chance it was having her. Not today. After what he'd done to her—twice—no matter how eager she was, she needed at least a couple of days to recuperate.

He got to his feet. "Gemma?"

Silence. He called again, and this time, when the same absence of any sound or movement answered him, the lips that had twitched at imagining her soaking away the aches of his initiation in his tub tightened with alarm. He rushed to the bathroom, burst through the slightly open door.

He almost slumped to the floor at finding it empty. He was in worse shape than he thought. Being with Gemma had just masked his condition. He'd imagined a dozen macabre scenarios during the minute his calls had met with silence.

She had to be in the kitchen. There was no way she could hear him there. Images of her tousled and glowing from a shower, dressed in one of his shirts or lost in one of his bathrobes filled his mind. And she'd be awkward and swollen in all the places that would make him ache until he could barely speak.

He considered walking to her naked, then pulled on pants. She'd let him expose her to every intimacy, had responded with every fiber of her being, but she was still shy when she wasn't in the throes of pleasure. He didn't want to test her more, for now. He'd already rushed her in so many ways. So what if she'd asked him to? That didn't mean he should be so eager to comply. He was the experienced one here, and he shouldn't behave like an overeager teenager.

Seconds after this self-lecture, he was almost running to the kitchen. *Aih,* he *would* embarrass her again.

The premonition hit him before he stepped into the kitchen. All through his penthouse. The feeling of... emptiness. Absence.

The feeling became fact in seconds. The kitchen was also empty.

He didn't stop this time. He whirled around and bolted to inspect each room. Nothing.

Gemma was gone.

He stood in the middle of his living room, overlooking Manhattan, unable to process the knowledge.

She couldn't have just left!

She must have had an overwhelming reason for leaving. Maybe some emergency. Yes. That made sense. But...if something had happened, why hadn't she woken him up? To tell him, to let him help? She knew what kind of power he wielded. If any of her loved ones were in trouble, she knew he'd be the most qualified to help.

Was it possible she didn't realize he'd do anything for her? Was it possible she didn't believe, as he did, that they'd transcended all the conventions of relationship development, had taken a short cut to the highest level one could attain? Or was she so independent that she couldn't bring herself to ask for help because she was determined to deal with whatever problem had cropped up on her own? Or maybe it hadn't occurred to her to ask, in her rush to whatever the emergency was?

Stop. He was probably off base in all of his assumptions, was assigning a ludicrous interpretation to something that would be clear the moment she contacted him.

Something else hit him like a sledgehammer.

He hadn't exchanged any contact info with her.

And it was even worse. He didn't know her last name.

Just what had he been thinking last night?

That was it. He hadn't been thinking. Of anything but her, what they'd shared from first sight onward. He had, for the first time in his life, lived totally in the moment.

He'd always held back from fully trusting others, even his closest people, despite believing in their best intentions. He'd guarded himself against the consequences of their mistakes and misdemeanors. But with Gemma, he hadn't only dropped his guard—it hadn't been raised in the first place. He'd not had a moment of doubt. She was the woman he'd dreamed of but never truly thought he'd find.

The one.

And she was gone. After giving him the most perfect night of his life, after giving him herself and a glimpse of a magnificent future filled with an unprecedented connection, she was just...gone.

Calm down. She'd have an explanation, a perfectly reasonable one, for leaving without waking him up. It had to be the only thing she could have done, or she wouldn't have done it. She wouldn't have left him like that if it weren't.

So he should cool it. He might not know her last name

or her whereabouts, but she knew his. All he had to do was wait for her.

She'd come back the moment she could.

Gemma didn't come back.

It seemed she'd disappeared off the face of the earth.

He'd thought his security detail would have kept tabs on her. But when they'd seen her leave in the early-morning hours, all they'd worried about was him. They'd called to make sure he was okay, and when he'd answered, what he'd remembered doing only when they reminded him, clearly fine but sleepy and brooking no further interruption, they'd let her go. They hadn't seen any reason to follow her. That had destroyed his biggest hope of finding her, and the hope of doing so was becoming dimmer by the minute.

He'd widened his search until it had encompassed the whole United States. No one had heard of her.

With the evidence suggesting that she'd never existed on American soil, he'd begun to think that she and the enchanted night they'd spent together had been a figment of his imagination. Even with his one proof of her existence—the photo he'd taken of her—everyone insisted they'd never seen her. Everyone his people had questioned had commented that they would have remembered someone like her. And they didn't. As for her name, it rang no bells.

It *was* as if she'd never existed.

An explanation had reared its head constantly during his frantic search. He'd knocked it out of the way, determined not to let it have a hearing. But once he'd breathed again with the certainty that she hadn't had an accident or worse, he found his options narrowing down until they'd dwindled to nothing.

Nothing but that explanation made sense.

There was no escaping it anymore. He had to face it, no matter how mutilating it was.

She didn't want to see him again.

She might have been the woman who'd turned his life upside down, but it seemed he'd been nothing to her but a one-night stand. A man she'd chosen to initiate her nubile body into the rites of passion and unlock her limitless sexual potential. Perhaps he'd seemed exotic to her, a man from a different culture and country whom she could cut out of her life once the adventure was over.

Now that resignation had replaced desperation and he'd given up on the dream of her, there was nothing to fight for anymore, nothing to keep him here.

It was time he returned to Zohayd to confront his duty.

To embrace his nightmare.

"Shaheen."

That was all his father said, minutes after Shaheen had walked into his office.

It was enough. Disappointment and exasperation blared in the toneless delivery of his name.

Shaheen didn't blame him. He had ignored his father and the rest of the world for the past eight weeks. After that single phone call telling his father he was not coming home as promised, he'd made himself unavailable to anyone. He hadn't explained why.

His father had left him a dozen messages, had sent emissaries to bring him back or to at least get him to explain his reneging on the decision he'd arrived at only days before.

His father rose from behind his desk, majestic and packed with power and ire and wreathed in the full-blown regalia of the King of Zohayd.

Shaheen held his gaze as his father approached him. King Atef Aal Shalaan made no attempt to hug him as he usually did, but instead stood there, flaying him with his displeasure-radiating glower. His father was a couple of inches shorter, yet broader with more than three decades head start in maturity and responsibility. Shaheen had always thought his shoulders broad enough to carry the weight of the kingdom's fate on them. And that was not to mention his overwhelming presence.

Yet King Atef needed far more than presence to keep the kingdom at peace, to keep his enemies in check and his allies in line. More than ever, he had to appease the most powerful of those who constantly snapped at the heels of the ruling house, demanding their cut of power, prestige and proceeds. And that was something only Shaheen could deliver by sacrificing himself at the literal altar.

His father exhaled, the golden eyes he'd passed down only to Shaheen's brother Harres glittering from below intimidating eyebrows. "I won't ask what made you disappear. Or what brought you back."

"Good." Shaheen didn't attempt to temper his terse mutter. His father would have to be content that he *had* come back. Nothing else was his business.

"But," his father went on, "I'm letting it go only because this is not the time to take you to task over your potentially catastrophic behavior. The reception is in full swing."

The reception. Aka the bridal parade his father had

put together the moment he'd been informed Shaheen was on his way to Zohayd onboard his private jet. He was trapping him into it, before he had a chance to change his mind again.

And there it was, brewing in the main ceremony hall—the storm that would destroy his life. Two thousand people were in attendance, all those with a stake in the marriage and all those involved in the negotiations and manipulations and coercions.

But Shaheen wasn't expected to just flip through the women like he might a mail-order catalog and circle the model he thought most bearable. He was supposed to assess the merchandise in a more comprehensive fashion.

With marriages being what they were in Zohayd—especially the higher you went up the social scale—it was families who married, not individuals. He would have an extended family for a wife. And every potential family was here so that he could decide which one he could best stomach having as a constant presence in his life through their influence on his wife's and children's every thought and action.

"You're not dressed appropriately." His father's reprimand brought him out of his distasteful musings. "I told your *kabeer el yaweran* what was expected of you tonight."

Shaheen's head of entourage *had* said his father wanted him to wear Zohaydan royal garb. He'd scowled at the man and resumed staring blindly at the clauses in his latest business contract.

Now he scowled at his business suit and then at his father with the same leashed aggravation followed by the same pointed dismissal.

His father drew in an equally annoyed breath. "Since

you're flaunting yet another expectation, I demand that you at least wear an expression that doesn't reveal your abhorrence for being here."

Shaheen exhaled in resignation. "Don't ask more of me, Father. A pretense that this isn't torture is foremost among the things I don't have to give."

"You're being unreasonable. You're not the first or last royal to enter a marriage of state for his kingdom's sake."

"And you did it twice, so why not me, eh?" Shaheen knew he was stepping over the line talking to his father, *and* king, this harshly. But he didn't care. He had no more stamina for observing protocol. "And I *am* here to do it, Father. So why should I even attend this farce at all? Why not spare me this added torment? I'd rather not choose the method of my own execution. I'll leave it up to you to pick the most humane one."

King Atef winced at his analogy. "That's the problem. Many candidates have pros and cons that weigh each other out. It has to be your personal preference that tips the balance in one's favor."

"You think I care if I'm shot or electrocuted or cut to pieces? They're all equal and interchangeable to me. Just pick one."

"You're exaggerating now. All your bridal candidates are fine young women. Beautiful, well-bred, highly educated, pleasant. You'll get to like your bride, and maybe in time love her."

"Like you love Queen Sondoss? And loved my mother?"

His father's scowl deepened at Shaheen's ready counter. The best he'd reached with Shaheen's mother was peaceful coexistence. As for Queen Sondoss, leashed hostility was all he could hope for on a good day.

"There are Aliyah and Kamal. I believe no one can be any happier than they are."

"Don't bring them up, Father. They were already crazy in love when they married. Circumstances just forced them apart, and thankfully, forced them back together."

His father's gaze wavered. Then he let go of his kingly veneer.

Nothing remained but the loving father who looked and sounded pained at what he couldn't save his son from. "I can't tell you how much I regret that you'll have to walk in my footsteps. But there's no way around it. And that is why I'm asking you to pay attention to the candidates. At least you have more than one to choose from. I had no say in choosing either your mother or Sondoss. You may have better luck finding someone who's compatible with you among the dozen possible brides."

Shaheen's teeth ground together. He'd already found someone who was compatible with him in every way.

Gemma had clearly not thought the same. She hadn't even thought him worthy of a goodbye.

That didn't change anything for him. He knew now that everything he'd ever dreamed of existed, even if she didn't want him, even if he could never have her. What were the chances that fate would gift him with another woman who was even close?

He not only believed it wouldn't, he didn't want it to.

He refrained from saying anything. His father would have to roll the dice and decide Shaheen's fate himself.

Finally his father gave up, brushed past him and walked out with heavy steps.

Shaheen watched him, compassion flickering through the deadness inside him.

His father hadn't had an easy life. Certainly not a contented one. Shaheen had grown up believing that his father had never known happiness or love outside of what he felt for his job and children. It had been only a couple of years ago that they'd found out he'd once tasted that happiness and love, with a woman. Anna Beaumont.

He'd had an affair with her during his separation from Queen Sondoss two years after Haidar and Jalal were born. Then Anna had fallen pregnant, and his efforts to end his marriage to Sondoss had failed. And though it had nearly destroyed him, he'd left Anna, telling her he could never be with her again, due to the threat of war with Sondoss's home kingdom of Azmahar, and that it was imperative to abort their child.

Instead, Anna had put her baby up for adoption. Shaheen's aunt Bahiyah, secretly knowing about her brother's affair, had adopted Aliyah and passed her off as hers.

It was only many years later, while his father was recovering from a heart attack, that he'd searched for Anna again and discovered the truth. It was a timely discovery, as another flare of unrest in the region could only be resolved if a daughter of King Atef's married the king of Judar. Now Aliyah was King Kamal's worshipped wife and Judar's beloved queen, and Anna Beaumont had become a constant presence in Aliyah's and, by association, his father's lives.

Shaheen believed that had only deepened his father's unhappiness. For he could never have the only woman he'd ever wanted, and as Shaheen sensed, still did.

He and his father had that in common, too.

Shaheen kept his eyes fixed on his father's slumped shoulders as they reached their destination, braced himself as they stepped into the ceremony hall.

Brightness and buzzing seemed to rise at their entry, but he couldn't register the magnificent surroundings beyond the darkness and ugliness inside him. It was reflected on every surface, on every face that turned to look at him.

Suddenly every hair on his body stood on end.

What now?

His eyes panned the room, seeking the source of the disturbance that had drenched him. It now felt as if a laser beam was drilling through his gut.

Then everything came to a grinding halt.

His heart almost ruptured with one startled detonation.

There, at the farthest end of the hall…

Gemma.

Five

Shaheen's mind had snapped. It must have.

He was seeing things.

He swallowed the lump of shock that had lodged into his throat, shuddered as it landed like a brick in his stomach.

He was seeing Gemma.

But he couldn't be. His mind must be projecting the one thing it wanted most, the woman whose memory and taste and touch had been driving him insane and whom he'd despaired of seeing again.

He closed his eyes.

He opened them. She was still there.

"Shaheen, why did you stop?"

He heard his father's concern as if it were coming from a mile away. Gemma, who was at the far end of the two-hundred-foot space, felt mere inches away.

Her gaze snared his across the distance, just like that

first time, was roiling with the same intensity, the same awareness. One thing was missing. Shock.

Of course. She was expecting to see him. There was no element of surprise for her this time. But there was more in her expression. Apprehension. Aversion even.

She was that loath to see him? Then why was she here?

The relevant question hit him harder than the shock of her being here.

How was she here? In Zohayd, in the palace, at this function?

He felt himself moving again, his body activated and steered by his father's hand on his forearm as he led him deeper into the throngs of people gathered to watch his sacrifice.

Moving forced him to relinquish his eye lock with Gemma. He rushed ahead to gain another direct path to her. But she evaded his eyes now, hid from him.

Frustration seethed through him, questions. The urge to cleave through the crowd, push everyone out of the way till he got to her overwhelmed him. He imagined hauling her over his shoulder and storming through the palace to his quarters, pressing her to the nearest upright surface and devouring her.

It wasn't consideration for his father's guests, the most influential people in Zohayd and the region, that stopped him. It was her avoidance. The knowledge that she didn't want him as he wanted her. That whatever had brought her here wasn't him.

For an interminable time, he believed he responded when addressed, monosyllables that he vaguely thought were appropriate, shook hands and grimaced at eager female faces and fawning family members, all the time trying to catch glimpses of her, desperately trying to get her to look at him again.

At one point, his older brother Harres appeared at his side.

"You look out of it, bro. Got stoned to get through this?"

Shaheen felt the urge to deck him. "And what if I did, Mr. Immune-From-This-Abominable-Fate Minister of Interior?"

Harres grimaced. "I did offer to do it myself again. I told them that, unlike you, I don't care one way or another, and I'd certainly remain neutral in my post since I would never get attached to whatever wife they saddled me with. They still refused."

Shaheen's aggression drained. Harres *had* tried to take his place time and again. He would spare him if he could.

He exhaled. "They know you'd get attached to your children."

Harres shrugged. "Maybe. Probably. I don't know. I really can't imagine being a husband let alone a father." He put an arm around Shaheen's shoulder, gave him a hard squeeze of consolation, the golden eyes that could have been their father's flaring with empathy. "I would have done anything to spare you this."

Which Shaheen had just thought. "*Aih,* I know."

He again caught sight of Gemma among the shifting crowd, took an involuntary step nearer as if to force her acknowledgment, resurrect her hunger with his eagerness.

"And *I* know who you're looking at. Who would have thought our little Johara would turn out to be such a stunner?"

Harres's words made no sense. Had Shaheen's mind started to deteriorate from the stress?

Shaheen looked at Harres, *seeing* him for the first time since they'd started talking, the juggernaut knight the kingdom had entrusted with its security, and who'd done the best job in its history. An expression softened his hewn, desert-weathered features, one Shaheen had never seen there except around their female family members. A rare gentleness, a proud indulgence.

And he'd thought Harres had said... No. He couldn't have said that name. Where would it come from, anyway?

He shook his head, desperate to clear it. "What are you talking about?"

"The vision in gold over there. Our Johara...or I should say *your* Johara all grown-up." Harres gave a nod in Gemma's direction. "You've been looking nowhere else since you walked in. And I can't blame you. I gaped at her for a solid ten seconds when Nazaryan greeted me with her on his arm. Who would have thought, eh?"

Shaheen stared at Harres as if he'd started talking in a language he'd never heard before. "Nazaryan?"

Harres snapped his fingers in front of his eyes. "Snap out of it. You're scaring me."

Shaheen shook his head again. "What do you mean Nazaryan?"

"I mean Berj Nazaryan, our royal jeweler, her father."

Shaheen's eyes slid from Harres's, as sluggish and impeded as his thoughts, followed the direction of his earlier nod.

Gemma was the only one in that direction dressed in gold. Harres was talking about her. And he was calling her...calling her...

Johara.

The bubble of incomprehension trembled inside Shaheen. Then it burst.

Gemma was Johara.

Shock mushroomed through him like a nuclear detonation.

His mysterious Gemma was Johara. Berj Nazaryan's daughter. Aram's sister. The girl he'd known since she was six. Who'd become his shadow since the day he'd plucked her out of the air from a thirty-foot fall.

No wonder he'd felt he'd known her forever. *He had.* He *had* recognized her with that first look, even if not consciously.

And no wonder. She looked nothing like the fourteen-year-old she'd been when he'd last seen her. Skinny with glasses and braces, with no ability to wield her femininity the way girls in Zohayd learned to from a very early age. She hadn't only realized her potential, she'd become the total opposite of her former self.

He'd thought he'd seen every brand of beauty this world had to offer. But she was something he'd never thought would be gathered in one woman, all his tastes and fantasies come to life. And that was just on the surface. Deeper, where it counted most, little Johara, as Harres had called her, had become the woman who'd seduced Shaheen on sight, had possessed him in a single night.

He rocked on his feet with the mushrooming realization. Only Harres's hand on his arm steadied him.

Among the storm tossing him about, he managed to answer Harres's worried question. "No, I don't need air. I'm fine."

But he was so far from fine he could be on another planet. He might never be fine again.

He'd taken Johara to his bed.

He'd taken her, in every way, repeatedly.

Just as he thought shock couldn't engulf him any further, his eyes captured her incredible dark ones again. And the final piece of the puzzle crashed down in place. It should have been the first thing he understood the moment he realized who she really was.

He might not have recognized her, but she had known who he was from the first moment. She'd given him enough clues. Her first word to him had been a gasp of his name. She'd later told him all about herself, which had amounted to what he *did* know of her family history, without the names, dates and places.

And when he hadn't clued in, so bowled over by her he hadn't even connected the sun-size dots, she'd chosen to leave him in the dark. The apprehension he felt from her must be her anxiety about his reaction now that she knew he'd finally wised up.

"Now that you've met your potential brides, how is your stomach holding up?"

"Can we give you tips who *not* to choose?"

Shaheen dazedly turned toward the two warm, musical female voices. Aliyah and Laylah flowed to him, hugging him on both sides, reaching up to kiss a cheek each, their exquisite faces brimming with vitality and joie de vivre.

He automatically hugged and kissed them back as the ramifications of what had happened between him and Gemma…*Johara* expanded inside him, squeezing all his vitals.

"The beauty in emerald over there, the one with the incredible black hair down to her feet?" Laylah pinched his cheek playfully as she turned his head in the direction of the woman she was describing, before turning his face back to her quickly. "Don't even look at her again. Her unbelievable locks will turn to serpents at the first opportune moment."

"And the redhead over there." Aliyah directed his gaze toward the woman she was mentioning with more discreet taps on his cheek. "Run if you ever see her again. She grows scales and blowtorches anyone within a mile radius."

Harres laughed. "If you're trying to make Shaheen feel better about this, you're going about it in bizarro fashion."

Laylah poked a teasing elbow into Harres's abdomen. "Hey, we're saving him from settling on the prettiest flower and being devoured alive."

"So now that you've eliminated the most beautiful flowers, do I surmise you think he should go for the ugliest one?"

Aliyah gave a horrified shudder. "Oh, no, *that* one is just as monstrous, without the advantage of being nice to look at. What's inside is on the outside in her case. In fact, we've narrowed down his choices to two."

Harres huffed a sound of pure sarcasm. "Don't tell me. The candidates with the *least* monstrous qualities."

"Actually they're both pretty decent. One is not as accomplished or worldly as Shaheen would prefer, but we believe she would become so as his wife. The other one is really nice, but doesn't have much of a sense of humor. Again, with Shaheen for a husband, she'll definitely develop one."

Shaheen felt as if he'd fallen into the twilight zone, expected to hear a laughter track burst into the background any moment now.

He cleared his throat. "*Shaheen* is right here." The two women squeezed him again, sheepishness coating their expressions. "Thank you, my dears, for vetting my bridal nightmares as only you two discerning ladies could. Write down your choices and hand them to Father. But if he decides one of the monsters is more beneficial to the negotiations, that is who I'll end up with. Anyway, my life as I know and want it is over. So, as I told Father earlier, one catastrophe with which to meet my end is as good as another."

A pall fell on the duo in the wake of his words.

Horror dawned in Aliyah's and Laylah's eyes, contrition twisting their features. They really hadn't realized how much Shaheen hated this, were now mortified that they'd been oblivious to his own distress and teased him about it.

"Oh, Shaheen, I didn't know you were…"

"Oh, Shaheen, I didn't realize…"

Aliyah's and Laylah's apologies stumbled over each other. They fell silent, Aliyah biting her lip, Laylah's eyes filling with tears.

His focus flowed back to its captor, to Gem—to *Johara*. Her eyes darted away the moment his fell on her. She'd been watching him.

A bubble of agitation and elation expanded inside him.

She might be avoiding him, but she *wanted* to look at him and did so the moment she could.

Harres's phone rang.

He answered. After a few terse sentences, he turned his eyes to Shaheen. "I'm sorry to leave you. But something's brewing at our borders. It may take hours or even days to defuse."

Shaheen nodded, accepted Harres's bolstering hug, watched him hug the women and stride away.

Shaheen looked back at the fidgeting Aliyah and

Laylah, a calculating smile spreading his lips even as his heart twisted inside his chest. "How about you atone for your sins by granting this doomed man a last request?"

They both jumped, voices intertwining with promises of anything at all if it would make him feel better.

He looked back at Johara, who again turned her eyes away and bestowed a brittle smile on the group surrounding her.

"Remember Johara Nazaryan?"

Both women looked to Johara.

"Oh, yes," Laylah said. "My mother used to drag me away every time I tried to talk to her. Now look at her, flitting around Johara as if she were an A-list movie star."

Aliyah smirked. "It's not only your mother. All our female relatives and acquaintances who never deemed to speak to her or her mother before are falling over themselves to be reintroduced."

Laylah giggled. "Bless their superficial souls. They never acknowledged what a classy, talented woman Jacqueline Nazaryan was, or what a sweet girl Johara was. But now that Johara has become *the* new designer on the cusp of international stardom, they all want to secure a chance to be the first to wear her latest exclusive designs."

"It's amazing to see that they consider their next outfit more important than their husbands." Aliyah's lips twisted. "Their men are about to flood the ceremony hall in drool, and the women can't care less."

Shaheen blinked, noting the people gathered around Johara for the first time. Women who'd treated her with condescension, or at best the dismissive courtesy due to a valuable employee's family member, were now treating her not just as an equal but as a celebrity.

But it was the men's behavior that made aggression swirl inside him. Many were openly ogling her and courting her attention and favor. His muscles turned to steel as every territorial cell in his body primed for a to-the-death fight for his mate.

Yes. No matter what she'd done or how impossible it all was, his body, his very being, considered her his mate. Accepted nothing else.

Aliyah turned back to him. "What about Johara?"

His burning conviction seemed to force Johara's gaze to him. He muttered, low and hungry, "Bring her to me."

Shaheen was about to combust.

With frustration.

It had been two hours since he'd told Aliyah and Laylah to pluck Johara from her new rabid fans and bring her to him.

After a brief surprise, the two women, who clearly weren't aware of the seriousness of the situation that necessitated his making a marriage of state, thought it a brilliant idea.

They thought he *should* flaunt the royal council's decrees and marry whomever he liked. And with their former connection, who better than Johara?

They'd gone after her as dozens of people inundated Shaheen again. He'd fended them off as he struggled to track the two women's efforts to disentangle Johara from her companions.

After sinking in the quicksand of the court's convoluted maneuvers, the two women could only look on as they lost Johara to another tide of eager fans until she exited the hall.

He had no doubt she'd thwarted them on purpose, had escaped. He had no idea where she'd gone, or if she'd even remain in Zohayd.

By the time he'd freed himself, he'd had a choice between interrogating guards and servants and having the news that he was looking for her spread like wildfire throughout the kingdom, or inspecting every guest suite in the palace himself and causing an even bigger scandal for his—and her—father.

So here he was, pacing his quarters, barely stopping himself from driving his fist through a wall.

He couldn't let her avoid him. He had to confront her. If only for one last time.

Plans were ricocheting in his mind, each seeming more ludicrous than the next, when a knock floated to his ears from his apartment's door.

"Go away," he growled at the top of his voice.

He'd thought whomever was unfortunate enough to seek him now had heeded his order when the knock came again, more urgent.

He stormed to the door, flung it open, ready to blast whomever it was off the face of the earth.

And there she was. Gemma. Johara.

She stood there, in the gold dress that echoed her hair's incredible shades and luster, looking up at him with anxiety in her gaze, a tremor strumming those lush, petal-soft lips he'd been going mad from needing beneath his for eight agonizing weeks.

"Shaheen…"

The memory of that night when she'd said his name, looked at him like that and changed his life forever ripped through him.

He didn't give her a chance to say anything else.

He swooped down on her with the same speed and determination he had two decades ago, when he'd snatched her away from death's snapping jaws. He hauled her into the room, his feet feeling as if they were leaving the ground in his desperation to have her against him, beneath him, *with* him.

Everything merged into a dream sequence. Gemma, Johara, filled his arms, her sweet breath mingling with his, her lips pressing desperately against his own, her flesh cushioning his, her heat and hunger enveloping him.

But questions gnawed at him, eating a hole through his gut as big as the one her disappearance had left in his heart. Why had she withheld the truth from him, why had she left him that way, why had she chosen now to come back, and the most important question of all—had she come back for him?

Nothing came out but an agonized, *"How could you?"*

She jerked as if the words singed her. She wrenched away, pressed her face into the bed. "You're angry."

"Angry?" He rose on one elbow, gazed down at her trembling profile. "You think I'm *angry?*"

"N-no." The tears he could see glittering in her eyes welled, spilled over to drench her cheek, making a wet track down to lips that trembled. "You're way more than angry. You're enraged. And outraged. And y-you have every right to be both."

"I'm none of those things. I'm…I'm…" He sat up, raked his hands through his hair, felt close to tearing it out. "I still can't believe you did this to me."

"I'm so sorry. I know I should have told you who I was…"

"Yes, you should have. But that isn't what I meant. How could you leave me like that? Didn't you realize how I'd feel? I felt…" He paused as she hesitantly turned to face him, searched for the words to describe his desperation and desolation after her disappearance. Nothing came to him but one word. It gashed out of him *"Bereaved."*

She lurched as if he'd shot her. Emotion crumpled her face, and more tears poured from her.

He studied her, paralyzed by the enormity of the distress radiating from her, then he reached for her, even now fearing he'd grab thin air. He groaned his remembered anguish as he pressed her harder into him, lost the ability to breathe as her precious body filled his empty arms, when he'd despaired he'd ever hold her this close again.

"I never intended for any of that to happen." She sobbed on his shoulder. "I-I only came to the party to see you, didn't dream you wouldn't recognize me. But when you didn't…when you were…"

He pulled back to watch her, to fill his eyes with the reality of her, her nearness, threaded his aching fingers into her hair. "Were what? All over you? Out of my mind with wanting you on sight?"

"I never imagined things could go that far. I thought I'd see you one last time before you got married and I no longer had the right to…to… I should have told you who I am, but I knew if I did, you would pull back, treat me like an old acquaintance, and I couldn't give up that time with you. If I'd told you, you certainly wouldn't have made love to me. So I didn't, and I-I compromised you. And I had to leave before I did anything even worse."

Shaheen stared down at her, life flooding back into him.

This was why she'd left. She'd thought she had to. For his sake. It had been as magical for her as it had been for him. She wanted him as much as he wanted her, and it had killed her as much as it had him when she'd walked away.

But one thing stopped his elation in its tracks. Her mortification, her self-blame. Setting her straight took precedence over every other consideration.

He grabbed her hands, covered them in kisses. "You're wrong, my Gemma, *ya joharti,* my Johara. You didn't compromise me—you energized me, stabilized me. You liberated and elated me. And you were wrong about your doubts, too. I might have hesitated when I found out who you were, mostly from surprise, but *nothing* would have stopped me from taking you. Nothing but you, if you didn't want me."

Her tears stopped abruptly, the remorse dimming her eyes then giving way to the fragility of disbelief, relief and finally the radiance of wonder.

His heart expanded, his world righting itself. A hand behind her head and another behind her back gathered her to him, fitting her into him, the half he'd felt had been torn away from his flesh.

"But you wanted me," he murmured into her mouth, tasting her, plucking at her clinging lips, over and over. "You still want me."

She moaned, opened to him, let him into her recesses, the most potent admission of desire. He took it all, gave more, one thing filling his awareness. His Johara was back in his arms. And he planned to keep her there, to never let her go again.

He told her. "And I'll never stop wanting you."

* * *

Johara cried out as Shaheen's lips came down on hers in full possession. Her world spun in a kaleidoscope of delight, her body in a maelstrom of sensation.

But she wasn't here for this.

No matter that she'd been dying for him, shriveling up from deprivation.

She dug her shaking fingers into the vital waves of his hair, tried to tug at them, to have him allow her a breath that didn't pass through both their bodies. Before he dragged her any deeper into pleasure, submerged her into union with him. She failed.

But as if sensing her struggle, he withdrew his lips from hers lingeringly, rose to look down at her, his eyes a mixture of tenderness and ferocious possession. "What is it, *ya joharti?* Your heart is flapping so hard I can feel it inside my own chest."

"Th-this isn't why I came here, Shaheen. I just wanted to explain, to say goodbye—"

"There will be no goodbyes between us, *ya galbi.* Never."

Before she could cry out that there would be, no matter what either of them wanted, he claimed her lips again.

And she drowned. In him, in her need, in a realm where only he existed and mattered. She let herself sink, promising herself it would be the last time...

"I'm sorry. I did knock. Repeatedly."

Johara jerked as the soft apology came from far, far away, shattering the cocoon enveloping her and Shaheen. She shuddered, felt Shaheen stiffen above her.

"Get out of here, Aliyah."

Silence met his growl, then a distressed intake of breath.

"I'm really sorry, Shaheen, but this can't wait."

Johara lurched again as Aliyah's strained words brought the outside world crashing back on her like an avalanche.

Earlier, Aliyah and Laylah had tried to cajole her into speaking with Shaheen. She'd made her escape then, thinking she'd saved him from making more compromising mistakes because of her. But if she'd feared any suspicion of their relationship would tarnish his image and hurt his marriage plans, she'd done far worse now. She'd just given Aliyah evidence.

She lay beneath Shaheen, her dress riding up to her waist, her splayed legs accommodating his bulk as his hands cupped her buttocks through her panties and his hardness ground against her. Her dress hung off one shoulder exposing half a breast that had just been engulfed in his mouth.

Mortification drenched her, all the more so because the arousal coursing through her didn't even slow down. She wouldn't have been able to bolt out of the room even if she wasn't pinned down by Shaheen. She couldn't move.

She didn't need to. Shaheen relinquished his possession of her flesh with utmost tranquility, rearranged her clothes with supreme care. Then he scooped her up from the bed and steadied her on her feet, smoothing her mussed hair, gently massaging her worried features.

With one last look of reassurance, one last, lingering kiss, he turned to his sister.

Aliyah looked an apology at Johara. It was clear she did have a paramount reason for being there. One she wasn't about to divulge in Johara's presence.

Seeing this unfortunate development as an opportunity to escape, Johara rushed forward to leave.

Shaheen's hand on her arm stopped her.

"Please, Shaheen," she choked out, hoping that Aliyah, who'd moved away discreetly, wouldn't hear. "Let me go. I'll soon be gone and you won't see me again, for real this time. I beg you, for as long as I must stay in Zohayd, you must stay away from me."

She bolted away, gathering the heavy layers of her silk dress in her hands so her stumbling legs wouldn't snarl in their folds.

She still almost fell on her face when she heard his beloved voice behind her, intense, low, permeated with voracity and finality.

"There is no way I will stay away from you, *ya joharti.*"

Six

"This had better be good, Aliyah."

Shaheen heard irritation sharpening his voice as he closed the door. He stood there, vibrating with the need to storm after Johara. Instead, he turned to Aliyah. He'd never been upset with her in his life, but he was furious with her now. Not because she'd interrupted his and Johara's surrender to their deepening bond, or because he was seething with frustration. But because her intrusion had upset Johara, had given her another reason to pull back from him.

Johara evidently knew about the gravity of his situation, as often the families of those who worked in sensitive areas in the palace did. And she had extreme feelings about compromising him. She'd put them both through hell so she wouldn't. She must think Aliyah witnessing their lovemaking the ultimate exposure.

And instead of only fighting the world for her, he

now had to fight against her own anxieties, too. He had to convince her to stop trying to do what she thought was right for him, to let him worry about his problems, to realize his best interests lay in having her with him.

He still had no idea how he'd achieve that, but now that he knew she'd never really left him, still wanted him, he would renege on his promise to his father, to his kingdom. He would face anything on earth to be with her, come what may.

"Actually this is bad. As bad as can be," Aliyah finally answered his exasperation, her voice measured.

And in spite of the situation and what she'd just said, his heart softened with love and admiration for her.

Aliyah had had the harshest life of them all, had triumphed over impossible odds. He still couldn't believe how she'd come back from a prescription drug addiction that doctors' misdiagnoses and overanxious parents had plunged her into, how she'd made the decision to face her addiction and the world alone at the tender age of sixteen. It never ceased to be a pleasure for him to see her so healthy, to watch her blossoming daily with Kamal's love, settling deeper in contentment with the blessing of their happiness and two children and filling her position as one of the most beloved queens in the world.

He watched her as she approached with the grace of the old supermodel and the new queen. She was truly regal, dressed in honeyed-chocolate, the color of her eyes; she was as tall as Johara, if differently proportioned. But her every step closer struck a chord of foreboding in his heart.

She stopped before him, her turmoil more obvious close up. She gestured to herself. "See anything wrong with this picture?"

"Is this about you?" He took her by the shoulders, his eyes feverishly scanning her. "Are you…" He stopped, swallowed the ball of panic that suddenly blocked his throat. "Are you okay?"

She reached out an urgent hand to his face. "Oh, I'm fine. It's not about me. It's about these."

His gaze followed her hand to where it rested on the magnificent diamond-and-precious-stone necklace gracing her swanlike neck. Matching earrings dangled to her shoulders and an elaborate web-ring bracelet adorned her wrist.

"What about them?" he asked, mystified. "Apart from looking more incredible with your beauty showcasing them?"

"Father did give them to me to showcase for this function. They are part of the Pride of Zohayd." Shaheen nodded. He recognized them as part of the royal jewels, Zohayd's foremost national treasure. "I was supposed to return them as soon as I took them off, as you know, but as I did I…"

"What? You…damaged them?"

If she had, Berj Nazaryan would fix them, and no one should be the wiser. Because if anyone found out, the situation *would* be grave.

Her gaze grew darker. "No. I discovered they're fake."

He gaped at her.

Fake. *Fake.*

The word revolved in his mind, gaining momentum, until it catapulted him forward to touch the jewels, to inspect them.

He raised confused eyes to her. "They look the same."

"That's the whole idea of good fakes. And these are nothing short of *incredible*."

Logic tried to make a stand. "But you're not a jewelry expert. And you probably haven't worn those before."

"I did far more than wear them. You remember I was almost catatonic when I was in my early teens? Well, my shrinks recommended I have a creative outlet as part of my 'therapy.' I wanted to paint, and the only thing I wanted to paint was the jewels. Mother Bahiyah got me into the vaults regularly to paint them."

So she did know the jewels intimately.

Denial took over from logic. "But it's been so many years since you saw them."

"Time doesn't make any difference with my photographic memory. Tiny discrepancies screamed at me from the moment I took a good look at them. But without comparing them to detailed photos of the originals, I'm sure no one else would notice. No one but the experts, that is."

Shaheen felt the frost of dread spread through him. He'd seen evidence of her infallible memory. As a supremely talented professional artist, Aliyah used it now to produce paintings with uncanny detail.

If she thought the jewels were fakes, they were.

His shoulders slumped under the enormity of the conviction.

Aliyah joined him in the deflation of defeat, lowered her eyes, then exhaled and tucked a mahogany tress behind her ear. She lifted her gaze back to his. "My first instinct was to rush to Harres with this. I did try to call him, but he's incommunicado. I then thought of Amjad as our eldest, but I realized it should be you I told first. For now."

He blinked, nothing making sense anymore. "What do you mean?"

"My decision was based on your past connection

to Johara and the special interest you showed in her tonight. But then I came here and discovered it was far more than special interest. This isn't the first time this happened between you. I could tell. Your passion, the depth of your involvement, almost burned me from twenty feet away. You're her lover, aren't you?"

"You..." Shaheen shook his head, still trying to assimilate her revelations. And assumptions. "You think Johara has something to do with this?"

Aliyah let her shoulders drop. "I honestly don't know what to think. Between father and daughter, Berj and Johara are not only among the few who have access to the jewels, they're among the few in the *world* capable of faking them. And then, there is her sudden reappearance in Zohayd and in the palace."

Shaheen's numbness evaporated under the ferocity of the need to defend Johara. "She came back for *me*."

Aliyah's gaze grew wary. "Is this what she told you?" He looked at her helplessly, because Johara hadn't said that. Aliyah went on, her voice more subdued. "She came back three weeks ago. I was here visiting mother Bahiyah the day after her arrival. And I met her. She said she came back to see her father. The father who resigned his post as royal jeweler just before the reception."

This time when she fell silent, Shaheen felt he'd never be able to talk ever again.

When the silence grew too suffocating, she sighed. "I can't believe either of them could do something like this, either. But then, who knows what's been going on with Berj? Mother Bahiyah told me tonight she wasn't surprised when he quit, said he hasn't been himself for a while. She said he'd been getting more morose, withdrawn, empty-eyed. And then he had a heart attack."

The new shock forced his voice to work. "*Ya Ullah*, when?"

"Three months ago."

"Why did no one tell me?" Berj, the endlessly kind and patient, stunningly creative man, like his son and daughter, had always been one of the dearest people to Shaheen. He loved him more than he loved any of his uncles.

"According to mother Bahiyah, he made Father promise not to tell anyone, even his family," she assured him. Then she reluctantly added, "But maybe he felt his mortality, knew he wouldn't be able to work for much longer. Maybe our enemies got to him."

"To offer him what? Financial security? Do you think Father didn't reward his two-decade career with our family more generously than anything anyone else could offer? Though the job has never been about money for Berj, he can now live a retired life of leisure and luxury. And if he doesn't want that, he can afford to start his own business. He doesn't even have any dependents to worry about. All his family are financially independent in their own right."

"He might have a problem that depleted his funds—gambling, for instance." Aliyah shrugged. "I'm as confused as you are. I'm just pointing out that he hasn't been himself. And then, Johara has changed beyond all recognition, on the surface. What if she's changed on the inside, too, and—"

He growled his unconditional belief in Johara, cutting Aliyah off. "*No.* No, she hasn't. She's still our Johara. *My* Johara."

Aliyah looked at him with the same caution she would look at an enraged tiger who might lash out at any second. "I never really knew her, but I always got good vibes from her. I only met her again that day three weeks ago, then again tonight. I did like her again on sight, much more now that we're both grown-up. But though I don't see her as a manipulator, I do get the feeling she's hiding something. Something big."

"It's her relationship with me."

"No. I felt it again just now, when there was…nothing to hide about *that* anymore."

He glowered down at her. "You won't make me doubt her."

"I'm just presenting you with the facts. I'd hate to think anything bad, let alone something that bad, of Berj and Johara, but right now I'm at a loss to come up with another explanation."

"There *is* another explanation. Everything you mentioned is circumstantial evidence. Nothing more."

"True. But we can't afford to overlook any possibilities. This is too huge, Shaheen. The fate of the royal house—the whole kingdom—depends on it."

Silence crashed again.

At last, Aliyah drew in a ragged breath. "What shall we do?"

"*You* will hand back the jewels as if you didn't notice anything. And you will *not* say anything to anyone. Starting with Amjad and Harres. Give me a few days to sort this out."

"Are you sure, Shaheen?"

There were no hesitation in him. "Yes."

Aliyah chewed her lip, worry etched on her face. "I did want to give you a chance to sort this out. But that was before I walked in on you and Johara. You're in love with her, aren't you?" Shaheen only nodded. He was. Irrevocably. She exhaled. "Are you sure you can handle this? Do you think you can be objective?"

He wouldn't even dignify that with an answer. "Give me your word that you'll let me handle this, will let me recruit Harres and Amjad into the matter at my discretion."

"You're going to search for proof Johara and Berj have nothing to do with it, aren't you? What if you don't find any? What if we don't have the time for you to investigate?"

"We have time."

"How do you know that?"

"Think about it, Aliyah. The forgers probably faked all of the Pride of Zohayd collection, or they would have somehow made sure you were handed authentic pieces to wear tonight. But since no claim has been leaked that we failed to protect the jewels from theft, the thieves and forgers are waiting for the time when the biggest scandal can be achieved."

Horror dawned on Aliyah's face. "The Exhibition Ceremony!"

He nodded grimly. "Yes. And that's still months away. So we have time. And I *will* take every possible second of it. Give me your word that you'll let me have it, Aliyah."

Aliyah's expression filled with conflict as she met his gaze head-on. He struggled to bring his emotions under control so he wouldn't give her more cause to doubt his judgment.

She finally nodded. "You have it. And Kamal's, too."

"You told him!"

"I tell him everything." She suddenly dragged him into a fierce hug. "If you love her like I love Kamal, I wish nothing more than for you to prove her innocence, that you can have her and love her."

He hugged her back for a long moment. Then he kissed the top of her head. She looked up at him one last time then walked out.

Shaheen staggered to the nearest chair, sank down onto it.

It was all too much to take in.

The bridal ordeal, finding Johara here, what happened since. Now Aliyah's discoveries. Their possible explanations and ramifications. Yet one thing trumped it all.

Johara wasn't here for him. She was here for her father.

Yet the realization didn't pain him. She thought she had no place in his life. She hadn't thought she *could* come back for him. In fact, it must have been torture for her to attend the reception tonight. To not only know he was getting married to someone else, but to watch him pick that wife.

And Berj had chosen tonight of all nights to hand in his resignation, and hours later, Aliyah discovered that his paramount duty, safeguarding the jewels, had been compromised.

No. He couldn't doubt him. And he would never doubt Johara. There *was* another explanation.

But until he found it, this was a catastrophe in the making.

The Pride of Zohayd jewels were far more than the foremost national treasure.

Legend had it that each piece of jewelry opened doors where none existed, attained coveted results where they had seemed impossible, courted monarchs' favor, brought true love, achieved undying glory and even cheated death.

Five hundred years ago, when tribal wars in the territories that had yet to become Zohayd were at their peak, Ezzat ben Qassem Aal Shalaan knew that on the day the leadership of his tribe fell to him, he'd need more than wisdom, power and military triumphs to bring an end to the conflicts and gather the tribes under his rule.

He'd followed the history of each jewel, charted an infallible plan to possess them all and wield unparalleled authority. To his father's horror, he left the tribe when he was only eighteen and went on his quest to collect those jewels from all over the Asian continent.

It took him twelve years to do it, but on his return, the tide turned in his tribe's favor, and within months, he'd united the tribes and became the first king of Zohayd. Together, he and the jewels had become known as the Pride of Zohayd.

The jewels became the symbol of the royal family's entitlement to the throne. Legend went on to say that they remained in no one's hands if unworthy of the privilege and power.

Each year for the past five centuries, Aal Shalaan monarchs had held a week of festivities to renew their claim to the throne, culminating in a grand ceremony to exhibit the jewels to representatives of the Zohaydan people as proof that the Aal Shalaans remained the rightful rulers of the land.

There was only one reason the jewels would be stolen and replaced by fakes.

This was an insidious plot to overthrow the ruling family.

For what felt like hours, his mind raged with scenarios and solutions. Each time one started to seem possible, he slammed into a dead end.

He felt he'd been battered by the time he got to his

feet, a basic plan—the only one he believed could
work—in mind.

To set it in motion, he had to get away from the
palace.

And get Johara out, too.

She had to get out of here.

That was the only thing on Johara's mind since she'd
stumbled away from Shaheen.

All through the palace to her quarters, she'd struggled
to walk naturally and greet the workers who were
everywhere in the aftermath of the reception, undoing
its havoc.

By the time she reached her room, she couldn't
remain upright, slumped against the door to stop herself
from collapsing to the ground.

Her body was still in turmoil, her whole being rioting.
She wanted to run back to Shaheen's quarters and throw
herself in his arms. Come what may.

But she couldn't. Ever again.

And not only would she be deprived of him forever,
she'd probably be here to witness his marriage, if her
father still needed her by the time it came to pass.

"I did it."

Johara's heart almost burst through her ribs. She
swung around, found her father walking in from her
suite's kitchenette. He looked as if he'd aged another
ten years.

"I handed in my resignation to the king."

So he'd finally done it! He'd attended the reception
with her, stood beside her for most of it, and hadn't said
a word. He hadn't said a word, period. He was taking
this even harder than she'd thought.

The desolation in his voice sent compassion surging

through her, propelling her to him so she could hug him, absorb his misery.

He let out a ragged breath, accepted her silent embrace.

Then he pulled back with a sad smile, love shining in the eyes he'd passed down to her. "You always know what to do and say. And more important, what *not* to do and say. I don't think I could have stomached platitudes about how it's for the best, how it's time to start a new life."

A smile trembled on her face in an attempt at teasing. "Even though it's true."

He pinched her cheek softly. "Especially since it is."

She smiled back into his eyes, thankful that he was letting her steer him away from moroseness.

She'd been urging him to resign for the past three weeks, since the day she'd come back and he'd told her he was thinking it was the solution to everything, to sever his connection to Zohayd. And he'd had no idea of *her* dilemma.

She couldn't have agreed more. Yet it had taken him this long to bring himself to do it.

"This place, these people, are far more than a job to me." He walked to the nearest couch, sat down with a heavy exhalation.

She nodded. "Mother always said they held your heart as much as we did, but with the added feeling that you were doing something far bigger than yourself, playing a major part in maintaining the peace and prosperity of Zohayd."

"It's not a feeling, it's a fact." A faraway look of bittersweet reminiscence came over his face. "She once told me I was delusional, considering myself a knight who swore undying allegiance to a great king. But it's not a delusion. I am, and he is." He looked back at her, dejection dimming his gaze. "The only reason I'm ending my service is because I'm no longer in any shape to deliver what he deserves. Even as I lost my family, first Jacqueline, then you, then Aram, I still… functioned. But lately, I seem to have lost my focus, my skills, my stamina."

"You never lost *us*. We love you!"

"But you're no longer with me. Did you know I've been begging your mother to come back to me and to convince you to return, too?"

No. That was news to her. Her parents' relationship had always been a mystery.

"My efforts intensified after Aram went back to the States six years ago. She always refused, so I came to see you both more, stayed longer each time. When he realized my need to be with you, King Atef went out of his way to afford me extended leaves."

She'd wondered how he'd been able to visit them for such long periods. Each visit had always left Jacqueline Nazaryan distraught.

"Your mother has never stopped loving me, you know?"

Johara looked at him helplessly. It seemed he had suddenly decided to answer all the questions he and her mother had always evaded. It had always been impossible to fathom her mother when it came to her father. Jacqueline talked about him and to him with such ire and intensity, but she'd never asked for divorce, or hooked up with another man.

Now Johara watched her father smile to himself, the smile of a man remembering the woman he loved, a sensual pain filling his eyes and lips. "We're still lovers."

She inhaled. Now that was something they'd both left her in the dark about. Very efficiently. She doubted she and Shaheen could hide the intimate nature of their relationship that well. Or at all. Which was why she must never be seen with him again.

She exhaled. "Why won't she come back?"

That would have saved *her* from coming back herself and seeing Shaheen again, driving the lance in her heart deeper.

Her father's lips twisted. "Because she's angry at me. She's been angry at me for a decade and a half. There was a time when I thought she might come back, but then you joined her and she's been adamant ever since about not returning to Zohayd, even for a visit."

"That's why you didn't tell her about your heart attack. Or your depression."

His nod was defeated. "I won't pressure her by playing on her sympathy, Johara. And I certainly don't want her pitying me. I chose my duty over her. I've made a mess of things, and that won't be how I win her back. But I intend to. Or die trying, anyway."

She gasped and he made an apologetic wave of his hand as he rose from the couch. "Don't listen to me, I'm feeling sorry for myself. I'll snap out of it. All the faster because you're here. I've never felt this fragile, and I think my condition makes me more prone to clinging to what I have here. It was your presence that gave me the strength to do what I did tonight. Will you please stay until I serve my notice?"

Her father had never asked anything of her until he'd asked her to come be by his side through this.

She couldn't say no then. She couldn't say it now. She nodded, surged to hug him again.

As she watched him walking out of her suite, her heart churned out thick, slow thuds.

She was trapped. She'd survived being in Zohayd with Shaheen out of the kingdom, but now...

Even after the night of magic they'd shared, she hadn't really believed he might react that way when he saw her again. During the past eight weeks, she'd tormented herself that, with his impending marriage in motion, when they met, he'd pretend she was the acquaintance he hadn't seen in years and then ignore her.

But he hadn't. He'd been every bit as incredible as he'd been that night. She had the same effect on him that he had on her, making him forget caution and trample on reason.

She couldn't let him do that.

Until she could escape Zohayd, this time forever, she had to do everything she could to stop him from destroying his and his family's credibility and weakening their power.

Most of all, she had to keep her secret intact.

A secret that, if discovered, might cost the Aal Shalaans their throne.

Seven

After coming to his decision, Shaheen had ambushed his father as he'd prepared to sleep.

He'd told King Atef he'd changed his mind. He was relieving him of the burden of choosing his bride. But he wanted more choices. Or more reason to choose one of the existing candidates over the others. Surely the families didn't think a prettier dress or a more practiced smile would sway him? Didn't they have more... incentives? For him, personally? He was not just the king's son, a body with the required genes. He was a force to be reckoned with throughout the world. It was his life they were bartering away, after all, and they'd better make it worth his while.

His father had only closed his eyes then risen from his bed and walked out of his room without looking at Shaheen.

Shaheen shut his own eyes now. He hated to add to

his father's strife. But he couldn't include him in his plan. Not yet.

His plan was simple. Kick up a controversy, drag in all those involved in his dilemma and stand back and watch. People showed their true colors in conflicts.

And that was what had been missing so far. After they'd agreed that Shaheen would pick a family through its representative bride, the tribes had fallen into a peaceful coexistence, thinking that, with Shaheen's reputation for being completely incorruptible, there was nothing they could do beyond parading their daughters before him to influence his decision.

Now he'd as good as told them he wasn't just acting the king's obedient son in this matter and they should indeed fight dirty for said favor.

The reactions to this new development—and most important, the nonreactions—would expose who among their so-called allies who had access inside the palace were after new treaties within the current ruling regimen, and who was planning a coup.

He'd thrown his bomb and retreated, gone to his villa on the waters of the Arabian Sea, a hundred miles from the palace. He'd be inaccessible yet still be able to monitor the developments as the reactions of those involved reached him one way or another. Most important, he'd see Johara away from the scrutiny of the court.

She was coming to him now.

His heart expanded at the thought of her. It had taken every iota of his negotiating skills to secure her agreement. And she'd amazed him all over again.

She hadn't resisted because she was feeling jealous or slighted or even heartbroken that he was seeking her out even as he went ahead with his marriage plans.

She'd done so because she didn't want to stir up trouble for him.

But though making everyone believe he was still in the game was paramount for his plan's success, none of that mattered. Not when weighed against protecting her from hurt.

He couldn't leave her in the dark about his feelings and about what he had planned.

She'd agreed to come only when he'd told her he'd come to her publicly if she didn't. She'd believed he was desperate enough to do it. But she'd insisted on making her own way. She'd said no one would think anything of her driving away from the palace on her own, but if she left in his chauffeured car, it would probably be on the national news within the hour. She'd even asked him to send his entourage away while she visited him. Since there was nothing he wanted more than to be alone with her, he'd emptied the immediate two-mile radius.

He was now standing on his second-floor bedroom suite's veranda, awaiting her arrival. He cast his impatience across the tranquil emerald waters, followed the curve of the bay that hugged them and the villa, untouched by human hands except for the road that arced along its edge and that would bring her to him.

The sea winked diamonds in the pre-sunset rays as it lapped froth on the white-gold shore, its mass rocking gently back and forth, its rumble a hypnotic loop. The dense palm trees embracing the villa on its eastern and northern sides swayed in the strong autumn breeze in a dance of rustling elegance and harmony.

The magnificence and serenity felt lifeless, lacking. When she arrived everything would come alive, would be complete.

A cloud of dust swirled at the edge of his vision. In moments it parted on a streak of silver. A speeding car.

"Johara."

He whispered her name, again and again, as he ran through the villa and grounds to await her at the gates.

In minutes, she pulled the car to a gentle stop, feet from him. He covered the remaining distance, holding her eyes through the windshield. He ended up leaning down to plant his palms flat on the hood of her father's Mercedes, trying to bring the longing under control. Then he saw her mouth his name, the feelings echoing his trembling over her face. And he failed.

He rushed to her side, yanked her door open. Then she was in his arms, and he was in hers.

He took her from gravity as he wished to from everything that caused her worry. She surrendered herself to his haven, arms enveloping him from neck to back. He savored their connection, letting their eyes embrace, mate, love welling through him as he pressed her closer and closer. Then he took her lips.

She whimpered his name and he groaned hers between kisses so urgent they grew from barely letting their flesh connect, to sealing their lips in wrenching fusions.

They only broke apart when he placed her on his bed.

He loomed above her, looking down into her eyes, waiting for her to show him, to ask him.

She did, in every way. Her swollen lips joined her misty eyes in their demands, trembled on his name, begging for him.

He'd promised himself he'd talk to her first. But while he could have denied his own craving, he couldn't deny hers.

He rose and her arms fell off his body. They thudded on the dark brown silk he'd draped his bed with for her, graceful arcs of surrender surrounding her head and fanned golden hair. Then she arched upward sinuously, in a wave of white-hot desire stroking him from thighs to chest.

He shuddered with the effort not to tear her out of her clothes and ram into her. His hands trembled when he forced gentleness into them as he stripped her out of her beige pantsuit, which could have been the most outrageous lingerie for its effect on him. He descended deeper into mindlessness as her twists and undulations helped him expose her lushness for his voracity.

"You have no idea, my Gemma…" He kissed and suckled his way from her feet, up her endless satin legs, turning her on her stomach to devour the firmness of her thighs and buttocks, to dig massaging fingers and mouth into the grace of her back and neck. "No idea, what I went through, when you disappeared. Worry almost destroyed my sanity. Then misery, when I thought you didn't want me."

"No." Her cry tore through him as he ground himself against her back, finesse and restraint evaporating. Moans filled his head, high and deep, hers and his. Her flesh burned him with its own torment as she struggled beneath him, demanding he let her face him. He did, and she sank her fingers in his hair, tugged, her eyes urgent, adamant, solemn. "I've never wanted anything but you, Shaheen."

"And I never knew what wanting was until you." Her tears spilled at his declaration. He kissed them away, put her hands to his shirt. "Show me how much you want me, *ya galbi*."

The hunger that spread over her face made him unable to bear the speed with which she exposed him. He ripped anything that couldn't be undone fast enough, hoping she wouldn't be alarmed at his savagery. Relief flooded him when it only inflamed her more.

But it wasn't every dig of her fingers, nip of her teeth, pull of her lips, or even that she overcame her shyness and stroked and tasted his manhood that made him almost berserk. It was her words that singed him through to his soul and served as the ultimate aphrodisiac.

"I always thought you the most beautiful thing in the world, Shaheen," she sobbed. "I want you all over me, inside me."

"Give me your pleasure first, *ya galbi*."

Before she could protest, he clamped one nipple between his lips, suckled her, nipped her, gorging on the feel and taste. Her cries of pleasure amplified in his inflamed brain as her body begged for his invasion. He glided the length of his nakedness against hers, reveling in how her satin firmness cushioned his rougher hardness. He pushed her legs apart with his knees, opened her folds with one hand. He stumbled to the brink just gliding his fingers along her molten heat, just smelling her arousal.

He drew harder on her nipple, giving her two fingers to suckle, while his other hand rubbed shaking circles over the knot of flesh where her nerves converged. She writhed, moaned, rippled beneath him, demanding more. He gave her more, two fingers pumping into her tight, flowing heat. After a few languorous thrusts, she bowed up on a stifled cry. Then she came apart.

"*Aih, ya galbi*, show me how much you want everything I do to you." He feasted on the sight as she took her fill of pleasure, her inhibitions almost gone. Each grip and release of her inner flesh on his fingers transmitted to his arousal.

He still waited until she subsided, then stimulated her again. She pushed his hand away with a sharp cry of impatience, snared him with her legs, trying to get him to mount her.

He smiled his approval into her stormy eyes. "*Aih,* show me what you want of me, tell me how you want it."

"I want you to take me, hard. Don't you dare hold anything back this time. Give me all of you—" her fingers dug into his shoulders, wrenching him down on top of her with all the power of her fervor "—*now!*"

Before he complied, he reached for the bedside drawer. He was ready with protection this time. She stayed his hand, shook her head. Holding her heavy-with-need gaze, he read her message. She was telling him it was safe to take her. And he couldn't draw another breath if he didn't, if he didn't give her all of him. He gripped her buttocks, tilted her, growled, "*Khodini kolli…take all of me, ya joharti,*" and plunged.

He hit her womb on that first thrust, obeying her need for his total invasion, secure she was ready, that any discomfort would only sharpen her pleasure. She engulfed him back with a piercing keen, consumed him in what felt like a velvet inferno.

He rested his forehead on hers, feeling like he was truly home, his hold on consciousness loosening.

Then she arched beneath him, until he felt she took him into her core, her streaming eyes making him feel she'd taken him into her heart. She was embedded in his.

With a pledge that he'd never let her go, he withdrew all the way then thrust back, fierce and full.

He rode every satin scream as hard as she'd demanded, his rumbling echoing her cries. Her tightness clamped harder around his length, pouring more red-hot pleasure over his flesh, until she convulsed beneath him.

Seeing her abandon, feeling the force of her pleasure, shattered him. He plummeted after her into the abyss of ecstasy, slid himself all the way inside her and released his essence.

Time ceased to matter, to exist, as he came down on top of her as she demanded, anchoring her after the tumult.

Then he brought her over him, a drape of satisfaction, everything he wanted wanting him back, and back in his arms.

"Ahebbek, ya joharti. Aashagek. Enti hayati kollaha."

She jerked at the words he whispered against her cooling forehead. Then she pushed feebly against him, demanding to be released from their union.

It took a moment before he could bring himself to release her, worry replacing satiation and bliss at her agitated breathing and renewed tears, which he was sure didn't indicate renewed arousal.

"Don't…say things like that again." She wiped tears away, half stricken, half furious. "I believe you want me like you've never wanted another, but don't say what you can't possibly feel."

He sat up, caught her face in both hands, made her look at him. "That *is* how I feel. And more."

Thicker tears overflowed from her reddened eyes. "How can you? How can you love me, worship me, think that I'm all your life? Before today, we had only one night together."

"We had eight *years.* And all the years we've been apart. I loved you each moment of those." A sob tore through her as she shook her head, tried to escape his grip again. He wouldn't release her, persisted. "Why do you find it unbelievable? *You* loved me each moment of those years."

She dipped her head, her hair swishing forward in waves that looked like sun rays spun into glossy satin, obscuring her expression. "I...never said I loved you."

"Yes, because you're trying not to 'compromise' me, or 'impose' on me, by keeping this on the level of the senses, and away from the domains of the heart and soul."

She bit her trembling lower lip. "W-why do you think that?"

"Because I know you. I've known everything about you since you were six and grew up under my proud eyes. You didn't just share everything you thought with me, you shared *how* you thought. I can predict everything that goes inside your brilliant if misguided mind and your magnanimous, self-sacrificing heart. That's why I love you so completely. And you love me as totally, as fiercely. I feel it. I felt it from the first moment I met you again. I might not have recognized you consciously, but everything in me knew you, and knew I had always loved you."

She gaped at him. And gaped at him. Then she burst in tears.

"Oh, Shaheen...I n-never dreamed you c-could feel the same." Words tore from her between sobs. "If I'd known, I wouldn't have tried to see you again. I don't want to complicate your life."

He pressed her hard, stopping her self-blame again.

"As I told you last night, you've done nothing but make my life worthwhile. In the past, being with you was the best thing that ever happened to me...until Aram made me feel like a dirty old man." She jerked at that. He almost kicked himself for bringing it up. He tried to divert her. "Then, from the night we met again—"

She wouldn't be diverted. "How did Aram make you feel like that?" He shrugged. She clung to his arm, ebony eyes entreating, undeniable. "Tell me, please."

How could he resist her when she looked at him that way?

And then, he wanted no secrets between them. Ever again.

He exhaled. "You remember how I used to spend every possible second with you and Aram, either individually or together. Then one day, after a squash match—he'd trounced me, too—I related something clever that you'd said to me the day before, and he tore into me. Called me a cruel, spoiled prince, accused me of ignoring him for years whenever he'd tried to warn me about treating you too indulgently, to stop encouraging your hopeless crush on me. Then he threatened me."

"Wh-what did he threaten you with?"

"Not death or serious injury, don't worry. But that was actually what shook me most—how intense but nonviolent he was. It was as if he hated me, and had for a long time. I would have preferred it if he'd beaten me up, broken a few bones. I would have healed from that. But I never healed from losing his friendship. He told me that if I didn't keep you away from me, he'd make my father order me to never come near you again."

"So that was why you suddenly shunned us!"

He nodded. "I tried to defend myself at first, said you

were the little sister I never had and how dare he say I'd think of you—or encourage you to think of me—*that* way."

"So you never thought of me…that way?"

"*No.*" She seemed dismayed at his emphatic negation. "Come on, Johara, I was a man of twenty-two, you were a kid of fourteen. I would have been a pervert if I had thought of you that way. But you were *my* girl, the only one who 'got' me. I had to explain myself to everyone else, even to Aram and my family, but not to you. I loved you, in every way but *that* way. I love you in every way now."

He poured his emotions into her eyes, then her lips. She surfaced from the mating of their mouths, panting. Then pleasure drained from her face as the pall of what they'd been discussing resurfaced. "What happened after that?"

He sighed again. "Aram said he didn't give a damn what I thought or felt. He only cared that I was emotionally exploiting you. And he couldn't stand by until I damaged you irrevocably. I realized he was doing what he thought best to protect you, which is why I was never really angry at him. Perhaps subconsciously, I *was* waiting for you to grow up so that I could feel that way about you. So in a fit of mortification, I swore I'd never talk to you, *or* him, again, that neither of you would have to put up with the 'cruel, spoiled prince' anymore. That's why I pulled away, in a misguided effort to keep my word to him.

"Then, as I agonized over how much I'd inadvertently hurt my best friends, you left Zohayd, and your father announced that you wouldn't be coming back. My last memory of you was of your forlorn face as you left the palace. I felt I'd betrayed our friendship. I left Zohayd soon afterward, and came back only sporadically through the years, until Aram left Zohayd a few years back. I felt I didn't have the right to try to heal our friendship."

She stared at him, chest heaving, emotions flashing in dizzying succession over her ultra-expressive face.

Then she threw herself at him, crushed him to her. "Ah, *ya habibi,* I'm so sorry. Aram was *so* wrong."

His lips twisted as he looked down at their entwined nakedness. "I think he was *so* right."

"He was wrong *then.* That's what counts. You never led me on, never hurt me. I owe most of what I am today to your friendship. I think I'm not as messed up as he feared I'd be."

"You're perfection itself, inside and out."

"See? He was absolutely wrong. Ooh!" She punched a pillow. "And the rat even told me you said you stopped talking to us because we were 'the help.'"

"What?" he shouted. "All right, *now* I am angry at him."

"Makes two of us. Just wait until I get ahold of him. I'm going to have his overprotective hide!"

"I hope you didn't believe him!"

She slid a leg between his, stroked his face, laying everything inside her wide-open for him to read, to drink deeply of. "Does it look like I did?"

"No, *alhamdulel'lah,* thank God." He stroked her back in wonder. "You're all I want. It's all I want, to be with you."

A grimace wiped away her loving expression. "Wanting it and being able to do it are polar opposites here."

He threaded his fingers through her hair, cupped her head through its thickness, took her lips in a fierce kiss.

"Things might be complicated now, but I will resolve everything—"

"Please, don't. Don't promise me anything. I don't want you burdening yourself with what you can't accomplish, or with the guilt when you fail to. I will take what I can have with you, and I'll always be happy that I did. That I love you. That you love me."

Before he could protest, she dragged him to her, drowned him in delirious passion, taking the reins this time.

In the aftermath of pleasure, she slept in his arms. He remained awake, watching her.

And he knew he couldn't tell her. About the jewels, or about his plan. He couldn't bring the ugliness of the outside world into their happiness now. He wouldn't sully hers if at all possible.

It was up to him to make it so.

For the next two weeks, Johara spent a few hours every morning helping her father pack, resolve any standing issues and train his replacements before she slipped away to Shaheen's villa to throw herself in his arms.

He told her again and again not to worry, that he was working on securing a way for them to be together.

She believed he'd fail. That her time with him was counting down. Again. On a slower scale than that night she'd thought would be all she'd have of him, but counting down still. And when their time ran out, it would break them both.

But she couldn't think of that now. She was bound on filling every second they had left with wonder and happiness and pleasure. Maybe if they charged every cell they could with love and closeness and cherishing, they might be able to endure the desolation of a life without each other.

She opened the front door to his villa, knowing she'd find it empty. He wasn't here. A message ten minutes ago had told her he'd been detained, but would be there soon. And that he adored her.

She sighed in anticipation, soaking up the masculine elegance surrounding her. Acres of polished marble the color of the awe-inspiring beaches just steps from the back porch, whitewashed walls, deep brown furniture the color of the palm trees that seemed to form a natural fortress wall around the villa, and accents in gradations of emerald like the breathtaking sea that greeted her from every window, spreading to the horizon.

"I was told, but I couldn't believe it."

For the moment it took the words to sink into her brain, she had the conviction that Shaheen's voice was the one that caressed her ears and slid down every inch of her skin, his presence that reached out to envelop her.

But even before she spun around, she knew. It was almost Shaheen's voice, almost his presence. But it wasn't him.

This voice had the same beauty and depth and influence, but instead of warmth it held an arctic chill, instead of emotion there was a void. This presence wasn't permeated by humor and gentleness and compassion, but by sarcasm and aggression and cruelty. She knew who it was before she saw him.

Amjad.

Shaheen's oldest brother. The crown prince of Zohayd. One of the most unstoppable forces in the world of finance.

And the most feared man in the region.

Her jaw almost dropped as she watched him approach her with the languid, majestic prowl of a stalking tiger.

This must be what a fallen angel looked like. Impossible beauty, hair-raising aura. His luminescent emerald eyes were said to be the only of their kind in the Aal Shalaan family in five centuries, inherited directly from Ezzat Aal Shalaan, the founder of Zohayd. Many even said Amjad was his replica, with the same imposing physique, frightening intelligence and overwhelming charisma. Some believed he was Ezzat reincarnated.

It was also said their lives followed much the same lines. Ezzat's first wife had also plotted to murder him.

But that was where their destinies diverged. Ezzat had found his true love only a year after aborting the plot against his life, had lived with her in harmony from the time he'd married her at thirty-one till the day he'd died at eighty-five.

Amjad had exposed his treacherous wife eight years ago, and there was no sign that he'd find someone to love. In fact, from what she'd heard, he seemed determined to wrestle destiny into submission, thwarting any of its attempts to bring him any measure of closeness again.

"Now I see that what I thought to be ridiculous hyperbole is actually pathetic understatement. You've become a goddess, Johara."

Johara blinked at Amjad, stunned.

His smile would probably cause a meltdown were any of Zohayd's female population within sight and earshot. But it shocked her to see that predatory sensuality on the face of the man she'd always considered her oldest brother.

Not knowing what to say to that, she said what she did feel. "It's so good to see you, Amjad."

His eyes crinkled, making them even more chilling. "Is it?"

She swallowed, suddenly feeling like a mouse about to be made a bored cat's swatting toy. "Yes, of course. It's been so many years. You're looking well."

"Just well?" Amjad's spectacular lips turned down in a pout. "I usually get a more…enthusiastic response from the ladies."

She cleared her throat. "You know how you look, Amjad. Surely the last thing a man of your caliber needs is an ego stroke."

"Ouch." He winced, looking anything but hurt, the calculation in his eyes growing more cutting. "But then again, an ego stroke from a woman of your caliber is something to be coveted. Any kind of stroke would be… most welcome."

She gaped as he stopped barely a foot away, tried to step back. He stepped forward, maintaining the suffo-cating nearness.

She, too, had thought the tales she'd heard about him had been exaggerations. They were absolute under-statements. This close, she got a good look at what Amjad had become.

It was as if his magnificent body was a shell, housing an entity of overpowering intellect and annihilating disdain. He'd used to be a loving, outgoing, deeply passionate and committed man. The woman who'd tried to poison him might have failed to kill him, but she'd poisoned his soul and killed off everything that had made him the incredible force for good he'd once been.

Regret squeezed her heart.

Suddenly every hair on her body stood on end, in sheer shock.

His hand slid around her waist, tugged her flush against his hardness from breast to knee.

She froze, unable to even breathe.

At last, she choked out, "Amjad, please, don't—"

He pressed her closer. "Don't what, *ya joharti?*"

Hearing Shaheen's endearment for her from anyone else would have startled her. Hearing it from Amjad, spoken with that insolent familiarity, seriously disturbed her.

He didn't disgust her. It was impossible for him to do so; he was Shaheen's flesh and blood. He was like *her* brother, even if he was behaving as anything but. She only felt so sad she wanted to weep. Then she got mad.

She pushed at him with all her strength. "Don't call me that. I'm not your anything."

She could have been fighting a brick wall. His hold didn't even loosen. He even pulled her closer. "Not yet. But I can be. Your everything, if you only say the word. I can give you everything, Johara. Just name it and it's yours."

Mortification washed over her as the full realization of what he was doing here radiated outward, drenching her in a storm of goose bumps. "Please...don't do this."

He caught her hands, dragged her arms around his neck, held them in place with one hand, the other keeping her head prisoner as he swooped down and latched his lips to her exposed neck. She might have cried out, but the next second, thunder drowned out all her efforts.

"*B'haggej'jaheem*, what are you *doing?*"

Eight

Johara's heart stopped the moment Shaheen's enraged voice slammed into her back.

But it wasn't only her heart that plunged into deep freeze. The paralysis was total as Amjad straightened in degrees, not in any hurry to turn to face Shaheen. She could only stare up at him as he raised his head, releasing her neck from the coldness of his lips, which may as well have been draining her life away. Then she met his eyes and the ice encasing her turned to stone as he let her see what he felt toward her for the first time. Sheer abhorrence.

One hand was still locking both of hers around his neck. He brought the other one up and her horror deepened. To any onlooker—to Shaheen—it would seem as if he were unclasping the hands she had clamped there of her own will.

Then Amjad moved aside, affording her a direct look

at Shaheen. He was standing under the arch between the foyer and the expansive sitting area. She would have sobbed if she hadn't been struck mute. She'd never imagined Shaheen looking like that. He looked... frightening.

"Shaheen, you're home early." Amjad turned to his younger brother in a sweep of pure grace and power, unperturbed, imperturbable. "Johara and I were getting...reacquainted."

Inside, she was screaming. *Don't believe him.* Outside, she could only watch his reaction in mounting horror. Then realization descended and she gave up trying to break out of her paralysis.

Maybe this was for the best. Shaheen's best. If he believed Amjad, he'd be hurt, betrayed. But he'd eventually be free of his love for her. Free of her. She wished that for him, the peace and freedom she'd never have.

Shaheen moved then, walked up to them. Even with desperation descending on her, his every step closer thudded in her now stampeding heart like the ticking of a time bomb. And he didn't even meet her eyes. He kept his locked on his older brother's.

Then he stopped, his gaze moving to the arm maintaining a hold on her waist. Without raising his eyes again he said, "Take your hand off Johara, Amjad. Or have every bone in it broken."

She shuddered. His voice was now as pitiless as Amjad's. Worse. Laden with barely contained aggression.

Amjad finally let go of her, raised both hands up in a cross between mock placation and false surrender. "Intense. And here I thought you were gentleman enough not to make this more...awkward than it is. So, little brother, is this your way of laying claim to a woman? Threatening other men off? Afraid if you let her choose which man best fulfills her…needs, she won't choose you? So it is like Johara said. You are leaving her no choice but to succumb to your…attentions."

"One more word and you'll be flat on your back with a broken jaw, spitting out blood and teeth."

"I should have believed you when you told me what a caveman he was being." Amjad's ruthlessly handsome face shifted from chillingly sincere as he addressed her to devilishly goading as he turned to Shaheen. "That was over a dozen words, by the way."

Shaheen pounced, grabbed Amjad by his casual yet superbly cut zippered black sweater. Every nerve in her body slackened as the two majestic forces of nature prepared to collide.

They were equal in every way, so similar, yet seemed like opposites. Even in his fury, Shaheen's spirit shone untarnished, radiating a spectrum of positive vibes and influences, while Amjad's emptiness seemed to suck all light and life from his surroundings, to turn everything dark and hopeless.

After a breathless moment of tension as she trembled with the need to throw herself between them but forced herself to let this unfold without her intervention, with a mutter of disgust, Shaheen pushed Amjad away so hard that his older brother took several steps backward to steady himself.

"You're not worth it," Shaheen hissed.

"Go ahead, make me the villain here. But this was mutual."

Shaheen bared his teeth on a fed-up grimace. "Shut *up*."

"Or what? You've already decided not to sully your

hands with my blood." Amjad straightened his clothes, swept the hair that had rained down his face to frame his slashed cheekbones back in place. "I didn't know you were that involved, but maybe it's for the best. You really have to be objective, Shaheen. A woman has a right to look out for her best interests. Johara is justified in looking out for number one and going out *for* number one. And let's face it. With your problems, you don't make the grade."

Shaheen gave a vicious snort. "Save your venom, Amjad, even if you have an unlimited supply of it. You must be far less shrewd and insightful than I gave you credit for if you believe for a second I'm buying this farce you staged."

Amjad gave him a pitying glance. "Is that what you're hoping this is? Something I staged? How would I have staged her arms around me when you walked in?"

"Knowing you, you bulldozed her into it. Knowing her, she was too considerate of who you are—to me, and to her in the past—to blast you off the face of the earth as you deserve." Shaheen suddenly seemed to think Amjad deserved no more attention, swung to her, his face transforming in a heartbeat from intolerant and unforgiving to the very sight of tenderness and concern. "I'm so sorry, *ya joharet galbi,* that I exposed you to this indignity."

Overwhelmed, she whispered, "You didn't do anything…"

"It is on my account that Amjad has insulted you, in an effort to plant doubt in my mind about your feelings and intentions toward me."

"You realized what he… You know that I…" She choked, unable to go on. That he trusted her, didn't even pause to question…

All thought of giving him up for his own good forgotten, she threw herself into his arms, breath gone, her heart fracturing at his feet from too much love. He soothed her with gentle caresses, his words of love and apology unceasing. "I'll always know what's in your heart. You *are* my heart."

"My, Shaheen…" Amjad's sarcasm fractured their moment of communion. "This has to set a new world record for patheticness. Think, little brother. Why is she back now of all times? Contrary to you, she knows you're not as clever as you think you are, that we were bound to find out about your 'secret' arrangement."

Shaheen turned to Amjad, never loosening his hold on her. "We? You mean Father knows, too?"

Amjad gave a denigrating huff. "With the hoops you're making him hop through and the condition he's been in since Aliyah and Anna returned? Nah. But if *I* put his and hers together when I saw her coming back to the palace all flushed and flustered yesterday while you were pointedly away, I'm sure others of lesser insight will catch on and connect the dots."

Shaheen shook his head in amazement. "So enlighten me, Amjad. What is Johara's plan, in your opinion?"

Amjad sighed as if he had to explain that things fell down or water was wet to a moron. "She's after a ransom. Yours. I was pretending to offer her myself in return for unhooking you from her claws when you interrupted."

Shaheen massaged her waist, as if to erase Amjad's accusations and disdain. "But I didn't interrupt. You dragged me away on a wild-goose chase, waited for Johara, timed your performance so I'd walk in to see her presumably in your arms. And you thought I'd charge in and accuse her of betraying me."

Amjad looked the image of uncaring boredom. "Would have been less…traumatic for you lovebirds if you had. Pity. I gave 'nice' a shot. I should have stuck with my forte—nasty. Now I will."

"First, you'll do nothing, Amjad. Second, if Johara wanted to be bribed to leave gullible me alone, why do you think she insisted on all this secrecy?"

Amjad gave him a ridiculing look. "Because letting you loose when you believe she walks on water will fetch a far higher price. And it worked. I was willing to pay top dollar."

Shaheen only laughed at that, looked down at her, no longer seething with affront, but highly entertained. "What would it cost for you to let go of me, *ya jo-harti?*"

A smile twisted with a wince on her lips. "You know."

Shaheen stilled them in a fierce kiss before he looked back at Amjad. "Only I can make her let go of me, Amjad. And I'm never letting her go. So why don't you get down on your knees and beg Johara's forgiveness, then get out of here?"

Amjad huffed in disgust. "She really has you clinging around her pinky with your face smashed against it, doesn't she? Fine. Every man has a right to choose his poison. But risking war for her? Tsk."

"If you're so concerned about war, why don't you do something about it? Break your pathetic vow never to marry again and take one of those brides they want to shove down my throat."

"Oh, I did break it, when I saw you kicking and screaming. I thought as crown prince they'd jump at my offer. But father came back to me with the consensus within an hour. No bride will have me. They believe

I'll go all Shahrayar or Othello on them. Even if their families are willing to sacrifice their daughters at the altar of my madness, the families think I'll turn on the next of kin. Comes from being viewed as a force that can't be approached let alone harnessed and profited from, I guess."

Shaheen guffawed. "Aw, thanks for trying to spare me *that* at least. But I'm so glad you're not shocked that you were turned down. You *have* been tearing through the kingdom—and the world—with borderline sane actions and insane gambles."

Amjad's gaze grew more ridiculing. "Really? Then how has each one paid off big-time? Maybe I'm not as irrational as you all like to think I am. Digest this and gain new insight into your mad brother's actions and convictions. You'll find I'm right about other things, too." He flicked Johara a just-wait-until-I'm-through-with-you look. "Her, for instance. Even if you can't think so now, being caught in her love spell."

Johara saw Shaheen's eyes soften. "It's you who are under a spell—of hatred. You knew and loved Johara once, too. Yet you can't access that knowledge or that love because of the paranoia you've been trapped in since Salmah. You will never understand that I'd mistrust myself before I would Johara. I trust her with my life, and far more."

Amjad pretended to dust himself off. "Yuck. All that sticky nonsense will take some heavy-duty sense to wash off. Well, you go ahead and smother yourself in her honey trap for now, while I—"

He stopped, turned his head. Then she, too, heard what had caught his attention. A faraway drone. It was getting louder, nearer by the second. In moments, it was unmistakable.

A helicopter.

Amjad turned back, derision turning his beauty into that of an unrepentant devil. "Uh-oh. Sounds like the cavalry have realized what you're up to and are charging here to save you from your mushy heart and malfunctioning mind."

Giving him one last impatient look, Shaheen clasped her hand and led her to the western veranda, where she noticed for the first time a clearance that must be a launching/landing pad.

It was. In seconds, the helicopter landed there. As the rotors winded down, a very tall, broad man jumped down from the pilot's side. He rushed to the passenger's side to help a woman down, his movements as tender as Shaheen's were with her. She worked out the woman's identity when she recognized the man. Kamal Aal Masood, the king of Judar.

Sure enough, Aliyah came into view, proving Johara's deduction. And deepening her agitation.

From the grim expression on Aliyah's face as she approached the villa with her juggernaut of a husband, Johara knew that her reason for interrupting them the other night hadn't been resolved. And Johara was certain that it concerned her. Probably Amjad's same concern. And Aliyah was back to broach the subject with Shaheen, with a one-man army as reinforcement.

The regal couple walked into the villa. Shaheen received them with her at his side, hugging them both and introducing her to Kamal. Kamal gallantly kissed her hand. Aliyah gave her the accustomed three kisses, one on one cheek, two on the other. It all seemed genial enough, but Johara vibrated with the tension radiating from the couple, from the whole scene.

Amjad advanced on them, pulled Aliyah in for a

quick kiss, thumped Kamal on the back, then got to the point without preamble, breaking the stilted cordiality. "So, Kamal, what warrants the presence of the king of Judar on our soil and on such a clandestine visit, too?"

Kamal gave Amjad a smile that echoed his own, that of a man who knew his own power to its last iota, was versed in wielding it to its most destructive limits, who tolerated nothing but his own way, always. "So which part of 'clandestine' don't you get, Amjad?"

Aliyah arched an exquisite eyebrow at him. "Yes, Amjad, if we wanted you to be involved, we wouldn't have come here."

Amjad held a hand to his heart as if Aliyah had shot him there with a barb. "Whoa. My little cousin-turned-sister has grown some sharp fangs. Especially with your weapon-of-mass-destruction husband at hand."

Kamal coughed a laugh. "If you think she's baring her fangs because I'm here, then you should be reintroduced to your little cousin-turned-sister. I'm the one who holds her back when she wants to rip you to shreds. You remind her too much of me before she...unscrambled me."

Amjad gave him a look of mock sweetness, belittlment blaring in it. "Yes, I can see you're all 'fixed.'"

Aliyah harrumphed. "You should be so lucky to find someone who'd 'fix' you, too, Amjad."

"How about I pass, sis? For the next few reincarnations."

Kamal stepped nearer, his smile becoming as confrontational as Amjad's was disparaging. "How about I 'fix' you myself?"

Amjad's smile grew more provoking. He was clearly spoiling for the fight Shaheen had denied him. "That's how you get your kicks nowadays, Kamal? You can't win against the lady who has you whipped, so you pick fights to win her lenience? Shaheen just finished attempting the same thing, by the way."

"You know, Amjad, I've been wanting to deck you for a long time. Now is as good a time as any to finally act on the impulse."

As the two men squared off, Johara found herself absently thinking they could have been brothers, too. And it wasn't just their height and looks. Kamal had more in common with Amjad than Shaheen did. There was the same harshness about him, chiseled into his face and carved into his being. This man could be ruthless. Must regularly be so, to be able to govern Zohayd's big sister kingdom so well, to be obeyed so completely in this volatile region.

Aliyah pushed the two men apart, one hand perpendicular to the other. "Okay, testosterone timeout. In your corners, boys."

Johara blinked at the transformation that came over Kamal as he looked at Aliyah. It was a shock to see softness melting him, love and devotion possessing his every feature and move. Johara recognized the emotions that she and Shaheen shared. She had no doubt Aliyah was everything to Kamal, that he'd die for her. And vice versa.

Kamal gave Aliyah a loving squeeze. "Just because you wish it, *ya rohi*. But next time you want to shred him, let me know."

Amjad snorted. "So apart from airing the fond fantasies you all have of beating me up, can I hope you're here on an undercover mission to save Shaheen from his stupidity, too?"

Kamal's lips twisted. "Maybe I'm here to show him

some youngest-brother solidarity, sharing my expertise in swatting off nuisance older brothers."

"You mean Farooq and Shehab?" Amjad huffed. "Those softies who left you the throne to be with their sweethearts? I almost feel it's my duty to coach them in how to make your life harder. You have it way too easy." At Aliyah's jab in his gut, Amjad rolled his eyes, exhaled. "Fine. Keep your regal secrets. For now. I'll leave you foursome to your sickeningly sweet double date." He nodded at Johara as a parting shot. "I'll be watching you."

The other three bristled. Johara almost blurted out that he wouldn't have to, not for long. But Shaheen hugged her closer to him, his protective gesture deepening her muteness.

As soon as Amjad was out of earshot, strolling non-chalantly to the door, Kamal gave a heavy exhalation. "We came here for an update on the progress of your plan and to give you our input, but…" He paused, looked apologetically at Aliyah then Shaheen. "I know I promised, and Amjad is a world-class and probably one-of-a-kind pain, but he's an extensively powerful one, not to mention he's got a major stake in this. Though I agree secrecy is paramount, I do believe he and Harres should be brought in now, not later. We need them."

Shaheen's eyes flared with alarm. "I need more time. My plan is working. I'm gathering more information every day."

Kamal shook his head, emphatic, final. "It's not working well enough or fast enough, Shaheen, and you know it."

"What plan?" Johara clutched Shaheen's arm, her heart thudding with dread. "What's going on, Shaheen?"

Shaheen looked down at her, entreaty setting his eyes ablaze. "It's nothing to concern yourself with, *ya habibati.*"

Aliyah placed her hand on his other arm. "No, Shaheen. I now believe Johara has nothing to do with this. And since she doesn't, she needs to know. This involves her, too, as much as or even more than it does any of us."

Johara's heart almost uprooted itself as she watched Shaheen close his eyes for a long moment, confusion and worst-case scenarios crashing through her mind.

Then he let out a ragged exhalation. "Fine. Call Amjad back."

In moments, Kamal walked back with Amjad. Before Amjad could voice the speculation evident on his face, Shaheen began to talk.

Johara could only stare at him as he revealed shock after shock. The jewels. The Pride of Zohayd. Stolen. Replaced by fakes. She filled in the blanks he left out with all present intimately aware of them. The projected consequences.

After he finished talking, the only thing that could do the ominous revelations justice descended on their quintet. Decimating silence. Even Amjad was lost for words.

It was she, who'd been practically mute since Shaheen had walked in, who finally found her voice, a chafing whisper. "Why didn't you tell me?"

Shaheen cupped her cheek, concern seizing his face. "I didn't want to burden you with this before I discovered the culprits."

"Give me a break!" Amjad erupted. "I can forgive you being blind when it's your own life at stake, even if your actions could cause an internal crisis. But civil war pales in comparison to what this could mean to the whole region. Can you even imagine the instability a coup and a new ruling house in Zohayd would cause? Can you even project what could be far worse, a new 'democratic' dictatorship sprouting in the middle of the kingdoms? Are you totally out of your mind? What culprits are you trying to discover? One is standing right before you, the only one who had the opportunity and the means to carry this out. What more do you need? A Dear John videotaped gloating confession from her after she's destroyed us all?"

"I swear I *will* knock you down, Amjad," Shaheen growled.

"Have at it, Shaheen." Amjad threw his hands in the air, calculation gone, agitation taking hold. "I thought Johara's return was the plot of a woman out to get all she can out of the royal family she grew up among. But this is far worse. It's clear how it all happened. Berj summoned her to help him stage his plan and faked his heart attack as motive to call her back. He must have sent her after you to guarantee that no one would think to question her return, not with her double-pronged alibi of being the distraught daughter and hopeless lover. It would have worked spectacularly if Aliyah hadn't discovered the theft."

Shaheen slammed both palms flat into Amjad's shoulders, shouted at him, "You see betrayal everywhere, Amjad. You're so poisoned by it you can't hear how your suspicions cancel each other out. One moment you think Berj and Johara are so stupid they'd do something like this when they'd be the first the fingers point to, the next you accuse them of being consummate manipulators. *You're* the one who's so blind you don't see how flimsy the circumstantial evidence against them is, and the frame up it all reeks of."

"That makes the most sense," Aliyah agreed. "Someone thought Berj and Johara would be the perfect fall guys if the plot was discovered."

"If Aliyah's—and Shaheen's—instincts say you and your father are innocent—" Kamal looked at Johara, a pledge glittering in his golden eyes "—then that's my proof that you are. You have my word I'll do everything in my power to defend you, to discover those who sought to frame you, and to punish them for it."

Amjad put both hands up. "Since the voice of sanity is having no effect in breaking up this mutual admiration society, I'll do more than any of you is willing to even consider. I'll concede that I may have gotten it wrong. But in case I didn't, consider the consequences you might be inviting, chasing fictional culprits while letting the real ones get away. With the jewels, the throne and the region's stability."

"Your concern is noted, Amjad," Shaheen muttered. "And dismissed. Now give me your word you will not go after either Johara or Berj in any way."

Amjad held his brother's eyes for one last moment, before he shrugged. "I can only promise you this—once Harres is brought up to speed, if he believes the same as you, since you're the one who has more to lose than any of us, I'll let you steer this."

Shaheen gave him a curt nod. "Good enough for me."

Aliyah spoke then, in what felt like a summation. "Now that we're not fighting amongst ourselves, I don't think we can be careful enough handling this. Even though the thieves know we wouldn't be able to conduct an open investigation if we did discover the fakes, giving

them the false security of believing we haven't will
help us uncover them and retrieve the jewels before the
Exhibition Ceremony."

After that, the men and Aliyah determined the mea-
sures each of them would undertake in the investigation,
with Kamal, as the most neutral party, chosen to be the
one to inform Harres.

Johara stood by Shaheen, numb, as they departed.

After the last echo of Aliyah's and Kamal's helicopter
and Amjad's roaring sports car faded in the distance,
Johara remained staring blindly into nothingness.

She'd thought she'd already imagined the worst that
could happen, thought she'd done everything she could
to protect Shaheen from any consequences. She knew
nothing...

She jumped as Shaheen's hands came down on her
shoulders. "Come inside from the chill, *ya galbi*. You
need to sit down and I need to help you digest it all."

As she nodded, she heard another rumble in the
distance. In seconds, she saw what it was. A procession of
imposing stretch limos gleaming black in the declining
sun, each flaunting Zohayd's gold and emerald flag on
its hood.

Shaheen stiffened. "This is all I need to top off this
day. Father." He turned to her. "Please, wait in our room.
I'll sort this out, whatever it is, as soon as I can."

She could only nod and turn like an automaton to do
his bidding.

In minutes, she was sitting on the edge of his bed—
theirs for now—every nerve in her body jerking at each
sound as she documented the cavalcade's movements,
the voices she distinguished to be Shaheen's and his
father's rising, then the sound of urgent footsteps up the
stairs, coming nearer and nearer.

The door to Shaheen's bedroom burst open.

Shaheen stood behind his father looking like he might shove the king out of the way. Then King Atef, in full royal garb, advanced into the expansive room, dismissing his son's protests.

She rose from the bed, feeling she was about to receive the ultimate blow. Then the king delivered it.

"Is it true, Johara? Are you pregnant with Shaheen's child?"

Nine

Shaheen stared at the back of his father's head, the question reverberating in his mind. His gaze moved to settle on Johara's frozen face. Her eyes were holding his father's, shocked denial filling them.

Then she quavered, "No, I'm not."

And he got his confirmation.

Johara *was* pregnant.

He felt his heart spiral inside him, as if he were plummeting down a never-ending roller coaster.

From the moment he'd found her gone, he'd wondered if there'd been consequences to their surrender to passion without a thought for precautions. Thinking she could discover her pregnancy while she was alone had exacerbated his misery at her disappearance. But she'd said nothing since they'd been together again, making him certain she wasn't pregnant. Then after that first time when she'd stopped him from using precautions, making him believe she'd taken her own, they'd made love again and again through the past two weeks, and he'd believed there was no chance of their passion bearing fruit.

But she hadn't taken precautions because she was already pregnant. And she hadn't told him due to her seemingly unwavering decision to never compromise him or impose on him with demands she believed she had no right to make, and that he'd be incapable of meeting.

From what felt like the bottom of an abyss he heard his father's voice, thickened with regret and apology.

"I'm sorry, *ya b'nayti,* if I'm relieved to hear that. I couldn't wish for a better woman for Shaheen, but as king, the last thing I can consider are my wishes. With the current situation and Shaheen's commitment to defusing the brewing unrest, I am forced to consider only that, at whatever cost to myself and my family."

Shaheen saw Johara nod, her golden hair a gentle wave of resignation around her face. And he moved, pushed past his father.

He stopped before her. Unable to touch her as his emotions mushroomed, he heard a bass rumble bleed out of him. "You didn't believe me. When I pledged that we would be together, that I am yours and will never be anyone else's. And this is why you never told me. You were planning on leaving me 'to my destiny' without telling me. You planned to have our baby on your own."

She cast her eyes down, as if to misdirect him from the knowledge now coursing through his blood, as if he needed to look into her eyes to see through to her soul. "I s-said I'm not pregnant."

He touched her then, just a finger below her chin,

bringing up those eyes that he needed to look into to feel alive now. "Yes, because you're terminally heroic and misguided and want to sacrifice yourself for my so-called best interests and those of Zohayd. Your eyes are still promising me freedom, when my only freedom is to be yours."

His father advanced, confusion and foreboding warring over his weathered, noble face. "So, is it true?"

Johara held Shaheen's eyes, the attempt to hide the truth trembling for one last moment before it fractured. And it came flooding out with a cascade of beseeching tears. "I'm sorry…"

He snatched her into his arms, crushed her to him. "Be sorry only for hiding this from me, for thinking of denying me not only you, but our child, too. Don't you understand I'd rather die than be without you?"

"I would, too." She sobbed in his chest. "But I never wanted to cause you trouble. Now I've caused you nothing but. Oh, Shaheen, I shouldn't have come to that party…"

He held her away to scowl his exasperation down on her. "And what am I? A boy with no will of my own, who didn't realize the consequences of my actions? Everything I did, I'd do again in the exact same way. The only thing I'd change would be to tie you to my wrist so you wouldn't leave me for my 'own good,' so I'd be there to celebrate the discovery of your pregnancy with you." Anger at her efforts to protect him frothed on a new surge. "You slept in my arms every day, told me everything…but *that*. Would you have ever told me?"

"*No.*" Her eyes melted with entreaty. "I never wanted to keep this from you, but I can't think beyond the moment with you, can't imagine a time when you'll no longer be part of my life or that you won't be part of our baby's. All I know is that my pregnancy will do what the king is saying it will. I can't even imagine the damages if people know you have an heir on the way."

"And the damages to us, to our baby? You didn't imagine those?"

A rumble penetrated their cocoon of agitation. Shaheen turned to look at his father, winced at the mess of love and regret and finality that congealed on his face.

Then in a voice heavy with them all, the king said, "I am beyond happy that you have a woman you want—"

Shaheen interrupted him. "I *love* Johara. Always have, always will. There will be no negotiations about that."

His father continued, a king who wouldn't let even his son, or his pain on his behalf, stop him from seeing his duty through. "That this woman is Johara makes it infinitely better. But there is no stopping the chain reaction this will set off." He turned to Johara, gaze heavy with the remorse of being unable to put her before everything. "News of your pregnancy came to me through servants, so it must be all over the region by now. All we can do is rewrite history and hope for the least possible consequences."

Johara darted a look into Shaheen's eyes before her gaze went back to his father. "What do you mean?"

His father exhaled raggedly. "I will announce that you're already married in a *zawaj orfi*. Even if it is a secret marriage and frowned upon—and in royal circles in Zohayd, unprecedented—it remains binding. We'll say this is why you followed Shaheen to Zohayd after such a long absence. It will legitimize your baby, and we'll have a marriage ritual to make the marriage public and fully legal."

Shaheen felt Johara tremble in his arms, saw hope quiver on her face before doubt snuffed it out again. "What about the marriage of state Shaheen is required to enter? How will this affect your negotiations and peace in Zohayd?"

His father's shoulder slumped lower. "I'll try to convince any tribe to consent to giving their daughter as a second wife."

Shaheen had known what the condition to his father's damage control solution could be. It still outraged him to hear it. "They can consent all they like. *I'm* not taking a second wife."

"Don't be so quick to dismiss this option, Shaheen."

"I never intended to marry anyone but Johara. I was only biding my time until—" Shaheen stopped. He'd almost blurted out the reason he'd appeared to be going along with the negotiations "—until I found a way out with the least repercussions. But now that I've seen the price I could have paid for not confronting this, I'm no longer pretending."

"What choice do we have, Shaheen? If you don't meet them halfway at least, there will be fallout into the next century. I would have given anything apart from the kingdom's peace for you to have Johara. But no matter what happens now, you'll at least have your child, raise it as your own, and not be deprived of it as I was deprived of Aliyah until lately."

"Are you even listening to yourself, Father? You sacrificed your one true love and ended up thinking your daughter was your niece, and only because *Ammeti* Bahiyah rescued her from a life of anonymity. But what did your sacrifices ever gain you, or the kingdom? You've been battling one potential uprising after another ever since, the last one two years ago when only Aliyah's and Kamal's marriage defused it at the last moment. And here they are, threatening another, and you think sacrificing me will appease them? For how long? They're like tantrum-throwing brats and the more you give them the more they'll demand and the louder they'll scream for it. You can never placate them. So I'm marrying Johara now, not later as I was determined to. And not as a damage-control measure, but because being with her is the one thing I've ever wanted for myself. And I will be with her for the rest of my life. You and the rest of the tribes must deal with it."

Johara clung to him. "I can't let you do that to yourself and your father and kingdom, Shaheen. Not on my account—"

"It's on all our accounts—yours, mine and our baby's. Trust me, *ya joharet galbi*. I will resolve this."

Her fingers dug into his arms, her eyes unwavering with determination. "Then promise me...if you can't, you'll let me go."

"I promise I never will."

Before she could protest more, his father spoke, his voice like a knell of doom. "Don't make promises you can't afford to keep, Shaheen." Before Shaheen could interrupt, his father forged on. "Now you will come back to the palace with me. Your marriage ceremony must be arranged at once."

"My deepest admiration, Johara, from one master manipulator to another. You're the very best I've seen."

Johara stiffened at Amjad's drawling sneer. Shaheen

gave her a bolstering squeeze before he turned to his brother.

It was Harres, who'd met them at the palace's main entrance, who answered him. "It was I who recommended you be one of the two witnesses to the marriage, Amjad. I can easily replace you with Father. Or anyone off the street."

"And deprive me of the pleasure of handing Shaheen over to the lioness he's so eager to be devoured by? Can you be so cruel?" Amjad put his arm around Shaheen's shoulder, looked Johara in the eyes. "So how do you think Johara leaked the info about her pregnancy? She must be rubbing her hands in glee that it created the desired scandal and results. You aren't the only one who can't wait for you to marry her now. Everyone— including me—is shoving you at her."

Shaheen looked heavenward before leveling pitying eyes on him. "Do you drink two cups of hot paranoia first thing each morning?"

Amjad cracked a laugh, gave him a hard tug before letting him go. "I bet they have better taste and effect than the cups of insipid sentimentality you're guzzling down nonstop."

"Then how about you try a sip of common, if rare to you, sense?" Shaheen said. "The palace is crawling with aides whose favorite pastime is to monitor the palace's inmates, and who have nothing but sex scandals on the brain. A female versed in signs of early pregnancy must have guessed Johara's condition and put the same 'his and hers' together that you did and spread the word. Father's *kabeer el yaweran* thought the rumor too dangerous to ignore and relayed it. Happy now?"

"Ecstatic." Amjad folded one hand on top of the

other over his heart in mock delight. "I'm going to be an uncle!"

Shaheen grimaced. "In theory. In practice, I'm not letting you near your niece or nephew if you don't revert to being human."

"You mean I ever was one? Flatterer. But I'll leave humanity to you. With all the associated stupidities of the condition. Which, I admit, have most entertaining facets. It was very enlightening to learn that you don't care about sending the region to hell in a handcart as long as you have Johara and your impending offspring. Such a relief to know you're not perfect after all, Shaheen. I was beginning to really worry about you."

Shaheen only gave him a serene look. "So, any new accusations for Johara and her father, Amjad? Get them all off your chest."

Amjad shrugged his shoulders, which were immaculately draped in a navy silk shirt. "Oh, just variations on the old themes according to the developments." He turned his gaze to Johara. "She's full of surprises, isn't she, our Johara?"

Harres punched him in the arm, pointed two fingers to his own eyes. "You keep your eyes here, *faahem?*"

Amjad massaged away his brother's punch, his grin goading. "I understand. You're now one of Johara's lackeys."

Harres narrowed his eyes. "I *can* order my special forces to take you someplace where you can stew in your poisonous brew until the ceremony is over."

"You think they'd obey you and not their crown prince? I'm almost tempted to let you see where their loyalties lie."

"I'll say it's on grounds of insanity. You've paved

those, so it won't be hard to convince them to cart you away."

"But-but…mo-*om!*" Amjad did a spectacular impression of a sullen boy and it only made Johara think she'd never been in the presence of someone more dangerous. Or more…lonely. "I'm the only fun one around. What would this party be without me?"

Harres shook his head, intense fondness mixing with exasperation and even regret. "I swear, sometimes I feel you're the youngest, not the oldest."

Amjad's provocation rose another notch. "But you remain stuck in the middle either way, bro."

"You *said* you'd defer to my opinion. I should have known you would only if it coincided with yours." Harres turned to Johara with long-suffering apology in his eyes. "I told Amjad that his theories of you being behind the jewel conspiracy and creating a scandal to force Shaheen to marry you cancel each other out. If the conspiracy bore fruit, Shaheen wouldn't be prince. Why sabotage the status Amjad thinks you're marrying him for?"

Amjad raised his hand in another impression of an overeager student in class. "I know that one!" Johara turned reluctant eyes to him. The man was electrically charismatic even when he insulted her with every breath. He met her eyes, and still talked about her as if she wasn't there. "It's a win-win situation for her. If the conspiracy works, she gets paid off big-time, Shaheen loses the title but retains his wealth and power as a businessman and sheikh, and she retains her chokehold on him in every way. Then, once she has all power in her hands, she negotiates the return of the jewels, at whatever price, through a third party, and has it all."

Harres gave a hearty snort. "Sheesh, Amjad. You

actually live with that thing you call a brain inside your head?"

"You envy me because you live with nothing inside yours? That must be how our head of homeland security and secret service got to be so trusting. I almost feel compelled to report this to the council. I bet they'd expel you from your post and toss you out on your ear if they got a whiff of you being such an oblivious romantic."

Shaheen grinned at him. "Crown prince or not, Amjad, we outnumber you. How about we throw you out on *your* ear?"

Amjad swept his brothers a bedeviling smile, so secure in his power that he couldn't be goaded into posturing. "Chill, boys. Haven't you ever heard of the esteemed position of devil's advocate?"

"You mean devil's assistant." Harres tsked. "Now of all times. You're sick, Amjad."

"I'll live. But really, when better? Afterward, I'll have to forever hold my aggression. And with Shaheen thinking with body parts that don't include his brain, you were my last hope of someone seeing beyond the star-crossed drama unfolding here."

At that moment the king called Shaheen and Harres away, leaving Amjad alone with Johara.

She waited until they were out of earshot. Then she pounced.

She grabbed Amjad's forearm, dug her fingers into it with all her strength. She heard his surprise in the sharpness of his indrawn breath, saw it in the pupils that jerked to full expansion, engulfing the uncanny emerald of his eyes.

"Listen, Amjad," she hissed. "I'm not in any condition to listen to more of your delightful theories about my cunning and long-term treachery. I've loved Shaheen since the moment I laid eyes on him, even before he saved my life. I thought living with my hopeless love was the worst thing that I'd ever feel. Then I came back into his life and realized he's loved me as long and as fiercely, and my pain became agony. I feel like I've fallen into a nightmare, getting my impossible dream of having Shaheen, but in this terrible way. All I have to look forward to is a few months with him, if that, then a life without him, when he'll love and need me and our baby as much as we do him, but be forced to live without us.

"So thank your demons that *you've* never loved like this and evidently *can't* love anyone. You'll never suffer the agonies and ecstasies of our soul-deep connection, or the despair I'm anticipating when I have to leave him. And I'm *not* letting you add to his troubles. So, to quote Shaheen, from now on, Amjad, shut *up!*"

She fell silent, glaring up at him, trembling with the emotions tearing through her, and thought if stupefaction took human form, it would be Amjad now.

When he remained silent, she let out the air in her lungs on a choppy exhalation. "Now take your mind off of me and concentrate those formidable powers of yours on the most important thing. The jewels."

He shook his head, as if to wake up from a trance. Then he finally drawled, "It has always paid for me to think the worst and make amends later if need be. So I will do anything I can to atone for my attitude when—*and if*—I become convinced you are innocent." He bent closer, as if to give her a mind and psyche scan. "So just answer me this, Johara—if you and your father *are* innocent, why didn't you recognize the fakes?"

"I know why." Johara jerked around at Shaheen's declaration. He and Harres reached her and Amjad's side again. "Berj has been sliding into depression, and his inability to focus on his job—and therefore his failure to notice the fakes—is the reason he's retiring. Johara hasn't been near the jewels since she left Zohayd twelve years ago."

Amjad pursed his lips as he considered those rationalizations. "I still need to interrogate Berj."

Shaheen exhaled. "The one thing saving you from a right hook to that implacable jaw of yours is that I don't want to put a swollen hand in Johara's during the marriage ceremony."

"I can be your witness with swollen knuckles." Harres's feral eyes flashed on a mixture of sheer deviltry and pure danger.

Amjad whistled in mock admiration. "My, aren't you two full of fine male aggression. Down boys. I'm going to question him as a legitimate party in the investigation, not as a suspect."

Johara intercepted any reaction from Shaheen or Harres, stuck her face in Amjad's. "You can interrogate *me* all you like, but don't you dare go near my father."

"We need him to examine the fakes," Amjad persisted.

Johara shook her head emphatically. "*I'll* do that."

"Are you qualified?" She glared at him. He raised his hands in concession. "So you are. Fine. What's your plan?"

"I'll analyze the craftsmanship and come up with a list of possible forgers. There is a limited number of artists in the world capable of producing such almost undetectable duplicates. I've studied each extensively and can distinguish their signature styles."

After Shaheen and Harres agreed that this was the best plan, Amjad stepped closer, curved his arm at her.

She blinked up at him. What was this confounding man up to now?

"What are you up to now?" Shaheen echoed her suspicion.

Amjad eyes crinkled at him on what seemed to be an actual smile. "Johara needs to choose the jewels she'll wear for your wedding. And since you, as her groom, are forbidden to see her from now till then—" Amjad looked at her "—I'm petitioning that she bestow the honor of escorting her to the vaults on me."

After a long moment of stunned silence, Harres guffawed. "Wonders will never cease."

Shaheen seemed to wrestle with indecision before he nodded to her to accept Amjad's offer. He still put a protective hand on top of the one she hooked in Amjad's arm, giving his brother a hard glare. "If you say one more word to upset her…"

"Don't worry, Shaheen." Amjad winked at her. "When I called Johara a lioness, I didn't know the half of it. She can evidently defend herself, and you, against a whole army."

"I heard you wore black for your wedding."

Aliyah laughed at Johara's comment, turned from sorting through the outfits that had been brought in for Johara to pick from. "My choice of the color of mourning and power in Judar was my way of showing Kamal what I thought of being forced into marriage. His, uh, *very* favorable reaction was an early sign that we *are* made for each other." Aliyah stopped, alarmed. "Don't tell me you're thinking of copying me!"

"Oh, no. I just hope you don't expect me to wear white." Johara ran palms down her still flat belly. "It would feel funny when everyone knows we're getting married because I'm pregnant."

"You're getting married because you're in love." That was Laylah, already dressed in the outfit she'd attend the ceremony in, a two-piece dream of gleaming satin and ethereal chiffon in gradations of emerald and turquoise, heavily worked in sequins, beads and pearls. "Don't let the circumstances fool you."

Johara conveyed her gratitude with a look. Laylah and Aliyah had been with her all morning, defusing her agitation at the upcoming events. Not that she'd ever visualized her and Shaheen's wedding, since she'd never thought there would be one, but she'd barely slept all night, dreading the stilted, subdued ceremony that *would* see them married.

Now it was only two hours away. And she still couldn't bring herself to pick a dress. She shook her head at yet another suggestion of Aliyah's.

Aliyah sighed as she put the outfit back on the packed rack. "You're right. None of these are...*you*."

"Maybe you should attend the ceremony wearing only your jewels." Laylah winked at her. "Who needs clothes when she's adorned in the priceless pieces of the Pride of Zohayd?"

Aliyah exchanged a glance with Johara. Laylah hadn't been told.

Before more could be said, a knock rapped on the door of Johara's suite, where she'd insisted on remaining until after the ceremony.

Aliyah rushed to answer the door.

After a moment, she swung around with eyes and smile practically tap-dancing in excitement. "Close your eyes, Johara!"

"What...?" Johara said dazedly, eyes widening instead.

Laylah rushed behind the couch Johara was sitting on and placed her hands over her eyes.

"They're closed," she called out to Aliyah.

After moments of hearing the giggles of the two women, Aliyah chirped "Ta-da!" and Laylah removed her hands.

Johara blinked. Then she gaped. And gaped.

Held high in Aliyah's hand was the most incredible outfit she'd ever seen in her life. And in her line of work, she'd seen the best that human creativity and craftsmanship could offer.

"Now *that's* you," Aliyah announced proudly. "Courtesy of the man who knows you best and values you most, your smitten groom. It has a note attached, too."

That ended Johara's paralysis. She zoomed up and pounced on the truly invaluable part of this gift, the thoughtfulness behind it. Her hands trembled and her eyes surged with tears as she saw Shaheen's elegant, powerful print, almost heard him whisper the words into her ear, against her cheek, her lips, each inch of her.

Lan ustatee abaddan ann oteeki ma yoofi jamalek huqqun, fahal turdeen an ta'khothi nafsi kollaha awadan, ya joharet hayati?

I can never give you what will do your beauty justice, so will you accept taking all of me instead, jewel of my life?

She was useless for an indeterminate time afterward as Aliyah and Laylah surrounded her, sharing her agitated delight.

Then Laylah finally pulled back. "If you *don't* want

to attend your wedding in only jewels, you better hop
into that miracle."

And miracle was right. One of every gradation of gold
and brown that reflected her coloring down to the last
hair, amalgamated from finest silk, georgette, chiffon,
lace and tulle, flowing into a three-piece outfit that she
molded into as if it had been sculpted for her, on her.

Aliyah and Laylah commented that that was the
doing of another miracle. A man who knew every inch
of his woman, and who could translate that intimate
knowledge into such a precise fit.

Burning with embarrassment and joy, Johara rushed
to the full-length mirror to inspect herself, unable to
even guess how Shaheen had managed to get this outfit,
and on such short notice, too.

She'd worn incredible dresses since she'd turned
sixteen, but this one wasn't only her, this was the best
her she could be.

The top was corsetlike, accentuating the nip of her
waist and the lushness of her breasts, with tiny sleeves
and a deep décolleté that showcased the clarity of her
complexion and the wonder of each piece of jewelry she
wore on her neck and arms.

The jacquard *lehenga* skirt was gathered to one side,
hugging her hips in upward sweeps before falling in
tight pleats to the floor. The embroidery and cutwork
was on a level she'd never seen before, in sequins, silk
thread, pearls and gemstones, all Zohaydan traditional
motifs built around the first letter of both her name and
Shaheen's in Arabic, boggling her mind more, since
it proved this had been made in the past twenty-four
hours specifically for her. The finishing touch was a
flowing silk and chiffon *dupatta* with the same motifs
scalloping its edge and that hung from the middle of her

head, secured there with a tiara that would have been worth a queen's ransom had it been authentic.

She stood there as the picture was completed, her pleasure at the beauty of it all dipping then dissipating.

All this for such a sterile ceremony.

"It's time, Johara."

She shook off her dejection, rushed to precede Laylah and Aliyah out of the room. No matter what this was, as she'd told Amjad, it was far more than she'd ever dreamed of.

She was marrying Shaheen. She was having his baby.

Those were the true miracles.

Ten

Johara's tiny procession started to pick up followers as soon as they stepped out of the corridor leading from her quarters.

Each time she looked behind her, more women had joined the queue, and soon there were a few dozen of them, smiling from ear to ear and giggling in her wake.

Each group of four was dressed in the same outfit, with the colors of each group's attire a variation in deeper shades of the same cream and beige colors. By the time she looked back before they reached the main palace floor, the formation of the queue and the gradation in colors from lightest right behind her to the deepest at the end of it left her in no doubt.

They were her bridal procession.

She heard Laylah groaning. "Oh, man. I feel like a peacock!"

Aliyah looked down at her dress of deep reds and oranges. "And I feel like a fire breathing dragon. Someone should have told us what the color scheme was going to be."

"By someone," Laylah put in, in case Johara missed it, which in her condition, she *had,* "we mean your groom, who's going to pay big-time for deciding your bridal procession outfits based on the dress he picked for you, and leaving us in the dark. Or I should say, in Technicolor."

"Years from now," Aliyah groaned, "your children are going to look at your wedding album and ask you why their aunties were perched on your sides looking like parrots."

"You're actually the splash of color bringing all this to life." They both gave her yeah, *sure,* looks and she insisted, "I could never carry off those colors, and Shaheen knew it. But your brand of vivid beauty should never be subjected to anything less fiery and vital. And that is my professional opinion. I would never pick anything but bold, vibrant colors for either of you. And I can't wait to design you some outfits that only you can do justice!"

"I always thought I'd like you if I got to know you. I was wrong." Laylah hugged her exuberantly. "I'm going to *love* you."

Aliyah hugged her on the other side. "I already do. It's enough to feel how much you love Shaheen."

Johara met Aliyah's eyes and realized that was why Aliyah had decided she was innocent of stealing the jewels. As a woman in love herself, Aliyah had recognized that Johara would rather die than cause Shaheen heartache or harm.

Feeling her tears welling, she distracted herself

by focusing on her surroundings. She wasn't going to Shaheen with red eyes and streaked makeup.

Soon, the splendor she was rushing through occupied her focus for real—the palace she'd considered home, where she'd lived for most of her childhood, the best part of her life.

It was growing up here that had fanned the flames of the artistic tendencies she'd inherited from her parents. Moving from the plain practicality of New Jersey to this wonderland of embellishments and exoticness and grandeur blended from Persian, Ottoman and Mughal influences had fired her imagination from her first day here.

The palace had taken thousands of artisans and craftsmen three decades to finish in the mid-seventeenth century, and it had always felt to her as if the accumulation of history resonated in its halls, inhabited it walls. As much as the ancient bloodlines with all their trials and triumphs coursed through Shaheen's and his family's veins and stamped their bearing and characters, each inch of this place had been maintained as a testament to Zohayd's greatness and the prosperity of its ruling house.

But all that would be for nothing if the jewels were not found. If she couldn't figure out who'd forged them...

"We're here!"

"Here" was before the doors to the ceremony hall where the bridal parade had been held for Shaheen. Though it had been agony to be there that night, she'd still felt the wonder of being there again.

As a child she hadn't been allowed to attend royal functions held there. But when all was quiet, Shaheen had taken her there as frequently as she wished, to stay as long as she wanted, having the place all to herself to draw each corner of it, each inlay detail, each pierce work, each calligraphy panel.

The octagonal hall had always felt as if all the greatness, purpose and philosophy of the palace's design converged there. It was the palace hub, gracefully enclosed by its central marble one-hundred-foot wide and high dome, its walls spread with intricate, geometric shapes, its eight soaring arches defining its space at ground level, each crowned by a second arch midway up the wall with the upper arches forming balconies. It was from those that she'd learned her best lessons of drawing perspective.

A few dozen feet from the hall's soaring double doors, which were heavily worked in embossed bronze, gold and silver Zohaydan motifs, the music became louder. The quartertone-dominated Zohaydan music with its Indian, Turkish and Arabian influences and exotic instrumental arrangement and rhythm swept through the air, riding the fumes and scents of incense.

Then four footmen in black outfits embroidered with gold thread pulled back the massive doors by their circular knobs.

She stumbled to a stop, everything falling away.

She'd thought the ceremony would be a damage-control affair that would boil down to two purposes—the king's to publicize their so-called secret marriage, and theirs, to get her hands on the fake jewels. But this… this…

She hadn't, couldn't have expected *this*.

She moved again, propelled by the momentum of her companions across a threshold that felt as if it opened into another realm. Into a scene lifted right out of the most lavish of *One Thousand and One Nights*.

From every arch hung rows of incense burners and

flaming torches, against every wall rested miraculous arrangements of white and golden roses among backgrounds of lush foliage. Each pillar was wrapped in bronze satin that rained silver tassels and was worked heavily in gold patterns. Sparkling gold dust covered the marble floor. Everything shimmered under the ambient light like Midas's vault, among the swirling sweetness of *ood,* musk and amber fumes.

And studding the scene were far more than the two thousand people who'd populated the first and only ceremony she'd attended here. A mind-boggling assortment, from those dressed in the latest exclusive fashions to those who did look as if they'd just stepped out of *Arabian Nights.*

Her feverish eyes made erratic stops as she recognized faces. King Atef and King Kamal, sitting on a platform to one side on thronelike seats. Dozens of highest-order international political figures and celebrities. Queen Sondoss and Shaheen's half brothers, Haidar and Jalal, among probably every other adult Aal Shalaan and their relatives.

The only one she couldn't see was Shaheen.

Shaheen…he'd done all this. For her. But when? How? Where was he? She couldn't be here, face all this, without him…

"Johara! Breathe!"

She gulped a breath at Laylah's prodding. Then another.

"*Stop.* You've hyperventilating," Aliyah exclaimed.

She forced herself to regulate her breathing. She could just see the headlines if she fainted.

Pregnant Aal Shalaan Bride Passes Out At Wedding Ceremony.

Her vision had cleared and her steps had firmed when

the openly gawking crowd parted to stand on two sides as she and her procession made their way through. She felt she was treading the insubstantial ground of a dream as the thunder of clapping rose and the music, which she realized issued from an extensive live ensemble, began the distinctive percussive melody of the most popular Zohaydan wedding song, the one that called everyone to come wonder at the bride's splendor and her groom's phenomenal luck. By the time Aliyah and Laylah were singing along, she was floating on auto.

Then she saw her father.

He was mounting three gold-satin covered steps to a gold-satin-covered platform at the epicenter of the hall. She'd chosen him to act as her proxy, the one who would put his hand in Shaheen's during the ritual. She'd thought they'd all sit down and it would be over in minutes. Now it seemed his role included taking her to her groom with all the ceremony of this carefully choreographed piece.

She'd seen him for minutes last night with Shaheen and the king and only to tell him of the situation. To say he'd been shocked would be the understatement of the century.

He now waited for her, the litheness of his figure accentuated in a tight-fitting bronze silk tunic and pants, his chest heavy with the shining and colorful medals of honor and distinction he'd received throughout his service, his broad shoulders bearing the tags of the highest rank he'd quit. She felt Aliyah and Laylah fall behind as she climbed the steps, each diverging on one side of the platform to lead a portion of her procession to form a circle around it. As she reached the top, her father took her hands in his, his earlier shock replaced by lingering bewilderment tinged by guarded joy.

But it was the apology that lurked in the depths of his black eyes that made her pull him to her in a fierce hug.

He let out a ragged breath as his arms trembled around her. "I'm sorry I was so absorbed in my own problems I didn't notice what was going on with you. Is that why you felt you couldn't tell me? You thought I couldn't be there for you?"

Mortification rose inside her. She wasn't letting him in on more than he could think. She hugged him tighter. "*No*. If it concerns only me, I will always let you in, Daddy."

"But it concerned Shaheen, too, and you were protecting him." She nodded into his shoulder. He sighed, pulled back to look at her, his eyes level with hers. "You love him?" She nodded again, knew she didn't have to say how much or for how long. It was there in her eyes. "Then this is the best thing that ever happened to me, to see you marry the man you love. I can't think of a better man for you, or a better man, period. I do think Shaheen is the best of all the princes. And you know how highly I think of them all."

"Even me, Berj? You think highly of me?" Johara jerked as Amjad descended on her and father's tête-à-tête, clamping her father's shoulder and tugging him under his, looking down into his startled eyes, his radiating that ruthless shrewdness and uncanny emerald fire. "Now, where could I have possibly gone wrong?"

"Crown Prince Amjad..." Her father looked totally confused. "I meant no offense..."

"Oh, don't apologize to him, Dad." Johara glared up into Amjad's merciless teasing, trying to gauge if he was going to do more than tease, all but baring her teeth, warning him off.

"My impending sister-in-law has spoken." Amjad did that thing he did so well, looking one in the eye and talking about them in third person, sidelining them. "Seems you've been granted license to offend, Berj. And I hope you'll also reconsider your high opinion. We wouldn't want to give me a good name, now would we?"

As her father smiled like someone who'd just walked into the middle of a conversation and was too embarrassed to ask what it was about, Amjad's eyes traveled down the mind-boggling simulation of the pure gold cascading choker necklace, encrusted in two hundred fifty carats of diamonds ranging from pure ice to golden yellow, that covered her from high on her neck to the edge of her décolleté. "So which, in your opinion, is the *real* Pride of Zohayd, Berj? Your daughter or this?"

He touched the necklace. She stamped her foot on top of his.

Amjad didn't even wince as her high heel jammed between his bones, his only response an intensifying of the bedeviling in his eyes. The tug of war had been subtle enough to go unnoticed by all, so her father almost jerked in shock when Amjad threw his head back on a guffaw as if out of the blue. The sound was so predatory it would have scared her if she weren't so furious.

She was about to hiss to Amjad that she wasn't above making a more overt retaliation if he dared renege on their deal when a storm of murmurs mushroomed, drowning out the music and her intentions.

As the crowd turned in a wave toward the new focus of attention, she knew. It was Shaheen.

"Grandstander," Amjad murmured. Then he bent to

deliver his next words in her ears. "Enjoy. But not so much that you forget what this is all about."

"And don't *you* forget my special forces gathered right outside this hall."

Harres had materialized on her other side. He gave her a bolstering smile and Amjad a subtle tug, making him fall back, gesturing for her and Berj to precede them.

The moment their quartet descended from the other side of the platform, the lights dimmed, until the hall was dipped in darkness with only a spotlight following her procession, focused on her. She couldn't see anything beyond her next step.

Her stampeding heart shifted into higher gear. She could feel that she was moving deeper into Shaheen's orbit, felt his eyes on her, caressing her, loving her.

And though she couldn't see him, she opened herself, letting him see everything inside her. Along with all of her that he knew he had, she gave him her gratitude that he hadn't let this be a rushed apology of a ceremony. Even if she was dying of embarrassment, would have preferred something far more private and far, far less extravagant, she knew this was his way of shouting to the world his pride of being hers the loudest he could.

And she knew it was already causing untold damages.

She'd noted the pointed absence of all the tribes they'd been negotiating with. She could only surmise the worst.

But for now, he was giving her more miracles by the moment. And she would take them all and treasure each forever.

The music changed into a hotter rhythm. Her heart followed suit as the spotlight following her split in two, the duplicate inching away, leading her gaze with its sweep.

Then it fell on him.

She stopped, yanked her father to a halt with her, heard Amjad snort as he and Harres almost walked into them. But nothing mattered. Nothing but Shaheen.

It was the first time she'd seen him like this. And she'd thought he looked like a desert god in modern clothes!

Now, swathed in the trappings of his heritage, the distillation of its art and chivalry and history, he was beyond description. And his eyes were telling her he cared about only one thing. Becoming hers.

She moved again, the desire to examine his every detail more closely galvanizing her.

The vigorous waves of his hair, now brushing his collar, gleamed deepest mahogany under the spotlight, which struck tongues of flame from his fiery-brown eyes. His face had never looked more noble, more potent, with every slash of character carved deeper in the stark light. The rest of his perfection was encased in a three-piece outfit fashioned from heavy *jamawar* silk in browns and golds echoing her own clothing. A scarf printed with the royal insignia in an ingenious repetition and gathered by a dazzling brooch, another piece from the Pride of Zohayd, overlaid his high-collared, fitted golden top. A wide bronze satin sash connected the top to deeper bronze pants that stretched over the power of his thighs and legs, billowing at their ends to gather into burnt brown polished leather boots.

But it was the cloak on top of it all that that made her feel he'd come to her from a trip through the past.

The color of darkest, richest earth, it fell from his endless shoulders in relaxed pleats to his feet, looked as if it were constantly sighing in pleasure to be surrounding him. Embroidery on its front panel descended in a wide V to his waist level, the gold thread and beads forming such elaborate motifs, the artist in her salivated for the chance to examine their formation and realization. The embellishments seemed to accentuate his masculinity, if that was possible.

With her every step nearer, he tensed, and the cloak seemed to bate its breath with him for her arrival. She wished he'd hide her within it, transport her away from all the pomp and attention.

But she knew he was doing this for her, to honor her, to show her that this was no damage-control maneuver but the one thing he wanted to do, was proud to, and was doing with as much fanfare as possible so no one would mistake his desire and pride.

Before she could throw herself into his arms, a blonde woman in a cream sarilike outfit and a man as tall as Shaheen in all-black with midnight hair down to his shoulders stepped out of the darkness into the circle of light.

Johara almost choked.

She'd been sad that this would be too rushed, too hushed, not even a real wedding, that she wouldn't have them here. But Shaheen…he…he…

He'd brought her mother and brother to her!

For a stunned moment, her mind compensated for her body's inability to move, streaked.

She hadn't seen Aram face-to-face in over a year. She'd missed him terribly, drank in the sight of him now. He looked more like a pirate than ever, seeming to grow more imposing with each passing year, her total opposite in coloring, having inherited her mother's dazzling turquoise eyes and their father's swarthy complexion and night-black hair, and combining their mother's family's height with the sturdiness and breadth of their father's. Her mother looked her eternally beautiful self.

And she surged to them, encompassed them with Shaheen in her delight. Her kisses moved from her mother to Aram, ended all over Shaheen's face with a reiteration of thanks, for this gift, his best yet.

The music changed yet again, to take on a more solemn and momentous timber, to herald the next stage in the ceremony.

Her mother caught her closer, kissed her again. "*Ma cherie,* I never thought this day would come to pass. I was so worried about you."

Johara pulled back from her, stunned. "You knew?"

"I always knew." Her mother's eyes grew more brilliant with tears. "It's why I never wanted to come back here. I didn't want you exposed to heartache. I thought your love for Shaheen would only hurt you, since it was impossible. I can't tell you how relieved I am, how happy that I was wrong."

She surrendered to her mother's fierce hug again, processing this new knowledge. Seemed she was totally useless in keeping a secret. Everyone except her father had read her like an open book.

Then a thought struck her and she pushed out of her mother's arms and rounded on Aram. "Which reminds me!" She glowered her displeasure at him. "*You* were wrong."

He looked taken aback for a second, his eyes flying accusingly to Shaheen, before he looked back at her, smirking. "If this doesn't prove I was right, I don't know what does."

"You were wrong *then*. And I want an apology!"

"I won't apologize for doing what I had to, to protect you."

"Oh, you *will* apologize. To Shaheen! How could you accuse him of…any of that? You of all people, his *supposed* best friend?"

"You're not going to have *another* sibling fight right here, are you?" Harres groaned. "I thought we've had enough of those."

"No such thing as enough sibling fights," Amjad said, his very voice an incitement. "And again, when better? I say this is long overdue. Have at it, boys and girls."

Aram bared his teeth. "I didn't realize how much I missed you, Amjad."

Amjad grinned back, baring the demon inhabiting his own body. "Was that my cue to say I missed you, too? Oops, missed it."

Johara's father cleared his throat. "I'm realizing with each passing second that I know nothing about what's been going on around me, but will you take pity on me and not make me feel more like the deaf in the parade here?"

Johara and Aram hugged him in apology. Shaheen let it last a moment, then he put his arms around the quartet of her family.

"There will be no more fights among us." He looked emphatically among them. He meant all of them. Him and Aram, her and Aram, her mother and father. He didn't continue until he got their consenting nods. "Now we need to put the *ma'zoon* out of his misery. After he finishes marrying us, he will spend the rest of the night printing our royal book of matrimony."

With that, they broke apart, and her father placed her hand in Shaheen's. Shaheen hugged her to his side as he led her and their procession to their final destination, a gilded woodwork miniature of the palace—the *kousha*—where the *ma'zoon* awaited them, and where they'd sit throughout the wedding proceedings.

As they sat down on the silk brocade couch, Johara between Shaheen and her father and the rest of their family on either side, she exchanged a look of total love and alliance with him.

Then the ritual began.

Three hours of escalating festivities later, Johara stood jangling in the aftermath of it all in Shaheen's bedroom, at his dresser, taking off the jewels.

He'd told her he'd wanted to take her to their home by the sea, or even fly them away and have their wedding night on board his jet. But the jewels were prohibited from leaving the palace.

She was completely okay with it. She'd been imagining being with him in this room ever since their aborted time together the night he'd come back to Zohayd.

He'd gone to inform their fathers that the jewels would be returned in the morning. When she asked what excuse he'd given for that, he made her wish she hadn't. She blushed now thinking about it.

"Take your *dupatta* off, *ya joharti*."

She spun around as the hunger in his bass rumble licked her back. She watched as he approached, her hands automatically rising to obey him.

As her *dupatta* slid off her head, he snapped his scarf off his neck, hurled it to the floor. "Now your *lehenga*."

She obeyed again, at once, unable to wait to be free

of her clothes and crushed beneath him, taken, invaded, made whole.

He covered more of the two dozen feet between them, giving up his cloak for her skirt, then his top for hers. She swallowed over and over at the sight as each move gave her a show of rippling strength and symmetry. Soon all that remained were her panties, and she gave him those for his sash. All she had left on were her three-inch sandals.

"This is the ultimate unfairness," she croaked as he stopped before her in his low-riding pants and boots, a colossus carved by gods of virility. "You always have more clothes."

His eyes crinkled as they swept over her, the fire in them rising, singeing her. "I wish I can take credit for that. There's no higher cause than feasting on your nakedness."

"You can take credit this time." She cupped her breasts, trying to assuage their aching. "For everything. Today was beyond anything I ever dreamed of, *ya habibi*. The outfit, the thought behind it, the note, every last detail of this night, Mom and Aram. I have no words to tell you what your thoughtfulness meant to me. What *you* mean to me. You've always meant…everything. Now…now… No…there are no words. I only hope you'll always let me show you how much I love you, as you keep showing me."

She trembled with the magnitude of her love and gratitude, that he existed, that he was now hers, no matter how fleetingly. She'd loved him with everything in her from the moment he'd touched her. She'd wanted him even more when she'd felt his baby growing inside her. And now he was her husband. Her *husband*.

The knowledge made it all deeper, all-encompassing, turning her hunger for him almost into distress.

Then he put what she felt into words and made it much worse, and infinitely better. "Anything I can think of to show you my love, prove your ownership of me, will never be enough. I thought I wanted you as much as I possibly could before. But now, knowing our baby is growing inside you, knowing you're my *wife*...my desire for you makes my former ferocity seem tame and my worry of losing control an easily curbed impulse. My mind is shooting to all kinds of fanciful fears, that our union this time, with us feeling this way, might take us all the way to the edge of survival."

"So what?"

Her reckless challenge cracked his control. He dragged her by the hand, slammed her against him, breast to thigh. "So what indeed. How about we see what the edge of survival feels like?"

"Oh, yes. Yes, take me there, Shaheen, and beyond." She slithered from his hold onto her knees before him, her hands worshipping his hardness through his pants, shaking on his zipper.

As she slid it down he whipped one hand to his back, snapped something from the band of his pants before they fell to mid-thigh, allowing him to spring free, thick and daunting, dark and glistening with craving, throbbing with control.

She'd barely taken him into her mouth, licking the addictive taste of his desire from his silk-smooth crown when he pulled her up, gathering her from the ground in one arm. She cried her protest and he growled as he saluted each of her nipples with a devouring suckle. She cried out again as another wave of arousal crashed through her, her core pouring its demand for his invasion.

"You always say it's punishment, not reward, giving you pleasure without giving you me." He pressed her to the capitoné wall beside his bed. "Tonight you get reward first, then punishment later."

He made a lightning-fast move with his left hand as his right one secured her against the wall, his bulk opening her around him. She felt a sharp tug, heard a sharper click.

She tried to turn her head, to investigate, but his eyes caught hers, and everything ceased to matter, to exist.

Lava simmered in his eyes and from the erection that found her entrance. His hiss felt even hotter. "I want to invade you, finish you, perish inside you."

"Then do it, finish us both...*please*..."

He rammed into her. All his power and love and hunger behind the thrust. He slid against all the right places, places he'd created inside her, abrading nerves into an agony of response, stimulating receptors for all the sensations they could transmit. Then he moved as hard and fast as she was dying for him to.

Almost too soon she started shaking, arched against him in a deep bow, hovering at the edge of a paroxysm as the world diffused, only his beloved face in focus, clenched in pleasure, his eyes vehement with his greed for hers.

She tried to bring both arms around him to hold him as she gave everything to him, but her right hand snagged, wrenched back.

She looked down in her haze, found it shackled to his left one in a gilded handcuff.

Just the idea—that he'd done this, bound her to himself, thought of it, wanted to show her how inseparable he wanted them to be, how mind-blowingly deep, how decadently *wicked* it all was… Her senses went haywire, sent overload shearing through her.

"I did tell you I'd tie you to my wrist, didn't I?" he growled as he gave her his fiercest thrust yet and her body all but exploded in the most powerful climax he'd ever given her.

Her shriek of his name came in bursts as the convulsions of release ripped through her. Discharge after discharge of pleasure pummeled her, squeezing all of her muscles, inside and out over every part of him, his heat and weight bearing down on her and within her in waves, stimulating her to her limits and beyond.

She raved, begged. "Can't…can't…please…you… you…"

And he gave her what she needed. The sight of his face, the feel of him succumbing to the ecstasy she gave him, the pulse of his own climax inside her. They hit her at her peak, had her thrashing, weeping, unable to endure the spike in pleasure. Everything blipped, faded…

Heavy breathing and sluggish heartbeats seemed to echo from the end of a long tunnel as the scent of sex and satisfaction flooded her lungs. Awareness trickled into her body, a mess of tremors so sated she was practically numb. She felt one thing. Shaheen. Still inside her.

She opened lids weighing a ton each, saw him swim in and out of focus. She was on her back on the bed, with him kneeling between her legs, her hips on his thighs, his free palm kneading her breasts, gliding over her shoulders, her arms, her belly.

She watched him watch her, her position the image of wantonness, of surrender and trust, her free arm thrown above her head, her back arched, breasts jutting, legs opened over his hips, his shaft half-buried inside her, stretching her glistening entrance, wrapped around him in the most intimate kiss.

"So how did you like your...reward?"

"You were right..." she slurred at his deepening occupation. "This was...the edge of survival. I felt... my every cell...burst."

He set his teeth as he rocked another inch inside her. "See why I always insist on taking the edge off?" He rose off the bed, scooped her up with him, his smile all satisfaction and indulgence. "But now that I have, I can really turn to your punishment."

And for the rest of the night, among a few more rewards, he punished her with escalating inventiveness. And in continued captivity.

Johara jumped when something dropped into her lap.

She looked down and saw the handcuffs at the same moment she felt Shaheen surrounding her.

She'd been so absorbed that she hadn't felt his approach for the first time ever.

"The best morning in history to you, my crafty Gemma."

She beamed up at him, opened her mouth for his luxuriant invasion. She'd undone the handcuffs and slipped out of bed two hours ago. She couldn't bring herself to wake him up, but had been burning to examine the jewels. And she had.

He let her surface from his kiss, slid a loving touch down her cheek. "I see you've filled a whole notebook with observations. Can I hope that you have a list for us?"

"No." She saw dismay gather in his eyes and rushed to deliver the rest of her verdict. "I have better than that. I know exactly who forged these jewels."

Eleven

"Are you sure about this, *ya joharti?*"

Johara turned her eyes away from the streets of Geneva zooming by the window of their car. She'd been looking blindly outside since they'd left the airport. Shaheen's worried gaze had been touching her ever since. Now that he'd voiced his concern, she could no longer look away.

She met his solicitude and again wanted to tell him that she wasn't sure. And again dismissed the thought as it formed.

She nodded to him, kissed the hand that swept down her cheek. His eyes softened even more before they snapped back to the road.

They'd flown here on his private jet hours after she'd delivered her verdict. Not that he was asking her if she was sure of *that*. Shaheen, as she became more certain with each passing moment, took everything she said as incontrovertible fact. He had absolute faith not only in her integrity but also in her expertise. He was confident that her deduction of the identity of the forger was incontestable. Equally because he believed she knew her business, and that she wouldn't accuse someone if she wasn't certain beyond a shadow of doubt.

She was. Although she'd been tempted to say she wasn't. Because she felt the moment her role in uncovering the conspiracy was over, her time with Shaheen would be over, too.

Nothing worked to allay that fear. Not even when he said they had time to abort the conspiracy and had forever together. In fact, the more he said that, the more desperate she became. All this bliss couldn't possibly continue. Not at anything less than a terrible price. One she would be unable to let Shaheen or Zohayd pay.

She'd started counting down her remaining time with him from the moment she'd given him her verdict.

He and Harres and Amjad had at first said they'd handle it. They would besiege the forger with their special influence and force a confession. She'd insisted on being the one to approach him. She believed no coercion would be needed. Shaheen had at once trusted her judgment, supported her decision.

But he sensed her agitation, was worried that she was outside her comfort zone. And she was, if not for the reason he thought.

They stopped at a gated parking lot. The attendant recognized both of them and at once let them into the area reserved for the exclusive establishment's most elite clientele.

Shaheen stopped the car, turned to her. *"Kolloh zain?"*

She pulled him to her for a brief, fierce kiss. "Yes, everything's all right. Let's do this."

In moments they were walking hand in hand into the avant garde reception area of the showroom of LaSalle, one of the most celebrated designers of original jewelry in the world.

As more people recognized them, they were given the treatment only a star fashion designer and a billionaire prince could be given. In seconds they were let into the sanctum of Théodore LaSalle, the establishment's owner and the brand's namesake.

Dressed in fifties-movie-star elegance, the David Niven look-alike rushed to meet them in the foyer leading to his office, his face split into a wide smile of someone expecting an unrepeatable honor and a transaction worth a year of magnificent sales.

"Doesn't look as if he suspects why we're here," Shaheen muttered under his breath as the man ushered them into his office and rushed to his desk. "Or he's a superlative actor."

"What can I offer you, *mes cheries?*" LaSalle asked, one finger on his intercom. "All refreshments are available."

"That won't be necessary, *Monsieur* LaSalle," Johara said. "Please, come sit with us. We have something of extreme importance to discuss with you."

LaSalle's face fell as he walked to his sitting area, where Shaheen had led her to a love seat opposite the seat he gestured for the man to take.

Trepidation seized LaSalle's face. Shaheen said something to her in Arabic. That this looked like a guilty man. She squeezed his hand, and he nodded. Whatever he thought, he would let her deal with LaSalle. She'd told him she believed not only in the man's artistry but in his integrity, too. She would give him every benefit of the doubt first.

She started, careful not to make her words either a question or an accusation. "It's about the duplicates of the Pride of Zohayd collection, Monsieur LaSalle."

The man didn't even look at her, his gaze pinned nervously on Shaheen. Johara could imagine how her husband looked to the man, a lethal predator crouched in deceptive calm, but clearly only on a tight leash, and would launch into a slashing attack at a word from her.

"Are there any complaints about any of the pieces, Prince Aal Shalaan? I am, of course, willing to replace any that have been damaged, even if due to negligence. I produce my pieces with a lifetime guarantee. But if this is about the quality, in my defense—" he swung his gaze to her, as if asking her support "—you of all people, Mademoiselle Nazaryan—*pardonnez moi,* Princess Aal Shalaan—know the difficulty of working from photographs, even the most detailed and multiangled of close-ups."

Johara sat forward, placed a placating hand on the man's trembling one. "The quality is what only you can achieve, Monsieur. It was the sheer genius of the duplication that narrowed down my options to you. It's imperative that you tell us everything about how you came to make those duplicates."

"You mean you don't *know?*" LaSalle gaped at her. "But it was the royal house who commissioned the duplicates."

After a stunned moment when Johara thought they'd gotten this all wrong, she asked slowly, "You mean King Atef personally commissioned them?"

The man shook his expressive hands. "Of course not. I don't even know who did, but it was understood it was the royal house."

"How was it understood?" Shaheen grated.

The man gave a helpless, eloquent shrug. "Owners of invaluable treasures frequently wish to have duplicates to use if their jewelry will be worn or displayed in less than totally secure conditions."

"So who approached you from the royal house?" Shaheen asked.

"I wasn't approached directly. In fact, it was through a quite convoluted method of double blinds."

"And you still thought this was aboveboard?" Shaheen hissed.

The man was looking more mortified by the moment. "Yes. The rich and royal always wish to hide their true dealings, and it made sense that the royal house would not want it to be known that the duplicates existed. And then, who else could have provided me with all those photographs? Who could afford to pay the astronomical fee I was given?"

"Who indeed." Shaheen huffed. "But didn't it seem suspicious that they didn't entrust their own royal jeweler with the chore?"

The man nodded vigorously. "But I was told Berj was not well, and I even called him to make sure of that. My contacts said they didn't want to burden him in his state. They also feared if he heard a whiff of this, he'd feel slighted that he'd been bypassed for this assignment, that he'd feel his usefulness to the royal house had come to an end. As a fellow master craftsman, this was even more incentive for me to keep silent than the money I was paid. I appreciated my clients' need for absolute accuracy more when it was their effort not to tip him off to the fact that he'd be maintaining duplicates. I did warn them that he would know, no matter how accurate the replicas, but I was assured he was in no condition to notice, if I made them close enough."

She stared at LaSalle, a terrible suspicion spreading through her. She turned to Shaheen only to see it reflected in his eyes.

Then he put it into words. "They were certain of his inability to recognize the fakes because they've been drugging him. This explains his deteriorating condition of late. And when he believed there was something wrong with him and started taking medication for his so-called depression, the drug interactions must have caused his heart attack."

"They could have killed him!" Johara cried out, her heart rattling with rage.

Shaheen gave a solemn nod, eloquent with his determination to punish those responsible for this most of all. "But since they didn't want a new jeweler, a younger and more vigilant one in his place, they pulled back, counted on his unwarranted medications to confuse him enough for their purposes."

"This is appalling!" Monsieur LaSalle exclaimed, horror seizing his face. "I've been party not only to a fraud, but to almost having a hand in Berj's death?"

"You are not in any way accountable," Shaheen assured him. "But we need you to tell us every detail about how you were contacted, how you were paid and how you delivered the duplicates. Any information you give us will be the only leads we have toward apprehending the culprits and returning the real jewels."

The man exploded to his feet. "You have my full cooperation. And if they approach me again, I will keep playing the game, so they'll either give me more information or grow secure and do something that will help you expose them."

After they'd obtained every possible detail from LaSalle, Johara and Shaheen drove straight back to the airport.

As they approached Shaheen's jet, she saw a black Jaguar parked near its stairs. Amjad and Harres were leaning against it.

As soon as she and Shaheen stepped out of the car, Harres met them. Amjad remained where he was, hips braced against the hood, legs crossed at the ankles and hands deep in his pockets.

"Any news?" Harres asked.

"What we can use only, please," Amjad interjected.

Shaheen shot him an exasperated glance then answered Harres. "The forger is a reputable jeweler who was duped like the rest of us. He offered to do all he can and promised to keep working with us."

Amjad sighed. "If you say so. Or is it Johara who does?"

Shaheen ignored him. "The thieves have access to funds on par with us. And they have infiltrated the palace on every level." He gave Harres the tape with LaSalle's recorded details. "I think this has enough threads to lead us to the mastermind."

Harres put the tape in his pocket. "I've already started investigating everyone who was in the palace during the past year. But this will narrow down my search. It will narrow down your sweep, too, Amjad."

Amjad shrugged, the picture of nonchalance. "Why should I narrow it down? I'm having a ball tracing every transaction that occurred in the accounts of everyone who was *ever* in the palace and cross-referencing those with just about everyone in the region and their dogs. Even after I find the funds exchanged in the conspiracy and the hands that exchanged them, I'm keeping this up. Seems the Pride of Zohayd is not the only treasure to be found here. I'm exposing dozens of priceless secrets. I now have something ruinous on just about everyone, it's just sublime."

Harres thumped Amjad on the back. "What he meant by all that is that he, like all of us, is forever in your debt, Johara."

Johara looked Amjad in the eye. "I'll accept his gratitude when he actually proves effective in getting the jewels back."

Amjad's lethal smile acknowledged her third-person payback. "Oh, I will. But now it's time to return to Zohayd and face the music. Harres should have stayed back and announced code red. Your wedding has the tribes up in arms. Expect the worst."

The moment they touched down in Zohayd, the king summoned them. And it was clear the worst *was* to be expected.

It still took hearing it to make it real, to tip her from the edge and into the nightmare.

"The council is in session right now, Shaheen," King Atef said as soon as they entered his stateroom, his voice heavy with sorrow. "They have made a final decree. You are to dissolve your marriage to Johara. A bride has been unanimously chosen for you, and neither she nor her family will accept her being a second wife. And they demand that her offspring be your heir, not your child from Johara. They are gathering their people on our borders, in all the hubs of unrest within the kingdom. They say your answer would decide their next actions."

Johara felt as if a scythe had cut her down at the knees. Shaheen's arm came around her, held her up, hugged to him.

"Don't worry about those thugs, Father," Harres growled. "I'll send them running with their tails between their legs."

"And afterward, Harres?" Everyone, including Harres was startled when Shaheen spoke up. Johara shuddered at his calmness. "You think force will create any long-term or real peace?"

Harres's scowl was spectacular. She could see him fighting to the death over this. "They're bluffing, and I'll show them that I don't take kindly to bluffs. And if they're not, I'll show them I'm even less forgiving of threats. This same council entrusted me with the peacekeeping of this kingdom, and *B'Ellahi*, I'm keeping it."

"This is not a bluff, Harres," King Atef said. "And if they carry out their threats, it is my fault. I've misled them for too long. Now they're enraged. And unreasonable."

Aggression blazed in Harres's feral eyes. "Give me the word, and I'll show them unreasonable!"

Amjad stayed pointedly silent through it all. Watching her.

Shaheen only shook his head at Harres. "There will be no need for any of that." He turned to his father. "I wish you'd let them tell me that to my face instead of hiding behind you and burdening you with their pompous and insane demands." Then he turned to her. "Stay here, *ya galbi*. I'll be back in minutes."

Johara watched Shaheen walk away and felt as if she'd lost him already. He would try to talk the council out of their decision. And he'd fail.

Her vision swam as it wavered to the men who'd been a major part of her life. They were Shaheen's family, were hers, too. Harres growled that he'd beat back any attempt at an uprising so hard, the dead would reconsider their mutinies. The king argued that he couldn't give the order to plunge the kingdom into war. Amjad watched her. She sank deeper in despair.

Then Shaheen came back. His *kabeer el yaweran* was behind him, laden in dossiers.

He took her hand to his lips then folded her arm through the crook of his. "Shall we, *ya joharet galbi?*"

She walked only because he steered her, could barely see the route they took through the palace to the council hall or the Roman senatelike assembly all around them once they entered it, barely heard the din die down as Shaheen brought her to a stop in the middle of the floor.

He spoke at once, his voice an awe-striking boom. "I will never divorce Johara. Or take a second wife. And this is final."

The hall exploded.

Shaheen raised his voice over the cacophony. "But…I have a solution."

The clamor again died down as everyone recognized the determination and certainty in Shaheen's voice and demeanor.

He went on once there was total silence. "My solution will exonerate my king, my family and my tribe of my actions, end any ill will you now bear toward them."

He let a beat pass when everyone and everything seemed to hold their breath. Then he said, "Exile me."

Johara's heart stopped.

She felt every heart in the gigantic hall follow suit.

Then Shaheen continued, and her heart burst into thundering shock and horror. "I offer that my family disown me, strip me of my name, and for the kingdom of Zohayd to forever forbid me, and my children, entry to its soil."

As the uproar rose again, his voice again drowned it out. "But this will only appease the insult I've dealt you by breaking my vows. To compensate you, my venerable lords, for any loss you may suffer from my refusal to enter the beneficial union you demanded…" He beckoned for his *kabeer el yaweran* to come forward. "I give you all my assets."

Silence crashed over the hall.

Nothingness roared inside Johara.

Shaheen was saying…offering…

Suddenly, a voice rent the silence. "Yes, make an example of Shaheen Aal Shalaan!"

Another roared, "It's the only way to appease our tribes. Exile him!"

More voices rose, tangled.

"Prove that not even the king's son can renege on his word."

"Show every royal they cannot play with us all and get away with it."

Shaheen only smiled down at her. The smile of someone who'd achieved exactly what he was after. Then he steered her away and out of the council hall.

They might have walked two steps or two miles when it all sank in. She wrenched on his hand, bringing him to a stop.

"Are you out of your *mind?*"

His smile broadened, his face the picture of relief. "I've never been more in it, and I—"

She cut him off, words colliding as they spilled out of her. "*This* is what you meant every time you told me you'll resolve this? *This* was your solution all along?"

"Yes. It took me a while to work out the details that will hand everything I own and control over to others without causing the businesses to collapse or the people populating them to go bankrupt or lose their jobs—"

She barged in on his explanation, panting now, almost raving. "But that is not a solution! That…this… is a *catastrophe.* You're sacrificing everything that you *are!*"

"And I'm so relieved this is over. It's *not* a sacrifice, by the way, just a tiny price to have you and our baby. But you don't have to worry. I'll rebuild my success and my fortune."

"I'm not worried about *that.*" She stamped her foot, feeling her brain overheating, her body shaking apart. "I'm making more money all the time and I have enough for both of us, which you can use as capital to rebuild your empire. What I am is *devastated* at the enormity of the sacrifices you just offered—your name, your family, your country, everything you've worked for…"

And he dared chuckle. "So what? I have a wife who'll support me."

She gave a chagrined shriek. "You…you…" Words shriveled to ashes in her mouth. Only one hope remained. "They'll say no."

"Oh, no, they won't. If we'd stayed one more minute, we'd have been flooded in the drool of their eagerness to grab my assets. I'm worth far more to them dead and gone, figuratively speaking, than alive and begetting children of their blood."

And she grabbed him by the arms and shook him. "Go back right now and say you take it all back! You tell them that you—"

He hugged her off the ground, ending her tirade. Before she could twist out of his arms, he buried his face in her neck. "I'm not repeating my father's mistakes, *ya galbi*. He gave up his only chance at love, married women he could barely tolerate for the sake of his kingdom and throne. But I'm giving away replaceable things, just giving the tribes what they want so I can be what I want to be. Yours. It doesn't matter what else I am." She squirmed in his arms, sobbed, and he only pressed her closer. "I'll always remain who I am, in my heart, to my loved ones. As for my success, it might have been in part due to my status before, but now I am formidable in my own right with my knowledge and experience. Even if I never attain the same success or wealth again, what does it matter when I have the ultimate treasure—you and our baby?"

She at last made him put some distance between them, took his face in her trembling hands. "But you'll *always* have us, no price needed. Divorce me, Shaheen, give them the marriage they want. Both I and our baby will be yours forever, no matter what."

"Okay, Romeo and Juliet, move it."

Johara jerked as a hand clamped her arm. It was Amjad. He was also holding Shaheen's arm. Before either of them could say anything, he dragged them back into the council hall.

In the middle of the floor where they'd stood minutes ago, he stopped and stepped in front of them.

"All right, *venerable* lords, listen carefully." The noise again dissipated at Amjad's terrifying growl. "You always called me the Mad Prince, and now's your chance to find out just how crazy I am. All you have to do is vote against Shaheen, and I'll make each and every one of you and your spawn into the next five generations sorry to have ever been born."

"I second that." Harres came forward to stand beside Amjad.

Shaheen's younger half brothers, Haidar and Jalal, joined the lineup, forming a barricade of towering manhood and power in front of her and Shaheen.

"Third and fourth, here," Haidar said for both him and his twin. "You might be all-powerful tribal lords here, but let us remind you *we* are not just the king's sons. Each of us packs more power in the world at large than you can probably imagine."

"You *don't* want to make enemies of us." Jalal's face was reminiscent of Amjad's cruel handsomeness, a younger and even more reckless version of Amjad's demon evidently incubating inside him.

Harres gave his younger brothers a look of approval. "So to sum up, if you vote to exile Shaheen, if you touch a cent of his assets, we will all be your enemies until the day you die."

"*But,* if you free him and apologize for all you've put him through," Haidar elaborated, "you'll have our… gratitude."

Amjad gave a loud, irreverent snort. "Yeah. And you do want to see me grateful, I assure you. You will love it."

Harres nodded. "So either join us in the twenty-first

century, forget the blood-mixing rituals and do business through more…lucrative means, or…piss us off. Your choice."

With that, the brothers turned and started to walk out.

Shaheen pushed at them. "I *won't* let you do this—"

Amjad grabbed Shaheen's arm, dragged him along, hissing, "Ever heard of a strategic withdrawal, Romeo? Walk with me."

Once outside, Amjad flicked a hand at the guards and they all scattered. Then he hooked his hands low on his powerful hips, twisting his lips at Shaheen. "What's wrong with you? We were driving a bargain in there. You don't outbid your team."

Harres gave a harsh laugh. "And the greedy blowhards are having mini heart attacks in there, thinking of all they could milk out of our carte blanche."

Shaheen shook his head, adamant. "I won't let you do this. This is my responsibility."

Amjad rolled his eyes. "Bored now."

Harres turned to Haidar and Jalal, sent them back into the hall to find out the council's verdict.

Once they left, Johara realized he'd sent his younger brothers away so that he could talk freely. "I only wish we could tell the council they actually *owe* you, and more so Johara, more than they could ever repay, for giving us the first solid leads to abort the conspiracy that would tear apart the kingdom they're squabbling over pieces of."

Haidar and Jalal came back almost as soon as they'd gone in, their faces spread with cynical smiles.

"That had to be the fastest decision in the history of the kingdom," Jalal chuckled. "Money sure talks, and talks big."

Amjad slapped him on the back. "Shut up and spit it out."

Jalal smirked at him. "They release Shaheen of his vows, demand no punishment. And to 'give peace a chance,' they're 'willing' to negotiate a 'suitable' compensation."

Johara shook with relief and confusion, still unsure what this meant for all of them, what kind of losses they'd sustain so she and Shaheen could remain together.

"That's it?" She heard her voice trembling on the question. "They want…money? Why didn't they just ask for it in the first place?"

Shaheen put a finger below her chin, raised her face to his, his eyes adoring. "You would have ransomed me, *ya joharti?*"

She gave a vigorous nod. "I certainly would have. I will pay all I have now as part of this compensation."

Shaheen hugged her closer, delighted, defusing her turmoil. "They wouldn't have taken anything in settlement without reaching this point of crisis. The ways of tradition are too demanding, and people in our region have entered grueling and needless wars to keep a vow or save face." He turned to his brothers. "I know they wouldn't have agreed no matter how much they had to gain if you hadn't stood together and scared them off. You have my and Johara's gratitude, but now that they've given up the macho posturing, I'll be the one to negotiate with them. Money, as Jalal said, and massive favors are more potent than magic."

"And let you give up your right as the 'middle' child to always cause us the most trouble?" Jalal winked at him.

"It is more cost effective to give those vultures bites of each of us rather than help you rebuild your empire." Haidar grabbed Jalal and turned back to the hall. "Now excuse us as we get to the nitty gritty on the bite sizes expected."

Shaheen called out after them, "If I'd let those vultures pick apart said empire, I wouldn't have needed your help. I have a standing offer from my princess to bail me out of anything."

Johara heard their laughter until they disappeared.

Then Shaheen turned to Amjad and Harres. "Before they come back again, let's get this out of the way. Now, I'll take care of our so-called allies, while you root out our hidden enemies."

Amjad patted him on the back, all condescension. "Yeah, you two run along now and leave this to the grown-ups."

Shaheen grinned at him, then turned to exchange some last details with Harres.

Johara put her hand on Amjad's arm. "You helped Shaheen and I stay together, at a great price to yourself. Is that your way of 'atoning'? Of saying you're taking back everything you said about me?"

Amjad's eyes looked even more ruthless for their mock chagrin. "How can I possibly do that? You're a woman, aren't you?"

"Your mother was a woman."

Amjad cracked a guffaw. "And you've just made my case."

"What about your aunt? Your sister and cousin?"

Amjad made a simulation of being deep in thought. "There *might* be some anomalies in the species."

"Any hope I fall into the same anomalous category?"

"Could be." Amjad's eyes grew pondering, penetrating. "I'll reserve my final verdict. For a couple of... decades."

"Don't listen to this doomsayer, Johara." Harres put his arm around her shoulder. "You're our Johara and we all love you."

Amjad gave him an abrasive look. "And some of us would not only die for you, they were about to delete themselves from existence for you, too." His gaze moved to Shaheen. "Idiot."

Shaheen threw his head back on an exhilarated laugh. "And I can't wait for the day a woman comes along and makes you wish to delete yourself for her."

"She already came along. And almost did the job herself."

Johara's heart convulsed. The sarcasm in Amjad's voice only made her see how deep the scar went. All the way through him. She was mortified to remember how she'd accused him of being unable to love. What if this wasn't only betrayal and anger, but mortally wounded love, too?

Then Amjad opened his mouth and snuffed any compassion. "So we're off to see about our enemies, and you sleep lightly next to your bride. Now that you're all hers with a cherry on top, she might kill you—with too much love."

Harres guffawed. "One day, Amjad, a woman will make you beg her to kill you the same way. She's out there for you."

Amjad gave him one of those demolishing looks she was sure would disintegrate others. "Says the man who's gone through every unattached woman in the northern hemisphere from the age of twenty-five to forty and hasn't found 'the one' for him yet."

"I'll leave you to debate the existence of women for either of you. I'm taking the one I was born to love—"
Shaheen paused for Amjad to oblige him with a snort

"—to have our honeymoon, away from all snorters and conspirators."

With one last thankful glance at them, one she shared, he swept her up in his arms.

Ecstatic, overcome, she buried her face in his neck, her heart too full to do anything but murmur her love over and over.

A long time later, entangled in the luxury of their intimacy with the sea breeze caressing their cooling bodies, Shaheen rose on his elbow beside her.

He ran his hand lovingly over her still flat belly. "You know, I'm only sorry my plan didn't work. If they'd exiled me, I would have proved to you that you *are* far more precious than everything I am or have, than life itself. But I have the rest of my life to prove this to you."

"You already did. You do, with every breath." She caressed his beloved face, bliss running down her cheeks. "And I'll spend my life proving to you that you are as precious to me."

He hugged her to him. "You already did, the day you let go and trusted me to catch you. How many times have you trusted me since? With your heart, your body, your happiness, your future? And your helping us expose the conspiracy when you know whoever is plotting it will do anything to keep it hushed, putting yourself on the line with us."

"We're in this together, all of it, for better or for worse." She kissed him with all the fierceness of her love, the profundity of her pledge. "Thank you, *ya habibi,* for saving me, for loving me, for existing and being everything to me."

He drowned her in another kiss before he pulled back.

"And I have one more thing I haven't thanked *you* for yet."

She gazed up at him, awash in love and ecstasy, waited for him to tell her one more thing that would hone the perfection.

And he did. "Thank you for never forgetting me, for seeking me out again, and giving me my life's reason. You, and our baby."

* * * * *

Much more is in store for the powerful
Aal Shalaan brothers!
Look for Olivia Gates's next
PRIDE OF ZOHAYD book
To Tempt a Sheikh.
Coming in February 2012.
Only from Desire™ *!*

"I want you to wear my engagement ring."

Shock unfurled in Kate's toes. She didn't know what Duarte was up to. Right now he held all the cards.

"Seems to me like you have a fine sense of humor to suggest something as ridiculous as this. What do you really hope to accomplish?"

"If my father thinks I'm already locked into a relationship—" he skimmed his knuckles up her arm "—he will stop pressing me to marry one of his friends' daughters."

"Why choose me? Surely there must be plenty of women who would be quite happy to pretend to be your fiancée?"

"There are women who want to be my fiancée, but not pretend."

"What a shame you're suffering from such ego problems."

"I fully realize my bank balance offers a hefty enticer. With you, however, we both know where we stand."

Dear Reader,

Welcome to book two in my RICH, RUGGED & ROYAL series about the mysterious Medina family!

What would you do if you crossed paths with a man who just happened to be a prince from a deposed royal family? And what if a photograph of that immensely hunky guy could be worth millions? How far would you go to snag that picture?

Photojournalist Kate Harper faces just that dilemma when she discovers the true identity of resort mogul Duarte Medina.

Duarte Medina is a man who will do anything to protect his family's privacy, and Kate Harper will stop at nothing to find out everything she can about the elusive Medina heir. In fact, the life of someone very dear to her depends on Kate's success in exposing the Medina secrets. All too soon, she finds herself unable to stop exposing her own heart to the dark and brooding royal!

Thank you for picking up Duarte and Kate's story. And don't miss the final installment of RICH, RUGGED & ROYAL, *His Heir, Her Honor*, with Dr Carlos Medina, in January.

Cheers!

Catherine Mann

www.catherinemann.com

HIS THIRTY-DAY FIANCÉE

BY
CATHERINE MANN

Published in Great Britain 2011
by Mills & Boon, an imprint of Harlequin (UK) Limited,
Eton House, 18-24 Paradise Road, Richmond, Surrey TW9 1SR

ISBN: 978 0 263 88326 8

51-1211

Harlequin (UK) policy is to use papers that are natural, renewable and
recyclable products and made from wood grown in sustainable forests. The
logging and manufacturing processes conform to the legal environmental
regulations of the country of origin.

Printed and bound in Spain
by Blackprint CPI, Barcelona

USA TODAY bestselling author **Catherine Mann** is living out her own fairy-tale ending on a sunny Florida beach with her Prince Charming husband and their four children. With more than thirty-five books in print in more than twenty countries, she has also celebrated wins for both a RITA® Award and a Booksellers' Best Award. Catherine enjoys chatting with readers online—thanks to the wonders of the wireless internet that allows her to network with her laptop by the water! To learn more about her work, visit her website, www.catherinemann. com, or reach her by snail mail at PO Box 6065, Navarre, FL 32566, USA.

To Mollie Saunders,
a real-life princess and a magical storyteller!

One

Catching a royal was tough. But catching an elusive Medina was damn near impossible.

Teeth chattering, photojournalist Kate Harper inched along the third-story ledge leading to Prince Duarte Medina's living quarters. The planked exterior of his Martha's Vineyard resort offered precious little to grab hold of as she felt her way across in the dark, but she'd never been one to admit defeat.

Come hell or high water, she would snag her top-dollar picture. Her sister's future teetered even more precariously than Kate's balance on the twelve-inch beam.

Wind whipped in off the harbor, slapping her mossy green Dolce & Gabbana knockoff around her legs. Her cold toes curled along the wooden ridge since she'd ditched her heels on the balcony next door before climbing out. Thank God it wasn't snowing tonight.

Wrangling her way into an event at the posh Medina resort hadn't been easy. But she'd nabbed a ticket to a Fortune 500 mogul's rehearsal dinner for his son by promising a dimwit dilettante to run a tabloid piece on her ex in exchange for the woman's invitation. Once in, however, Kate was on her own to dodge security, locate Prince Duarte and snap the shot. As best she could tell, this was her only hope to enter his suite. Too bad her coat and gloves had been checked at the door.

The minicameras embedded in her earrings were about to tear her darn earlobes in half. She'd transformed a couple old button cameras into what looked like gold-and-emerald jewelry.

The lighthouse swooped a dim beam through the cottony-thick fog, Klaxon wailing every twenty seconds and temporarily drowning out the sound of wedding-party guests mingling on the first floor. She scooched closer to the prince's balcony.

Kate stretched her leg farther, farther still until… Pay dirt. Her pounding heart threatened to pop a seam on her thrift-shop satin gown. She grabbed the railing fast and swung her leg over.

A hand clamped around her wrist. A strong hand. A *masculine* hand.

She yelped as another hand grabbed her ankle and hauled, grip strong on her arm and calf. His fingers seared her freezing skin just over her anklet made by her sister. A good-luck charm to match the earrings. She sure hoped it helped.

A swift yank sent her tumbling over onto the balcony. Her dress twisted around her thighs and hopefully not higher. She scrambled for firm footing, her arms flailing as her gown slid back into place. She landed hard against a wall.

No, wait. Walls didn't have crisp chest hair and defined muscles, and smell of musky perspiration. Under normal circumstances, she'd have been more than a little turned on. If she wasn't so focused on her sister's future and her lips weren't turning blue from the cold.

Kate peeked…and found a broad male torso an inch from her nose. A black shirt or robe hung open, exposing darkly tanned skin and brown hair. Her fingers clenched in the silky fabric. Some kind of karate workout clothes?

Good God, did Medina actually hire ninjas for protection like monarchs in movies?

Kate looked up the strong column of the ninja's neck, the tensed line of his square jaw in need of a shave. Then, holy crap, she met the same coal-black eyes she'd been planning to photograph.

"You're not a ninja," she blurted.

"And you are not much of an acrobat." Prince Duarte Medina didn't smile, much less say cheese.

"Not since I flunked out of kinder-gym." This was the strangest conversation ever, but at least he hadn't pitched her over the railing. Yet.

He also didn't let go of her arms. The restrained strength of his calloused fingers sparked an unwelcomed shiver of awareness along her chilled skin.

Duarte glanced down at her bare feet. "Were you booted for a balance beam infraction?"

"Actually, I broke another kid's nose." She'd tripped the nasty little boy after he'd called her sister a moron.

Kate fingered her earring. She had to snap her pictures and punch out. This was an opportunity rarer than a red diamond.

The Medina monarchy had pretty much fallen off the map twenty-seven years ago after King Enrique Medina was deposed in a coup that left his wife dead. For decades rumors swirled that the old widower had walled up with his three sons in an Argentinean fortress. After a while, people stopped wondering about the Medinas at all. Until she'd felt the journalistic twitch to research an individual in the background of a photo she'd taken. That twitch had led to her news story which popped the top off a genie bottle. She'd exposed the secret lives of three now-grown princes who were hiding in plain sight in the United States.

But that hadn't been enough. The paycheck on that story hadn't come close to hauling her out of the financial difficulties life had thrust upon her.

Her window of opportunity to grab an up-close picture was shrinking. Already paparazzi from every corner of the globe were scrambling for a photo op now that news of her initial find leaked like water through a crumbling sandcastle.

Yet somehow, she'd beaten them all because Duarte Medina was really here. In the flesh. In front of her. And so much hotter in person. She swayed and couldn't even blame it on vertigo.

He scooped her into his arms, apparently sporting real strength to go with those ninja workout clothes.

"You are turning to a block of ice." His voice rumbled with the barest hint of an exotic accent, the bedroom sort of inflection perfect for voice-overs in commercials that would convince a woman to buy anything if he came with it. "You need to come in from the cold before you pass out."

So he could call security to lock her up? Her angle with the earring cameras wasn't great, but she hoped she'd snagged some workable shots while she jostled around in his arms.

"Uh, thanks for the save." Should she call him Prince Duarte or Your Majesty?

Coming into this, she'd envisioned getting her photos on the sly and hadn't thought to brush up on protocol when confronted with a prince in karate pajamas. A very hot, swarthy prince carrying her inside to his suite.

Now that she studied his face inches from hers, his ancestry was unmistakable. The Medina monarchy had originated on the small island of San Rinaldo off the coast of Spain. And in the charged moment she could see his bold Mediterranean heritage as clearly as his arrogance. With fog rolling along the rocky shore at his back through the open balcony doors, she could envision him reigning over his native land. In fact it was difficult to remember at all that he'd lived for so many years in the United States.

He set her on her feet again, her toes sinking for miles into the plush rug. The whole room spoke of understated wealth and power from the pristine white sofas, to the mahogany antique armoire, to a mammoth four-poster bed with posts as thick as tree trunks.

A bed? She tried to swallow. Her throat went dry.

Duarte smiled tightly, heavy lidded eyes assessing. "Ramon has really outdone himself this time."

"Ramon?" Her editor's name was Harold. "I'm not sure what you mean." But she would play along if it meant staying put a few minutes more. To get her pictures, of course.

"The father of the groom has a reputation for supplying the best, uh—" his pulse beat slowly along his bronzed neck "—companionship to woo his business associates, but you surpass them all in originality."

"Companionship?" Shock stunned her silent. He couldn't be implying what she thought.

"I assume he paid you well, given the whole elaborate entrance." His upper lip curled with a hint of disdain.

Paid companionship. Ah, hell. He thought she was a high-priced call girl. Or at least she hoped he thought high-priced. Well, she wasn't going that far for her sister, but maybe she could scavenge another angle for the story by sticking around just a question or two longer.

Kate placed a tentative hand on his shoulder. No way she touching his bared chest. "How many times has he so generously gifted you?"

His smoky dark eyes streamed over the tops of her breasts darn near spilling out of the wretched thrift-store dress. "I have never availed myself of—how shall we say? Paid services."

A good journalist would ask. "Not even once?" Maybe she could inch just her pinky past his open neckline.

"Never." His hard tone left no room for doubt.

She held back her sigh of relief and let herself savor the heat of his skin under her touch.

Her fingers curled. "Oh, uh…just oh."

"I am a gentleman, after all. And as such, I can't simply send you back onto the balcony. Stay while I make arrangements to slip you out." His palm lay low on her waist. "Would you like a drink?"

Her stomach squeezed into an even tighter ball of anticipation. Why was she this hyped-up over an assignment? This was her job, one she was well-trained to do. Thoughts of her days as a photojournalist for news magazines bombarded her. Days when her assignments ranged from a Jerusalem pilgrimage to the aftermath of an earthquake in Indonesia.

Now, she worked for GlobalIntruder.com.

She stifled a hysterical laugh. God, what had she

sunk to? And what choice did she have with a shrinking newspaper industry?

Sure, she was nervous, damn it. This photo was about more than staying in the media game. It was about finding enough cash fast to make sure her special-needs sister wasn't booted out of her assisted-living facility next month. Jennifer had a grown-up's body with a child's mind. She needed protection and Kate was all she had left keeping her from becoming an adult ward of the state.

Too bad Kate was only a couple of rent payments away from bankruptcy court.

The prince's hand slid up her spine, clasping the back of her neck. Her traitorous body tingled.

She needed a moment to regroup—away from this guy's surprising allure—if she hoped to get the information she needed. "Is there a powder room nearby where I can freshen up while you pour the drinks? When I leave your suite, I shouldn't *look* like I climbed around outside the balcony."

"I'll show you the way."

Not what she had in mind. But she'd kept her cool during a mortar attack before. She could handle this. "Just point, please. I've got good internal navigational skills."

"I imagine you're good at a great many things." His breath heated over her neck as he dipped his head closer to speak. "I may have never had use for offers such as yours before, but I have to confess, there is something captivating about you."

Oh, boy.

His warm breath grazed her exposed shoulder, his lips so close to touching her skin without closing that final whisper for connection. Her breasts beaded against the already snug bodice of her gown. She pushed her heels deeper into the carpet to keep her balance. Her anklet rubbed against her other leg. Her good-luck charm from Jennifer. Remember her sister.

"About that bathroom?" Frantically, she looked around the bedroom suite with too many tall, paneled doors, all closed.

"Right over here." His words heated over her neck, raising goose bumps along her arms.

"Uh, but…" Was that breathy gasp hers? "I prefer to go solo."

"We wouldn't want you to get lost on your way." He stopped just at her earlobe as if to share a secret.

Had he touched her? His breath against her skin left her light-headed. He cupped the other side of her head. Hunger gnawed deep within her as she ached to lean into his cradling touch.

Then he backed away, his hand teasing a tempting trail and his black workout clothes rustling a lethal whisper. "Just through that door, Ms. Kate Harper."

Duarte gestured right, both of her earrings dangling from between his fingers.

Duarte had been waiting for this moment since the second he'd learned which tabloid scumbag had blown apart his family's carefully crafted privacy. He held Kate Harper's earrings in his hands along with her hopes of a new scoop. He'd been alerted she might be on the premises and determined her hidden cameras' locations before they'd left the balcony.

He'd spent his whole life dodging the press. He knew their tricks. His father had drummed into his sons at a young age how their safety depended on anonymity. They'd been protected, educated and, above all, trained.

Sweat trickled between his shoulder blades from his workout—a regimen that had been interrupted by security concerns.

One look at the intruder on the screen and he'd decided to see how far she would go.

In that form-fitting dress, she personified seduction. Like a pinup girl from days past, she had a timeless air and feminine allure that called to the primal male inside him. Good Lord, what a striking picture she would make draped on the white sofa just behind her. Or better yet, in his bed.

But he was an expert at self-control. And just calling to mind her two-bit profession made it easier to rein in his more instinctive thoughts.

Kate Harper perched a hand on her hip. "I can't believe you knew who I really was the whole time."

"From the second you left the party." He'd been sent pictures of her when he'd investigated the photojournalist who cracked a cover story that had survived intense scrutiny for decades.

Background photos of her portrayed something very different: an earthy woman in khaki pants and generic white T-shirts, no makeup, her sleek brown hair in an unpretentious ponytail as opposed to the windswept twist she wore now. A hint of cinnamon apple fragrance drifted his way.

Her bright red lips pursed tight with irritation. "Then why pretend I'm a call girl?"

"That's too high-class for the garbage you peddle." He pocketed her earrings, blocking thoughts of her pretty pout.

His family's life had been torn apart just when his father needed peace more than ever. Too much stress could kill Enrique Medina faster than any extremist assassin from San Rinaldo.

"So the gloves are off." She folded her arms over her chest, rubbing her hands along her skin. From fear or the cold ocean wind blasting through the open French doors? "What do you intend to do? Call your security or the police?"

"I have to admit, I wouldn't mind seeing more than gloves come off your deceitful body." Duarte closed the balcony doors with a click and a snick of a lock.

"Uh, listen, Prince Duarte, or Your Majesty, or whatever I'm supposed to call you." Her words tumbled faster and faster. "Let's both calm down."

He glanced over his shoulder, cocking an eyebrow.

"Okay, *I* will be calm. You be whatever you want." She swiped back a straggling hair with a shaky hand. "My point is I'm here. You don't want invasive media coverage. So why not pose for just one picture? It can be staged any way you choose. You can be in total control."

"Control? Is this some kind of game to you, like a child's video system where we pass the controller back and forth?" He stalked closer, his feet as bare as hers on the carpet. "Because for me, this isn't anywhere near a game. This is about my family's privacy, our safety."

Royals—even ones without a country—were never safe from threats. His mother had been killed in the rebellion overthrowing San Rinaldo, his older brother severely injured trying to save her. As a result, his father—King Enrique Medina—became obsessed with security. He'd constructed an impenetrable fortress on an island off the coast of St. Augustine, Florida, where he'd brought up his three young sons. Only when they'd become adults had Duarte and his brothers been able to break free. By scattering to the far corners of the U.S., they'd kept low profiles and were able to lead normal adult lives—with him on Martha's Vineyard, Antonio in Galveston Bay and Carlos in Tacoma.

Kate touched his wrist lightly. "I'm sorry about what has happened to your family, how you lost your mother."

Her touch seared at a raw spot hidden deep inside, prompting him to lash out in defense. Duarte sketched his knuckles over her bare ears. "How sorry are you?"

He had to give her credit. She didn't back down. She met his gaze dead-on with eyes bluer than the San Rinaldo waters he just barely remembered.

Kate pulled her hand away. "What about a picture of you in your ninja clothes lounging against the balcony railing?"

"How about a photo of you naked in my arms?"

She gasped. "Of all the arrogant, self-aggrandizing, pompous—"

"I'm a prince." He held up a finger. "But of course everyone knows that now, thanks to your top-notch journalistic instincts."

"You're angry. I get that." She inched behind the sofa as if putting a barrier between them, yet her spine stayed rigid, her eyes sparking icicles. "But just because you're royalty doesn't give you a free pass along with all these plush trappings."

He'd left his father's Florida fortress with nothing more than a suitcase full of clothes. Not that he intended to dole out that nugget for her next exposé. "Can't blame a prince for trying."

She didn't laugh. "Why did you let me in here? Am I simply around for your amusement so you can watch me flinch when you flush my camera?"

Kate Harper was a woman who regained her balance fast. He admired that. "You really want this picture."

Her fingers sunk so deep in the sofa that her short red nails disappeared. "More than you can possibly know."

How far would she go to get it?

For an immoral moment he considered testing those boundaries. His identity had been exposed already anyway, a reality that drained his father's waning strength. Anger singed the edges of his control, fueling memories of how soft Kate's skin had felt under his touch when he'd pulled her onto the balcony, how perfectly her curves had shaped themselves to his chest.

Turning away, he forced his more civilized nature to quench the heat. "You should leave now. Use the door directly behind you. The guard in the corridor will escort you out."

"You're not going to give me my camera back, are you?"

He pivoted toward her again. "No." He slid his hand in his pocket and toyed with her earrings. "Although, you're more than welcome to try to retrieve your jewelry."

"I prefer battles I have a chance of winning." Her lips tipped in a half smile. "Can I at least have a cigar to hock on eBay?"

Again she'd surprised him. He wasn't often entertained anymore. "You're funny. I like that."

"Give me my camera and I'll become a stand-up comedian—" she snapped her fingers "—that fast."

Who was this woman in an ill-fitting gown with an anklet made of silver yarn and white plastic beads? Most would have been nervous as hell or sucking up.

Although, perhaps she was smarter than the rest, in spite of her dubious profession.

This woman had cost him more than could be regained. He would forge ahead, but already his father feared for his sons' safety, a concern the ailing old man didn't need. An alarming possibility snaked through his mind, one he should have considered before. Damn the way she took the oxygen and reason from a room. What if her minicamera sent the photos instantly by remote to a portal? Photos already on their way to flood the media?

Photos of the two of them?

Duarte sifted the earrings between his fingers. A plan formed in his mind to safeguard against all possibilities, a way to satisfy his urges on every level—lust and revenge without any annoying loose ends. Some might think over such a large decision, but his father had taught him to trust his instincts.

"Ms. Harper," he said, closing in on her, following her behind the sofa. "I have another proposition instead."

"Uh, a *proposition?*" She stepped backed, bumping an end table, rattling the glass lamp filled with coins. "I thought we already cleared the air on that subject. Even I have limits."

"Too bad for both of us. That could have been…" He stopped mid-sentence and steadied the lamp—a gift from his brother Antonio—filled with Spanish doubloons from a shipwreck off San Rinaldo. No need to torment her for the hell of it, not when he had a more complex plan in mind. "It's not that kind of proposition. Believe me, I don't have to trade money—or media exclusives—for sex."

She eyed him warily, surreptitiously hitching up the

sinking neckline of her gown. "Then what kind of trade are we talking about here?"

He watched her every move. The way she picked at her painted thumbnail with her forefinger. How she rubbed her heel over the silly little anklet she wore. He savored up every bit of reeling her in, the plan growing more fulfilling by the second.

This was the best way. The only way. "I have a bit of a, uh, shall we say 'family situation.' My father is in ill health—as the world now knows thanks to your invasive investigative skills."

She winced visibly for the first time. "I'm very sorry about that. Truly." Then her nervousness fell away and her azure-blues gleamed with intelligence. "About the trade?"

"My father wants to see me settled down, married and ready to produce the next Medina heir. He even has a woman chosen—"

Her eyes went wide. "You have a fiancée?"

"My, how you reporters gobble up tidbits like fish snapping at crumbs on the water. But no. I do not have a fiancée." Irritation nipped, annoying him all the more since it signaled a bit of control sliding to her side. "If you want another bread crumb, don't anger me."

"My apologies again." She fingered her empty earlobe. "What about our trade?"

Back to the intriguing problem in front of him.

He would indulge those impulses with her later. When she was ready. And gauging by her air of desperation, it wouldn't take much persuasion. Just a little time he could buy while settling a score and easing his father's concerns about future heirs.

"As I said, my father is quite ill." Near death from the damage caused by hepatitis contracted during his days on the run. The doctors feared liver failure at any time. He shut off distracting images of his pale father. "Obviously I don't want to upset him while his health is so delicate."

"Of course not. Family is important." Her eyes filled with sympathy.

Ah. He'd found her weakness. The rest would be easy.

"Exactly. So, I have something you want, and you can give me something in return." He lifted her chilly hand and kissed her short red nails. Judging by the way her pupils dilated, this revenge would be a pleasure for them both. "You cost our family much with your photos, destroying our carefully crafted anonymity. Now, let's discuss how you're going to repay that debt."

Two

"Repay the debt," Kate repeated, certain he couldn't be implying what she'd thought. And she would look like a fool if she let him know what she'd assumed. She inched her chilly hand from his encompassing grip. "I'm going to work for you?"

"Nice try." He stepped closer, his ninja workout pants whispering a dark, sexy hello.

Holding her silence, she crossed her arms to hide her shivery response and keep him from moving closer. This man's magnetism was mighty inconvenient. Her toes curled into the Aubusson rug.

He tipped his head regally, drawing her attention to the strong column of his neck, his pulse steady and strong. "I want you to be my fiancée."

Shock unfurled her toes. "Are you smoking crack?"

"Never have. Never intend to." He clasped her wrists

and unfolded her arms slowly, deliberately until they stood closer still. His eyes bored into hers. "I'm stone-cold sober and completely serious. In case you haven't noticed, I do not joke."

Her breasts strained against the bodice of her dress with each breath growing deeper, more erratic. She didn't know what he was up to. Right now, he held all the cards, including all her photos.

Any hope of salvaging an article from this required playing with fire. "Seems to me like you have a fine sense of humor to suggest something as ridiculous as this. What do you really hope to accomplish?"

"If my father thinks I'm already locked into a relationship—" he skimmed his knuckles up her arm "—with you, he will quit pressing me to hook up with one of the daughters of his old pals from San Rinaldo."

"Why choose me?" She plucked his hand away with a nonchalance she certainly didn't feel inside. "Surely there must be plenty of women who would be quite happy to pretend to be your fiancée."

He leaned on the back of the sofa, muscular legs mouth-wateringly showcased in his ninja pants. "There are women who want to be my fiancée, but not pretend."

"What a shame you're suffering from such ego problems." She playfully kicked his bare foot with hers.

Oops. Wrong move. Her skin flamed from the simple touch. An answering heat sparked in his eyes.

It was just their feet, for pity's sake. Still, she'd never felt such an intense and instantaneous draw to a man in her life, and she resented her body's betrayal.

Heels staying on the ground, Duarte toed her anklet, flicking at the beads. "I fully realize my bank balance offers a hefty enticer. With you, however, we both know where we stand."

Her yarn and plastic contrasted sharply with his suite sporting exclusive artwork. The seascape paintings weren't from some roadside stand bought simply to accent a Martha's Vineyard decor. She recognized the distinctive brushstrokes of Spanish master painter Joaquín Sorolla y Bastida from her college art classes.

She forced herself not to twitch away from Duarte's power play, not too tough actually since the simple strokes felt so good against her adrenaline-pumped nerves. "Won't your father wonder why he's never heard you mention me before now?"

"We're not a Sunday-dinners sort of family. You can use that as a quote for articles if you wish, once we're finished."

Articles. Plural. But would they be timely enough to generate the money to settle her sister's bill for next month? "How long from now until that finish date?"

"My father has asked for thirty days of my time to handle estate business around the country while he's ill. You can accompany and compile notes for your exclusive. I'll be hitting a number of hot spots around the U.S., including a stop in Washington, D.C., for a black-tie dinner with some politicians who could put your name on the map. And of course you'll get to meet my family along the way. I ask only that I get to approve any material you plan to submit."

Thirty days?

She did a quick mental calculation of her finances and Jennifer's bills. With some pinching she could squeak through until then. Except what kind of scoop would she have when every news industry out there could have jumped in ahead of her? "The story could be cold by then. I need some assurance of a payoff—at work—that will help advance my career."

Bleck, but that made her sound money-grubbing. How come men struck hard bargains and they were corporate wizards, but the same standards didn't apply to women? She had a career to look after and responsibilities to her sister.

Duarte's eyes brimmed with cynicism. "So we're going to barter here? Quite bold on your part."

"Arrest me, then. I'll text a story from my jail cell. I'll describe the inside of your personal suite along with details about your aftershave and that birthmark right above your belly button. People can draw their own conclusions and believe me, the click-throughs will be plentiful."

"You're willing to insinuate we had an affair? You're prepared to compromise your journalistic integrity?"

For her sister? She didn't have any choice. "I work for the *Global Intruder.* Obviously journalistic integrity isn't a high priority."

A glint of respect flecked his eyes. "You drive a hard bargain. Good for you." He straightened, topping her by at least half a foot. "Let's get down to business, then. There's going to be a family wedding at the end of the month at my father's estate. If you hold up your end of the bargain for the next thirty days, you get exclusive photos of the private ceremony. The payoff from those photos should be more than adequate to meet your needs."

A Medina wedding? Wow. Just. Wow.

Before she could push a resounding yes past her lips, he continued, "And in a show of good faith, you can submit a short personal interview about our engagement."

"All I have to do is *pretend* to be your fiancée?" It sounded too good to be true. Could this Hail Mary pass for Jennifer work out just right?

"Of course it's pretend. I most certainly do not want you to be my real fiancée."

"You're serious here. You're actually going to take me with you to your father's estate?" And give her photos of a family wedding.

"Ah, I can see the dollar signs in your lovely eyes."

"Sure I want a story and I have bills to pay like anybody else—well, anybody other than Medinas—but I work for that payday." Hey wait, he thought her eyes were lovely? "What reporter in their right mind would say no to this? But what's the catch? Because I can't imagine anyone would willingly invite a reporter into the intimate circle of their lives. Especially someone with as many secrets as you."

"Let's call it a preemptive strike. Better to know the snake's identity rather than wonder. And I also gain four weeks of your charming presence."

Suddenly an ugly suspicion bloomed in her mind. "I'm not going to sleep with you to land this exclusive."

Her eyes darted back to the bed, an image blossoming in her brain of the two of them tangled together in the sheets, their discarded clothes mating on the floor in a silky blend of green and black.

A humorless chuckle rumbled in his chest. "You really are obsessed with having sex with me. First, you believe I've mistaken you for a prostitute. Then, you think I want to trade my story for time in your bed. Truly, I'm not that hard up."

She blinked away the dizzying fantasy he'd painted of the two of them together. "This just seems so... bizarre."

"My life is far from normal." The luxury that wrapped so effortlessly around him confirmed that.

"I should simply accept what you're offering at face value?"

"It's a month of your life to make appearances with a prince while I settle Dad's estate. Our family is rather well connected. You'll have some very influential new contacts for future stories."

Now, didn't he know how to tempt a girl? On too many levels. "If we're not sleeping together, what do you get out of this?"

He held up one finger, tapping it on her shoulder. "I give my father peace." He added a second touch, thumbing her collarbone. "I retain control of my own personal life. And three—" he curled his whole hand around her in a hold that was both arousing and a little dangerous "—I manage all cameras, all the time. You don't have access to any shots unless I okay them. The press hears nothing without my approval. And before you get too excited, when we go to my father's, you will not know where he lives."

She laughed in hopes of dispersing the tingles tightening her breasts. "Do you intend to put a bag over my head before you stuff me in a limo?"

"Nothing so plebian, my dear." His thumb continued to work its magic. "Suffice it to say, you will get on an airplane and then land on a private island, somewhere warmer than here in Massachusetts. Beyond that…" He shrugged, sliding past her, a hint of cedar drifting along with him.

Pivoting, she watched him stride across the room, his steps silent, his hips trim and decidedly hot. "You're taking me to an untraceable island so you can kill me and dump my body in the ocean for exposing your

HIS THIRTY-DAY FIANCÉE

family—which, for the record, is just my job. Nothing personal."

Shaking his head, he stopped in front of a painting of a wooden sailboat beached on its side. "Pull a bag over your head? Feed you to the sharks? You are a bloodthirsty one." Pulling back the gold-framed artwork, he revealed a wall safe. Duarte punched in numbers and the door hissed open. "Nobody is going to kill anyone. We're going to let the world know we're engaged right away. Then if you disappear, all fingers will point to me."

"If they can find you on that 'warm island.'"

"Thanks to you, I'm sure my father's secluded hide-away will be found sooner or later." He pulled out one flat velvet box after another, each with an exclusive jeweler's name imprinted on the top. "One last point. If you break any of my rules about distribution of information, I will turn over the security footage of you breaking into my estate and press charges for unlawful entry. It won't matter that you've been my fiancée. The world will believe the tape was taken after our breakup and that you were a scorned woman bent on revenge."

The unrelenting line of his back, strong column of his neck exposed by closely shorn hair spoke of cool determination. She wasn't dealing with a rookie. "You would really send me to jail?"

"Only if you betray me. If you didn't want to play in the big leagues, then you shouldn't have climbed onto my balcony. You can always just walk away free and clear now." He plucked the smallest jewelry box from the back and creaked it open to reveal an emerald-cut ruby flanked with diamond baguettes. "Negotiations are over. Take it or leave it. That's my deal."

She eyed the platinum-set engagement ring, jewels

clearly perfect yet curiously understated. No gaudy Hollywood flash, but rather old-money class that appealed to her more than some princess-cut satellite dish in a six-pronged setting. For Jennifer's sake, she would make this work. She had to. She would regret it for the rest of her life if she didn't take this risk, a chance to provide for her sister forever.

Decision made, Kate extended her hand. "Why on earth would I betray you when we've obviously come to a mutually beneficial agreement?"

Duarte hardened his focus as he did in the workout room and plucked the ring out of the cushiony bed. Best not to think about any other kind of bed.

Cradling her left hand in his, he slid the ring in place, a ruby-and-diamond antique from the Medina family collection. He could buy her something more contemporary and ornate later, but now that he had Kate's agreement, he wasn't going to give her time to wriggle out. He had a month to exact revenge on her. And no, he wasn't going to dump her in the ocean or cause her any bodily harm.

Instead, he would seduce her completely, thoroughly and satisfyingly. He wanted this woman and would have pursued her regardless of how they'd crossed paths. But they hadn't met under normal circumstances. He couldn't forget what she'd done to his family. The best way to discredit any future reports from her would come from casting her in the role of a bitter ex.

A month should be plenty of time to accomplish all of his goals.

Closing his hand around hers, he sealed the ring in place. "The bride and groom have left the rehearsal dinner downstairs, so we will not be stealing their spotlight by showing up together."

"Together? Tonight?"

"Within the hour." He thumbed the ring until the ruby centered on top of her delicate finger. "I told you I wanted to spread the word soon."

"This is more than soon." She rubbed her foot against the yarn anklet, betraying nerves she didn't let show on her face.

"It's in your best interest that we establish ourselves as a couple right away." Just saying the word *couple* brought to mind images of how thoroughly he intended to couple with her. "Especially if you're still concerned about me feeding you to the fishes."

"Then, uh, okay. I guess there's no time like the present." She tugged up the bodice of her dress, drawing his eyes right back to her cleavage.

His teeth ached, he wanted her so much. He liked to think he appreciated the whole package when it came to women, mind as well as body. But good God, this woman had a chest that could send a strong man to his knees. He burned with the urge to ease down the sides of her gown and reveal each creamy swell, slowly taking his time to explore and appreciate with his hands, with his mouth.

Patience. "There's a large party downstairs with plenty of movers and shakers from social and political scenes. You'll get to share details with your boss. My word. Fifteen minutes downstairs and then I'll have the reassurance that you're committed. You'll have the reassurance that I can't kill you without pinging police radar."

"Okay, okay, I see your point." Her laughter tickled his ears. "It's just all moving so fast I want to make sure

I think of everything. I need to make one call before we go public."

"To your editor? I think not." He tugged her closer, the soft curves of her breasts grazing his chest. He could almost taste the milky softness of her skin. "I need your commitment to this plan first. Can't have you going rogue on me out there."

The fight crept back into her eyes, chasing away the nervousness he'd seen earlier. Her grit fired his insides every bit as much as her pinup-girl curves.

She locked his hand in a firm hold, her eyes meeting his dead-on. "I need to call my sister. We can put her on speakerphone if you don't trust me about what's being said, but I have to speak to her first. It's nonnegotiable. If the answer's no, then I'll accept your offer to walk away and settle for an exposé on your birthmark."

With the top of her head at nose level, he could smell the apple-fresh scent of her shampoo, see the rapid pulse in her neck bared by her upswept do. A simple slide of his hands around her back and he would be able to cup her bottom and cradle her between his legs before he kissed her. He couldn't remember when he'd wanted a woman this much. And although he tried to tell himself it had something to do with a stretch of abstinence since the Medina story broke, he knew full well he would have ached to have her anytime. Anywhere.

Why hadn't photos of her in the private investigator's report captured his attention the way she did now? He'd registered she was an attractive woman, but hadn't felt this gut-leveling kick. She chewed her bottom lip, and he realized he was staring.

His fingers tightened around her hand wearing his ring. "What about speaking to the rest of your family?"

"Just my sister," she said softly. Her eyes were wary but she didn't pull away. "What about *your* family?"

And would he tell his brothers the truth? He would have to decide on the best strategy for approaching them later. "They'll get the memo. You could call your sister immediately after we make our announcement downstairs."

She shook her head quickly, a light brown lock sliding loose to caress her cheek the way he longed to. "I don't want to risk any chance of her hearing it from someone else first." Kate tipped her chin defiantly, as if prepping for battle. "My sister is a special-needs adult. Okay? She will be confused if this leaks before I can speak to her. It's not like I would lie about something you can easily verify."

Every word she shared was so obviously against her will that his conscience engaged for the first time. But that couldn't change his course. Kate had set this in motion when she'd climbed onto the ledge, in fact back when she'd identified his face in a picture that launched an exposé on his family. Still, his inconvenient kick of conscience could be silenced by acquiescing to her request for a call.

"Fine, then." He unclipped his cell from his waistband and passed it to her. "Feel free to phone your sister before she finds out on Facebook. But I would hurry if I were you. We all know how quickly internet news can spread."

She scrunched her nose. "You cut me to the quick with your not-so-subtle reference to my news story of the century."

God, she was hot. And he wanted her.

While he would have to wait to have her, before the

night was over, he would claim a seal-the-deal kiss from his new fiancée.

Meanwhile, it wouldn't hurt to keep her on her toes. "Make your call quickly. You have until I've changed for our appearance downstairs."

With slow and unmistakably sexual deliberation, he untied the belt on his workout clothes.

Kate damn near swallowed her tongue. "Uh, do you want me to step into the hall?"

"You promised to use speakerphone, remember?" Duarte turned his back to her but he didn't leave. He simply strode toward the mahogany armoire.

The jacket slid from his shoulders.

Holy hell.

He draped the black silk over one of the open cabinet doors, muscles shifting along his back. She saw sparks like a camera flash snapping behind her retinas.

Oh. Right. She needed to breathe.

God, this man was ripped with long, lean—lethal—definition. She'd felt those muscles up close when she'd fallen against him on the balcony.

How much further would he carry this little display? Her fingers had been wowed, for sure, but her photographer eyes picked up everything she'd missed in that frantic moment earlier.

She was female. With a heartbeat. And swaying on her feet. The cell phone bit into her tight grip, reminding her of the reason she'd come here in the first place. Keeping Jennifer happy and secure was top priority.

Thumbing in her sister's number, she considered blowing off the whole speakerphone issue. But she'd probably pushed her luck far enough tonight. There was no reason not to let him hear and he would have

Jennifer's number anyway now that it was stored in his cell history.... And hey, might Jennifer have his as well after this call? Interesting. She would have to check once she could steal a moment away from him. She activated the speaker phone just as her sister picked up.

"Hello?" Jennifer's voice came through, hesitant, confused. "Who's this?"

"Jennifer? It's Katie, calling from a, uh, friend's phone." Her eyes zipped back to Duarte and his silky pants riding low on his trim hips. "I have some important news for you."

"Are you coming to see me?" She pictured Jennifer in her pj's, eating popcorn with other residents at the first-rate facility outside Boston.

"Not tonight, sweetie." She had a date with an honest-to-God prince. The absurdity of it all bubbled hysteria in her throat.

"Then when?"

That depended on a certain sexy stranger who was currently getting mouth-wateringly naked.

"I'm not sure, Jennifer, but I promise to try my best to make it as soon as possible."

Duarte pulled out a tuxedo and hung it on the door. She caught the reflection of his chest in the mirror inside the wardrobe. The expanse of chest she'd only seen a slice of from his open jacket—

"Katie?" Jennifer's voice cut through the airwaves. "What's your news?"

"Oh, uh…" She gulped in air for confidence—and to still her stuttering heart as Duarte knelt to select shoes. "I'm engaged."

"To be married?" Jennifer squealed. "When?"

Wincing, Kate opted to deliberately misunderstand

the whole timing question since there wasn't going to be a wedding. "He gave me a ring tonight."

"And you said yes." Her sister squealed again, her high-pitched excitement echoing around the room. "Who is he?"

At least she could answer the second question honestly. "He's someone I met through work. His name is Duarte."

"Duarte? That's a funny name. I've never heard it before. Do you think he would mind if I call him Artie? I like art class."

He glanced over his shoulder, an eyebrow arched, his first sign that he even noticed or cared that she was still in the room while he stripped.

Kate cradled the phone. "Artie is a nice name, but I think he prefers Duarte."

A quick smile chased across his face before he turned back to the tux. His thumbs hooked in the waistband of his whispery black workout pants. Oh, boy. Her breath went heavy in her lungs and she couldn't peel her eyes off him to save her soul. So silly. So wrong. And so compelling in his arrogant confidence.

Then she realized he was watching her watch him in the mirror. His eyes were dark and unreadable. But he wasn't laughing or mocking, because that would have shown, surely.

Silence stretched between them, his thumbs still hooked on the waistband. His biceps flexed in anticipation of motion.

She spun away, zeroing in on the conversation instead of the man. "You will probably see something in the paper, so I want you to understand. Duarte is a real-life Prince Charming."

God, it galled her to say that.

The whistle of sliding fabric carried, the squeak of the floor as he must have shuffled from foot to foot to step out of his pants.

"A Prince Charming? Like in the stories?" Jennifer gasped. "Cool. I can't wait to tell my friends."

What would all those friends think and say when they learned he was a prince in more than some fairy-tale fashion? Would people try to get to Duarte through especially vulnerable Jennifer? The increasing complications of what she'd committed to hit her. "Sweetie, please promise me that if people ask you any questions, you just tell them to ask your sister. Okay?"

Jennifer hesitated, background sounds of a television and bingo game bleeding through. "For how long?"

"I'll talk to you by tomorrow morning. I swear." And she always kept her promises to Jennifer. She always would.

"Okay, I promise, too. Not a word. Cross my heart. Love you, Katie."

"I love you, too, Jennifer. Forever and always."

The phone line went dead and Katie wondered if she'd done the right thing. Bottom line, she had to provide for her sister and right now her options were limited. The lure of those wedding photos tempted her. A family member, Duarte had said. One of his brothers? An unknown cousin? His father even?

A hanger clanked behind her and she resisted the urge to pivot back around. Right now she cursed her artistic imagination as it filled in the blanks. In her mind's eye, she could see those hard, long legs sliding into the fine fabric tailored to fit him. The zipper rasped and she decided it was safe to look.

Although that also put his chest back in her line of sight. He was facing her now, pulling his undershirt over his head, shoes on, his tuxedo pants a perfect fit as predicted. As the cotton cleared his face, his eyes were undiluted. And she could read him well now.

She saw desire.

Duarte was every bit as turned on as she was, which seemed ironic given she was wearing that god-awful dress and he was putting on a custom-cut tuxedo. Somewhere in that contrast, a compliment to her lurked if he could see past the thrift-store trappings of her unflattering dress.

"We need to talk about my sister," she blurted.

"Speak," he commanded.

Duarte carried this autocratic-prince thing a little far, but she wasn't in the mood to call him on it. She had other more pressing matters to address, making sure he fully understood about her sister.

"Earlier, I told you that my sister has special needs. I imagine you couldn't misunderstand after hearing our conversation." Hearing the childlike wordings with an adult pitch.

"I heard two sisters who are very close to each other," he said simply, striding toward the stack of jewelry boxes he'd set on a table beside the safe, his shirttails flapping. He creaked open the one on top to reveal shirt studs and cuff links, monogrammed, and no doubt platinum. "You said there's nobody else to call. What happened to the rest of your family?"

She watched his hands at work fastening his shirt and cuffs, struck again by the strange intimacy of watching a stranger dress. "Our mother died giving birth to Jennifer."

Glancing over at her, the first signs of some kind of genuine emotion flickered through his eyes. A hint of compassion turned his coal-dark eyes to more of a chocolate brown. "I am sorry to hear that."

The compassion lingered just for a second, but long enough to soften her stiff spine. "I wish I remembered more about her so I could tell Jennifer. I was seven when our mother died." Jennifer was twenty now. Kate had taken care of her since their father walked out once his youngest daughter turned eighteen. "We have a few photos and home videos of Mom."

"That is good." He nodded curtly, securing his cummerbund. "Did your mother's death have something to do with your sister's disability?"

She didn't like discussing this, and frankly considered it none of people's business, but if she would even consider being around this man for a full month, he needed to understand. Jennifer came first for her. "Our mother had an aneurysm during the delivery. The doctors delivered Jennifer as soon as possible, but she was deprived of oxygen for a long time. She's physically healthy, but suffered brain damage."

He looped his tie with an efficiency that could only come from frequent repetition. "How old is your sister?"

Now wasn't that a heartbreaking question? "She's an eight-year-old in a twenty-year-old's body."

"Where's your father?"

Sadly, not in hell yet. "He isn't in the picture."

"Not in the picture how?"

"As in, he's not a part of our lives now." Or ever again, if she had anything to say about contact with the self-centered jackass. Anger spiked through her so hot and furious she feared it might show in her eyes and reveal a major chink in her armor. "He skipped the country once

Jennifer turned eighteen. If you want to know more, hire a private investigator."

"You chose to be Jennifer's legal guardian." He slid his tuxedo coat off the hanger. "No law says you had to assume responsibility."

"Don't make it sound like she's a burden," she responded defensively. "She's my sister and I love her. Your family may not be close, but I am very close to Jennifer. If you do anything at all to hurt her, I will annihilate you in the press—"

"Hold on." He paused shrugging on his jacket. "No one said anything about hurting your sister. I will see to it that she's protected 24/7. Nobody will get near her."

How surprising that he would commit such resources to her family. She relaxed her guard partway, if not fully. She couldn't imagine ever being completely at ease around this man. "And you won't let your guards scare her?"

"They take into account the personality of whomever they're protecting. Your sister will be treated with sensitivity and professionalism."

"Thank you," she said softly, lacing her hands and resisting the urge to smooth his satiny lapels. She hadn't expected such quick and unreserved understanding from him.

"Turn around," he commanded softly, hypnotically, and without thinking she pivoted.

His hand grazed the back of her neck. Delicious awareness tingled along her skin. What was he doing? Hell, what was *she* doing?

Something chilly slithered over her heated skin, cold and metallic. Her fingers slid up to his fingers…

Jewels. Big ones. She gasped.

He cupped her shoulders and walked her toward the

full-length mirror inside the armoire door. "It's not bad for having to make do with what I had in the safe."

His eyes held hers as they had earlier when he'd been changing. Diamonds glinted around her neck in a platinum setting, enough jewels to take care of Jennifer for years.

"Stand still and I'll put on the matching earrings." They dangled from between his fingertips in much the same way her purloined camera earrings had earlier. Except these were worth a mint.

What if she lost one in a punch bowl?

"Can't I just have my own back?"

"I think not." He looped the earrings through effortlessly until a cascade of smaller diamonds shimmered from her ears almost to her shoulders. "I'll send a guard to retrieve your shoes, and then we can go."

"Go where?" she asked, her breath catching at his easy familiarity in dressing her. He sure knew his way around a woman's body.

Duarte offered his elbow. "Time to introduce my fiancée to the world."

Three

In a million years, he never would have guessed that tonight he would introduce a fiancée to Martha's Vineyard movers and shakers. Even though the engaged couple had left the rehearsal, the band, food and schmoozing would continue long into the night.

Duarte had expected to spend the bulk of his evening working out until he decided how to approach his father's request for a month of his time. He needed to simplify his life and instead he'd added a curvaceous complication.

No looking back, he reminded himself. And by introducing Kate to a ballroom full of people he ensured she couldn't fade away. Once in the Medina spotlight, always in the spotlight.

Kate stood at his side in the elevator—more private than the two flights of stairs. As the button for the ground level lit up, he slid his iPhone back into his pocket. He'd just sent a text to his head of security, ordering protection for Jennifer Harper, securing all the identification information for Kate. He would follow up on those instructions after the announcement.

The parting doors revealed the back hall, muffled sounds swelling inside. Clinking glasses and laughter mingled as guests downed crate after crate of Dom Perignon. A dance band finished a set and announced their break. His event planners oversaw these sorts of gigs, but he spot-checked details, especially for a seven-figure event.

Offering his arm to Kate, he gestured through the open elevator doors into the hall. This part of the resort was original to the hundred-year-old building, connecting to the newly constructed ballroom he'd added to accommodate larger events. He'd started his chain of resorts as a way to build a cash base of his own, independent of the Medina fortune.

While he spent most of his time in Martha's Vineyard, scooping up properties around the U.S. allowed him to move frequently, a key to staying undetected. There was no chain name for his acquisitions. Each establishment stood on its own as an exclusive getaway for hosting private events. He didn't have any interest in owning a home—his had been taken away long ago—so moving from hotel to hotel throughout the year posed no problem for him.

Kate's hand on his arm seared through his tuxedo, making him ache to feel her touch on his bare skin. His body was still on edge from the glide of her eyes on him as he changed.

Yet, listening to her on the phone with her sister, he'd been intrigued on a deeper level than just sex and revenge. Suddenly Kate's anklet of yarn and plastic beads made sense. There were layers to this woman that intrigued him, made him want her even more.

And he intended to make sure she wanted him every bit as much before he took her to bed.

Duarte stopped in front of the side door that would open into the ballroom reception area. He reached for the knob.

Her feet stumbled, ensconced in her retrieved black high heels. "You're really going to go through with this."

"The ring did not come out of a gum-ball machine."

"No kidding." She held it up, the light refracting off the ruby and diamonds. "Looks more like an heirloom, actually."

"It is, Katie."

"I'm Kate," she snapped. "Only Jennifer calls me Katie."

Jennifer, the sister who'd wanted to call him Artie. If his brothers heard, they would never let him live that one down.

"All right then, Kate, time to announce our arrival." He wondered what Kate thought of his other name, the one he'd called himself after leaving the island at eighteen. An assumed name he could no longer use thanks to her internet exposé. Now people would always think of him as Duarte Medina instead of Duarte Moreno, the name he'd assumed after leaving his father's island.

Sweeping the ballroom doors open, he scanned the tables and dance floor illuminated by crystal chandeliers, searching for the father of the groom. He spotted Ramon with his wife a few feet away.

The pharmaceutical heir smiled his welcome and

reached for the microphone. "Dear friends and family," he called for his guests' attention.

Some still milled over their dinner of beef tenderloin, stuffed with crab and scallops. Others collected around the stage waiting for the band to return from their break.

Ramon continued, "—please welcome our special guest who has generously graced us with his presence—"

Bowing and scraping was highly overrated.

"—Prince Duarte Medina."

Applause, gasps and the general crap he'd already grown weary of bounced around the half-toasted wedding guests who'd been whooping it up for a week's worth of celebration. Times like these he almost understood his father's decision to live in total seclusion.

Once the hubbub died down, Ramon pulled the mic to his mouth again. "A hearty welcome as well to his lovely date for the evening—"

Duarte stopped alongside Ramon and spoke, filling the room without artificial aid. "I hope you will all join me in celebrating a second happy event this evening. This lovely woman at my side, Kate Harper, has agreed to be my wife."

Lifting her left hand, he kissed her fingers, strategically displaying the ring. Cameras flashed, thanks to the select media that had been invited. Kate had been on target by calling her sister. This news would be all over the internet within the hour—just as he intended.

Comments jumbled on top of each other from the partyers, while Kate stayed silent, a smile pasted on her face. Smart woman. The less said, the better.

"Congratulations!"

"How did you two m—?"

"No wonder he dumped Chelsea—"

"Oh, you both must come to our—"

"Why haven't we heard anything about her before now?"

Duarte decided that last question deserved addressing. "Why would I let the press chew Kate alive before I could persuade her to marry me?"

Good-natured laughter increased, as did the curiosity in the sea of faces. He needed to divert their thoughts. And the best way?

Claim that kiss he'd been craving since the second he'd felt the give of Kate's soft body against him on the balcony.

Her ring hand still clasped in his, he folded her arm against his chest. The pulse in her wrist beat faster under his thumb, her pupils widening with a clear signal of awakening desire. She didn't like him, and he didn't like her much either after what she'd put his family through.

But neither of them could look away.

The whispers and shuffling from the guests dulled in his ears as he focused only on her. He brushed his mouth across hers, lightly, only close enough to graze the barest friction across her bottom lip. She gasped, opening just enough to send a surge of success through him. As much as he wanted to draw this out and see how long it would take her to melt fully against him, they did have an audience and this kiss served a purpose other than seduction.

Time to seal the deal.

A second after Duarte sealed his mouth to hers, Kate had to grab the front of his tuxedo jacket to keep from stumbling. Shock. It must be shock.

But her tingling body called her a great big liar.

The seductive rasp of his calloused hand cupping her face, the light tug on her bottom lip between his teeth threatened her balance far more than any surprise. Her fingers twisted tighter in the fine weave of fabric. Tingles sparked until her eyes fluttered closed, blocking out their audience, the very reason for this display in the first place. But whatever the reason, she wanted his mouth on hers.

Sure, the attraction had been evident from the start, but still she hadn't been prepared for this. There were kisses...

And then there were *kisses*.

Duarte's slow and deliberate intensity clearly qualified as one of the latter. Tension from the whole crazy night unfurled inside her, flooding her body with a roaring need that blocked out the gawkers and whispers. The cool firm pressure of his lips to hers—confident and persuasive—had her swaying against him, her clenched hands between them.

Memories of his bronzed flesh flashed through her mind. How much more of him would she see in the coming month? And if she was this tempted after a mere couple of hours together, how much worse might the attraction become with a month of these pretend fiancée kisses and touches?

His mandarin-cedar scent enfolded her as seductively as his arms. She splayed her fingers on the hard wall of his chest. The twitch of muscles under her touch offered a cold splash of reality.

What in the world was wrong with her that she could be so thoroughly entranced by a guy she'd just met? Her bank balance, her career, her sister's very future demanded she keep a level head.

Easier said than done when the stroke of his tongue along the seam of her lips sent a lightning bolt straight through her.

She pulled away sharply before she did something reckless, like ask him to continue this later. Kate scavenged a smile and gave Duarte a playful pat on the chest for the benefit of their witnesses, people dressed in designer clothes and wearing jewels that rivaled even those around her neck. This was his world, not hers. She was just a thirty-day guest and she would do well to remember that.

This party alone offered plenty of lavish reminders. Duarte took her arm and excused them both from the festivities. A legion of uniformed staff gathered the remains of the meal as she walked past. Her mouth watered at the leftover beef tenderloin, stuffed lobster tail…and wedding cake. Okay, technically it was a groom's cake for the rehearsal dinner, but still.

Her empty stomach grumbled. Embarrassed, she clapped a hand over it.

Lord, she loved wedding cake, had a serious weakness for it, which totally pissed her off since she considered herself far from a romantic. It was as if the cake called to her, laughing the whole time. *Mock me, will you?*

And speaking of negative vibes, more than one woman shot daggers with her eyes as Kate made her way back to the door with Duarte. She wanted to reassure them. She would be out of the picture soon. But somehow she didn't think that would help these females who'd set their hopes on a wealthy prince. One wafer-thin woman even dabbed at tears with a napkin.

Could that be the one somebody had said he'd dumped?

Arching up on her toes, Kate whispered against his chin, "Who's Chelsea?"

The question fell out of her mouth before she could think.

"Chelsea?" He glanced down. "Are you taking notes for the *Intruder* already?"

"Just curious." She shrugged more nonchalantly than she felt. "I am not a popular person among the young and eligible female crowd."

Duarte squeezed her hand on his elbow. "No one will dare be rude to you. They believe you're going to be a princess."

"For the next month anyway." With his kiss still singing on her lips, thirty days seemed like a very long time to resist him.

"I think we've milled around enough for now." He pushed through the side door back into the hall, deserted but for a security guard. The elevator doors stood open, at Duarte's beck and call as everyone else appeared to be around this place.

Once inside the private elevator, Kate stomped her foot. "What were you doing out there with that whole kiss?"

Duarte tapped his floor number. "They expected a kiss. We gave them a kiss."

"That wasn't a kiss." Her toes curled in her high-heeled pumps until the joints popped. "That was, well, a lot more than it needed to be to make your point."

His heated gaze swept down, his lashes longer than she'd noticed before. "How much more was it?"

The elevator cab shrunk in size, canned music suddenly romantic and mood setting. What a time to realize she'd never had sex in an elevator. Worse yet, what a time to realize she *wanted* to have sex in an elevator.

With Duarte.

She reached behind her neck to unhook the necklace. "Call me a cab so I can leave."

"How did you get here in the first place?" He caught the necklace that she all but threw at him to keep their hands from accidentally brushing. "Slow down before you tear off your earlobes."

"I came in a taxi." She slid the second cascade of diamonds from her earlobe. "I paid him to wait for an hour but that's long past, and I'm sure he's left."

"For the best, because really—" he extended his palm as she dropped the rest of the jewelry there "—do you think I trust you'll walk out of here and come back? We're past the point where you're free to punch out of our plan."

"I'll leave your damn ruby ring behind, too, and you can assign more of your guards to watch me." Would he threaten again to have her arrested? Would that really even hold up after the announcement they'd just made?

"That's not the point, and if you take off that engagement ring, you'll be losing the chance for those wedding photos."

The elevator doors swooshed open to his private quarters. He motioned for her to enter ahead of him. Going forward meant committing to the plan.

She stepped into the hall but no farther. Was this the point where he would turn into a jerk and proposition her? He had kissed her with skilled deliberation. "A part of our deal included no sex."

"I always keep my word. We will not have sex—unless you ask." He stepped closer. "Although be aware, there will be more kisses in the coming weeks. It's expected that I would shower my fiancée with affection. It's also expected that you would reciprocate."

"Fair enough," she conceded, then rushed to add, "but only when we're in public."

"That's logical. Know, too, though, that we will have to spend time alone with each other. This evening, for example, we need to get our stories straight before we face the world on a larger scale."

So much for her assumption of darker motives for his refusal to call a cab. What he said made sense. "Know that I'm staying under duress."

"Duly noted. Just keep remembering that black-tie dinner in D.C. with politicians and ambassadors."

"You're wicked bad with the temptation."

He steamed her with another smoky once-over. "You're one to lecture on that subject."

"I thought we were going to talk."

"We will. Soon." He stepped away and she exhaled. Hard. "I have a quick errand to take care of, but I'll have dinner sent up to your room while you wait. I hear tonight's special is tenderloin and stuffed lobster."

"And cake," she demanded, even knowing it wouldn't come close to satisfying the hunger gnawing as her insides tonight. "I really need a slice of that groom's cake."

Duarte watched his head of security shovel a bite of chocolate cake in his mouth in between reviewing surveillance footage and internet headlines on the multiple screens. A workaholic, Javier Cortez frequently ate on the job, rather than take off so much as a half hour for a meal. He even kept an extra suit in his office for days he didn't make it home.

Wheeling out a chair from the monitor station, Duarte

took a seat. "What were you able to pull together on security for Jennifer Harper?"

Javier swiped a napkin across his mouth before draping the white linen over his knee again. "Two members of our team are currently en route to her assisted-living facility outside Boston. They're already in phone contact with security there and will be reporting back to me within the hour."

"Excellent work, as always." He didn't dispense praise lightly, but Javier deserved it.

The head of security had also endured a crappy month every bit as bad as Duarte's. Javier's cousin, Alys, had betrayed the Medina family by confirming the *Global Intruder*'s suspicions about Duarte's identity. She had served as the inside source for other leaks as well, even offering up Enrique Medina's "love child" he'd fathered shortly after arriving in the U.S.

Javier had weathered intense scrutiny after Alys's betrayal had been discovered. He'd turned in his resignation the second his cousin had been confronted, vowing he bore no ill will against the Medinas and was shamed by his cousin's behavior.

Duarte had torn up the resignation. He trusted his instincts on this one.

How odd that he found it easier to trust Javier than his own father. That could have something to do with Enrique Medina's "love child" the whole world now knew about. Their grief-stricken widower father hadn't taken long to hook up with another woman. The affair had only lasted long enough to produce Eloisa. Duarte made a point of not blaming his half sister. He tried not to judge his father, but that part was tougher.

Making peace with the old man was more pressing than ever with Enrique's failing health.

Javier set aside his plate with a clink of the fork. "No disrespect, my friend, but are you sure you know what you're doing?"

Most wouldn't risk asking him such a personal question, but Javier's past wasn't that different from Duarte's. Javier's family had escaped San Rinaldo along with the king. Enrique had set up a compound in Argentina as a red herring. The press had believed the deposed king and his family had settled there.

However, the highly secured estate in South America had housed the close circle who'd been forced out of San Rinaldo with the Medinas—including the Reyes de la Cortez family. Javier understood fully the importance of security as well as the burning need to break free of smothering seclusion.

Duarte tapped a screen displaying an image of Kate at the antique dinner cart, plucking the long-stem red rose from the bud vase. "I know exactly what I was doing. I was introducing my fiancée to the world."

"Oh, really?" Javier leaned closer, pulling his tie from over his shoulder, where he must have draped it when he started his dinner. "Less than two hours ago she was scaling the side of the building to get a photo of you."

His eyes cruised back to the screen. Kate stroked the rose under her nose as she settled in the chair. Her brown hair tousled, her feet bare, she had the look of a woman who'd been thoroughly kissed and seduced.

Thinking of the way she'd made her entrance on the balcony earlier… He couldn't help but smile at her audacity. "Quite an entrance she makes."

"Now you've invited her into your inner sanctum?" Javier shook his head. "Why not simply hand over a journal with your life story?"

"What better way to watch your enemy than keeping

her close?" In his room. Where she waited for him now, savoring the beef tenderloin with the gusto of a woman who appreciated pleasures of the senses. "She will only see what I want her to see. The world will only know what I want it to know."

"And if she goes to the press later with the whole fake engagement?" Javier's eyes followed his to the screen, to Kate.

Duarte clicked off the image and the monitor went blank. "By then, people will label anything she says as the ramblings of a scorned woman. And if a handful of people believe her, what does that matter to me?"

"You really don't care." Javier tapped the now-dark screen, a skeptical look on his face.

"She will have served her purpose."

"You're a cold one."

"And you are not very deferential to the man who signs your extremely generous paychecks," he retorted, not at all irritated since he knew his friend was right. And a man needed people like that in his inner circle, individuals unafraid to declare when the emperor wore no clothes. "I assume you want to continue working for me?"

"You keep me on because I don't kowtow to you." Javier picked up his cake plate again. "You've never thought much of brownnosers. Perhaps that's why she intrigues you."

"I told you already—"

"Yeah, yeah, inner sanctum, blah-blah-blah." He shoveled a bite of the chocolate rum cake, smearing basket-weave frosting into the fork tines.

"Perhaps I am not as cold as you say. Revenge is sweet." So why wasn't he seeking this sort of "revenge" with Javier's cousin? Alys was attractive. They'd even dated briefly in the past.

"If you wanted revenge you could have gotten Kate Harper fired or arrested. She's snagged your interest."

Javier was too astute, part of what made him excel at his job as head of security. But then what was wrong with sleeping with Kate? In fact, an affair made perfect sense, lending credibility to their engagement.

"Kate is…entertaining. I'll grant her that." And his life was so damn boring of late.

Work did not provide a challenge. How many millions did a man need to make? He was a warrior without an army.

If he'd grown up in San Rinaldo, he would have served in her military. But with his history, he'd never had the option of signing on for service in his new home.

How ironic to be a thirty-five-year-old billionaire suffering from a career crisis? "She's also helping take heat off me with my father. The old man is in a frenzy to ensure the next generation of Medinas before he dies."

"Whatever you say, my friend." Javier tipped back a bottled water.

Ah, hell. He couldn't hide the truth from himself any more than from his friend. Duarte was off balance, tied up in knots over his father because he'd promised his mother he would watch Enrique's back. But how did a person defend someone against a failing liver?

He sometimes wondered why Beatriz had asked him when Carlos had been older, when Carlos had been the one to come through for her. She'd reminded him then he had always been the family's little soldier. He'd done his best to protect his family, a drive he saw equaled in Kate's eyes when she spoke of her sister. How ironic that their similar goals of protecting family put them so at odds.

Standing, Duarte returned the rolling chair under the console of monitors and tapped the blank screen that had held an image of Kate relishing her dinner. "Make sure you leave that one off. I'll take care of security in Kate's suite."

Four

Thank goodness no one was looking, because she'd tossed out table manners halfway through the lobster tail. Kate washed down the bite of chocolate rum cake with sparkling water. She was hungrier than she'd realized, having skipped supper due to nerves over crashing the Medina party.

Sipping from her crystal goblet, she opted for the Fuiggi water rather than the red wine. She needed to keep her mind clear around Duarte, especially after that kiss.

A promise of temporary pleasures that could lead to a host of regrets.

Footsteps sounded in the hall, a near-silent tread she was beginning to recognize as his. Would he go to his suite or stop by her room? He'd said he wanted to talk through details about their supposed dating past before they faced the world.

He stopped outside her door. Her toes curled. She licked her fork clean quickly and pushed away from the small table. Her shoes? Where had she ditched them before digging into her meal?

The door swung open.

Time had run out so she stayed seated, tucking her bare feet underneath the chair. Duarte filled the open frame to her room, blocking out the world behind him, reminding her that they were completely alone with each other and the memory of one unforgettable kiss. She straightened with as much nonchalance as she could, given her heart pumped as fast as a rapid-shot camera.

"Supper is to your liking?" He draped his tuxedo coat over the back of a carved mahogany chair.

"It's amazing and you know it." She wished she could take a slice of the cake to Jennifer.

"You were hungry." He loosened his tie.

Her heart stuttered. "How about you keep your pants on this time, cowboy."

"Whatever makes you happy, my dear."

Smiling, he slid the tie from his collar slowly, a sleigh bed with a fluffy comforter warm and inviting behind him. Then he stopped across from her at the intimate table for two, complete with silver and roses. Thank heaven he was still clothed—for the most part.

She placed her fork precisely along the top of her dessert china, the gold-rimmed pattern gleaming in the candlelight. "My compliments to your chef."

"I'll let him know." He scooped up her cut crystal glass of untasted wine and swirled the red vintage along the sides. "I have to confess, it's refreshing to hear a woman admit to appreciating a full dinner rather than models who starve themselves." He eyed her over the top of the Waterford goblet. "Eating can be a sensual experience."

Just the way he lingered over the word *sensual* with the slightest hint of an exotic accent made her mouth go moist. She swallowed hard and reminded herself to gather as much information as possible for future articles. While her primary job focused on taking the photos, an inside scoop could only help sell those shots.

This time with Duarte wasn't about her. She was here for her job, for her sister. "You don't strike me as the sort to overindulge when the dinner bell clangs. You seem very self-disciplined."

"How so?" He tipped back the glass.

She watched his throat work with a long swallow, his every move precise. "I would peg you as a health-food nut, a workout fiend."

"Do you have a problem with a sweaty round in the gym?"

"I don't love it, but I adore food more than I dislike exercise. So I log a few miles on a stationary bike when I can." Wait, how had this suddenly become about her when she was determined to learn more about him?

"You need to stay in shape for scaling ledges." He tapped the rim of his glass to her water goblet, right over the spot where her mouth had rested.

The *ting* of crystal against crystal resonated through her. "You said you saw me on security footage before I ever entered your room. What if those tapes of me crawling around outside somehow leak to the media? Won't that shoot a hole in our engagement story? And what about the part I played in exposing your half sister?"

"About the balcony incident, we'll blame it on the

paparazzi chasing you out of your room. As for Alys, we can always say you let it slip at work." He dropped into the chair across from her, lean and long, his power harnessed but humming.

"What's to stop me from claiming any of that if you decide to use the video feed against me?"

"Do you think I've revealed all the ammunition in my arsenal?" He turned the glass on the table, the thin stem so fragile in his hand.

"Are you trying to worry me?" She refused to be intimidated.

His breathing stayed even, but his eyes narrowed. "Only letting you know I play at an entirely different level than anyone you've ever come up against. I have to. The stakes are higher."

"I don't know about that." An image of Jennifer's smile when she'd passed over the braided anklet filled Kate's mind. "My stakes feel pretty high to me."

He set aside his drink and reached back into his tux jacket. His hand came back with a computer disc in a case. He slid it across the table toward her. "Copies of the photos from your camera and from my own press team for you to share with the *Intruder*."

"All of my photos?" she asked with surprise—and skepticism.

"Most of your photos." The hard angles of his face creased into a half smile. "You can pass these along to your editor. If he questions why you're still speaking to him when you have a rich fiancé, tell him that we want to control the release of information and as long as he plays nice, the flow will continue. I'll have a laptop computer sent up for you. I keep my word."

She traced an intricate *M* scrolled on a label, the

gilded letter taking on the shape of a crown. Her brain spun headlines... Medina Men. Medina Monarchs.

Medina Money, because without question pure gold rested under her fingertips. And he'd promised her so much more in four weeks. "I need to stop by my apartment tomorrow before we leave."

"Cat or dog?"

"What?" She glanced up quickly.

"Do you have a cat or a dog? What kind?" He cradled his iPhone in his broad palm. "I'll pass along the details to my assistant and your animal will be boarded."

His arrogance almost managed to overshadow his thoughtfulness. Almost, but not quite. "I didn't know that ninjas read minds. And it's a cat. I'm away from home too much to have a dog. My neighbor usually watches him for me."

"No need to bother your neighbor. My people will see to everything, like with your sister's security." He began tapping in instructions.

How easy it would be to let him take charge, especially when what he offered was actually helpful...even thoughtful. "That's nice of you. Thanks."

He waved aside her gratitude and continued texting. "Before you mention packing clothes, forget it. I'm already ordering everything you'll need. You'll have some of the new wardrobe by morning."

She glanced down at her green Gabbana knockoff. "Cinderella makeover time?"

"Believe me, you don't need a makeover. Even wearing a, uh—" He stumbled over his words for the first time, his brow furrowing....

"A secondhand-store bargain, you mean?" She found his hesitation, this first sign of human emotion, unsettling...and a little charming. "You don't have to worry about offending me. I'm not embarrassed by the fact my bank balance is smaller than yours. That's just a fact."

"Very good that you're not going to waste our time with ridiculous arguments. What's your dress size?"

"Eight for dresses, pants, shirts."

"Got it." He input the information. "Shoe size."

"Seven. Narrow."

"Bra?"

She gasped. "Excuse me?"

"What is your bra size?" He quirked an eyebrow, without raising his onyx gaze. "Some of the evening gowns will have a fitted bodice and special cut. Last-minute alterations in person can be made, but it's helpful to have a ballpark number to start with."

Resisting the urge to flatten her hands to her breasts required a Herculean effort. "Thirty-four C."

He didn't look away from his iPhone, but a slow sexy smile creased his face. The air between them crackled and her nipples ached inside her strapless pushup. This man was entirely too audacious. And enticing. Finally, he put away his phone and returned his focus to her.

"A new 'princess' wardrobe will be waiting in the morning with enough garments to see you through our first few days of travel. The rest of your clothing for the month will arrive before the end of the week." He thumbed the engagement ring on her finger, nudging the ruby back to the center again.

His simple touch stirred her as much now as his kiss had earlier, and this time they were alone rather than in a ballroom full of onlookers. His gaze fell to her mouth, brown eyes turning lava-dark with desire.

He'd told her the engagement was mutually beneficial for practical reasons, but at the moment she wondered if he had a different agenda. Could he really be so interested in getting her into his bed that he would expose himself to press coverage? That he would want her so much after one meeting was mind-blowing. Who wouldn't be complimented?

Except it also felt so far out of the realm of possibility that she felt conceited for considering it. Revenge seemed a far more logical reason for the seductive gleam he directed at her.

Either way, she needed to keep her guard up at all times. "Thank you. I will be certain the reporter who pens the stories accompanying my photos notes that you have impeccable, princely manners."

"No thanks or credit needed. I won't even notice the expense of a few dresses and 34C bras."

Her fingers curved into a fist under his touch. "I was referring to your consideration in looking after my cat before we leave."

"Again, that has nothing to do with being nice." He enfolded her curled hand in his until it disappeared. "I'm only taking care of loose ends so we can move forward."

This man was such a strong presence he could eclipse a person as fully as his palm covered her hand. "Of course I'll also have to make note in the article that you're bossy."

"I prefer to think I'm a take-charge sort of man."

"You would have made a great general."

He traced from her ring finger around to the vein leading to the pulse in her wrist. "Why do I feel like you're not complimenting me?"

"Don't you worry about how I'll present you in stories once this is over? Photography may be my main focus, but I do write articles on occasion."

The warmth of his clasp seared her skin. They were

just linking fingers, for crying out loud, something as innocent as two teens in a movie theater. But they weren't in some public locale.

They were alone, and she questioned the wisdom of letting him touch her in private. The heated look in his eyes was most definitely anything but innocent.

"You'll be the ex-fiancée. It'll all sound like sour grapes." He released her fist and stood before she could pull away. "Regardless, I don't give a flying f—"

"Right. Got it." She raised both hands. "You don't care what people think of you."

"I only cared about privacy, and now that's a moot point." He walked around the table, stopping beside her and tipping her chin with a knuckle. "So let's get back to talking about how smoking-hot you look regardless of what you wear, and how much better you must look in nothing at all."

She saw this for what it was, a gauntlet moment where she could either back down—or let him know she wasn't a pushover. No dancing around the subject or pretending to ignore his seductive moves to keep some kind of peace. She'd always met life head-on and now wouldn't be any different.

"Stop trying to throw me off balance." She stared at him without flinching or pulling away. "I've kept a steady hand taking pictures through bomb blasts in a war zone and during aftershocks in earthquake rubble. I think I can handle a come-on from you."

A flicker of approval mingled with the desire in his dark eyes at her moxie. And how silly to be excited because she'd impressed him with something other than her cup size. She wasn't interested in the man beyond what he had to offer in a photo op.

Okay, not totally true. Truth be told, just looking at

him turned her on. Hearing his light Spanish accent stoked that a notch. He was a handsome man, and a big-time winner in the genetic gene pool when it came to charisma.

But that didn't mean she intended to act on the attraction.

"I can handle you," she repeated, just as much to reassure herself as to convince him.

"Good, an easy victory isn't nearly as much fun." He reached behind her, his hand coming back with a thick white robe. He passed the folded terry cloth bearing the resort logo to her. "Enjoy your shower."

Kate was naked under the robe.

The terry cloth was thick and long and covered her completely from Duarte's eyes as he lounged in her suite. But deep in his gut, he knew. She wore nothing more.

He went utterly still in his chair by her fireplace. He'd waited for a half hour in her suite, a large room with a sitting area in the bay window, sleigh bed across the room. She stood in the doorway from her bathroom, her fluffy robe accenting the crisp blue-and-white decor. Her wet hair was gathered in a low ponytail draped over one shoulder.

It was longer than he'd expected. He also expected her to demand that he leave. But she simply tucked her feet into the complimentary slippers by the door and padded across the room toward him.

Unflinching, she stared back at him, her eyes sweeping down him as if taking in every detail of his tuxedo shirt open at the neck, dark pants sans cummerbund, feet propped on the ottoman. She stopped alongside him and sank smoothly into the blue checkered chair on the other side of the fireplace. She was fearless.

And magnificent.

She crossed her legs, baring a creamy calf. "What else do we need to cover before facing the world tomorrow?"

The fire crackled and warmed. He'd started the blaze to set a more intimate tone. Except now it tormented him by heating her pale leg to an even more tempting rosy pink. "Let's discuss how we met. You spin mythical stories from a thread of truth. How about take a stab at it by creating our dating history?"

"Hmm…" Her foot swung slowly, slipper dangling from her toes, her yarn jewelry still circling her ankle. "After I broke the story about your family, you confronted me…at my apartment… You didn't want to risk being seen at my office. You know where I live, right? Since you knew to send someone to take care of my cat."

"You're based out of Boston, but travel frequently," he confirmed correctly. "So you just keep a studio apartment."

"Your detectives have done their homework well." Her smile went tight, her plump lips thinning. "Did you already know about Jennifer?"

"No, I only know your address and work history."

Perhaps there he'd dropped the ball. He, above all people, should know how family concerns shaped a person's perspective. Pieces of the Kate puzzle readjusted in his mind, and he resolved to get back to the issue of her sister.

Although Kate's tight mouth let him know he would have to tread warily. "Tell me, Ms. Harper, how does someone who covered the wars in Iraq and Afghanistan end up working for the *Global Intruder?*"

"Downsizing in the newspaper industry." She blinked fast as if working hard not to look away nervously.

"Taking care of your sister had nothing to do with your decisions?" He understood her protectiveness when it came to her sibling. The bond was admirable, but he wouldn't let softer feelings blur his goal.

"Jennifer needs me." Kate picked at the white piping along the club chair.

"There were plenty of people willing to roll out for an assignment at the drop of the hat." Unanswered questions about her career descent now made perfect sense. "By the time you settled your sister, you'd lost out on assignments. Other reporters moved ahead of you. Have I got it right?"

Fire snapped in her eyes as hotly as the flames popping in the fireplace. "How does this pertain to fielding questions about our engagement? If the subject of Jennifer comes up, we'll tell the media it's none of their business."

"Well, damn." He thumped himself on the forehead. "Why didn't my family and I come up with that idea ourselves? To think we hid out and changed our identity for nothing."

"Are you sure we'll be able to convince anyone we even like each other, much less that we're in love?"

He tamped down the anger that would only serve to distract. This woman was too adept at crawling under his skin. "We're only talking about your basic life story. Surely you can trust me with that."

"Give me a good reason why I should trust you with anything. I don't really know you." She toyed with the tip of her damp ponytail, releasing a waft of shower-fresh *woman*. "Perhaps if you would tell me more about your past, I'll feel more comfortable opening up in return."

"Touché," he said softly as a lighthouse horn wailed in the distance. "Instead, we'll move back to creating our dating history."

She dropped her ponytail and stared upward as if plucking the story from the air. "On the day we met, I was wearing khaki pants, a Bob Marley T-shirt, and Teva sandals. You remember it perfectly because you were entranced by my purple toenail polish." Her gaze zipped and locked with his again. "You get bonus points if you remember the polish had glitter. We ended up talking for hours."

"What was *I* wearing?"

"A scowl." She grinned wickedly.

"You sound positively besotted."

She flattened a hand to her chest dramatically, drawing his eyes to the sweet curves of her breasts. "I *swooned*." Kate leaned forward, her robe gaping enough to tease him with a creamy swell but not enough to give him a clear view. "I took your picture because I found you darkly intriguing and the feeling increased when you came to confront me about exposing your identity. The attraction was instantaneous. Undeniable."

"That part will be very easy to remember." His groin tightened the longer he looked at the peekaboo flesh of her generous breasts.

"You wooed me. I resisted, of course." Clasping the neck of her robe closed, she sat back. Had she tormented him on purpose? "But ultimately I fell for you."

"Do tell what I did to convince you." Any edge with Kate would be helpful.

Her grin turned mischievous. "You won me over with your love poem."

He leaned back. "Afraid not."

"I was joking." She toe-tapped his feet, propped and crossed on the ottoman.

"Oh. Okay. I see that now. I'm not artistic." His family also said he lacked a sense of humor, which had never bothered him before, but could prove problematic in dealing with this woman. He needed to turn the tables back in his favor. "I can be romantic without resorting to sappy sonnets."

"Then let's hear how you spin the story of our first date." She waved with a flourish for him to take over. "How did it go?"

"I picked you up in my Jaguar."

Kate crinkled her nose, shaking her head. "Nuh-uh. Too flashy to wow me."

"It's vintage."

"That's better," she conceded.

"And red."

"Even better yet."

He searched his mental catalogue of information about her for the right detail… "I brought you catnip and *cat*viar, instead of flowers and candy."

"You remembered I have a cat?" The delighted surprise in her voice rewarded his effort.

"I remembered everything you told me, although you neglected to mention her name and breed."

"*He* is a gray tabby named Ansel."

"As in Ansel Adams, the photographer. Nice." He filed away another piece of information about the intriguing woman in front of him.

"No flowers and candy at all, though. I'm surprised. I would expect you to be the exotic bouquet and expensive truffle sort."

"Too obvious. I can see you're intrigued by my unusual choice, which makes my point." That little strip of braided yarn she wore told him that Kate had a sentimental side. "Moving on. We ate a catered dinner on my private jet, so as not to attract attention in a restaurant."

"Your airplane? Where were we going?"

"The Museum of Contemporary Photography in Chicago."

"I haven't been there before," she said wistfully.

He vowed then and there to take her before the month was over. "We learned a lot about each other, such as food preferences—" He paused.

"Chili dogs with onions and a thick slice of wedding cake, extra frosting," she answered, toying with the tassel on the tapestry wall hanging behind her. "What about you?"

"Paella for me, a Spanish rice dish." Although he'd never been able to find a chef who could replicate the taste he remembered from San Rinaldo. "And your favorite color?"

"Red. And yours?"

"Don't have one." His world was a clear-cut image of black and white, right and wrong. Colors were irrelevant. "Coffee or tea drinker?"

"Coffee, thick and black served with New Orleans–style beignets."

"We're in agreement on the coffee, churros for me." Now on to the important details. "Favorite place to be kissed?"

She gasped, fidgeting with the tie to her robe. "Not for public knowledge."

"Just want to make sure I get it right when the cameras start. For the record, we kissed on the first date but you wouldn't let me get to second base until—"

"I don't intend for any interview to reach that point and neither will you."

"But we did kiss on our first date." He swung his feet to the floor and leaned forward, elbows on his knees. Closer to her.

"After your display in the ballroom, the whole world knows we've, uh, kissed."

He clamped his fingers around her ankle, over the beaded yarn. "From what I've learned about you tonight, kissing you, touching you, I think you have very sensitive earlobes."

Her pupils widened, her lips parting and for a moment he thought she would sway forward, against him, into him. The memory of her curves pressed to his chest earlier imprinted his memory. How much more mind-blowing the sensation would be bare flesh to flesh.

Kate drew in a shuddering breath. "I think we've learned quite enough about each other for one evening." She crossed her arms just below her breasts. "You should go so I can get some sleep."

The finality in her tone left no room for doubt. He'd pushed her as far as he could for one night. And while he would have preferred to end the evening revealing every inch of her body beneath that robe, he took consolation in knowing he had a month to win her over.

Easing back, he shoved to his feet. Was that regret in her eyes? Good. That would heighten things for them both when he won her over.

Five

The next morning, Kate pulled on her borrowed clothes, made of fabric so fine it felt like she wore nothing at all.

The silk lined linen pants were both warm and whispery. A turtleneck, cool against her skin, still insulated her from the crisp nip in the winter air leaching into her suite. They'd gotten everything right from the size of the clothes to her favored cinnamon-apple fragrance. Had he noticed even that detail about her?

Everything fit perfectly, from the brown leather ankle boots—to her bra. Toying with the clasp between her breasts, she wondered how much he knew about the selections.

All had been brought to her by the resort staff, along with a note, beignets and black coffee. The aftertaste of her breakfast stirred something deeper inside her, a place already jittery at the notion of him envisioning her underwear. He'd listened to her preferences about food choices. He'd remembered.

He'd even come through on his promise to deliver a secured laptop for her to send her photos to Harold Hough, her editor at the *Global Intruder*. Duarte had kept his word on everything he'd promised.

She trailed her fingers over the two packed bags with her other new clothes neatly folded and organized, along with shoes and toiletries. She plucked out a brush and copper hair clamp. What a different world, having anything appear with the snap of his fingers.

Sweeping the brush through her hair, she shook it loose around her shoulders. Excitement twirled in her belly like the snowflakes sifting from the clouds. She scooped up the fur-lined trench and matching suede gloves, wondering where they would go after stopping by her place for her cameras.

How could she want to spend time with a man who, underneath the trappings, was all but blackmailing her? She churned the dichotomy around in her brain until finally resolving to look at this as a business deal. She'd agreed to that deal wholeheartedly out of desperation, and she would make the best of her choice.

Kate stepped into the hall and locked her door behind her. Duarte's note with her breakfast had instructed her to meet him in his office after she ate and dressed.

Pivoting, she nearly slammed into a man who seemed to have materialized out of nowhere.

"Excuse me." She jolted back a step, away from the guy in a dark suit with an even darker glower.

"Javier Cortez—I work for Duarte Medina," he introduced himself, his accent thicker than his boss's. "I am here to escort you to his office." Javier was even more somber than his employer.

Duarte was intense. This guy was downright severe.

Something about his name tugged at her memory—and was that a gun strapped to his belt? "What exactly do you do here for Duarte?"

"I am head of security."

That explained the gun, at least. "Thank you for the help. I don't know my way around the resort yet."

His footsteps thudded menacingly down the Persian runner. "You managed quite well last night."

She winced. He must be the keeper of the video footage from her not-so-successful entrance. Which meant he also likely knew the engagement was a farce. She thumbed the ring and gauged her words.

"Last night was a memorable evening for many reasons, Mr. Cortez."

Pausing outside a paneled wood door, Javier faced her down. Why did he look so familiar? The other two Medina brothers were named Antonio and Carlos, not Javier. Roughly the same age and bearing as Duarte, still Javier didn't look like a relative.

And she couldn't help but notice that while he was undoubtedly handsome, this guy didn't entice her in the least.

"Is this his office?"

"The back entrance. Yes." His arm stretched across it barred her from entering—and parted his jacket enough to put his gun in plain sight. "Betray my friend and you will regret it."

She started to tell him to drop the B-grade-movie melodrama, then realized he was serious. She didn't give ground. Bullies never respected a wimp anyway. "So he tells me."

"This time, *I* am telling you. Know that I will be

watching your every step. Duarte may trust you with your cameras and that secure laptop, but I'm not so easily fooled."

Irritation itched through two dings of the elevator down the hall before she cleared her brain enough to realize what had bothered her about the man's name and why he looked familiar. "You're angry about your cousin getting booted out of royal favor for tipping me off."

His jaw flexed with restraint, his eyes cold. "Alys is an adult. She chose wrong. My cousin was disloyal not only to our family and the Medinas, but she also betrayed our entire country. I'm angry with *her*. Alys must accept responsibility for her actions, and you can feel free to cite me on that in your gossip e-zine."

"Thank you for the quote. I'll be sure they spell your name correctly." She hitched her hands on her hips. "I'm just curious about clarifying one point. If you're only mad at her and realize I was just doing my job, why are you reading me the riot act about not hurting Duarte?"

"Because I do not trust you." Javier stepped closer, his intent obviously to intimidate. "I understand you made your decision for practical reasons. Yes, you were doing your job. Understand, I am doing mine, and I am far more ruthless than you could ever hope to be."

As much as she resented being towered over, she understood and respected the need to protect the people you cared about. Javier might be a bully, but he wasn't just looking out for himself.

"You know what, Javier Cortez? Everybody should have a friend like you."

"Compliments won't work with me." He stared down his sharp nose at her. "Remember, I'll be watching you."

The door swung open abruptly. The security guru jerked upright.

Duarte frowned, looking from one to the other. "Is something wrong here, Javier?"

"Not at all," he answered. "I was only introducing myself to your fiancée."

"Kate?" Duarte asked her, his gaze skeptical.

She stepped in front of Javier and a little too close to Duarte. His hair still damp, she caught a whiff of her faux fiancé's aftershave and a hint of crisp air. Had he already been for a walk outside?

And ouch, how silly to wonder how he'd spent his morning.

A cleared throat behind her reminded Kate of the bodyguard. "Your buddy Javier was just giving me the lowdown on security around here."

As much as she wanted to tell Javier to shove it, the guy had a point. She needed to watch her step.

She couldn't allow herself to be swayed by Duarte's charming images of jet-setting dates and catnip gifts. This was a man who lived with security cameras and ruthless armed guards. He was every bit as driven as she was. She needed to harden her resolve and shore up her defenses if she expected to survive this month unscathed.

Which meant keeping tempting touches to a minimum.

Outside Kate's Boston apartment, Duarte slid inside the limousine, heater gusting full blast. The door closed, locking him in the vehicle with Kate and his frustration over finding her with Javier earlier. Not that he was jealous. He didn't do that emotion. However, seeing them standing close together made him…

Hell, he didn't know what it made him feel, but he didn't like the way his collar suddenly seemed too tight. He swiped the sleet from his coat sleeves.

After they'd taken the ferry from Martha's Vineyard, they'd spent the past couple hours driving through snow turned to sleet on their way to her place. She'd insisted on retrieving her cameras herself, stating she didn't want one of his "people" pawing through her things. He understood the need for privacy and had agreed. He controlled his own travel plans, after all. A few hours' wiggle room didn't pose a problem.

A hand's reach away, Kate sorted through her camera bag she'd retrieved from her tiny efficiency. The bland space where she lived had relayed clearly how little time she spent there.

She looked up from her voluminous black bag as ice and packed snow crunched under the limo's tires. "May I ask what's next on the agenda or are we going to an undisclosed location?"

"I have a private jet fueled and waiting to fly us to D.C. as soon as the weather clears. After we land, we'll stay at one of my hotels." He selected a card from his wallet and passed it to her. "Here's the address, in case you want to let your sister—or the *Intruder*—know."

Not that anyone would get past his security.

He'd bought the nineteenth-century manor home in D.C. ten years ago. With renovations and an addition, he'd turned it into an elite hotel. He catered to the wealthy who spent too much time on the road and appreciated the feeling of an exclusive home away from home while doing business in the nation's capital.

Silently, she pulled out her cell phone from her bag and began texting, her silky hair sliding forward over one shoulder. She was a part of the press. He couldn't forget for a second that he walked a fine line with her.

He needed to be sure she remembered, as well. "Don't make the mistake of thinking Javier is cut from the same cloth as his cousin. You were able to trick Alys, but Javier is another matter."

She kept texting without answering, sleet pinging off the roof. He studied her until she glanced over at him, tight-lipped.

Anger frosted Kate's blue eyes as chilly as the bits of melted sleet still spiking her eyelashes. "For your information, I didn't have to trick your pal Alys. Yes, I approached her about the photo I accidentally snapped of you at Senator Landis's beach house. But *she* came to *me* about your half sister."

Duarte registered her words, but he could only think about her determination, her drive...and her 34C breasts. He wondered what his assistant had chosen for Kate. As much as he wanted to know, checking out the clothes before they were sent to her felt...invasive. Privacy was important.

He understood that firsthand. "You made the contact with Alys when you chased her down about that photo of me with the senator."

"Believe what you want." She changed out the lens on a camera with the twist of her wrist. "I merely traced people in the picture until one of them was willing to give up more information on the mysterious past of a guy who called himself Duarte Moreno."

Hearing how easily someone in his father's inner circle could turn angered him. But it also affirmed what he'd thought during his entire isolated childhood on the island. There was no hiding from the Medina legacy. "You'll be wise to remember how easy it is to misstep. If our secret is out, I'll have no reason to keep you around until the wedding."

A small yellow rag in hand, she cleaned a lens. "One screwup and that's it? No room for mistakes and forgiveness? Everyone deserves an occasional do over."

"Not when the stakes are so high." A single mistake, a break in security, could cost a life. His mother had died and Carlos still carried scars from that day.

"Aren't you curious as to why Alys was willing to sell out your family?"

"The 'why' doesn't matter."

"There, you are wrong." She handled her camera reverently. "The 'why' can matter very much."

"What happened to neutral reporting of the facts?" He hooked a finger along her black camera strap.

"The 'why' can help a good journalist get more information from a source."

"All right, then. Why did Alys turn on us?"

Kate raised the camera to her face, lens pointed in his direction, and when he didn't protest, she clicked.

He forced himself not to flinch, tough to do after so long hiding from having his image captured as if the camera could steal his spirit. "Kate?"

"Alys wanted to be a Medina princess." Kate lowered the camera to her lap. "But how much fun would the tiara be worth if she couldn't show it off to the world? She wanted everyone to know about the Medinas, and my camera made that possible."

"Don't even try to say she had feelings for one of us. She wouldn't have betrayed us if she cared."

"True enough." Her voice drifted off and he could all but see the investigative wheels turning in her mind. "Did *you* love *her?* Is that why you're so edgy today?"

His restlessness had everything to do with Kate and nothing to do with Alys, a woman he considered past history. "What do you think?"

"I believe it must have hurt seeing a trusted friend turn on your family, especially if she meant something more to you."

"I'm not interested in Alys, never was beyond a couple dates. Any princess dreams she may have harbored were of her own making."

In a flash of insight, he realized she was curious about his past relationships, and not as a reporter, but as a woman. Suddenly his frustration over finding her with Javier didn't irritate him nearly as much.

He slid his arm along the back of the leather seat.

"Uh…" Kate jumped nervously. "What do you think you're doing?"

Dipping his face toward her hair, he nuzzled her ear. When she purred softly, he continued, "Kissing my fiancée, or I will be," he said on his way toward her parted lips, "momentarily."

Catching her gasp, his mouth met hers. His hand between her shoulder blades drew her closer. The rigid set of her spine eased and she flowed into him, her lips softening. The tip of her tongue touched his with the first tentative sweep. Then more boldly.

Carefully, he moved her camera from her lap to the seat. He untied her belt and pushed her coat from her shoulders. The turtleneck hugged her body to perfection, the fabric so thin he could almost imagine the feel of her skin under his hands. He cupped her rib cage, just below her breasts. If his thumb just twitched even an inch, he could explore the lush softness pressed against him.

Heat surged through his veins so quickly he could have sworn it would melt the sleet outside. Shivering, she brushed against him, her breasts pebbling against his chest in unmistakable arousal.

Kate's breathy gasp caressed his face and she wriggled closer. "What are we doing?"

"I want to reassure you. You have no worries where Alys is concerned." He swept her hair from her face, silky strands gliding between his fingers, catching on calluses. "You have my complete and undivided attention."

"Whoa, hold on there a minute, Prince Charming." She eased away. "That's quite an ego you're sporting there."

"You wanted to know if I had a relationship with Alys. And you weren't asking for some article. Am I wrong?"

"I'm the one who's wrong. I should have stopped that kiss sooner. I'm not even sure why..." She pulled her coat back over her shoulders. "Last night was a different matter. That display was for the public."

"I had no idea you were into voyeurism."

"Don't be dense."

"I'm complimenting you. I enjoyed that kiss so much I want a repeat."

"To what end?"

He simply smiled.

Her pupils widened in unmistakable arousal even as she scooted away, crossing her arms firmly and defensively across her chest. "We made a month-long business deal, and then we walk away. You said sleeping together wasn't a part of the plan unless I asked. And I do not intend to ask. I don't do casual sex."

He eased her tight arms from her chest and looped the trench tie closed again. "Then we'll have to make sure there's nothing casual about it."

Six

Two days later, Kate let the live band's waltz number sweep her away on the dance floor with Duarte in his D.C. hotel. The tuxedoed musicians played a mix of slower show tunes, segueing out of a *Moulin Rouge* hit and into a classic from *Oklahoma*. Duarte's hand linked with hers, his other at her back. Crystal chandeliers dimming, he guided her through the steps with an effortless lead. For the moment, at least, she was content to pass over control and simply enjoy the dazzling evening with her handsome date.

She'd been endlessly impressed by all she'd seen of his restored hotel and this ballroom was no exception. Greco-Roman architectural details mirrored many of the Capital City's earliest buildings. Wide Doric columns soared high to murals painted on the ceilings, depicting characters from classic American literature. Huck Finn stared down at her alongside Rip Van Winkle. Moby Dick rode a wave on another wall.

The black-tie dinner packed with politicians and embassy officials had been a journalistic dream come true. The five-course meal now over, she one-two-threed past a senator partnered with an undersecretary in the State department. Her fingers had been itching all night long to snap pictures, but Duarte had been generous with allowing other photographs while they were in D.C. She had to play by his rules and be patient.

And he'd been open to her sharing tips with her boss at the *Global Intruder*. Duarte had spent the past two days meeting with embassy officials from San Rinaldo and neighboring countries. He'd delivered a press conference on behalf of his family. She'd racked up plenty of tips and images to send on the laptop.

Although, sticky politics had quickly taken a backseat to questions about the fiancée at his side. Kate had to applaud his savvy. He'd been right in deciding an engagement could prove useful as he steered the media dialogue.

The press as a whole was having a field day with the notion of a Medina prince engaged to the woman who'd first broken his cover. Their concocted courtship story packed the blogosphere.

Undoubtedly images of them waltzing together would continue the Cinderella theme in the society pages. Her off-the-shoulder designer dress tonight was a world away from the ill-fitting gown she'd worn when breaking into Duarte's Martha's Vineyard resort. The shimmer of champagne-colored satin slithered over her with each sweeping step, giving her skin a warm glow. Duarte's hand on her back, his even breaths brushing her brow, took that warm glow to a whole new and deeper level.

She glanced up into his dark eyes and saw past the somber air to the thoughtfulness he tried so hard to hide. "Thank you for the clothes and the dinner. You really have come through on what you promised."

"Of course." He swept her toward the outer edges of the dance floor, around a marble pillar, farther from the swell of music. "I gave you my word."

"People lie to the press all the time." People lied period. "I accept it."

"I never expected to meet a woman as jaded as myself." His hand on her back splayed wider, firmer. "Who broke your heart?"

She angled closer, resting her head against his jaw so she wouldn't have to look in his too-perceptive eyes. "Let's not wreck this perfect evening with talk about my past." With talk about her father. "Just because you've got a packed romantic history doesn't mean everyone else does."

Wait! Where had that come from? It seemed they bumped into his old girlfriends around every corner. Not that she cared other than making sure they kept their stories straight about the engagement.

Maybe if she told herself that often enough, she might start believing it. Somewhere over the past few days, she'd started enjoying his presence. She really didn't want him to be a jerk.

"Hmm…" He nuzzled her upswept hair, a loose bundle of fat curls dotted with tiny yellow diamonds, courtesy of a personal stylist brought in for her for the afternoon. "What do you know about my dating history?"

"You're like a royal George Clooney. Except younger." And hotter. And somehow here, with her.

"Did you expect me to be a monk just because I had

to live under the radar?" His hand on her back pressed slightly, urging her closer as the music slowed.

"Best as I can tell from the women I've met during our time in D.C.—" she paused, her brain scrambling with each teasing brush of his body against hers, nothing overt, but just enough to make her ache for a firmer pressure "—you've never had a relationship that lasted more than three months."

His ex-girlfriends had wished her luck, *lots* of luck. Their skepticism was obvious. Women he hadn't dated were equally restrained in their good wishes.

"Would you prefer I led someone on by continuing a relationship beyond the obvious end?"

"Don't you care that you broke hearts?" Money and good looks, too, not fair. And then she realized… "Those women didn't even know you're a prince. You're positively a dangerous weapon now."

Why was she pushing this? Old news wouldn't make for much of a media tip. It shouldn't matter that this man who collected luxury hotels around the country had never committed to a single house, much less a particular woman.

He exhaled dismissively. "Anyone who's interested in me because of my bank balance or defunct title isn't worth your concern. Now can we discuss something else? There's the U.S. ambassador to Spain."

"I've already met him. Thank you." She had nabbed award-winning photos by never backing down. She wouldn't change now. "Didn't it bother you, lying to women about your past?"

"Perhaps that's why I never stayed in a relationship." He tucked their clasped hands closer and flicked her dangling earring. Yellow diamonds in a filigree gold setting tickled her shoulder. "Now there are no more constraints."

Her heart hitched in her chest at his outlandish implication. Even knowing he couldn't possibly be serious, she couldn't resist asking, "Are you trying to seduce me?"

"Absolutely. And I intend to make sure you enjoy every minute of it."

With a quick squeeze of their linked hands, he stepped back. The song faded to an end. He applauded along with the rest of the guests while she stood stunned and tingling.

Only seventy-two hours since she'd climbed onto his balcony and already she was wondering just how much longer she could hold out against Duarte Medina.

Abruptly, Duarte frowned and reached into his tuxedo coat. His hand came back out with his iPhone.

"Excuse me a second." The phone buzzed in his hand again. "Javier? Speak."

As he listened, his frown shifted to an outright scowl. His body tensed and his eyes scanned the room. Kate went on alert. Something was wrong. She looked around, but saw nothing out of the ordinary.

He disconnected with a low curse and slid an arm around her waist. His touch was different this time, not at all seductive, but rather proprietary.

Protective.

"What's wrong?" she asked.

"We need to duck out. Now." He hauled her toward a side exit. "Security alert. We have party crashers."

Duarte hurried Kate the rest of the way down the hall and into the elevator. No one followed, but he wasn't taking any chances or wasting a minute. Even a second's delay could prove catastrophic.

The old-fashioned iron grate rattled shut, then the doors slid closed on the wooden compartment, sealing him inside with Kate and jazz Muzak.

Finally, he had her safely alone, away from cameras, party crashers and the scores of other people wanting a piece of her simply because she wore his ring. Growing up, he'd resented like hell the island isolation his father had imposed on them all. But right now, he wouldn't have minded some of that seclusion.

He stabbed the stop button and reached for his phone to check for text updates from Javier.

"Duarte?" Kate gripped his wrist. "Why aren't we going upstairs?"

"Soon." He needed to ensure her security before he let himself enjoy how easily she touched him now. "We are going to hang out here until Javier gets the lowdown on those party crashers." Duarte scrolled through the incoming texts.

Inching closer, she eyed the corners of the wood elevator suspiciously. The side of her breast brushed his arm. His hand gripped the phone tighter.

Even if they were only in the elevator, he had her all to himself for the first time since he'd seen the shift in her eyes. He'd known she felt the same attraction from the start and seventy-two hours straight spent together had crammed months' worth of dates and familiarity into a short period.

On the dance floor, he'd sensed any residual resistance melting from her spine. However, he couldn't think of that now. He needed to get Kate to a secure location, and then find out how the pair of party crashers had slipped through security.

Picking nervously at the yellow diamond earring, Kate nodded toward his phone. "What's the report? Can we talk in here?"

"Yes." He tucked his phone back into his coat.

"You're sure? No bugs or cameras? Remember, I know how sneaky the press can be."

"This is my hotel, with my security." Although right now his security had suffered a serious breach in the form of two struggling actors seeking to increase their visibility. If the party crashers' confessions were even true. They had every reason to lie. "I stay in my own establishments whenever possible. Javier has two people in custody. He's checking their story and also making sure there aren't more people involved. Luckily, the initial pair never made it past the coat check."

"Sounds like Javier earned his Christmas bonus tonight."

"He's a valuable member of my staff."

Sighing, she sagged onto the small bench lining the back of the elevator, red velvet cushion giving slightly beneath her. "So the crisis is over?"

"We should know soon. Javier is questioning them directly." As security concerns eased, his other senses ramped into overdrive, taking in the scent of Kate's hair, the gentle rise and fall of her chest in her off-the-shoulder gown. "Anything more?"

Possibilities for that bench marched through his mind with unrelenting temptation.

"No, nothing, well, except you confuse me. You've been such a prince—in a good way—for the past three days. Then you go all autocratic on me." Her head fell back against the mirror behind her. "Never mind. It doesn't matter. A grumpy prince is easier to resist than a charming prince."

He stepped closer. "You're having trouble resisting me?"

Her fingers dug into the crushed velvet. "You have a certain appeal."

"Glad to hear it." He liked the way she didn't gush with overblown praise. Duarte sat beside her.

"What are you doing?"

"Waiting for the okay from Javier." He slid his arm around her shoulders and nuzzled her neck.

"What about the mirror? Are you sure it's not a two-way?" she asked but didn't pull back.

"Thinking like a journalist, I see. Smart." He grazed his knuckles along her bared collarbone, eliciting a sexy moan from her.

Flattening her hands against his chest, she dug her fingers in lightly. Possessively? "I'm thinking like the paranoid fiancée of a prince. Unless your whole intent is for someone to snap pictures of us making out in an elevator. I guess that would go a long way toward persuading the public we're a happily engaged couple."

"What I want to do with you right now goes beyond simple making out, and you can be sure, I don't want anyone seeing you like that except me. I pay top dollar to my security people. Everything from my phones, to my computers, to my hotels—this is *my* domain," he declared, his mouth just over hers. "Although you're right in that it's always wise to double-check the mirrors."

He reached behind her and ran his fingers along the frame. "This one is hung on the elevator wall rather than mounted in it. And when you press against the pane…" He angled toward her until their bodies met, her back to the glass. "Hear that? Not a hollow thump. A regular mirror for me to see the beautiful curve of your back."

"Duarte…" She nipped his lower lip.

"Not that I need to see your reflection when the real deal right in front of me is so damn mesmerizing," he growled.

Sliding his hands down, he cupped her waist and shifted her around until she straddled his lap. Champagne-colored satin pooled around them, her knees on either side of him. His groin tightened. The need to have her burned through him.

And then she smiled.

Her soft cool hands cupped either side of his face and she slanted her lips more firmly across his. Just as she gave no quarter in every word and moment of her day, she demanded equal time here and now. He was more than happy to accommodate.

Liquid heat pumped through him as finally he had unfettered access to her mouth. Champagne and strawberries from their dinner lingered. He was fast becoming drunk on the taste of Kate alone. Her fingers crawled under his coat, digging into his back, urgent, insistent.

Demanding.

He thrust his hand in her hair. Tiny diamonds *tink, tink, tinked* from her updo onto the floor.

"Duarte," she mumbled against his mouth.

"We'll find them later." To hell with anything but being with her. He couldn't remember when he'd ached so much to be inside a woman. This woman. He'd known her for three intense days that felt a lot longer than his three-month relationships of the past.

Of course he'd never met anyone like Kate.

His phone buzzed in his coat pocket. She stiffened against him. His phone vibrated again, her fingers between the cell and his chest, so the sensation buzzed through her and into him. She wriggled in his lap. He throbbed in response, so hard for her that he couldn't think of anything else.

"Ignore the phone." He gathered her closer, not near enough with the bunching satin of her evening gown between them.

"The call could be important," she said, regret tingeing her voice as she cupped his face and kissed him quickly again. "It could be Javier with an update. Or something even more important," she insisted between quick nibbles. "You said your father is sick. You don't want to be sorry you ignored a message."

Her words slowly penetrated his passion-fogged brain. What had he been thinking? Of course that was the whole point. Kate had a way of scrambling rational thought.

He pulled out his phone and checked the screen. His gut clenched with dread.

"Duarte?" Kate asked, sliding to sit beside him. "Is everything okay?"

"It's my brother Antonio." He reached for the elevator button, already preparing himself for the worst—that their father had died. "Let's go to our suite. I need to call him back."

Standing in her walk-in closet that rivaled the size of her studio apartment, Kate stepped out of her princess gown and hung it up carefully among the rest of her extravagant wardrobe. Another elaborate fiction, covering up the sham of her engagement with layers of beaded and embroidered fabrics. She smoothed the front of tonight's dress, releasing a whiff of Duarte's cedar scent and memories of the elevator.

As they'd returned to the suite, Duarte had asked

for privacy for his conversation with his brother and suggested she change clothes. Her heart ached to think what he might be hearing now. She wanted to stand beside him and offer silent comfort. Without question, the proud prince wouldn't stand for any overt signs of sympathy. Apparently he saved unrestrained emotions for elevator encounters.

Her body hummed with the memory of embracing him, straddling his lap with the hard press of his arousal evident even through the folds of her dress. Warm air from the vent whispered over her skin as she stood in her matching champagne-colored underwear with nothing more than diamond earrings and a lopsided updo.

How different the evening might have been if the call hadn't come through. She wouldn't have stopped at just a kiss. Right now they could have been living out her fantasy of making love in an elevator.

Or here, in her room, with him peeling off her thigh-high silk stockings. What came next for them now? Would they be leaving right away? Or staying overnight?

She was used to pulling up stakes in a heartbeat for a story. In fact, she kept a change of clothes in her camera case for just such occasions. A camera case that wasn't monogrammed or even made of real leather, for that matter. She was in over her head playing make-believe with a real live prince.

Her cell phone rang from across the room, and she almost jumped out of her skin. Oh, God. Her sister. They hadn't spoken today and Kate had promised. She snatched up an oversized T-shirt from the top of her camera case and yanked it over her head as she sprinted across the room.

She scooped her ringing phone from the antique dresser without looking at the screen. "Hello? Jennifer?"

"'Fraid not," answered her editor from the *Global Intruder.*

Harold Hough kept the e-zine afloat through his dogged determination. She should have known she couldn't avoid him for long.

"Is there some emergency, boss? It's a little late to be calling, don't you think?"

"You're a tough lady to reach now that you're famous. Hope you haven't forgotten us little people."

Sagging on the end of the bed, she puffed out her cheeks with a hefty sigh while she weighed her words. "I explained that my fiancé is fine with me talking to you. I will relay more snippets when Duarte and I have discussed what we're comfortable with the world knowing."

Resentment scratched inside her. Thank God she hadn't told him about her plans to sneak into Duarte's Martha's Vineyard resort. As far as Harold knew, she'd been hiding a relationship with Duarte these past few months and now was attempting to control the fallout with her leaks to him. And she sure wasn't going to tell him about a surprise call from Duarte's brother.

She stared at her closed door, her heart heavy for Duarte and what he might be facing in that conversation.

Harold's voice crackled over the line. "But you were at that exclusive embassy dinner tonight. I've already heard rumblings about some party crashers. I'd hoped to get more pictures from you. Did you receive my latest email tonight? Is there something you're not telling me?" he ended suspiciously.

"Have I ever been anything but honest? I've worked my tail off for the *Intruder*." She paused to apply a little pressure in hopes Harold would back off. "So hard, in fact, maybe I need a vacation."

Tucking the phone against her shoulder, she rolled down a thigh-high stocking while waiting for Harold's response.

"Right, you're distancing yourself from the *Intruder*." His chair squeaked in the background and she could picture him leaning back to grab a pack of gum, his crutch to help him through giving up cigarettes. "You've forgotten I'm the one who made it possible for you to pay your bills."

She rolled off the other stocking, back to her pre-Cinderella self in a familiar baggy T-shirt. "You know I'm grateful for the chance you gave me at the *Intruder*. I appreciate how flexible you've been with my work schedule." No question, she would have been screwed without this job. And she would still need it if things fell apart with Duarte. "I hope you'll remember the information I've shared exclusively with you."

"And I trust you'll remember that I know plenty about you, Ms. Harper." His voice went from lighthearted slimy to laser sharp. "If I don't get the headlines I need, I can send one of my other top-notch reporters to interview your sister. After all, you of all people should know that even royalty can't keep out an *Intruder* reporter."

Seven

Phone in hand, Duarte paced across the sitting area between the two bedrooms. While not as large as his Martha's Vineyard quarters, this suite would still accommodate him and Kate well enough for a few days.

If they even stayed in Washington, D.C., after this conversation with his youngest brother.

Duarte's restless feet took him to the blazing hearth. "How high is his fever?" he asked Antonio—Tony. "Do they know the source of the infection?"

They'd only recently learned that their father had suffered damage to his liver during his escape from San Rinaldo. Enrique had caught hepatitis during his weeks on the run in poor living conditions. His health had deteriorated over the years until their perpetually private father couldn't hide the problem from his children any longer.

"His fever's stabilized at 102, but he's developed pneumonia," Tony answered. "In his weakened condition, they fear he might not be able to fight it off."

"What hospital is he in?" He knelt to stoke the fire in the hearth. Windows on either side of the mantle revealed the night skyline, the nation's capital getting hammered by a blizzard. "Where are you?"

"We're all still at the island, not sure yet when we'll go back to Galveston." His brother's fiancée had a young son from her first marriage. "He's insisting on staying at his clinic, with his own doctors. The old man says they've kept him alive this long, so he trusts them."

Frustrated, Duarte jabbed the poker deeper into the logs, sparks showering. The other suites had gas fireplaces, but he preferred the smell of real wood burning. It reminded him of home—San Rinaldo, not his father's Florida island fortress. "Damn foolhardy, if you ask me. Our father's an agoraphobic, except his 'house' is that godforsaken island."

Tony sighed hard on the other end of the phone. "You may not be far off in your estimation, my brother."

"Okay, then. I'll scrap our next stop, and we'll head straight to the island instead once the snowstorm here clears." He hadn't planned to take Kate there for a few more weeks, but he wasn't ready to leave her behind. "Maybe meeting my charming new fiancé will give him a boost."

"He seemed to take heart from the wedding plans Shannon and I have been making." Tony had proposed only a couple weeks ago, but the pair didn't want to wait to tie the knot.

Duarte had been surprised they chose the island chapel for the ceremony, but Tony had pointed out that place offered the best security from the prying paparazzi. Good thing they'd been amenable to Duarte's suggestion of one reporter for a controlled press release. The *Intruder* wouldn't have been his first choice—or even a fiftieth choice—of outlets for such an important family event, but he'd resigned himself on that point since Kate would serve as the press envoy.

And if he could make a better job open up for her? He cut that thought short.

When Antonio got married at the end of the month, Kate would walk away with her pictures and her guaranteed top-dollar feature. Why should her leaving grate this much? He'd only known her a few days. Tony had dated his fiancée for months and everyone considered their engagement abrupt.

Duarte replaced the iron poker in the holder carefully rather than risk ramming the thing through the fireplace. "Congratulations, my brother," he said, standing, his eyes trained on his fiancée's door, "and I look forward to telling you in person as soon as Kate and I arrive."

"Be happy for yourself, too. Maybe this will help the old man get back on his feet again, then you can ditch the fake engagement."

"What makes you think it's fake?" Now why the hell had he said that?

"Hey now, I know we don't hang out every Friday, but we do communicate and I'm fairly sure you would have told me if you were seriously seeing someone, especially the individual who exposed our cover to the whole world."

"Maybe that's why I didn't tell you. Hooking up with Kate isn't the most logical move I've ever made." That was an understatement, to say the least. But he'd committed to this path, and he didn't intend to back away. "If I'd asked for your opinion you might not have given the answer I wanted to hear."

"Perhaps you have a point there." Tony's laughter faded. "So you really kept this relationship a secret for months? You've actually fallen for someone?"

Bottom line, he should tell Antonio about the setup. He and his brothers didn't live close by. They'd only had each other growing up, which led them to share a lot, trust only each other.

Yet, for some reason he couldn't bring himself to spill his guts about this. "As I said, we're engaged. Wait until you meet her."

"Hanging out with reporters has never been high on my list of fun ways to spend an evening. You sure you're not just looking to poke the old man in the eye?"

Dropping into an armchair and propping a foot on the brocade sofa, he considered Tony's question to see if deep down there was some validity, then quickly dismissed the possibility. It gave his father too much control over his life.

Being with Kate appeared to be more complex than some belated rebellion against his dad. "He will be charmed by her no-B.S. attitude. What's the word from Carlos?"

Their oldest brother kept to himself even more than their father did, immersed in his medical practice rather than on some island. It could well be hours before they heard from Carlos, given the sorts of painstaking reconstructive surgeries he performed on children.

"He's his regular workaholic self. Says he'll get to the island for the wedding, and that he will call Dad at the island clinic. God, I hope the old man can hold on long enough for Carlos to decide he can leave his patients. I'd considered moving up the wedding, but..."

"Enrique insists plans stay in place." His father was stubborn, and he didn't like surprises. For security purposes he preferred life remain as scheduled as possible. Life threw enough curveballs of its own.

Tony rambled on with updates about travel and wedding details. Duarte started to rib his brother over mentioning flower choices for the bride's bouquet—

Across the suite, Kate walked through the door in a knee-length nightshirt. His brain shut down all other thoughts and blood surged south.

"My brother," Duarte interrupted. "I'll get back to you later about my travel plans. I need to hang up."

Kate twisted her hair into a wet rope and hurried barefoot into the sitting area connecting her bedroom to Duarte's.

Almost certainly she should have gone straight to sleep after her conversation with Harold. Except her editor's threat of plastering Jennifer's picture all over a tabloid story sent bile frothing up Kate's throat. She'd played it cool on the phone while reminding Harold of how much she could deliver. Then she'd cut the conversation short rather than risk losing her temper.

Before she could think, she'd rushed to the door, knowing only that she needed the reassurance of Duarte's unflappable calm.

Setting aside his iPhone, he kept his eyes firmly planted on her. "I'm sorry my assistant forgot to order nightwear. The hotel does supply complimentary robes."

"Your assistant didn't forget. This belongs to me. I had it tucked away in my camera case." Kate tugged the hem of her well-worn sleep shirt down to her knees. A picture of a camera marked the middle, words below stating *Don't Be Negative*. "Did everything go all right with your phone call?"

Hopefully his was less upsetting than hers.

"My father has taken a turn for the worse." His body rippled with tension, his hands gripping the carved wood arms of his manor chair. "He has developed pneumonia. And yes, you can leak that to the press if you wish."

Her heart ached that he had to suspect her motives when she only wanted to comfort him. He seemed so distant in his tux against the backdrop of formal damask wallpaper. She searched for the right words to reach him.

"I wasn't thinking about my job. I was asking because you look worried." Seeing the shutters fall, Kate padded past the brocade sofa to the fireplace. She held her chilly hands in front of the blaze. "What do you plan to do?"

"Let's talk about something else."

Like what? She wasn't in the mood for superficial discussions about art. How long could they shoot the breeze about the oil paintings in her room, or the lithographs in his? She'd noticed sailing art in his Martha's Vineyard quarters. Maybe there could be something to those lighter conversations, and certainly she could use the distraction from worries about Jennifer.

"Hey," Duarte said softly from behind her.

She hadn't even heard him move.

The cedar scent of his aftershave sent her mind swirling with memories of how close they'd come to having sex in the elevator. She'd wanted him so much. The fire he'd stirred simmered still, just waiting to be rekindled. She was surprised to find herself with him so soon after. Had she come back in here purposely?

Had she used her frustration over the call from Harold as an excuse to indulge what she wanted?

She looked over her shoulder at him. "Yes?"

Or perhaps she meant *Yes!*

"Is something wrong? You seem upset."

How had this gone from his concerns to hers? Was he avoiding the subject because he didn't trust her? She decided to follow his lead for now and circle back around to discussing Enrique later.

"I'm just worried about Jennifer." She stared back at the fire. "And what will happen if the press decides to write something about her. I have to admit, it's more complicated than I expected, being on the other side of the camera lens."

His angular face hardened with determination. "No one will get past my security people to your sister. I promise."

If only it could be that simple. Nothing was simple about the achy longing inside her. "You and I both know I can't count on your protection long-term."

"After you publish those wedding photos, you'll be able to afford to hire your own security team."

No wonder he didn't trust her. She'd been chasing him down for photos from the start with no thought to the implications for his family. And now her family, as well. She was responsible for putting Jennifer in the crosshairs. Her emotions raw, Kate shivered.

His arms slid around her. "Do you need a robe?"

The cedar scent of his aftershave wrapped around her as temptingly as his hold.

"Is the shirt that ugly?" She looked back at him, attempting to make light, tough to do when she wanted to bury her face in his neck and inhale, taste, *take*.

"You look beautiful in whatever you wear." He eyed

her with the same onyx heat she'd seen during their elevator make-out moment. "I was only worried you might be cold."

"I'm, uh, plenty warm, right now, thank you."

His eyes flamed hotter. The barely banked craving spread throughout her. She couldn't hold back the flood of desire and she swayed toward him. Duarte's arms banded around her in a flash, hauling her toward him.

She met him halfway. Her arms looped around his neck, she opened her mouth and herself to him, to this moment. She couldn't remember when she'd been so attracted to someone so fast, but then nothing about this situation with Duarte qualified as normal.

The warm sweep of his tongue searched her mouth as he engaged her senses. He gathered up her hair in his hands, his fingers combing, massaging, seducing. She pressed closer, his pants against her bare legs a tempting abrasion that left her aching for closer contact. She stroked her bare foot upward, just under the pants hem along his ankle. Hunger gnawed at her insides.

Without breaking contact, he yanked at his loose tux tie and tossed it aside, leaving no doubts where they were headed. Her life was such a mess on so many levels, she couldn't bring herself to say no to this, to taking a few hours of stolen pleasure.

Her fingers crawled down the fastenings, sending studs and cuff links showering onto the floor like her hairpins in the elevator. She tore at his shirt. Finesse gave way to frenzy in her need to verify her memories of him undressing that first night. He took his hands from her long enough to flick aside the starched white cotton in a white flag of mutual surrender.

She peeled off his undershirt, bunching warm cotton in her hands and revealing his hard muscled chest.

The chandelier hanging from a ceiling medallion cast a mellow glow over his chest. He didn't need special photographer's lighting to make his bronzed body look good.

Duarte was a honed, toned *man*.

Kate swayed into him. Her stolen glance when he'd undressed had let loose butterflies in her stomach. Being able to look her fill fast-tracked those butterflies through her veins.

And his body called to her touch as much as it lured her eyes.

Entranced, she tapped down his chest in a rainfall path. Every light contact with the swirls of dark hair electrified the pads of her fingers. Pausing, she traced the small oval birthmark above his navel, an almost imperceptible darkening. Seeing it, learning the nuances of him, deepened the intimacy.

Her fingers fell to his pants.

Duarte covered her hands with his, stopping her for the moment. "We can stop this, if you wish. I don't want any question about why we're together if we take this the rest of the way. This has nothing to do with your job or my family."

Pulling her face back, she stared into his eyes. "No threat of charging me with breaking and entering?"

Even as she jokingly asked him, she knew in her heart he never would have pursued that angle. If he'd wanted to go that route, he would have done so at the start. Somehow, this attraction between them had caught him unaware, too.

He winced. "I want to sleep with you, no mistake about it." The hard length of him pressing against her stomach proved that quite well. "Now that it appears you're in agreement, I need to be sure you're here of your own free will. You have enough information and pictures to set yourself up for life. There's the door."

She could walk now. He was right. Except her life would never return to normal, not after the past few days. Leaving now versus in the morning or three weeks from now wouldn't make any difference for Jennifer.

But having tonight with Duarte felt like everything to Kate. "I'm a little underdressed to leave, don't you think?"

His hot gaze tracked over her, cataloguing every exposed inch and rousing a fiery response in its wake.

Bringing their clasped hands up between them, he kissed her wrists. "I'm serious, in case you hadn't noticed."

"It's tough to miss." She met and held his intense eyes. "Although in case you didn't know it, I'm serious, too."

"When did you figure out I was never going to turn over that tape to anyone?"

"A few minutes ago." Hearing Harold's threat against Jennifer, Kate realized what real evil sounded like. Duarte was tough, but he wasn't malicious. If he'd wanted to prosecute her, he would have done so up-front from the start.

She kissed him once, hard, before pulling back. "No more talking about anything outside the two of us in this suite. I need to be with you tonight, just you and me together in a way that has nothing to do with your last name or any contacts I may have. This is completely private."

"Then there's only one last thing to settle." His hands stroked down her sides until he cupped her hips. "Your bed or mine?"

She considered the question for a second before deciding. "I don't want to engage some power play. Let's meet here, on somewhat neutral ground."

Aside from the fact that they were in his hotel, the symbolism of not choosing one bed over the other still worked for her. She waited for his verdict.

"I'm good with that." He burrowed his hands under her T-shirt, whipping it up and off until she wore nothing but the champagne-colored satin strapless bra and matching panties.

The yellow diamond and filigree gold earrings teased her shoulders.

Like the sweep of Duarte's appreciative gaze. And for some wonderful reason, this hot-as-hell prince was every bit as turned on looking at her as she was looking at him.

She reached, half believing she'd fallen asleep back in her room and was dreaming. Beyond that, what if she'd somehow imagined the magnetic shimmer while kissing him in the elevator?

Her fingers connected with his chest and—*crackle*. A tingle radiated up her arm. This was real. He was real. And tonight was theirs.

This time when she reached for the fastening on his pants, he didn't stop her. His opening zipper echoed in the room along with the *pop, pop* of sparks in the fireplace. He toed off his shoes and socks as she caressed his pants down.

His hands made fast work of her bra and panties. "And now we're both wearing nothing."

He guided her toward him and pressed bare flesh to flesh. They tumbled back onto the sofa in a tangle of arms and legs. She nipped along his strong jaw, the brocade rough against her back, his touch gentle along her sides then away.

Following his hand, she saw him reach into the end table and come back with a condom. Thank goodness at least one of them was thinking clearly enough to take care of birth control. A momentary flash of fear swept through her at how much he affected her.

Then all thoughts scattered.

The thick pressure of him between her legs, poised and ready, almost sent her over the edge then and there. Her breath hitched as she worked to regain control. He thrust deep and full, holding while she adjusted to the newness of him, of them linked. She arched into the sensation, taking him farther inside her. Fingernails sinking deep half moons into his shoulders, she held on to the moment, held back release.

He kept his weight off her with one hand on the back of the couch, the other tucked under her. She rolled her hips under his and he took the cue, resuming the dance they'd started earlier, first in the ballroom, then in the elevator and now taking it to the ultimate level they'd both been craving.

Cedar and musk scented the air, and she buried her face deeper into his shoulder to breathe in the erotic blend. He kissed, nipped and laved his way up to her earlobe, his late-day beard rasping against her jaw. Her every nerve tingled with the memory of that first night in Martha's Vineyard when he'd stroked up her neck. She should have known then she wouldn't hold out long against the temptation to experience all of him.

Control shaky, she wrapped her legs around his waist and writhed harder, faster. Her knee bumped against the back of the sofa, unsettling their balance. She flung out her arms, desperate to hold on to to him, hold on to the moment.

"I've got you," he growled in her ear as they rolled from the brocade couch.

He twisted so his back hit the floor, cushioning her fall. He caught her gasp of surprise and thrust inside her. Her hair streamed over him as she straddled his hips, rug bristly under her knees. He cupped her bottom, guiding her until she recaptured their rhythm.

Were his hands shaking ever so slightly? She looked closer and saw tendons straining in his neck with restraint.

She braced herself, palms against his chest. Delicious tremors rippled up her arms as his muscles twitched and flexed with her caresses. His hands slid around and over her again. He cradled her breasts, teasing and plucking her to tightened peaks that pulled the tension tighter throughout.

Her head lolled and her spine bowed forward. Each thrust of his hips sent her hair teasing along her back. In a distant part of her mind, she heard his husky words detailing all the times he'd watched and wanted her. She tried to answer, truly did, but her answer came out in half-formed phrases until she gave up talking and just moved.

He traced her ribs, working his way down to her waist, over her stomach. Lower. He slid two fingers between them, slickening her taut bundle of aching nerves. She doubted she needed the help to finish, but enjoyed his talented touch all the same.

Carefully, precisely, he circled his thumb with the perfect pressure, taking her so close then easing back, only to nudge her closer.

She gasped out and didn't care how loud. She simply rode the pulsations rocking through her. He gripped her hips again, his hold firmer as he thrust a final time. His completion echoed with hers, sending a second round of lights sparking behind her eyelids and cascading around her until she went limp in the aftermath.

Sagging on top of him, she sealed their sweat-slicked bodies skin to skin. His hands stroked over her hair, his chest pumping beneath hers. She should move and she would, as soon as her arms and legs worked again.

She gazed at him in the half light, her eyes taking in the strong features of his noble lineage. God, even here in his arms she couldn't escape reminders of his heritage, his wealth. She was in so far over her head.

Being with him was different in a way she feared she could never recapture again. Would the rest of her life be spent as a second-best shadow?

And if he made this much of an impact in less than a week, how much more would he change her life if she dared spend the rest of the month with him?

Eight

Yellow moon sinking out of sight, Duarte cradled a sleeping Kate to his chest and carried her to his room. They hadn't spoken after their impulsive tangle. Instead, they'd simply moved closer to the fire for a slower, more thorough exploration. Afterward, she had dozed off in his arms.

Her legs dangled as he carried her. The simple yarn-and-bead-braided string stayed around her ankle. He'd asked her once why she never took it off. She'd told him Jennifer made it as a good luck charm. He didn't consider himself the sentimental type, but he couldn't help but be moved. That she wore the gift even when her sister wouldn't have known otherwise revealed more about her than anything she'd said or done since they'd been together.

Elbowing back the covers, he settled her on the carved four-poster bed and pulled the thick comforter over her.

He eyed the door. He should check his messages and make plans for a morning flight out to see his father, but his feet stayed put.

The allure of watching Kate sleep was too strong. He sat on the edge of the bed, *his* bed. Her hair splayed over the plump pillow, and his hands curved at the memory of silky strands sliding between his fingers.

He'd gotten what he wanted. They'd slept together. He should be celebrating and moving on. Except from the moment he'd been buried inside her, he'd known. Just once with Kate wouldn't be enough.

Already, he throbbed to have her again. The image of her bold and uninhibited over him replayed in his brain. He could watch her all night long.

Why hadn't he told her about going to the island when she'd walked in the room? The truth itched up his spine. After their impulsive kiss in the elevator, he'd sensed they were close to acting on the attraction. But he'd needed her to want him as much as he wanted her. He'd offered her a free pass to walk with all her photos and held back telling her about his imminent trip to see his father.

Now he knew. There was no mistaking her response. And instead of making things easier, his thoughts became more convoluted.

Kate rolled to her back, arm flung out in groggy abandon. Her lashes fluttered and she stared up at him, her eyes still purple-blue with foggy passion. "What time is it?"

"Just after four in the morning."

"Any further word about your father?" She sat up, sheet clutched to her chest her hair tumbling down her shoulders.

"Nothing new." He swallowed hard at the thought of

a world without his father's imposing presence. Time to invite her into a private corner of his life ahead of schedule. "But I'm putting the rest of the trip around the U.S. on hold to see my father first…just in case."

"That's a good idea." She squeezed his knee lightly. "You don't want to have regrets from waiting."

Resisting the urge to touch her proved impossible. He stroked a silken lock from her shoulder and lingered. As much as he wanted her here, he had to know. "My offer for you to take your pictures and walk away free and clear still stands."

Her hand slid from his knee, her eyes wary. "Are you telling me to go?"

Exhaling hard, he gripped her shoulders. "Hell, no. I want you right where you are. But you need to know that when we leave for the island, your life will be changed forever. Becoming a part of the Medina circle alters the way people treat you, even after you walk away, and not always in a good way."

Sheet still clutched to her chest, she studied him before answering. "I have one question."

His gut clenched. Could he really follow through on letting her go while the scent of her still clung to his skin? "Okay, then. That would be?"

"What time do we leave?"

Relief slammed through him so hard he wondered again how this woman could have crawled under his skin so deeply in such a short time. Not that he intended to turn her away. In fact, he even had an idea of how to make her life at the island easier. "We'll go in the morning, once the ice storm has cleared."

Jet engines whispering softly through the sky, Kate snuggled closer to Duarte's chest. Their clothes were scattered about the sleeping cabin in the back of the airplane.

Ten minutes after takeoff, she'd snapped photos of him, thinking the well-equipped aircraft with both a bedroom and an office would provide an interesting window into the Medina world. But she'd found her photographer's eye less engaged with his surroundings. Instead she'd increasingly closed in on his face as if she could capture the essence of him just by looking. Too soon, seeing him through the lens hadn't been enough and they'd reached for each other simultaneously, leaving their seats for the private bedroom. Yes, she was using sex to avoid thinking, and she suspected Duarte was, as well.

Tension rippled through his lean muscled body, and she could certainly empathize. Life had been spiraling out of control for her since they'd met.

And now they were winging to some unknown island. Shades covered all the windows so she didn't know if they were traveling over land or water. Duarte had told her the clothes appropriate for the "warmer climate" would be waiting.

What a mess she'd made of things. How was she supposed to report on a man she'd slept with? Should she have taken his offer to walk away?

Her fingers curled around his bare hip, his body now so intimately familiar to her. How much longer could she avoid weightier issues?

Duarte sketched the furrows in her brow. "What's bothering you?"

"Nothing," she said. She wasn't ready to let him know how being with him rocked her focus. Better to distract him. "I've never made love in a plane before."

"Neither have I." His fingers trailed from her brow to tap her nose. "You look surprised."

"Because I am." She expected this man had done all sorts of things she couldn't imagine. "I would have thought during all those three-month relationships, you would have joined the mile-high club at some point."

"You seem to have quite a few preconceived notions about me. I thought journalists were supposed to be objective."

"I am. Most of the time. You're just... Hell, I don't know."

He was different, but telling him that would give him too much power over her. Was she being unfair to Duarte out of her own fear? Was she making assumptions based on an image of a privileged playboy prince?

Swinging her feet off the bed, she plucked her underwear from floor.

Duarte stroked her spine. "Tell me about the man who broke your trust."

"It's not what you think." She pulled on her panties and bra. Where was her dress? And why was she letting his question rattle her? "I haven't had some wretched breakup or bad boyfriend."

"Your father?" Duarte said perceptively as he pulled on his boxers.

Kate slipped her kimono-sleeve dress over her head and swept it smooth before facing Duarte again. "He isn't an evil man or an abuser. He just...doesn't care." Parental indifference made for a deep kind of loneliness she couldn't put to words. Only through her camera had she been able to capture the hollow echo. "It doesn't matter so much for me, but Jennifer doesn't understand. How could she? He cropped himself right out of the family picture."

"Where is he now?" He stepped into his slacks and reached for his chambray shirt.

"He and his new wife have moved to Hawaii, where he can be sure not to bump into us."

"The kind to send his checks as long as he doesn't have to invest anything of himself?"

She stayed quiet, tugging on her leather knee boots.

His hand fell on her shoulder. "Your father does send help, right?"

Bitter words bubbled up her throat. "When Jennifer turned eighteen, he signed over his rights and all responsibility. They were going to put her in the state hospital since she can't live on her own. I couldn't let that happen, so I stepped in."

Duarte sat beside her, taking her hand lightly, carefully. "Have you considered taking him to court?"

"Leave it alone." She flinched away from him and the memories. "Bringing him back into her life only gives him the option to hurt her more than he already has. Jennifer and I will be fine. We'll manage. We always do."

Duarte cursed low. "Still, he should be helping with her care so you don't have to climb around on ledges snapping photos to pay the bills."

"I would do anything for her."

"Even sleep with me."

His emotionless voice snapped her attention back to his face. The coldness there chilled her skin. Confusion followed by shock rippled through her. Did he really believe she could be that calculating? Apparently what they'd shared wasn't as special to him if he thought so poorly of her.

Hurt to the core, she still met his gaze dead-on. "I'm here now because I want to be."

He didn't back down, his face cool and enigmatic. "But would you have slept with me to take care of her?"

And she'd thought she couldn't ache more. "Turn the plane around. I want to go back."

"Hey, now—" he held up his hands "—I'm not judging you. I don't know you well enough to make that call, which is why I'm asking questions in the first place."

Some of the starch flaked from her spine. Hadn't she thought the same thing herself, wondering about ways she may have misjudged him? "Fair enough."

"Has your father called you because of the publicity surrounding your engagement?" he asked, his eyes dark and protective. "People develop all sorts of, uh, creative crises when they think they can gain access to a royal treasure trove."

"I haven't heard a word from him." Although now that Duarte had given her the heads-up, she would be sure to let voice mail pick up if her father did phone. "Other than the obligatory holiday greeting, we haven't heard so much as a 'boo' from him. I guess that's better than having to explain his dropping in and out of our lives."

His hand slid up into her hair, cradling her head. "Your sister is lucky to have you."

"Jennifer and I are lucky to have each other." Kate stood abruptly, refusing to be distracted by his seductive touch.

This conversation reminded her too well that they knew precious little about each other. She'd known her jerk of a father all her life and still she'd been stunned when he dumped his special-needs daughter without a backward glance. What hurtful surprises might lurk under Duarte's handsome surface?

Watching her through narrowed eyes, Duarte pulled on his shoes and gestured her back toward the main cabin. "We'll have to put this conversation on hold. We should be landing soon. Would you like your first glance of the island?"

"The secrecy ends?"

"Revealing the specific location isn't my decision to make." He opened the window shade.

Hungry for a peek at where Duarte had grown up, she buckled into one of the large leather chairs and stared outside. An island stretched in the distance, nestled in miles and miles of sparkling ocean. Palm trees spiked from the landscape, lushly green and so very different from the leafless snowy winter they'd left behind. A dozen or so small outbuildings dotted a semicircle around a larger structure, what appeared to be the main house.

A white mansion faced the ocean in a U shape, constructed around a large courtyard with a pool. Details were spotty but she would get an up-close view soon enough of the place where Enrique Medina had lived in seclusion for over twenty-five years, a gilded cage to say the least. Even from a distance, she couldn't miss the grand scale of the sprawling estate, the unmistakable sort that housed royalty.

Engines whining louder, the plane banked, lining up with a thin islet alongside the larger island. A single strip of concrete marked the private runway, two other planes parked beside a hangar. As they neared, a ferry boat came into focus. To ride from the airport to the main island? They sure were serious about security. Duarte had said it wasn't his secret to reveal. She thought of his father, a man who'd been overthrown in a violent coup. And his brothers, Carlos and Antonio, had a stake in this, as well. None of the Medina heirs had signed on for the royal life.

God, she missed the days when her job had been about providing valuable information to the public. It had been two years since she'd been in the trenches uncovering dirty politics and the nuances of complicated wars as opposed to shining a public flashlight on good people who had every right to their privacy.

The intercom system crackled a second before the pilot announced, "We're about to begin our descent. Please return to your seats and secure your lap belts. Thank you, and we hope you had a pleasant flight."

A glass-smooth landing later, she climbed on board the ferry that would transport them to the main island. Crisp sea air replaced the recycled oxygen in the jet cabin. Her camera bag slung over her shoulder, she recorded the images with her eyes for now. Duarte would call the shots on when she could snap photos. Her stomach knotted even though there wasn't a wave in sight, a perfect day for boating. A dolphin led the way, fin slicing through the water, then submerging again.

An osprey circled over its nest and herons picked their way through sea oats along the shore like a pictorial feature straight out of *National Geographic*. Until you looked closer and saw the guard tower, the security cameras tucked in trees.

A guard waited on the dock, a gun strapped within easy reach to protect the small crowd gathered to greet them. She recognized the man and woman from recent coverage in the media. "That's your youngest brother, Antonio, and his fiancée."

Duarte nodded.

The wedding he had mentioned made perfect sense now. She'd started the ball rolling digging up information about the shipping magnate and his waitress mistress. But then they'd fallen off the map. Apparently Alys Cortez hadn't shared everything she knew about the Medinas.

The brothers shared the same dark hair, although Antonio's was longer with a hint of curl. Duarte had a lean runner's build, whereas she would have pegged his brother as a former high school wrestler.

What sort of school experience would the young princes have had on a secluded island?

As the boat docked, she realized another couple waited with Tony and Shannon. Javier Cortez stood with a woman just behind him. They couldn't possibly have permitted his cousin Alys to stay after she betrayed them. Although they allowed a reporter into their midst...

Duarte touched the small of her back as they walked down the gangplank. "There's someone here to see you."

She looked closer as Javier stepped aside and revealed—

Jennifer?

Disbelief rocked the plank under Kate's feet. What was going on? She looked back at Duarte and he simply smiled as if it was nothing unusual to scoop her sister out of her protective home without consulting Kate. Not that Jennifer seemed to notice anything unusual about this whole bizarre day.

Jumping with excitement, her sister waved from the dock, wearing jeans, layered tank tops and a lightweight jacket. Her ponytail lifted by the wind, she could have been any college coed on vacation. Physically, she showed no signs of the special challenges she faced. But Kate was all too aware of her sister's vulnerability.

A vulnerability that hit home all the harder now that Kate realized how easily someone could steal Jennifer away without her knowing. How could she ever hope to go on a remote shoot without worrying? What if her editor had been the one to pull this stunt?

Kate loved Jennifer more than anyone in the world. But the balance of that love wavered between sibling and motherly affection. The maternal drive to protect Jennifer burned fiercely inside her.

And Duarte had stepped over a line. How dare he use his security people to just scoop up Jennifer? He was supposed to be protecting her.

Her lips pursed tight, Kate held her anger, for now. She didn't want to upset her sister with a scene.

Jennifer hugged her tight before stepping back smiling. "Katie, are you surprised? We get to visit after all. Isn't it beautiful? Can we go swimming even though it's January? It's not snowing, like at home."

Kate forced a smile onto her own face, as well. "It might be a bit cool for that even now. But we could go for walks on the beach. Hope you brought comfy shoes."

"Oh, they have everything for me. He—" she pointed to Javier "—said so when he picked me up at school. I got to fly on an airplane and they had my favorite movie with popcorn. All these nice people were waiting to meet me when I got here a few minutes before you. Have you met them?"

Shaking her head, Kate let Jennifer continue with the introductions, which saved her from having to say anything for a while. More specifically, it offered her the perfect diversion to avoid looking at Duarte until she could get her emotions under control and him alone.

On the surface this seemed like a thoughtful gesture, but he should have consulted her, damn it. Thinking of Jennifer going off with people she didn't know scared the hell out of Kate.

As for the supposedly great assisted-living facility, they never should have let Jennifer leave without calling her first.

So much for giving him the benefit of the doubt, assuming he could be an ordinary, everyday kind of guy. Duarte assumed his way was best.

No worries about joining the ranks of his three-month-rejects club. Because she would be walking out on Duarte Medina on their one-month anniversary.

Nine

Duarte wasn't sure what had upset Kate, but without question, she'd gone into deep-freeze mode after the ferry crossing. He'd known the discussion about her dad made her uncomfortable, but not like this. He'd hoped seeing her sister would trump everything else and make her happy. He'd been wrong, and he intended to find out why—after he'd seen his father.

Two vehicles waited, as he'd requested. A limousine would take the women to the main house and Duarte would use the Porsche Cayenne four-wheel drive to visit the island clinic with Tony.

Watching Jennifer finish her introductions, Duarte was struck by how much she looked like her sister. They shared the same general build and rich brown hair, the strong island sun emphasizing caramel-colored highlights. But most of all, he couldn't miss how much Jennifer adored her older sister. The love and protectiveness Kate displayed was clearly returned.

Bringing them together had been the right thing. And here on his father's island he could offer the sisters some of the pampering they had been denied.

Duarte turned to Kate. "Javier will take you both back to the house. Shannon will help you settle in while I go see my father with Tony. Anything you need, just ask."

He dropped a quick kiss on Kate's cheek, playing the attentive fiancé.

Jennifer quickly hooked arms with her sister. "Let me see the ring…"

Their voices drifted off and Duarte faced his brother alone for the first time since he'd stepped off the ferry. Tony's normally lighthearted ways were nowhere in sight today.

Duarte took the keys from his younger brother's extended hand. "Any change in his condition?"

"His fever is down and the breathing treatments help him rest more comfortably." Tony closed the car door, sitting in the passenger seat. "But the core problem with his liver hasn't been solved."

He turned the key and the Porsche SUV purred to life. "Has he considered a transplant?"

"That's a sticky subject for the old guy." Tony hooked his arm out the open window as they pulled away from the ferry. "For starters, he would have to go to the mainland. His doctors are of mixed opinion as to whether he's a good candidate."

"So we just wait around for him to die?" What had happened to their father, the fighter? "That doesn't seem right."

Enrique may have turned into a recluse, but he'd

rebuilt a minikingdom of his own here off the coast of Florida. Duarte guided the vehicle along the narrow paved road paralleling the shore.

When he'd first arrived here as a kid, the tropical jungle had given him the perfect haven. He would evade the guards and run until his heart felt like it would burst. Over time he'd realized the pain had more to do with losing his mother, with watching her murder. Then he'd begun martial arts training as well so he could go back to San Rinaldo one day. So he could take out the people responsible for his mother's death.

By the time he reached adulthood, he realized he would never have the revenge he'd craved as a child. His only vengeance came in not letting them win. He wouldn't be conquered.

He'd thought his father carried the same resolve. Duarte forced his attention back on the present and his brother's words.

"His health concerns are complicated by more than just the remote locale. There's the whole issue of finding a donor. Chances are greatly increased when the donor is of the same ethnicity."

"Which means we should be tested. Maybe one of us can donate a lobe," Duarte said without hesitation.

"Again, he says no. He insists that route poses too great a risk to us." Tony stared out over the ocean. While Duarte had used running to burn off his frustration, the youngest Medina brother had gravitated to the shore for swimming, surfing and later, sailing.

"He's stubborn as hell."

Tony turned back, his grin wry. "You're one to talk. I'm surprised you actually brought Kate Harper here. And that you gave her our mother's ring. You're not exactly the forgiving sort."

It wasn't Beatriz's wedding ring—Carlos had that—and in fact Duarte hadn't remembered her wearing that one as clearly as he recalled the ruby she'd worn on her other hand. As a child, he'd toyed with it while she told him stories of her own family. She'd been of royal descent, but her parents had been of modest means. She'd wanted her sons to value hard work and empathize with the people of San Rinaldo.

What would life have been like if she'd made it out of the country with them?

But she hadn't, and what-ifs wasted time. Her death must be weighing heavier on his mind because of his father's failing health. And now, he would see his father for what could be the last time.

The clinic—a one-story building, white stucco with a red tile roof—sported two wings, perched like a bird on the manicured lawn. One side held the offices for regular checkups, eye exams and dental visits. The other side was reserved for hospital beds, testing and surgeries.

Duarte parked the car in front and pocketed the keys. Guards nodded a welcome without relaxing their stance. They weren't Buckingham Palace-stiff, but their dedication to their mission couldn't be missed.

Electric doors slid open. A blast of cool, antiseptic air drifted out. The clinic was fully staffed with doctors and nurses on hand to see to the health concerns of the small legion that ran Enrique's island home. Most were from San Rinaldo or relatives of the refugees.

Tony pointed to the correct door, although Duarte would have known from the fresh pair of heavily armed sentinels. Bracing, he stepped inside the hospital room.

The former king hadn't requested any special accommodations beyond privacy. There were no flowers or balloons or even cards to add color to the sterile space. The stark room held a simple chair, a rolling tray, a computer...

And a single bed.

Wearing paisley pajamas, Enrique Medina needed a shave. That alone told Duarte how ill the old man was.

He'd also lost weight since Duarte's last visit in May when he'd brought their half sister Eloisa over for her first trip to the island since she was a child. His father had been making a concerted effort to reconcile with his children.

A sigh rattled Enrique's chest and he adjusted the plastic tubes feeding oxygen into his nose. "Thank you for coming, *mi hijo*."

My son.

"Of course." He stepped deeper into the room. The old man had never been the hugging type. Duarte clapped him on the shoulder once. Damn, nothing but skin and bones. "Antonio says you're responding well to the treatment. When are you going to get a liver transplant?"

Scowling from one son to the other, Enrique said, "When did you become a nag like your brother?"

Tony spun on his heel. "I think I hear the guards calling me."

When the door closed, Duarte gave no quarter. "Still as stubborn as ever, I see, old man. I just didn't expect you to stop fighting."

"I'm still alive, am I not? My doctors wrote me off months ago." He waved a hand, veins bruised from IVs. "Enough about my health. I have no interest in discussing my every ache and ailment. I want to know more about your fiancée."

Duarte dropped into a chair. "Ah, so you held on long enough to meet her? Perhaps I should delay the introduction."

"If one of you promised a grandchild, you might get nine more months out of me."

"It's unfair to put your mortality on our shoulders."

"You are right," Enrique said, his calculating eyes still as sharp as ever in spite of his failing body. "What do you intend to do about it?"

Duarte weighed his next words. The old monarch passed on his sense of humor to Antonio and his intense drive to Carlos.

Duarte inherited his father's strategic abilities. Which told him exactly what he needed to say to get Enrique out of the hospital bed.

"You can meet Kate…when you get well enough to leave the clinic and come back to the house."

Kate had expected an amazing house. But nothing could have prepared her for the well-guarded opulence of the Medina mansion. Every *ooh* and *aah* from Jennifer as she caught her first glimpse reminded Kate of the awkward position Duarte had placed them in. Although she certainly didn't blame her sister.

Who wouldn't stare at the trees and the wildlife and the palatial residence? She and Jennifer had grown up in a small three-bedroom Cape Cod–style house outside Boston, comfortable in their second-story rooms. Kate had painted Jennifer's a bright yellow to go with photos she'd snapped of sunflowers and birds. She'd put a lot of effort into creating a space for her sister, the way a mother would have done. Jennifer had called the room her garden.

No wonder her sister was entranced by the botanical

explosion surrounding the Medina mansion. The place was the size of some hotels. Except she usually wasn't escorted to her hotel by a scowling head of security. Javier sat beside Shannon, eyeing Kate suspiciously the whole drive over.

The limousine slowed, easing past a towering marble fountain with a "welcome" pineapple on top—and wasn't that ironic in light of all those guards? Once the vehicle stopped, more uniformed security appeared from out of nowhere to open the limo.

Even a butler waited beside looming double doors.

Once inside, Kate couldn't hold back a gasp of her own. The cavernous circular hall sported gilded archways leading to open rooms. Two staircases stretched up either side, meeting in the middle. And she would bet good money that the Picasso on the wall wasn't a reproduction.

Shannon touched her elbow. "Everything will be taken up to the room."

"We don't have much." Kate passed her camera bag and Jennifer's backpack to the butler. "Duarte told me they—"

"—already have everything prepared. That's the Medina way," Shannon said, her words flavored with a light Texas twang. "Let's go straight through to the veranda. I'd like you to meet my son, Kolby."

Her footsteps echoing on the marble floor, Kate thought back to what she knew about Antonio Medina's fiancée and remembered the widowed Shannon had a three-year-old child from her first marriage, the boy she'd called Kolby.

Kate walked past what appeared to be a library. Books filled three walls, interspersed with windows and a sliding brass ladder. The smell of fresh citrus hung in the air, and not just because of the open windows. A tall potted orange tree nestled in one corner beneath a wide skylight. Mosaic tiles swirled outward on the floor, the ceiling filled with frescoes of globes and conquistadors. She pulled her eyes from the elaborate mural as they reached French doors leading out to a pool and seaside veranda.

A million-dollar view spread in front of her, and a towheaded little boy sprinted away from his sitter toward his mom. Shannon scooped up Kolby, the future princess completely natural and informal with her son.

Kate decided then and there that she liked the woman.

Shuffling Kolby to her hip, Shannon turned to Jennifer. "What would you like to do today?"

"What do I get to pick from?" Jennifer spun on her tennis shoes. "Are you sure it's too cold to go swimming in the ocean?"

Kate's heart warmed at Shannon's obvious ease with Jennifer.

"You could take a dip in the pool out here. It's heated." Shannon patted her son's back as he drooped against her, eyes lolling. "There's also a movie theater with anything you want to see. They've added a spa with pedicures and manicures even recently."

Jennifer clapped her hands. "Yes, that's what I want, painted toenails and no snow boots."

Laughing, Shannon set her groggy son on a lounger and walked to the drink bar. "You're a kindred spirit."

"What does that mean?" Jennifer asked.

Shannon poured servings of lemonade—fresh squeezed, no doubt. "We're sister spirits." She passed crystal goblets to each of them. Her eyes were curious behind retro black glasses. "I live to have my feet massaged."

"And when Katie marries Artie—" Jennifer's brown eyes lit with excitement as she clutched her drink "—we'll be sisters for real since you're marrying his brother."

Shannon spewed her sip. "Artie?"

Stifling a smile, Kate set aside her lemonade. "He prefers to be called Duarte."

Seeing how quickly Jennifer accepted these people into her heart sent a trickle of unease down Kate's spine. This was just the kind of thing she'd wanted to avoid. Explaining the breakup would have been difficult enough before. But now? It would be far more upsetting. Her frustration with Duarte grew.

Jennifer hooked arms with her sister. "I know you're the one who is going to marry Artie—uh, Duarte. But I already feel like a princess."

Duarte had done his best to leave his princely roots behind and lead his own life. But there was no escaping the Medina mantle here. Even the "informal" dinner at this place was outside the norm, something he realized more so when seeing the all-glass dining area through other people's eyes. Shannon's young son loved the room best since he said it was like eating in a jungle with trees visible through three walls and the ceiling.

Throughout the meal, Kate had stayed silent for the most part, only answering questions when directly asked. He wanted to tell himself she was simply tired. But now, watching her charge through her bedroom taking inventory of her surroundings and setting up her computer, she brimmed with frustrated energy. Her dress whipped around her leather knee boots.

No more waiting. He had to know what had set her off. "Tell me."

"Tell you what?" She spun away from the canopy bed, anger shooting icicles from her eyes. "It's helpful to a person when you elaborate rather than bark out one- and two-word orders."

He was completely clueless as to what pissed her off and that concerned him more than anything. He should at least have some idea. "Explain to me what has made you angry, and don't bother denying that you're upset."

"Oh, believe me." She sauntered closer, stopping by her camera case resting on a chaise at the end of her bed. "I wasn't planning to deny a thing. I was simply waiting for a private moment alone with you."

"Then let's have it."

She jabbed him in the chest, the kimono sleeves of her dress whispering against him. "You had no right to interfere in my life by bringing Jennifer here."

What the hell? Her accusation blindsided him. "I thought seeing your sister would make you happy."

"Do you have any idea how hard it was to get her into that facility, a place that fits her needs but also makes her happy?" Her words hissed through clenched teeth as she obviously tried to keep her voice down. "What if they give someone else her spot?"

That, he could fix. "I will make sure it doesn't happen."

"Argh!" She growled her frustration. "You can't just take over like that. You're not responsible for her. You have no say in her life. And while we're on that subject, how did you even arrange for her to leave? Good God, maybe I should move her anyway if security is that lax in the center. I'm shelling out a small fortune for Jennifer to live there. What if someone had kidnapped her?"

All right, he could see her point somewhat, even if he didn't agree. "I told you before. I had round-the-clock guards watching her *and* the facility—" he saw her jaw tighten and added "—which is quite nice by the way, like a boarding school. You've done an admirable job for your sister."

And she'd done it all alone without her father's help. That kind of pressure could explain her over-the-top reaction.

"I searched long and hard to find a place where she could live given how much I have to travel." Her chest heaved and her cheeks pinked with her rising emotions. "It wasn't easy and now you've jeopardized that. I simply can't let it pass that they released her to you without even consulting me."

Now he was starting to get pissed off himself. He'd been thinking of her and he wasn't accustomed to explaining himself to people. "I'm not a random stranger claiming a connection. It's well documented and, thanks to your job, highly publicized that I'm your fiancé. My name is known at that facility whether you like it or not and Javier was acting on my authority. We have the space for Jennifer here, as well as the staff on hand for anything she needs. In case you didn't notice, she's very happy with the arrangement."

"Of course she's happy. And that's going to make it all the tougher when we have to go back to our everyday, middle-class life. I can't afford—" she gestured around her wildly, her eyes lingering on a framed Esteban March battle painting "—all of this. I don't want her getting attached to the lifestyle."

Then it became clear. He stroked down her arm,

ready to entice her anger away in the canopy bed. "*You* don't want to get attached."

She dodged his touch. "You'll be out of my life in about three weeks. You've only been *in* my life less than a week. Be honest, you don't want a real relationship with me any more than I want to be a part of your crazy world. This needs to stop before someone gets hurt. We have to go back to our original arrangement."

Like hell. Anger kicked around inside him as hard as her words in his brain, her insistence that she didn't want to be involved with the Medina mess. "Do you think backing off will erase what happened last night and again today? Will you be able to forget? Because I damn well can't."

He could see those same memories scrolling across her mind.

Her gaze locked on him as firmly as his stayed on her. Moonlight played with hints of the caramel-colored highlights in her brown hair, glinted off the deepening blue of her eyes. He wanted her so much he went rock hard in a flash.

His life would be so much simpler without this attraction.

"Duarte, I haven't forgotten a second," she whispered.

Heat flared in her eyes as hot as the fire licking through his veins and he knew he wouldn't trade a second of the connection with Kate. He knew she couldn't ignore this any more than he could. Duarte started across the room just as Kate joined him, mouths meeting, passion exploding.

They fell back onto the canopy bed.

Ten

Duarte tucked Kate under him on the canopy bed, her frenetic kisses tapping into all the frustration burning his insides. Static lifted strands of her hair toward him, crackling off his face in an echo of the charged need snapping through him.

After their fight tonight, he hadn't expected another chance to be with her. Her seductive wriggle he now knew encouraged him to press his thigh closer. She sighed, urging him on with her gasps and fingers digging deeper into his back.

Their legs tangled in the spread. Without moving his mouth from hers, he wadded the coverlet and flung it on the floor. He tunneled his hand under the hem of her dress. The cool sheets slithered underneath them, the high thread count nowhere near as silky as her skin.

"Clothes," she whispered between nips, "we have too many."

He knew an invitation when he heard one.

"Let me help you with that."

Drawing his mouth from hers, he nuzzled down her body until he reached her long legs. She'd driven him crazy all day long with the killer boots. As he eased down one knee-high leather boot, he kissed along her calf, her skin creamy and soft. Her breathy moan, the impatient grapple of her hands on his shoulders encouraged him. He tugged the other boot down and sent it to the floor with a resounding thump.

Kate curled her toes, wriggling the painted white tips in a delicious stretch that called his fingers to her delicate arches. Stretching to the side, she switched on the bedside lamp.

He stroked along her arm and gathered her against him again. "You don't shy away from the light. That's a total turn-on."

She hooked a leg over his hip. "You're such a *guy*."

"Obviously." His erection throbbed between them.

Her eyes narrowed with purpose. "Lie back."

"We'll get there." He slanted his mouth over hers.

She flattened her palm against his chest. "I said for you to lie back." Determination resonated from her words as sure as the unremitting surf rolling outside the open veranda doors. "You give a lot of orders. I think it's time for someone to take charge of you."

"Are you challenging me to a power struggle?"

"I'm daring you to give your body over to me. Or does the prince always have to be in control?"

Her question hinted at their argument earlier, and damned if he would let this moment be derailed. His hand glided up to cradle her breast. "What do you have in mind?"

"No, no." She shook her head slowly, tousled hair

a sexy cloud of disarray around her face. "If I spell everything out, you're not taking much of a risk."

Her meaning crystallized in his mind. "So I trust you a little and you trust me a little?"

"You first," she said, the mix of vixen and vulnerability winning him over.

He whipped his shirt off, reclined back. And waited.

Standing at the foot of the bed, she bunched the hem of her dress in her hands, inch by inch exposing her thighs to his hungry gaze. Then showing her cranberry-red panties and bra he'd peeled from her earlier in the airplane.

Her dress covered her face for an instant before she flung it aside. The salty sea air through the French doors fluttered the canopy overhead and her breasts beaded visibly against the satin bra. His hands fisted in the sheets as he resisted the urge to haul her against him right then and there. She shook her hair from her face, flicking it over her shoulders.

"Your turn," she demanded.

God, she was hot and turned him inside out in a way no other woman had. He tugged his pants and boxers off, ready to cut short this game of dare or strip poker or whatever she wanted to call it.

She quirked a brow then reached for the center clasp—he swallowed hard—to unfasten her bra. Red satin fell away and he couldn't resist. He arched off the bed toward her.

Shaking her head, she covered her breasts and backed up. He reclined again, his arms behind his head. She lowered her hands and hooked her thumbs in her panties. A slow shimmy later, she kicked aside the underwear.

Her eyes blazed bold and determined as she knelt on

the bed. Crawling up the mattress, she climbed toward him. He slid his hands from behind his head, flattened along the sheets, but didn't touch her, not yet. The intensity in her eyes said she wanted to play this out a while longer. He didn't delude himself that this would magically fix their argument, and they might be better served talking.

But damned if he could find the words or will to stop her.

She fanned her fingers over his chest. A primitive growl rumbled free ahead of his thoughts. She dipped her head and flicked her tongue over his flat nipple. Again. She devoted every bit as much attention to him as he'd enjoyed lavishing on her beautiful body earlier in the plane. Drawing circles down his stomach, she scratched lightly down and down. His abs contracted under her touch.

Lower still she traced just beside his arousal until his teeth clenched. Then her cool hand curled around him and stroked, deliberately, continuing until his eyes slammed shut and his senses narrowed to just the glide of her touch. The caress of her thumb. The warmth of her mouth.

Dots specked behind his eyelids, the roar in his ears rivaling the crash of waves. His jaw clamped tight as he held back his release, fought the urge to move.

"Kate…" he hissed between clenched teeth.

Shifting, she stretched upward again, her lips leading the way as she kissed, licked, nipped until she reached his face.

Once he opened his eyes, she stared down at him. "Where do you keep the birth control?"

His desire-steamed brain raced to keep pace. "In my

wallet. I would reach for it, but someone told me not to move. Do you mind?"

With a fluid stretch over the side, she plucked his wallet from his pants and pulled out a condom. Flipping the packet between her fingers, she smiled at him with such a wicked glint in her now-near-purplish-blue eyes that he knew she wasn't through with her control game. Not by a long shot. She smoothed the condom down and took him inside her with such sweet torturous precision he almost came undone.

The restraints snapped and his hands shot up to cup her breasts. She pushed into his palms, tips harder and tighter than ever before. Her instant response to his touch sent a rush of possessiveness through him.

She cradled his face as she rocked her hips. "I would love to capture your expression on film."

"There I have to draw the line." He finger-combed her hair, bringing her mouth to his as he thrust again and again.

"I have to agree," she murmured against his lips, eyes wide, intimate as they watched, touched, even talked, both completely into each other and the moment. "As much as I would love to take your picture right now, the last thing we need is someone hacking into my computer and finding naked photos of you."

She'd surprised him there. But then he should be used to the way she lobbed bombshells his way. "You want to take risqué pictures of me?"

"I beg your pardon? I had something more artistic in mind." She ground her hips against his as she continued to whisper her fantasy. "But yes, you would be totally, gloriously, naked."

He throbbed inside the satiny clasp of her body. While he couldn't imagine himself pulling some pretty-boy naked modeling session even for Kate, he absolutely enjoyed hearing her fantasize. "Artistic how?"

"You're a mesmerizing man. The way light plays across the cut of your muscles in your arms, the six-pack ridges. Everything about you is stark angles. And shadows. The things I see when I look in your eyes..."

"Enough." He kissed her hard to break off her words, uncomfortable with the turn her scenario had taken. To hell with giving over control. He rolled her to her back and she didn't protest.

In a flash, she hooked her legs around his waist and took charge of her pleasure—of theirs—all over again. And it was every bit as combustible as before. The glide of sweat-slicked skin against skin, the scent of her with him lingering in the air. He couldn't get enough of her. Even as they thrust toward completion, he knew the sex between them would always be thus.

And it hadn't brought them any closer to resolving their argument.

A week later, Kate snapped a photo of Jennifer lounging in a hammock strung between two palm trees. Jennifer tucked in one earbud for her new iPod, boy-band music drifting from the other loose earpiece.

Click. Click.

Kate had photos galore, much to Harold Hough's delight, although in his emails he kept pressing for one of the king. She could answer honestly that she hadn't seen him. The monarch was still in the hospital. She hadn't been allowed access.

Focusing on her favorite Canon camera and her job rather than her confusing relationship with Duarte, Kate swung the lens toward her next subject. Antonio straddled a paddleboard in the shallow tides with little

Kolby in front of him, both of them wearing wet suits for the cooler waters. *Click. Click.*

These photos would be her wedding gifts to Shannon and Tony. Some pictures she considered off-limits to Harold Hough, the *Intruder* and the public in general. During the past week, she'd found herself more protective of the images than even Duarte. These people had welcomed her into their lives and they trusted her to represent them fairly in the media. She'd learned there were some moral lines she refused to cross, even for her sister.

Lifting the camera, she went back to work on images for her gift to the bride and groom. Two large dogs loped in the surf, the king's trained Rhodesian Ridgebacks named Benito and Diablo. *Click.* The dogs might look scary but they were pussycats around the little boy.

A strange squeeze wrapped around Kate's heart as she took a close-up of the child and his soon-to-be dad in matching wet suits. The towheaded little boy sported white zinc oxide on his nose and a big grin on his face.

Lowering her camera, she wondered how Duarte would act with his children someday. He wasn't the lighthearted playmate sort like Tony, but she'd seen his gentle patience and understanding with Jennifer over the past week. Her heart went tight again.

Don't think.

Duarte wore jeans and a lightweight pullover, wind threading in off the ocean and playing with his hair the way she longed to. From a distance he may have appeared casual, lounging back against a tree. But through her lens, Kate saw the iPhone in his hand and he sure wasn't playing music. His brow furrowed, he seemed intent on business.

Their week together had been guarded to say the least. While the king stayed isolated in the hospital, they'd settled into an unspoken standoff, participating in five-star family dinners. Smiling at movie nights in the home theater. Sailing. Swimming. Even going to the gym with a stationary bike for her to work off all the meals while Duarte completed a martial arts workout looking like sex personified.

Most would have considered the week a dream vacation.

Except Duarte hadn't apologized for his autocratic move in bringing Jennifer to the island without consulting her. And she simply couldn't tell him never mind, it didn't matter. Because it *was* important.

Although, she didn't understand why she felt so compelled to make her point. They would be out of each other's lives in another two weeks or so when she took the photos of Tony and Shannon's wedding. She should just enjoy the sex and let the deeper issues float away like palmetto fronds on the waves.

And the sex was most definitely enjoyable.

While their days together might be tension packed, the nights were passion filled. In her bed or his, they never planned ahead but somehow found their way into each other's arms by midnight, staying together until sunrise.

Pictures. Right. She'd forgotten.

Click, click, click. She captured Duarte in photos just for her personal collection when she left the island. After all, she would probably need proof for herself that it all happened in the first place. Every moment here felt surreal, a dream life she'd never been meant to live.

She shifted the lens.

Shannon sat cross-legged on a beach blanket with

a basket, arranging a picnic lunch. "Okay, y'all," she drawled, nudging her glasses in place, "we have roasted turkey and cheese with apricot-fig chutney on a baguette, spinach salad with champagne vinaigrette, and fresh fruit tarts for dessert. And for Kolby…" She pulled out what appeared to be lunch meat rolled in tortillas. Her blonde ponytail swished in the wind as she called out to her son and future husband. *Click. Click.* "Caterpillars and snakes."

Jennifer swung a leg over the side of the hammock and toe-tapped it into motion, rocking gently. "Tortillas as snakes? You're a fun mom, Shannon."

The young mother placed the deli rollups on a Thomas the Tank Engine plate. "Anything to make mealtime an adventure rather than a battle."

Swiping moisture off the lens, Kate refocused on her sister. "This reminds me of home in the summer, with picnics by the shore."

Before life had turned vastly complicated.

Jennifer adjusted her pink polka-dot visor. "Except it's January. I could get used to no snow." Her younger sister glanced at Duarte leaning against the tree at her feet. "Why did you wanna live somewhere so different from here? This is perfect."

"Not that different." He looked over patiently, tucking away his iPhone in a waterproof backpack. "Living on Martha's Vineyard reminds me of the parts of home that meant most to me, the rocky shore, the sailboats."

Something in his voice told Kate by "home" he meant San Rinaldo, not this island. For Duarte growing up, the luxury here must have seemed a poor substitute for all he'd lost. The sun dimmed behind a cloud.

Slipping from the hammock to stand beside Duarte, Jennifer pulled out her earbud and wrapped the cord around the iPod. "And when your toes get too cold, you can simply visit one of your other resorts."

"Like your sister travels with her job."

Kate's finger twitched on the next shot.

Her sister scrunched her nose. "Yeah, but the post-cards aren't as fun anymore." Jennifer's face cleared. "I still have the one she sent me from an airport in Paris when she was on her way to somewhere else. I don't remember where, but the postcard has the Eiffel Tower on it. Cool, huh?"

"Very cool, Jennifer."

"Hey." Shannon smiled from the blanket. "Duarte and Kate can fly you to the Eiffel Tower in their family jet."

Kate gasped and bit her tongue hard to keep from snapping back while Jennifer chattered excitedly about the possibility of such a trip. Shannon had no way of knowing she'd raised Jennifer's hopes for nothing. Kate nearly staggered under the weight of her deception. The future Medina bride had no idea this whole engagement was a farce. Kate hadn't foreseen how many people would be affected—would be hurt—by this charade.

Including herself.

What a time to realize she didn't want this to end in two weeks. She wasn't sure what the future held, but how amazing it would have been to date Duarte for real, let a real relationship follow its course. Her thumb went to the engagement ring, turning the stone round and round. Her camera slid from her slack grip to thud against the sand.

Oh, God. She dropped to her knees and dusted the camera frantically. She didn't have the money to replace her equipment. She knew better than to get caught up in some fairy-tale life that included flights to Paris and inherited family jewels, for crying out loud. What was the matter with her?

A shadow stretched beside her a second before Duarte knelt near her, offering her lens cloth. "Need this?"

"Thank you." She felt so confused. He'd given her nothing more than himself this week, making his body delectably available to her increasing demands, but never letting her have a glimpse of the heart within.

How long could they play this sensual teasing game before they hurt too many people to count?

"You miss it," he said. "The travel with your old job, before *Intruder* days of star chasing."

Ah. The least of her troubles right now. But then, Duarte had no idea he'd touched her heart in a way she could never seem to penetrate his.

Wary of being overheard, she checked on the rest of their party and found they'd moved away from the blanket, involved in setting up an elaborate new sunshade tent for Kolby's lunch. She looked back at Duarte quickly.

"My sister needs continuity," she responded and evaded his question. "This is the only way I can earn a living that provides for her."

"Perhaps there are different ways to find continuity than living in one particular place."

Did the man learn nothing? There he went again, presuming to handle Jennifer's life for her. Frustration from the past week boiled to life again. "Spoken like a man who lives in hotels, a man scared of having a real home."

A real connection, damn it.

They stared at each other in a standoff that had become all too common over the past seven days. Except with her heart aching she wondered how she could simply indulge in heated, no-strings sex with him tonight when they had failed to find common ground in every other arena of their lives.

Swallowing back a lump in her throat, she stood. "I should go and upload these photos. My editor's expecting an update and I would hate to miss a deadline."

Duarte clasped her arm, his eyes broadcasting his intent to press her for more...when a Jeep roared in the distance, rumbling across the sandy beach toward them. As the vehicle drove closer, Javier Cortez came into sight behind the wheel. The four-wheel drive skidded to a stop, spewing sand from the tires.

The head of security grabbed the roll bar and swung to the ground. "Duarte, I wanted to tell you in person."

Shannon shot to her feet, gasping. "Is it their father? Is he...?"

Tony rushed up the shore, his board under one arm, his other hand holding tight to little Kolby. "Javier?"

Cortez held a hand up. "Calm down, everyone. It's good news that I thought you should hear face-to-face. The king has recovered enough to be released from the hospital. He will be home by the end of the day."

The weight on Kate's shoulders increased as she thought of fooling yet another person with the fake engagement. This time, they added an old man in frail health to the list of people who would be hurt. And right now, she worried less about how she would be able to forgive Duarte and more about how she would ever forgive herself.

Eleven

His father was home.

Duarte had been as stunned as everyone else by Enrique's surge of energy. But the old man made it clear. He wanted to meet Kate.

Guiding her down the hall toward the wing housing his father's quarters, Duarte kept his hand on her back to steer her through the winding corridors. He barely registered the familiar antique wooden benches tucked here, a strategic table and guard posted there, too pre-occupied with the introduction to come.

What the hell was up with the edginess? He'd planned this from the start, to bring her along to appease the old man. They'd made a business proposition. So why did the whole thing suddenly feel off?

Because they'd clearly gone from business to personal in the past week and that rocked him to the core. He wanted more. Over the past weeks, she'd surprised him in ways he never could have foreseen. Like how she'd left her camera behind for this meeting with the king.

She'd told him that she planned to limit her photos of the king to the old man's appearance at Tony's wedding. For that matter, Duarte had been surprised at how few pictures she opted to send to the *Intruder* overall. Since the world was getting a steady flow of photos, news outlets ran those and weren't searching as hard for others. The interest hadn't gone away, but Javier's security team back home wasn't peeling as many reporters off the fences.

Now, entering the monarch's private suites, Duarte tried to focus on the present. While the mansion sported a small fortune in works of art by Spanish masters, Enrique saved his Salvador Dali collection for himself, a trio of the surrealist's "soft watches" melting over landscapes.

The old guy had become more obsessed with history after his had been stolen from him.

Cradling his antique Breguet pocket watch, Enrique waited in his bed, sitting on top of the cover, wearing a heavy blue robe and years of worries. His father's two Rhodesian Ridgebacks lounged on the floor at the foot of the bed. Brown, leggy and large, the dogs provided protection as well as companionship. Kate leaned down to pet Benito, the dogs accepting her because she was with Duarte.

Frail and pasty, Enrique appeared to be sleeping. Then his eyes snapped open with a sharp gleam in his gaze.

"Father." Duarte kept his hand planted on the small of her back. "This is Kate."

Enrique tucked his watch into his robe pocket and stayed silent, his coal-dark eyes assessing Kate. Duarte slid his arm farther around her, bringing her closer to his side. "Father?"

Kate rested a hand on his softly and stepped forward, facing the old man head-on and bold as always. "I'm glad you're well enough to return home, sir."

Still, his father didn't speak and Duarte began to wonder if Enrique had taken a turn for the worse. Was his once-sharp mind now failing, as well?

Kate stepped closer, magnificent in her unfailing confidence. "Do you mind if I sit?"

Still staring intently, Enrique motioned to the leather armchair beside his bed.

Sinking onto the seat, Kate perched a bit more formally than normal, her legs tucked demurely to the side. But other than that, she showed no sign of nerves in meeting the deposed king.

She pointed toward the framed painting closest to his bed. "I've always been a fan of Dali's melting watch works."

"You've studied the Masters?"

"I took art history classes in college along with my journalism degree. I can't paint or draw to save my soul, but I like to think I capture natural art and tell a story with my lens."

"I've seen some of your earlier photographs in our security file on you. You have an artist's eye."

She didn't even wince over the background check, something his father appeared to have noticed, too.

Pushing against the mattress, Enrique sat up straighter. "You're not upset that I had you investigated?"

"I investigated your family. It only seems fair you should have the same freedom."

Enrique laughed, rumbly but genuine. "I like the way you think, Kate Harper." He lifted her hand and eyed the ring, thumbing the top of the ruby once before nodding. "A good fit."

With that succinct endorsement, his father leaned back on the pillow, his eyes sliding closed again.

That was it? Duarte had expected…something more. Digs for specifics on a wedding date. Hints for grandchildren. Even a crack at her profession, and that made him wonder if perhaps there'd been something to Javier's accusation that he'd chosen Kate to jab back at the old man, after all.

If so, the joke was soundly on Duarte, because seeing Kate reach out to his father stirred a deeper sense of family than Duarte had ever felt before. Watching her in this setting finally pounded home what had been going on for weeks without him even noticing. Kate was more a part of his world than he was. She was a seamless fit in a high-stress environment, a strong but calming influence on the people around her, an intelligent and quick-witted woman who knew her mind and took care of her own.

What a kick in the ass to realize Kate was right about his lack of commitment to even a house, much less a relationship. He'd always prided himself on being a man of decisive action, yet when it had come to Kate, he'd been living in limbo—granted, a sex-saturated limbo—but limbo all the same.

Time to take action. He had about two weeks until his brother's wedding and he needed to utilize every second to persuade Kate to stay in his life after the thirty-day deadline.

Whatever the cost.

Gasping, Kate bolted upright in her bed. Alone. Her heart pounding out of her chest, she searched the room for him…but no luck. She'd fallen asleep in his arms, slipping into a nightmare where she'd melted away like a Dali watch, sliding from the ledge of Duarte's resort on Martha's Vineyard.

Sliding away from him.

She scraped her hair back from her face, the sheets slithering over her bare skin. The scent of his aftershave clung to the linens as surely as he lingered in her memories. He'd been so intense, so thorough tonight.

Stretching, her arm bumped something on the pillow. She jolted back and switched on the Tiffany lamp. A wrapped present waited in the cradle left by the imprint of his head. She clamped a hand to her mouth at the flat twelve-by-twelve package, a maroon box with a gold bow and no card. Not that she needed a card to know. Receiving a gift was different from the jewels and clothes he'd given her as part of the public charade. This was a private moment.

Why hadn't he stayed to see her reaction? Could he be as unsure as she was about where and how to proceed next?

Her stomach churned with excitement and fear. Maybe she was working herself up for nothing. Wouldn't she feel foolish if the present turned out to be a new gown to wear to the wedding? Or some other accoutrement to play out their fake engagement?

Her heart squeezed tight at the memory of meeting Enrique, a delightful old man who took her at face value and reeled her right in. Guilt had niggled at her ever since deceiving him—a warm and wonderful father figure to a woman so sorely lacking in that department. She hated to think about all the lies yet to come.

But there was only one way to find out what the box held. She swept the gift from the pillow, heavier than she'd expected. Curiosity overcame her fear and she tore off the crisp gold bow, then the thick maroon paper. Lifting the lid from the box, she found...

A small framed black-and-white photo—oh, God, an Ansel Adams of a moonrise over icy mountain peaks. Her hand shook as her fingers hovered over the image. He'd remembered. Just one conversation about her favorite photographer and he'd committed it to memory, choosing this gift with her preferences in mind.

Yes, he'd overstepped in spiriting Jennifer away, but he was obviously trying to woo her. And not with something generic that could have been ordered for any interchangeable woman.

Kate set the gift aside reverently and swept the covers away. She had to find him, to thank him, to see if she was reading too much into one gift. She stepped into the closet—good heavens, Duarte and his family had closet space to spare. She grabbed for the first pair of jeans and a pullover. Dressing on her way out of the room, she scanned the sitting area for Duarte.

The balcony door stood open.

Different from the wrought-iron railing she'd seen on the other side of the house when she'd arrived, this terrace sported a waist-high, white stucco wall with potted cacti and hanging ferns. In her time on the island, she'd realized the house had four large wings of private quarters, one for the king and three for his sons. Here, wide stone steps led down toward the beach, yellow moon and stars reflecting off the dark stretch of ocean.

She scanned and didn't see anything other than rolling waves and a small cluster of palm trees. As she turned away, a squeak stopped her short. She pivoted back and peered closer into the dark.

Moonlight peeked through the clouds long enough to stream over a hammock strung between two towering trees. The ghostly white light reminded her of the gorgeous photograph he'd given her. Duarte lounged with one leg draped off the side, swinging slowly. She couldn't think of when she'd seen him so unguarded.

Hand dragging along the wall, she raced down the steps. A chilly breeze off the water lifted her hair, night temperature dipping. The squeak slowed and she realized he must have heard her.

As she neared, her eyes adjusted to the dark. Duarte wore the same silky ninja workout clothes as the night they'd met. Looking closer, she saw a hint of perspiration still clung to his brow. He must have gone to the home gym after she'd fallen asleep. She was increasingly realizing he channeled martial arts moments to vent pent-up frustration.

Breathless—from the sight of him more than the jog—she leaned against the palm tree. "Thank you for the gift."

"You're welcome," he said softly, extending an arm for her to join him on the hammock.

Almost afraid to hope he might be reaching out to her on an even deeper level, she took his hand.

"It's such a perfect choice," she said as she settled against his warmth, the hammock jolting, rocking, finally steadying. "An Ansel Adams gift? Very nice."

"Any Joe with a big bank balance could have done that."

"But not just any Joe would have remembered what I named my cat." She brushed a kiss along his bristly jaw. "I can't wait to find just the right place to hang it."

Back at her apartment? Every time she looked at it,

she would be reminded of him. The air grew heavier as she breathed in the salt-tinged wind.

His arm under her shoulders, he fit her closer against him. "I'm glad you're happy."

It was one thing to talk in the course of a day or even in the aftermath of sex, but cuddling quietly in the moonlight was somehow more…intimate.

Furthermore, was she happy? At the moment, yes. But so much rode on the outcome of this month. She still feared disappointing so many people with a failed engagement.

"You're not what I expected, you know." She traced the V-neckline of his jacket. "But then that's my fault. It was easier to paint you as the arrogant rich prince. You try so hard, even when you screw up."

"Such as bringing Jennifer here without asking you." His deep voice rumbled over her hair, his chin resting on her head.

"Bonus points for admitting you were wrong." She stroked her toes over his bare feet beside hers.

"I *am* sorry for not consulting you before bringing Jennifer to the island."

She shifted to look up at him. "Did that apology hurt coming up?"

"I beg your pardon?"

Laughing, she swatted his chest. "I bet you've never begged for anything in your life. You're too proud."

"You would be wrong," he said so softly she almost missed the words. Then he squeezed her hand lightly. "I would give you an Ansel Adams gallery if you wish."

"Thank you, truly." She stretched to kiss him, just a closemouthed moment to linger and languish in the rightness of touching him. "But no need to go overboard.

The clothes, private planes, guards—I have to admit to feeling a little overwhelmed."

"You? Overwhelmed?" He sounded genuinely surprised. "I've only known one woman as bold as you."

For the first time that she could recall, he'd offered up a piece of personal information about himself. Another sign that he was trying to make amends? Get closer?

Her heart pounded so hard she wondered if he could feel it against his side. Was there a hidden, lost love in his past? "Who was the other woman?" she asked carefully. "The one as bold as I am?"

His heart beat so hard she *could* feel it under her palm. She waited, wondering if she'd misread his slip. And how would she feel if he suddenly revealed he'd been in love with someone else?

Finally, he answered, "My mother."

Everything inside her went still. Her senses pulled tightly into the world around her. The pulsing of her blood through her veins synched with the tide's gush and retreat. The palms overhead rustled as heavily as Duarte's breaths.

Kate stroked his chest lightly. "I would like to hear more about her."

"I would like to tell you…Carlos and I used to talk about her, verifying that our memories weren't becoming faulty with time. It's so easy for some moments to overtake others."

"The little things can be special."

"Actually, I'm talking about the bigger events." He paused, his neck moving against her in a long swallow. "Like the night she died."

She held her breath, terrified of saying something wrong. She'd covered dangerous and tragic situations in her job, back in the beginning, but she'd been seeing it all through a lens, as an observer. Her heart had ached for those suffering, but it was nothing compared to the wrenching pain of envisioning Duarte as a young boy living out one of those events.

"Kate? The fierce way my mother protected us reminds me of how you take care of Jennifer. I know you would lay down your life for her."

And he was right. But dear God, no woman should ever have to pay the price his mother had to look after her children. She closed her eyes to hold back the burning tears as she listened to Duarte.

"That night when the rebels caught us..." His chest pumped harder. "Carlos whispered for me to cover Antonio and he would look after our mother. When you said you couldn't imagine me ever begging..." He cleared his throat and continued, "I begged for my mother's life. I begged, but they shot her anyway. They shot Carlos because he tried to protect her..."

His voice cracked.

Her throat closed up with emotions, and now it wasn't a matter of searching for the right words because she couldn't speak at all. He'd planted an image so heartbreaking into her mind, it shattered her ability to reason. She just held him tighter.

"Once our mother died," he continued, his slight accent thickening with emotion, "time became a blur. I still can't remember how Antonio and I got away unscathed. Later I was told more of our father's guards arrived. After we left San Rinaldo, we spent a while in Argentina until we were reunited with our father."

Shivering more from the picture he painted than the cool night wind, she pushed words up and out. "Who was there to console you?"

He waved her question aside. "Once my father

arrived, we stayed long enough to establish rumors we'd relocated there. Then we left."

His sparse retelling left holes in the story, but regardless, it sounded as if there hadn't been much time for him to grieve such a huge loss. And to see his oldest brother shot, as well? That hadn't appeared in any news reports about the Medina family. What other horrifying details had they managed to keep secret?

Shadows cast by the trees and clouds grew murkier, dangerous. "It's no wonder that your father became obsessed with security and keeping his sons safe."

"And yet, he risked trips to the mainland those first couple years we were here."

"Your father left the island?" Where was Duarte going with this revelation? She had no idea, but she did know he never did anything without a purpose.

And she'd been so hungry for a peek inside his heart and his past for clues as to what made this man tick. She would be glad for whatever he cared to share tonight.

"My father had developed a relationship with another woman," he said, his voice flat and unemotional, overly so.

What he said merged with what she knew from covering his family. "You're talking about your half sister's mother." Kate knew the details, like the age of Enrique's daughter. Eloisa had been born less than two years after the coup in San Rinaldo. That affair had to have been tough for three boys still grieving the loss of their mother. "How did they meet?"

"Carlos's recovery from his gunshot wounds was lengthy. Between our time in Argentina and relocating here, Carlos had a setback. Our father met a nurse at the hospital." The muscles in Duarte's chest contracted. "He found distraction from his grief."

So much more made sense, like why Duarte and his brothers had little contact with their father. "His relationship with the nurse created a rift between you and your father."

It was easy to empathize with either side—a devastated man seeking comfort for an immeasurable loss. A boy resentful that his father had sought that comfort during such a confusing time of grief.

"You probably wonder why I'm telling you this."

She weighed the risks and figured the time had come to step out on an emotional ledge. "We've been naked together. While being with you is amazing, I would like to think we have more going for us than that."

"You've mentioned my numerous short relationships."

She hated the pinch of jealousy. "Your point?"

"I've had sex, but I don't have much experience with building relationships. Not with my family. Not with women. I've been told I'm an emotionless bastard."

"Emotionless? Good God, Duarte," she exclaimed, shifting over him, hammock lurching much like her feelings, "you're anything but detached. You're one of the most intense people I've ever met. Sure you don't crack a bunch of jokes and get teary eyed at commercials, but I see how deeply you feel things."

He silenced her with a finger to her mouth. "You're misunderstanding. I'm telling you I want more than just your body."

Her stomach bumped against her heart. Could he really mean...

"But, Kate, I can't be sure I have the follow-through. Given my history, I'm a risk to say the least."

Hearing this proud man lay himself bare before her this way tugged at her heart, already tender from images of a hurting young boy. She thought of the considerate gift, left on her pillow rather than presented in person. Could he be every bit as unsettled by their relationship as she was? He acted so confident, so in control.

Unease whispered over her like the night wind blowing in off the ocean. He'd said a relationship with him was a risk and she was just beginning to realize how much she had to lose—a chance with Duarte, a chance at his heart.

So much had changed so fast for both of them. If he was every bit as confused and stunned by the feelings erupting between them, perhaps the best answer would be a careful approach.

"Duarte," she whispered against his mouth, "how about we take it one day at a time until Tony and Shannon's wedding?"

Shadows drifted through his eyes like a stark Ansel Adams landscape playing out across Duarte's face. Then he smiled, cupping her head to draw her mouth to his.

The breeze blew over her again, chilling her through as she thought of how he'd opened up to her, and wondering if in her fear she'd fallen short in giving him her trust.

They'd eaten an honest-to-goodness family dinner. Working his kinked neck from side to side, Duarte cradled his post-meal brandy in the music room. Well, it was more of a ballroom actually, with wooden floors stretching across and a coffered ceiling that added texture as well as sound control. Crystal chandeliers and sconces glowed.

And the gang was all here, except for Carlos, of course. But their numbers had grown all the same.

Shannon played the piano, her son seated beside her

with his feet swinging. Tony leaned against the Steinway Grand, eyes locked on his fiancée. His brother was one hundred percent a goner.

Sweet Jennifer sat cross-legged on the floor by the mammoth gold harp, petting Benito and Diablo, blessedly oblivious that she played with trained guard dogs while armed security flanked the door. What the hell had he brought Kate and her sister into?

Enrique reclined in a tapestry wingback chair, his feet on an ottoman. The bottle of oxygen tucked by a stained glass window reminded Duarte how very ill their father still was. Kate sat in the chair beside him, her foot tapping in time with the "Ragtime Waltz" that Shannon whipped through on the ivory keyboard.

Kate.

His eyes lingered on her. Her basic little black dress looked anything but basic on her curves he knew so intimately well. His gaze skated down her legs to her sky-high heels. If only they could stay in bed, this attempt at a relationship would be a piece of cake.

It had been tougher than he'd expected spilling his guts for her last night in the hammock, but that's what women wanted. Right? Yet somehow he'd missed the mark because still she held something back.

The last ragtime note faded, and Duarte joined in the applause.

Tony retrieved his drink from beside the music. "Hey, Kate, maybe you can persuade Duarte to play for us."

She turned toward him, surprise stamped on her face. "You play the piano?"

"Not well." Duarte lifted his drink in mocking toast to his brother. "Thanks, Tony. I won't be forgetting that. Keep it up and I'll tell them about your harp lessons."

Laughing lightly, Tony returned the air toast. Carlos

was the only one of them to catch on during music class. Tony had never been able to sit still long enough to practice. The teacher had told Duarte he played like a robot.

Great. Tally another vote for his inability to make an emotional commitment—even to a piece of music.

Enrique angled toward Kate. "Duarte might not have been the best musician, but my goal was simply to give my sons a taste of the arts so they received a well-rounded education. We may have been isolated, but I made sure they had top-notch tutors."

"Hmm." Kate nodded. "I don't see you as the sort of person who sits back and turns over control. So tell me, what did you teach them?"

"You are a good reporter."

"That's gracious of you to say." She winked at Enrique, as at ease with him as if she spoke with the mailman. "Considering who I work for."

"I taught my sons art history." Enrique continued on about his favorite Spanish masters.

Duarte swirled brandy in the snifter. Kate's jab at the *Intruder* surprised him. But then he'd seen her scruples show in the photos she chose. Would she have taken a job she didn't like just for Jennifer?

Of course she would.

His determination to win her over multiplied. He still had ten days left. His mind churned with plans to romance her between now and the wedding. Time to fly her to the Museum of Contemporary Photography in Chicago, to live out the pretend courtship they'd concocted.

She might not have understood that he was reaching out last night. But he could tap every last resource in the coming days up to the wedding to ensure she stayed.

His will strengthened, Duarte looked forward to his first step—a surprise trip this weekend to woo her with art in the museum she'd never visited. He savored the vision of another plane ride with her until—

Tony waved for everyone's attention. He hefted Kolby up and slid his other arm around Shannon's waist. "We have an announcement to make. Since our family is here, why not proceed with the wedding? Or rather we will as soon as Carlos arrives in the morning."

Enrique's pocket watch slipped from his hand. Duarte lunged and scooped it up just shy of the floor.

"We don't want to wait until the end of the month," Tony said, his eyes zipping to their father just long enough for Duarte to catch his fear that any delay could be too late for Enrique. "We want to get married this weekend."

Duarte's brandy turned bitter in his mouth. They'd moved the wedding up, cutting short everything he needed to do to ensure Kate remained his forever. He only had her promise of cooperation until Tony and Shannon tied the knot. And after the wedding, Kate would have no reason to stay.

She'd asked for a day at a time. And his time with Kate had just been cut abruptly short.

Twelve

"You may kiss your bride," declared the priest, vestments draping from his arms as he blessed the newlyweds at the chapel's altar.

Kate blinked back tears, raised her camera and *click, clicked.* She'd photographed weddings to earn extra money in college, but she'd never witnessed a more emotional, heartfelt union. Tony and Shannon had exchanged their vows in a white stone church with a mission bell over the front doors. Duarte had told her the quaint chapel was the only thing on the island built to resemble a part of their old life. It wasn't large, but big enough to accommodate everyone here—Enrique, the rest of the Medina family, the island staff. Kate realized she and Jennifer were the only outsiders. Shannon had no family or friends attending other than her son, and Kate felt a kinship with the woman who'd faced the world alone.

Until now.

Once the embracing couple finished their kiss, they faced the select crowd, their happiness glowing as tangibly as the candlelight from their nighttime service. As Beethoven's "Ode to Joy" swelled from the pipe organ, Tony swept up the little ring bearer. Kolby hooked his arms around his new father's neck with complete trust and the happy family started down the aisle, wedding party trailing them.

The Medina princess Eloisa served as maid of honor in an emerald empire-waist gown. Her bouquet of evergreens and pink tropical flowers from the island was clasped over the barely visible bump of her newly announced pregnancy. As she passed her husband seated by the king on the front pew, she smiled with unabashed love.

Duarte followed, leanly intense and breathtakingly handsome in his tuxedo. She never in a million years would have sought out a mega-rich prince, yet the more she learned about Duarte the man, the more she wanted to be with him. To hell with day-by-day. She wanted to extend this beyond their deadline. She wanted to take that risk.

And then Duarte moved past her, followed by Carlos—the brother she hadn't met yet—ending the bridal party. Kate lowered her Canon. Carlos's steps were painstakingly slow as he limped down the aisle. He clearly could have used a cane. Something about the proud tilt of his chin told her that he'd opted to stand up for his brother on his own steam.

This wounded family was breaking her heart.

She brought her camera back to her face and kept it there all the way outside into the moonlit night. A flamenco guitarist played beneath the palm trees strung with tiny white lights.

Sweeping the crowd with her lens, she snapped photos randomly for the album she planned to give to Tony and Shannon. She would upload the images and burn a disc for the couple, presenting her gift at the reception in case she didn't see the newlyweds again.

Although maybe, just maybe... A wary thread of hope, of excitement whispered through her.

She adjusted her focus on Jennifer, her sister's face animated as she took in the lights twinkling overhead in the trees. Love for her sister filled her. Jennifer wasn't a burden, but protecting her innocence was a responsibility Kate didn't take lightly.

A wide smile creased Jennifer's cheeks and she waved enthusiastically until Duarte stepped into the picture.

"Yes, Jennifer?" His voice carried on the ocean wind. "What can I do for you?"

"I don't need anything," Jennifer answered. "You do lots for everybody. I wanted to do something for you."

Jennifer extended her fist. Duarte's face creased with confusion.

"This is for you," Jennifer continued, dropping into his hand a beaded string of braided gold thread with a metal ring at one end, "since you're going to be my brother soon. I didn't think you would like a bracelet or a necklace like I make for Katie. But you drive a car, so I made you a key chain. Kolby's nanny got me the supplies. Do you like it?"

He held it up, ring dangling from his finger as he made a big show of admiring it. "It's very nice, Jennifer. Thank you. I will think of you whenever I use it."

"You're welcome, Artie—uh, I mean—"

"You can call me Artie," he said solemnly. "But only you. Okay?"

"Okay." Her smile lit her eyes as she rose up on her toes to give him a quick peck on the cheek before she raced across the sand toward the bridal party.

More than a little choked up, Kate swung the lens back to Duarte just as he pulled his keys from his pocket. Her breath hitched in her chest... He couldn't actually be planning to actually use it...

But, oh, my God, he attached the beaded gold braid alongside keys to his high-end cars and an island mansion. Thoughts winged back to that first night in Martha's Vineyard when they'd made up their mythical first date, complete with a vintage Jaguar and *cat*viar.

Her hands fell to her side, camera dangling from her clenched fist. Tears burned her eyes as she fell totally, irrevocably in love with Duarte Medina.

And she couldn't wait to tell him once they were alone together tonight.

The rest of the evening passed in a blur of happiness until before she knew it, Kate was waving to the departing newlyweds. Everything had been magical from the wedding to the reception in the ballroom with a harpist. She had almost hated to miss even a second when she'd slipped away to her computer to burn the disc. But she'd been rewarded for the effort when she pressed the DVD into Shannon's hand. They'd insisted they didn't want gifts, but every bride deserved a wedding album.

Kate arched on her toes to whisper in Duarte's ear. "I'm going upstairs to change. Join me soon? I have a special night planned that involves you, me and a tub full of bubbles."

"I'll be there before the bath fills."

The glint in his eyes spurred her to finish up her last bit of business all the faster.

In her room, she sat in front of the computer to dispense with this last obligation to Harold. Duarte had even given her the thumbs-up to select the wedding photos on her own. He trusted her...

Her computer fired up to the homepage and she logged on to the internet, eager to be done with this as quickly as possible so she could freshen up in a bubble bath and dig through the drawers of lingerie for just the right pieces. The news headlines popped onto the screen with thumbnail images. She frowned, looking closer in disbelief. Déjà vu hit her as she stared at the strangely familiar images.

Pictures of Tony and Shannon's wedding.

The same photos she'd loaded to make the disc, but hadn't yet sent to Harold.

Not just any photos, but *her* work all stored on this computer.

Confusion built as she clicked on article after article from different news outlets, all with photos she'd just taken tonight. How could this be? She flattened her hands to the computer that both Duarte and Javier had assured her only she and Duarte could access.

Had Javier turned on the family like his cousin? She quickly dismissed that possibility. Before she'd made that fateful trip to Martha's Vineyard, the *Intruder* had tried more than once to get the inside scoop from everyone in Duarte's employ. No luck there. Javier had stayed loyal. Which only left Duarte, and he'd made it clear from the start that he sought revenge for what she'd done to his family with her photo exposé.

Her heart shattering, she felt like such a fool. Duarte had wanted retribution and he had succeeded. He'd maintained total control of how his family appeared in the press. And he'd ensured she didn't profit a dime off her efforts.

She'd been so close to admitting she'd fallen in love with him. But she would be damned before she let him know just how deeply he'd wounded her.

Five more minutes and Duarte would finally have Kate alone. He didn't hear the bath running, but then if all went according to schedule, he would have her on an airplane soon.

Tony and Shannon's early wedding hadn't left him much time to expedite his plans to take Kate to the Chicago museum. But he'd pulled it together. A jet was waiting, fueled up and ready to wing them away from here.

All he needed was her okay on plans for Jennifer—he'd learned his lesson well on not usurping Kate when it came to her sister. Hopefully, after tonight he would have a larger role in her life, one where they shared responsibilities. He was determined to make his pitch in Chicago, to persuade her that they should extend their relationship beyond tonight, beyond the island.

Looking through the open doors, he saw her still sitting at the desk in her room in front of her computer, not in the tub but every bit as alluring to him even with her clothes on. So many times they'd gone over her pictures together before she had sent them. She'd been careful about giving him a chance to veto photographs even though more often than not she nixed a picture first. He didn't even feel the need to look over her shoulder now.

He trusted her. What a novel feeling that almost had

him reeling on his feet. He turned away to gather his thoughts, bracing a hand on his four-poster bed.

Fast on the heels of one thought came another. He more than trusted her. He'd been mesmerized by the woman who'd stood toe-to-toe with him from the start. Someone he could envision by his side for life.

He'd known he wanted her with him long-term, but how had he missed the final piece of the puzzle? That he loved her.

The sense of being watched crawled up his spine and he turned around to find Kate standing in his open doorway. And she didn't look happy.

Pale, she stood barefoot, still wearing the midnight-blue dress with Medina sapphires and diamonds.

He straightened, alarms clanging in his brain. "What's wrong?"

Blinking back the shine of tears and disbelief in her eyes, she braced herself against the door frame. "You sold me out. You released my photos of the wedding to the press."

What the hell? He started toward her, then stopped short at the fury in her eyes. "Kate, I have no idea what you're talking about."

"Is that how you want to play this? Fine, then." She dropped her hands from the doorway, her fists shaking at her side. "I started to send the wedding photos, only to find they had already been released to every other media outlet. My big scoop stolen from me." She snapped her fingers. "That fast. You're the one who gave me that computer, totally secure you assured me. You were very specific about the fact that only you and I had access. What else am I supposed to think? If there's another explanation, please tell me."

Every word from her mouth pierced through him

like bullets, riddling him with disillusionment, pain, and hell, yes, anger. He may have decided he trusted her, but clearly that feeling wasn't returned.

"You seem to have everything figured out."

"You're not even going to deny it? You've had this planned from the start, your revenge on me for the story I broke exposing your family." Her composure brittle, she still stood her ground. "I was such a fool to trust you, to let myself care—"

Her throat moved with a long swallow as his plans crumbled around him. She'd clearly made up her mind about him. It was one thing if she had concerns or reservations, but for her to blatantly question his honor. She could ask for explanations all night long. Pride kept his mouth sealed shut.

Face tipped, she met his gaze without flinching. "I knew you were ruthless, but I never even saw this coming."

Was that a hint of hurt, a glint of regret in her watery blue eyes? If so, she had a damned strange way of showing it.

"You climbed onto my balcony to steal a picture." He tapped one of her earrings quickly before she could back away. "Sounds like we're a perfect, ruthless match."

She pulled off both earrings and slapped them into his palm. Her chin quivered for the first time and fool that he was, he couldn't bring himself to wound her further.

He pivoted away, hard and fast, earrings cutting into his fist. "There's a plane fueled up and ready on the runway. I'll send instructions to the pilot to take you and Jennifer back to Boston."

Watching her reflection in the mirror, he caught his last glimpse of Kate as she slipped the ruby engagement ring from her finger, placed it on his dresser and walked out of his life as barefoot as she'd entered.

Strapped into the private plane, Kate stared out the window at the fading view of the island lights. The shades would come down soon and the magical place would vanish like some Spanish Brigadoon.

Within an hour of her fight with Duarte, she and Jennifer were airborne as he'd promised. How could she have been so completely duped by him? From the second she'd found the internet explosion, she'd hoped he would explain how wrong she'd been. Even with the evidence barking that he'd set her up from the start, Kate had hoped he would reassure her of his love and come up with an explanation for the mysteriously leaked photos…

She didn't pretend to understand him. But then, he'd refused to explain himself, refused to give her even the satisfaction of knowing why he would choose this means for his revenge.

Jennifer sniffled beside her, a Kleenex wadded in her hand. "Why can't we stay at the island?"

Most of all, she hated the hurt she'd brought to her sister. How could plans to provide a better life for Jennifer have gone so wrong? "I have to work, honey. How about you just try to get some sleep. It's been an exhausting day."

They'd come a long way from the excitement of preparing for the wedding. She'd had such high hopes a few short hours ago.

"Why did you break up? If you're married to Duarte, you won't have to work anymore." She tore the wadded tissue then clumped it together again.

"It isn't that simple." Nothing about her time with Duarte had been simple.

"Then why did you get engaged?"

As hurt and angry as she felt, she couldn't put the entire blame on Duarte. She'd played her own part, going in with eyes wide-open, deceiving her sister and so many other good people. She deserved all the guilt Jennifer threw her way. "People change their minds, and it's good if that can happen before the couple walks down the aisle."

"But you love him, right?"

Unshed tears burned her eyes, tears that had been building since she'd stared at that computer. She didn't understand why he'd given her the Ansel Adams. Why he'd indulged her sister in a private moment with the key chain, never knowing Kate had been watching the whole time. Kate couldn't explain any of the moments he'd been so thoughtful and warm, appearing to share a piece of himself with her. But she understood the missing photographs hadn't sent themselves.

Her heart hurt so damn much.

Her sister thrust a fresh Kleenex into her hands. "Katie, I'm sorry. I didn't mean it." Jennifer hugged her hard. "You shouldn't marry him for me. You should only marry him if he loves you, like in Cinderella and Beauty and the Beast, except Duarte's not a beast. He just scowls a lot. But I think it's because he's unhappy."

"Jennifer." Kate eased back, clasping her sister's hand and searching for the right words to make her understand without hurting her more. "He doesn't love me. Okay? It's that simple, and I'm really sorry you got so attached to all the pampering and the people."

Most of all, the people.

"You're my family." Jennifer squeezed their clasped

hands. "We stick together. I don't need any spa stuff. I can paint my own fingernails."

The hovering tears welled over and down her cheeks. She didn't deserve such a dear sister. "We'll go shopping together for different colors."

"Blue," Jennifer said, her smile wide, her eyes concerned, "I want blue fingernails."

"It's a deal."

Jennifer hugged her a fast final time and reclined back in her seat, asleep before the steward came through to close the window shades. With a simple request for blue nail polish, Jennifer had given Kate a refresher course on the important things in life. Like her values. If she expected to be a true role model for her sister, she needed to reorganize her priorities. Jennifer deserved a better sister than someone who crept around on ledges to steal a private moment from someone's life.

Even if it meant hanging up her camera for good.

Thirteen

"Didn't you forget something?" Enrique asked from his bed.

His father's question stopped Duarte in his tracks halfway to the door. "And what would that be?" He pivoted toward Enrique, the old king perched on his comforter with his breakfast tray. "You asked me to bring your morning coffee and churros from the kitchen. If something's wrong you'll need to take that up with the chef."

"You forgot to bring your fiancée."

Was Enrique losing his memory? Duarte had already told him about the broken engagement when he'd asked for the tray in the first place. Concern for his dad's health momentarily pushed Duarte's mood aside. "She and I broke things off. I told you already. Don't you remember?"

His father pointed a sterling silver coffee spoon at

him. "I remember perfectly well the load of bull you fed me about going your separate ways. I think you screwed up, and you let her go."

He hadn't *let* her go. Kate had walked out on him, more like *stormed* away, actually. And even though he had a pretty good idea who'd stolen her photos and sold them to other outlets, that didn't change the way she'd believed the worst of him.

Not that he intended to let the individual who'd broken into her computer and taken her work get away with it. Since she had only used the computer for work while on the island, he would bet money her editor had had his IT department hack her account during communications about prior photos. Then Harold Hough had probably sold the pictures to other outlets for personal profit. The Medina computers had top-notch security, but no cyber system was completely immune to attack.

By the end of today, Javier and his team would hopefully have proof. Then Duarte would quietly make sure Harold Hough never took advantage of Kate again. While that wouldn't heal the hole in his heart over losing her, he couldn't ignore the need to protect her. More than his own hurt at losing her, he felt her losses so damn much. He hated the idea that she'd lost her big payday and was right back in a difficult situation with her sister's care.

"Well?" his father pressed.

Duarte dropped into a chair beside his father's bed with four posters as large as tree trunks. "Sorry to disappoint you." Best to come clean with the whole mess so his father wouldn't keep pestering him to chase after Kate. "We were never really engaged in the first place."

"And you think I didn't know that?" His father eyed him over the rim of his bone china coffee cup.

"Then why did you let me bring her here?" Maybe he could have been saved the stabbing pain over losing Kate.

Except that would have meant giving up these past weeks with her, and he couldn't bring himself to wish away their time together.

Enrique replaced his cup on the carved teak tray. "I was curious about the woman who enticed you to play such an elaborate charade."

"Has your curiosity been satisfied?"

"Does it matter?" His father broke a cakey churros stick in half and dipped it in his coffee. "You've disappointed me by letting her leave."

"I'm not five years old. I do not need your approval." And he did not have to sit here and take this off his dad just because Enrique was sick. Duarte gripped the arms of the chair and started to rise.

"Since you are grieving, I will forgive your rudeness. I understand the pain of losing a loved one."

Duarte reeled from his father's direct jab. He'd had enough of the old man's games. If he wanted a reconciliation, this was a weird way to go about it. "Strange thing about *my* grief, I don't feel the least bit compelled to jump in bed with another woman right now."

Flinching, Enrique nodded curtly. "Fair enough. I will give you that shot." Then his eyes narrowed with a sharpness that no illness could dull. "Interesting though that you do not deny loving Kate Harper."

Denying it wouldn't serve any purpose. "She has made her choice. She believes I betrayed her and there's no convincing her otherwise."

"It does not appear to me that you tried very hard to change her mind." Enrique fished in the pocket of his robe and pulled out his watch, chain jingling. "Pride can cost a man too much. I did not believe my advisers who told me my government would be overthrown, that I should take my family and leave. I was too proud. I considered myself, my rule, invincible and I waited too long."

Enrique's thumb swept over the glass faceplate on the antique timepiece, his eyes taking on a faraway look the deeper he waded into the past. "Your mother paid the price for my hubris. I may not have grieved for her in a manner that meets your approval, but never doubt for a minute that I loved her deeply."

His father's gaze cleared and he looked at Duarte, giving his son a rare peek inside the man he'd been, how much he'd lost.

"*Mi hijo,* my son," his father continued, "I have spent a lot of years replaying those days in my mind, thinking how I could have done things differently. It is easy to torment yourself with how life could be by changing just one moment." Gold chain between two fingers, he dangled the pocket watch. "But over time, I've come to realize our lives cannot be condensed into a single second. Rather we are the sum of all the choices we make along the way."

The Dali slippery-watch artwork spoke to him from the walls in a way he'd never imagined. Lost time had haunted his father more than Duarte had ever guessed. During all those art lessons his father had overseen, Enrique had been trying to share things about himself he'd been too wounded to put into words.

"Your Kate made a mistake in believing you would betray her. Are *you* going to let your whole life boil down to this moment where you make the mistake of letting your pride keep you from going after her?"

He'd always considered himself a man of action, yet he'd stumbled here when it counted most with Kate. Whether he'd held back out of pride or some holdover pain from losing his mother, he didn't know. But as he stared at the second hand *tick, tick, ticking* away on his watch, he *did* know he couldn't let Kate slip out of his life without a fight.

And now that he'd jump-started his mind out of limbo, he knew just the way to take care of Harold Hough and let Kate know how much faith he had in her. But first, he had barely enough time to extend his father an olive branch that was long overdue.

"Thank you, *mi padre.*" He clenched the old man's hand, grateful for the gift of a second chance.

January winds bitterly cold in Boston, Kate anchored her scarf, picking her way down the snowy sidewalk— toward the redbrick building that housed the *Global Intruder.* Not an overly large place, the *Intruder* head- quarters conducted most of its business online. She'd dreamed of a more auspicious retirement when the time came to hang up her media credentials.

But she didn't doubt her decision for a minute.

If she spent the rest of her life taking family portraits for tourists, then so be it. She had found a day facility for Jennifer, but her sister would be living with her. Hesitating at the front steps, Kate rubbed the braided charm that now hung on her camera case, the anklet she'd worn for luck not so long ago.

At least she would have her integrity, if not Duarte. She squeezed her eyes closed against the dull throbbing pain that hadn't eased one bit in spite of two nights spent soaking her pillow with tears.

A well-tuned car hummed in the distance, louder as it neared. She hopped farther onto the sidewalk to avoid a possible wave of sludge. How long had she stood on the curb of the one-way street?

She glanced over her shoulder just as a vintage Jaguar with tinted windows pulled alongside her. Her heart kicked up a notch as she wondered could it possibly be... A *red* vintage Jaguar, like the one Duarte had told her that he owned when they planned out their faux first date.

The driver's side door swept open and Duarte stepped out into the swirl of snowflakes. Long-legged, lean and every bit as darkly handsome as she remembered, he studied her over the roof of the car. She couldn't see his eyes behind the sunglasses, but his shoulders were braced with a determination she recognized well.

While she didn't know how to reconcile her heart to what he'd done with the photos, she couldn't stifle the joy she felt over seeing him here. Without question, he'd come for her. She hoped her weak knees would man-up before she did something crazy like walk right back into his arms.

Securing her camera bag on her shoulder, she walked closer to the car, appreciating the barrier between them. "Why are you here?"

"Because this is where you are. Jennifer told me."

"Not for much longer." She clutched her bag, too weary to give him a hard time for calling her sister. Jennifer missed "Artie" no matter what a brave face she put on. "I'm quitting my job at the *Intruder*."

"Why don't you hold off on that for a few minutes and take a ride with me first?" He peered over his sunglasses.

"You may not have noticed, but we're starting to attract a crowd."

Jolting, she looked around. Cars were slowing with rubberneckers, pedestrians who would normally hurry to get in out of the cold were staring curiously at the man who looked just like...

Heaven help her, they were celebrities.

Kate yanked open the passenger-side door. "Let's go."

Leaping into the low-slung vehicle, she clicked the seat belt into place, securing her into the pristinely restored Jag just as he slid the car into drive.

And didn't Duarte have a way of dragging her into his world when she least expected it? Sweeping snow from her coat, she cursed her weak knees, but she couldn't regret ditching the gathering throng. Funny how a red Jag drew attention. A Medina man beside it didn't hurt, either.

He dropped a large envelope onto her lap.

"What's this?" She thumbed the edge of what appeared to be a stack of papers.

"Documents transferring ownership of the *Global Intruder* to you."

Shock sparked through her, as blinding as the morning sun through the windshield.

"I don't understand." And she couldn't accept it if he offered it out of some sense of guilt over what he'd done to her. She thrust the papers back toward him. "No, thank you. I can't be bought."

Not anymore.

"That's not my intent at all." He guided the sports car effortlessly over the ice along narrow historic roads. "You lost out on the payment for your end of the bargain for the wedding photos. You even left behind the other pictures you took that the public hasn't seen. Why did you do that?"

"Why did you buy the *Intruder* for me?"

"You have a voice and honor I respect," he answered without hesitation. "I know you'll bring humanity to the stories you cover."

"You want me to work for you?"

"You're not listening." Pausing at a stoplight, he turned to face her and pulled off his sunglasses. Dark shadows of sleeplessness marked beneath his eyes much like the weariness on her face. "The *Intruder* is yours regardless. But it is my hope that you'll accept my apology for not clearing the air the minute you came into my room after the wedding."

The magnetism of his deep onyx eyes drew her even when she guarded her heart. Much longer alone with him and she would cave to the wary hope spiraling through her like smoke from the chimneys.

"All right." She hugged the papers to her chest like a protective shield, wondering how Duarte had managed this all so fast. But then he was a man of decisive action when he chose to be. "I accept the apology and the *Intruder*. You're off the hook. You can leave with a clear conscience."

He parked on the roadside within sight of Long Wharf and the Aquarium, the tinted windows shielding them from view.

Turning toward her, he pulled off his gloves and cupped her shoulders in a gentle grip. "I don't want to leave. I want you. And not just today, but forever if you'll have me."

Just like that, he thought he could drive up and buy her off with a big—albeit amazing—gift? She looked away from his magnetic eyes. Think, she needed to think.

She stared at his key chain swaying in the ignition. She struggled to be reasonable, for Jennifer's sake. Her sister had been so crushed over the breakup, Kate needed to be completely certain before she invited Duarte back into her life. Jennifer had braided that key chain for Duarte with such hope and love...

She tapped the swaying braid attached to Duarte's keys. "You kept Jennifer's present."

Frowning, he hooked his arm on the steering wheel. "Of course I did. What of it?"

The way he hadn't even considered hiding or tossing aside Jennifer's gift opened Kate's eyes in a way nothing else had. Like someone had taken off the lens cap, she saw him, really saw him for the first time. And in that flash she saw so many things clearly.

"*You* didn't distribute my photos," she said, her voice soft. "You didn't try to lash out at me for revenge."

He stroked back her hair with lingering, delicious attention to her sensitive earlobe. "I did not betray you, but I understand how it could be difficult for you to trust me."

What she'd realized—after seeing the key chain, hearing him say the words, witnessing the honesty in his eyes—felt so damn good. The love she'd only just found took root and began to flourish again. "Thank you for being the calm, reasonable one here. I don't even know how to begin to apologize for assuming the worst of you."

What it must have taken for a proud man like Duarte to overlook her accusation and come for her anyway. Regret burned right alongside the joy until she promised herself to make it up to him.

"Kate, I realize your father hasn't given you much reason to have faith in men or trust a man will be there for you." His palm sought the small of her back, drawing her closer. "I want the chance, I want the *time* to help you put that behind you. Most of all, I just want *you*."

Gripping the lapels of his wool coat, she brushed her lips over his. "I have one question for you."

The hard muscles along his chest tensed, bracing. "Okay, I'm ready."

"Can we spend a lot of that time making love?"

"Absolutely." He slanted his mouth over hers, familiar, stirring, a man confident in the knowledge of exactly what turned his lover inside out.

Five breathless heartbeats later, Kate rested her forehead against his. "I can't believe you bought the *Intruder*."

"I had to figure out a way to fire Harold Hough."

"You fired Harold?" Thinking of her boss's threat to expose Jennifer to the harsh light of the media, Kate didn't bother holding back the downright glee at hearing he'd gotten his just deserts.

"Inside that envelope you'll also see some of the proof Javier put together showing how Hough is responsible for selling all those photos to other media outlets. He pocketed the money for himself. He accessed your computer through a virus he sent in an email. After a, uh, discussion with me, he decided it was prudent to step aside and avoid a lawsuit."

"Why didn't you tell me this the second we got in the car together?"

"It was nice having you decide to trust me on your own. Although if you hadn't, I would have still pulled the plug on Harold for what he did to you and our family."

Our family.

He'd said it without hesitation, and she couldn't miss the significance.

"I want you to help me house hunt."

Now *that* declaration surprised her. He spoke like a man ready to put down roots, a man coming to peace with his past.

"You're really ready to give up the cushy hotel living?"

"I was thinking of something on the outskirts of Boston, large and on the water. Big enough for you to move in when you're ready, Jennifer, too." His accent thickened as it always did when emotion tugged at him.

"I love you, Kate. While I'm willing to give you all the time you need, I don't need more time to be sure of that."

He reached into his pocket and pulled out her ruby-and-diamond engagement ring. "This is yours now. Even if you walk away, no other woman will wear it. It will always be waiting for you."

The beauty of his words, his whole grand gesture in coming here and presenting her with the *Intruder,* offering to buy a house calmed any reservations. She peeled off her glove and offered her hand without a second thought. He slid the ring back in place and she knew this time, it would stay there.

Duarte closed his hand around hers and rested it over his heart. "Did you notice the car?"

"Your vintage Jaguar…" How far they'd come since that night she'd scaled the outside of his resort.

"I told you I would pick you up in it for our first date. Do you remember where we would go?"

"The Museum of Contemporary Photography in Chicago." How could she forget?

"And before you can protest, remember you own the *Intruder* so you can give yourself at least twenty-four hours off to regroup. If it's okay with you, I would like Jennifer to meet us at the plane. And lastly, you can bring your cat. It's my plane, after all. And—"

"No more details." She covered his mouth with her hand playfully. "Yes, I trust you completely with my life, my sister, my heart."

"Thank you." His eyes closed for a moment, the sigh shuddering through him telling her just how much her rejection had wounded him. She vowed to show him how dear he'd become to her in such a short time, and could only imagine how much more he would mean to her in the coming years.

His eyes opened again and he pressed a tender kiss into her palm. "So what about that trip to Chicago? Are you ready to leave?"

She slipped her arms around his neck and her heart into her eyes. "Yes, I will go to Chicago with you and house hunt after we return. I will wear your ring, be your princess, your wife, your friend for the next thirty days, thirty years and beyond."

Epilogue

Wind whipped in off the harbor, slapping the green bathrobe around Kate's legs. Her cold toes curled inside her slippers as she stood on the balcony of Duarte's Martha's Vineyard resort.

The lighthouse swooped a dim beam through the cottony-thick fog, Klaxon wailing every twenty seconds and temporarily drowning out the sounds from an early Valentine's party on the first floor.

A hand clamped around her wrist. A strong hand. A *masculine* hand.

Grinning, Kate turned slowly. His fingers seared her freezing skin just over her newest braided bracelet made by her sister. A good luck charm to celebrate her engagement. And Kate certainly hoped to get lucky in about five more minutes.

Nestled against the warm wall of her fiancé's chest, she savored the crisp chest hair, defined muscles and musky perspiration. Oh, yeah, she was more than a little turned on. Kate stared her fill at the broad male torso an inch from her nose. A black martial arts jacket hung open, exposing darkly tanned skin and brown hair. Her fingers clenched in the silky fabric of his ninja workout clothes.

Kate looked up the strong column of *her* ninja's neck, the tensed line of his square jaw in need of a shave, peering into the same coal-black eyes she'd photographed many times.

"You're not a ninja," she teased.

"And you are not much of an acrobat." Prince Duarte Medina didn't smile. But he winked.

The restrained strength of his calloused fingers sparked a welcomed shiver of awareness along her chilled skin.

"We should go back inside before you freeze out here."

"The moonlight on the water is just so beautiful." She leaned into the warmth of his chest, now plenty toasty thanks to the heat he generated with just a glance her way. "Let's stay for just another minute."

There hadn't been many seconds spent standing still over the past couple weeks. After returning from Chicago, they'd gone by the island to visit his father. Seated around the dinner table, Enrique had announced he intended to go to a mainland hospital for further assessment. A hospital in *Florida*.

If she'd put her mind to it, she probably could have guessed the Medina island was off the coast of St. Augustine, Florida, given the weather. And while the island sported a mix of English, Spanish and even a little French...her journalistic instincts said the place carried an American influence. But admitting that to herself then would have been more knowledge than she was comfortable having.

Knowledge that had far-reaching safety implications for the Medinas.

And now that she was a de facto Medina by engagement, she had a whole new perspective on the PR angle. No doubt, handling publicity for the Medina family would be a full-time job. She had retooled the *Global Intruder* into *Global Communications*.

Arching up, she kissed her fiancé, who also happened to be the proud new owner of a sprawling Boston mansion on the water, a forever home with room for Jennifer and any future little princes and princesses. "I love you, Duarte Medina."

"And I love you." He swept her up, sporting real strength to go with those ninja workout clothes. Strength and honor to count on for life.

* * * * *

*Look for Carlos's story,
coming soon from Desire™.*

PASSIONATE AND DRAMATIC

2 stories in each book – only **£5.30!**

My wish list for next month's titles...

In stores from 16th December 2011:

☐ Have Baby, Need Billionaire – Maureen Child

& The Boss's Baby Affair – Tessa Radley

☐ His Heir, Her Honour – Catherine Mann

& Meddling with a Millionaire – Cat Schield

☐ Seducing His Opposition – Katherine Garbera

& Secret Nights at Nine Oaks – Amy J. Fetzer

☐ Texas-Sized Temptation – Sara Orwig

& Star of His Heart – Brenda Jackson

Available at WHSmith, Tesco, Asda, Eason, Amazon and Apple

Just can't wait?

Visit us Online

You can buy our books online a month before they hit the shops! **www.millsandboon.co.uk**

1211/51

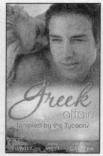

IMAGINED WORLDS

Paul Andersen
and Deborah Cadbury

'

Paul Andersen produced the original series of *Imagined Worlds* programmes in 1982 for BBC 2. A graduate in zoology he began working in television at ITV as a researcher in children's programmes. At the BBC he has worked as a producer on *Tomorrow's World*, *Open Secret* and *Horizon*.

Deborah Cadbury joined the BBC in 1978 as a psychology graduate, researching current affairs, music and arts and religious programmes. She moved to the science department in 1979 to work on *Tomorrow's World* and *Horizon*. Recently, she has produced *Q.E.D.*, *Inside Information*, the second series of *Imagined Worlds*, and *Doctor's Dilemmas*.

IMAGINED WORLDS

WORLDS

STORIES OF SCIENTIFIC DISCOVERY

PAUL ANDERSEN & DEBORAH CADBURY

ARIEL BOOKS

BRITISH BROADCASTING CORPORATION

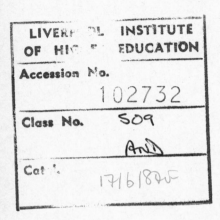
Published by the British Broadcasting Corporation
35 Marylebone High Street, London W1M 4AA

First published 1985
© Paul Andersen and Deborah Cadbury 1985

Typeset by Phoenix Photosetting, Chatham
Printed in England by Mackays of Chatham Ltd, Kent

ISBN 0 563 20386 2

Contents

Introduction

This century has experienced a growth in scientific knowledge unsurpassed by any other era in history. Space travel and test-tube babies have become accepted aspects of life in the developed world while esoteric concepts like Black Holes *and* DNA *have entered the popular language.*

The understanding of what lies behind these headline stories of our scientific advance is less well-known. Where do these ideas and discoveries come from? This book sets out to bring to life the often arcane world of research through nine personal stories of scientific endeavour. Each chapter gives an eminent scientist's own account of how his thinking has come to change the way we view the world.

Dr Tom Bower is acknowledged to be a leading pioneer in the field of child psychology – a subject which didn't exist when he started his career. Renowned especially for the subtlety of his experimental techniques, in The World of the Child *he describes his revolutionary new ideas about what an infant sees. His work has implications both for the parent-child relationship and for helping handicapped infants.*

In There's no Virtue in Timidity *Dr Tom Gold tells of how he and others produced a staggering new theory on the origin of the Universe just after the Second World War. Astronomy was just beginning to make use of the new technology of radio telescopes allowing man to look ever deeper into space. Cosmic rays, neutron stars and a trip to the Moon are all part of this story.*

Professor Patrick Wall and his colleagues have brought about a fundamental change in our understanding of pain. Their Gate Control theory finally dispelled the old Descartes model of pain which had survived for three hundred years. The Paradox of Pain *outlines ideas which have led to new treatments of pain, now in use in many pain clinics throughout the world.*

Molecular biology didn't exist as a subject when Sydney Brenner began his scientific career. From humble origins in South Africa he is now Director of the Medical Research Council Laboratory of Molecular Biology in Cambridge, the most prestigious scientific research institute in the world. He has been at the forefront of a pioneering group of scientists who put the nature of inheritance firmly on a biochemical footing. In The Entry of Molecular Biology *he describes the early discoveries which paved the way for the development of genetic engineering.*

Professor Abdus Salam began his path of discovery in Pakistan, learning the rudiments of science in a local school. His enthusiasm for mathematics, however, was to take him far beyond others, in East and West, to the frontiers of physics and a Nobel Prize. With a remarkable simplicity of ideas, he explains in Behind Reality *how everything in the Universe arises from a few principles and tackles the question, what is matter?*

For Dr Walter Gilbert it was the step from physics to biology that brought his fascinating story. In The Serpent in the Garden *he relates how the 1960s and '70s were the era of biological revolution. Genes, the chemicals of life, could now be seen and counted. Gilbert went ahead to find ways of adapting these messengers of life and so transformed the new concept of bioengineering. For this work he was awarded the Nobel Prize in 1980.*

Dr John Crook spent the same years observing the behaviour of animals. He describes in Programmed for Insight? *how the complex behaviour of social animals like baboons evolved and examines the pattern of sophisticated animal behaviour for clues as to why man behaves as he does.*

In The Day the Earth Moved *Dr Dan McKenzie reveals how he came to be enthralled by volcanoes and earthquakes. With all the confidence and determination of someone starting out in a subject he attacked the accepted view of the planet Earth and proposed a controversial new theory of how the continents came to be, which at the time made everyone in science stand still.*

Professor Roger Penrose has delved well beyond the Einsteinian Universe in his new mathematical view expressed in twistor theory. As he describes in Beyond Space-Time, *this branch of mathematics has stimulated a worldwide research programme, and extraordinary insights into the correspondence between mathematics and physics are now emerging.*

The aim of the BBC series was to discover how steps forward in science actually come about. By talking to scientists who have been the architects of contemporary thinking, it has been possible to uncover their imagined worlds which have paved the way to a new perspective. These pages capture this process of discovery, as each scientist recounts his story.

Finally, the authors would like to acknowledge the advice and support of David Paterson, the executive producer of Imagined Worlds, *John Lynch, who co-produced the first series of programmes, and Victoria Huxley and Hilary Duguid, the editors of this book.*

There was no science of child psychology twenty years ago when Tom Bower was a graduate at Cornell University, USA. So when he wanted to study infant development he was dispatched to the home economics department, since his interest was seen as closer to the study of cookery and housekeeping than anything else. No one considered it necessary to bring babies into the laboratory, after all what is the point in observing something which sleeps most of the time? In spite of this unscientific approach, theories – or in many cases, prejudices – of child behaviour abounded.

Bower married while still at university, and attempted to apply these theories to his own children. But none seemed to fit. Like any proud parent he would not accept that anything was wrong with his own children, so there had to be something wrong with the theories. And there was.

Today, thousands of experiments later, Bower has overturned many assumptions in child psychology, and all too frequently found himself at the centre of controversy. After receiving his Ph.D. from Cornell, he taught at Harvard and Stanford Universities. Since returning to Edinburgh in 1970, he and his colleagues built up what was the largest research centre for the study of infants in the world.

Over the years he has written on many aspects of development, especially the child's perceptual, social and intellectual skills. In this chapter are outlined the key experiments which have most influenced his thinking on perception, with descriptions of how an infant might see and understand the world.

Dr Tom Bower
Professor of Child Psychology,
University of Edinburgh

The World of the Child
Dr Tom Bower

Deborah Cadbury

When Tom Bower first studied child psychology he faced a vast array of conflicting theories. There was Freud, '. . . he saw infant development as some kind of X certificate movie. Babies were like his patients, seeing and understanding the world as an adult.' Then there was Piaget, '. . . he seemed to believe most babies were similar to his own, and constructed theories of intellectual development on the basis of his own children's behaviour.' Bowlby too was influential, '. . . he saw the new-born as an unsociable creature, but by some mysterious process of "attachment" to the mother the child becomes social.'

To Bower, most of the theories rested on shaky foundations. 'Before you can attempt to reach grand conclusions about intellectual, emotional or social behaviour you have to understand the starting point. What does a newly-born child perceive and understand of the world around it? Do the senses operate in the same way as an adult, with the child seeing what we see, hearing what we hear, smelling what we smell, or does it inhabit a very different world?' To find the answer, it was necessary to treat the infant as an object of scientific study, to experiment with and observe infants in the laboratory. But this was fraught with difficulties.

'When anyone – even a scientist – attempts "natural" observation on an infant, it rapidly becomes apparent that the baby sleeps most of the time. Not to be thwarted by this minor set-back, my senior tutor would carry on regardless, bringing sleeping babes into the labs to measure their abilities. It seemed quite obvious that the sleeping infants' abilities, just like a sleeping adult's, didn't amount to very much, but he wouldn't listen.' None the less, such unenlightened experiments went on in the early sixties. And that wasn't the only problem.

In the United States, where Bower was studying, ninety-five per cent of infants were born under anaesthesia. 'When I went to hospitals to look at new-born babies they seemed more like junkies waiting for their next fix . . . the drugs lasted a full six weeks, and during this time it was impossible to observe a baby's abilities.'

Even in the lab with a child that wasn't drugged, sleeping or crying, things weren't exactly straightforward. 'If you lay a baby, with rounded shoulders, rounded hips, on a flat table, it tends to roll. Babies don't like feeling unstable, so they put out their arms and then they are stuck, the arm holding them steady one way, and the elbow the other way. Unaware of this, experimenters might then try to observe the infants' motor and co-ordination skills. And of course, in this position, they don't have any.'

So Bower tried to obviate these problems by observing infants much more carefully in the laboratory, and working out how to put the question in a meaningful framework for them. The children were to dictate the pace and format of the experiments. He began with specifically human skills – reaching, grasping and imitating – trying to find out at what age they occur, and what perceptual abilities they require from the child.

'Reaching is very complex. Far from random thrashing about, it involves seeing and focusing on the object . . . controlling and slowing the arm movement on approach, opening the fingers and finally curling them around the desired object. According to standard texts this didn't happen until the baby was five months. So when mothers insisted that babies could perform this skill much earlier, I never believed them. It was part of my intellectual framework that babies only reach and grasp at five months, and I wouldn't listen to any alternative suggestion.' But one day his eyes were finally opened.

'It was when I went to visit my brother and his wife. While we were all talking there was a persistent noise of a bell ringing in the background, which everyone politely ignored. Eventually we asked about the noise and they said their new baby was banging a toy bell. I knew the baby was only seventeen days old, so it couldn't possibly be banging the bell. But I actually went and looked, and there was the child happily playing, bang, clang, bang, clang . . . innocently defying all the theories. It was quite shattering.' Bower finally accepted infants could reach within a few days of birth, and was instantly plunged into controversy, because very few other scientists accepted this.

The same argument arose with imitation. Here the mother sticks her tongue out, and if the child can imitate, it will do the same thing back, sticking its tongue out at the mother. Scientists thought that this was a reflex action, like a knee jerk, which a child couldn't perform until at least twelve months old.

'But when I repeated these experiments I was convinced imitation was much too complex a skill to be reflex. The child has to be able to focus on the mother's mouth, and notice the change in shape as her tongue comes out. This has to be mapped onto itself so he performs the same action, recognising that its mouth corresponds to hers, and its tongue to hers. The child has never looked in a mirror before, and yet it does exactly the same thing, transferring what it can see onto what it can feel in a very complicated way. This requires thought and intelligence. It may seem like a boring, tedious skill to us as adults, but not to babies. It is the acquisition of a new skill, and probably the first social gesture they make.' Unlike other scientists, Bower found infants could imitate within minutes of birth.

The more he studied these simple abilities, reaching and grasping, smiling and imitation, the more convinced he became that all of these skills are present in some form on the first day of life. Not only did this mean that the infant was much more capable than was previously assumed, but also it had major implications for our understanding of development.

Imitation: *Bower found a child can imitate its mother on the first day of life. 'It is mapping what it can see onto what it can feel in a very complicated way.'*

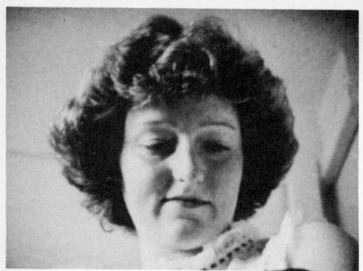

'For a nativist, a child at birth sees the world in the same way as an adult.' A face, for example, would appear to a baby exactly as it does for an adult. On the other hand, empiricists argue the child, 'is born into a world of complete chaos,' and a face would seem to it to be completely fragmented.

Philosophies of Development

Underlying all the different theories of development there were two main opposing philosophies: nativism and empiricism. 'For the nativist, from the moment of conception all our abilities and talents are fixed, determined by our genetic blueprint, and will never change. Therefore at birth the child sees the world in exactly the same way as an adult. Knowledge can be compared to the arrangement of our ribs; it is something we have because we are human. Skill can be compared with breathing; it is something that happens inevitably, given the structure of human brains and bodies. Development doesn't happen; it is simply a question of growth. This philosophy is expressed in many popular artefacts, for example in those nineteenth-century paintings where children are drawn as very small adults.'

By contrast, empiricists argue that 'the child is born into a world of complete chaos, where almost everything has to be learned. For them knowledge develops selectively as a result of experience. Skills develop as behaviour is modified through success, or failure, in coping with problems posed by the environment. Far from our visually ordered world, for the infant everything is fragmented . . . even its mother's face appears chaotic – the mouth, eyes and hair having no necessary connection.' Whereas the nativist might be pessimistic as far as the perfectibility of man is concerned, the empiricist argues that with the right environment, skills and knowledge will develop.

Given the experimental results on imitation, reaching and smiling on the first day of life, it was very tempting for Bower to conclude that the nativists' argument was closer to the truth. 'It seemed plausible that the new-born really does see what we see, smell what we smell, hear what we hear. Certainly its world couldn't be totally chaotic visually if it was capable of imitation – focusing on the mother's movement and mapping that onto its own body to repeat the same movement. But then I turned to experiments that showed the empiricist point of view could not be disregarded because it seemed that babies do learn, and change as they learn.'

The Reasons for Learning

The key method of development for an empiricist is conditioning, or learning, which is seen as the attachment of reward to the baby's activity. Classically, the baby is meant to show its learning ability by crying. It feels rewarded when mother or father attend to its needs, and learns to cry again when wanting the same result.

Initially, the baby is only interested in food, warmth or comfort and from these basic needs learning starts. Since it is not appropriate to analyse learning when the baby is hungry or crying, in the laboratory rather different set-ups are used.

'In a typical learning experiment we sit the child in front of an attractive toy, such as a mobile. The toy moves sometimes, depending on the child's activity. To stop the mobile it has to lower its foot, breaking a light beam and preventing it turning. To start it again, the child has to lift its foot out of the light beam. Most babies become interested in the stopping and starting of the mobile, analyse the situation quite quickly, and then notice that the movement is caused by something they've done with their feet. They play around with both feet, and rapidly realise what to do to make the event – the stopping and starting of the mobile – occur. . . .'

Up until now theorists assumed that the child was most interested in the event: the reinforcement or reward which encouraged the child to learn would be presumed in this case to be the mobile.

'Experimenters went to extraordinary lengths to understand what events make babies learn, designing different reinforcers, windmills, sweets, whole female persons popping out of boxes. But when I did these experiments I became convinced it wasn't the event, it was figuring out how to control what was going on that was important to the child. Learning itself was reinforcing, realising how to influence the outside world.'

By adjusting the experimental parameters Bower was able to test whether the child really was interested in its own control, rather than the event itself. 'If the child's control is made less than perfect, so that by moving its foot it doesn't always stop or start the mobile, then the child will carry on and on until it has solved the problem. Once it has the solution it can become bored quite rapidly, except occasionally to check that it still has power over the event.'

So rather than warmth, food or comfort being the critical factors to make babies learn, Bower reached the conclusion that the babies' own control of the outside world is more important. 'This seemed a surprising conclusion because "control" is a very abstract notion to attribute to young infants. And if something as abstract as "control" is critical for learning, possibly other aspects of child perception are regulated by equally intangible qualities?' Bower turned next to experiments on the child's intellectual development to see if these gave any insights into how the infant perceives its world.

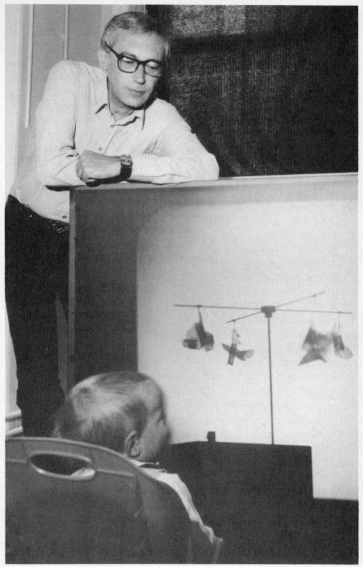

In a typical conditioning experiment the baby learns to control a mobile. By moving its foot down, the baby breaks a light beam which stops the mobile. To start it again the baby must lift up its foot.

The Clues from Intellectual Development

There comes a stage in development when infants pay less attention to sensory and perceptual information, and come to rely on
other kinds of information, such as that supplied by memory.
There is a progression away from dependence on immediate
sensory input, towards dependence on rules that combine
information coming in through the senses, with information from
memory. This progression is called by psychologists 'cognitive' or
intellectual development.

Piaget, one of the best-known writers on the child's intellectual
development, regarded the attainment of the 'object concept' as
crucial. How an infant perceives objects, and how he eventually
comes to understand objects as we do, requires the use of processes that will eventually generate mathematical reasoning and
logical thinking in adults. This is because initially babies have the
kind of problems with objects that adults would have difficulty
even envisaging.

'Suppose a baby sees its mother go out of the room and then
come back, how does the baby know that is the same mother? I
think it is possible that very young infants are not entirely certain
whether they have one mother, or lots of mothers. Consider an
even simpler case. Suppose an object, a toy, is moved from one
part of the room to another: how can the baby know that that is the
same toy? Is the baby able to say 'appearance' is more important
than 'place'? The toy has been in two places, that could mean
there are two of them.

'Problems can also arise with movement. We adults would be
extremely surprised if we saw an object zooming along a path of
movement, and suddenly turning into another object. Young
children are not. They have to work out that the same path of
movement doesn't imply the same object . . .' Tests had to be
designed which would show how the child is making judgements
about objects.

In a typical experiment, a colourful toy tracks along a particular
path and back again. At one point during this track, the object
disappears behind a screen. The baby is seated so that it can
follow the object, except of course when it is obscured by the
screen. The experimenter observes the child's eye movements. 'If
the infant knows that objects can go behind one another, it will
expect the object to reappear from the other side of the screen and
will show this by looking for the toy to reappear. A child which
doesn't yet realise the same object can disappear behind, or on top
of, or inside another object and then reappear, should perform

more randomly. When the object first disappears the child thinks it could have vanished, and should be quite surprised by its reappearance.'

Bower and his colleagues found that infants as young as eight weeks of age anticipate the reappearance of a toy that has vanished behind the screen. They do not look for the object after it emerges, rather the infants' eyes are at the exit point just as, or before, the object reappears. This seems to indicate anticipation of emergence rather than reaction to emergence.

Sceptics said the simplest possible explanation for this behaviour is the child's inability to arrest ongoing head movement. If the infant moves its head and eyes in pursuit of the object and is unable to stop its moving head, then it would appear to 'track' the object, due to a simple inability to control its own movement.

'So I tested this counter explanation by simply stopping the toy while it was still in view. The baby stopped moving its head with the object, and then looked to where the moving object ought to be, then back to the object, and again further along to where the moving object should be . . .

'Clearly the baby has perfect motor control in this situation, and looking backwards and forwards between where the object is, and where it ought to be if it were still tracking, illustrates the child is trying to solve a conceptual problem, rather than a motor problem. In this case, the child is possibly puzzling over whether it is the same toy once it has stopped – or whether a stopped object is different from a moving object.'

As the infant develops, it usually learns to transfer rules acquired in one situation to more complicated tasks. For instance, experiments can be designed to test whether the infant is aware of object movement, self movement, and the relationship between its point of view and the world.

'The child sits at a turntable on a chair which can also be moved around the table. We hide an attractive toy under one of three cups while the infant watches. Then the child is moved around the table and asked to find the toy. If the child fails in the task it is still egocentric. It has not appreciated its own movement in relation to the hidden object, and so it simply goes to the same position where it saw the object hidden, or it performs at random.' Bower found that most children over a year old could figure this out, and were well aware of the relationship between their own movement and object movement.

'After countless experiments on the acquisition of the object concept, I concluded that the child tries to solve complex conceptual problems from an early age. Is a stopped object the same as a moving object? Can a toy move and be transformed into something else at the same time? Can an object go inside, on top of, behind another object, and then reappear unchanged? To solve these problems, which the infant rapidly does, it is not preoccupied with the specific sensory qualities of objects – colours, textures, shapes and smells. I think the more intangible properties of the object – movement, place or position – are far more important in the child's thinking. The problem was how to analyse these intangible or abstract properties . . .'

The clues came several years later, when Bower was working on a different line of experimentation concerning social development and the concept of 'self'. He discovered, quite by surprise, that when a baby is trying to work out what is 'like me' and what is different, it can respond to very abstract patterns which are meaningless to adults.

The Clues from Social Development

Until recently it was thought that the infant was born non-social, interested only in basic needs such as food, liquid, warmth and comfort. This idea has come under attack in the last decade with psychologists arguing that the new-born shows many social behaviours. This is defined as behaviour which is produced in the presence of another human, and ceases when that human leaves the room. Imitation is a good example. It is specific to humans and is elicited by a child from the first day of life in the presence of its mother.

'To imitate, the infant has to be aware that it is human. You would hardly expect a response if you presented an infant with, say, an opening and closing matchbox – it can sense that no part of itself corresponds to a matchbox. But by imitating its mother, the infant is showing that it knows it has eyes, mouth, tongue, hands and that these parts correspond to the same part of the mother. It is the first stage in the affirmation of identity – evidence that the infant recognises that it is one of us.' But how does this become refined to a much clearer idea of self?

'The child starts life interested in anyone human. Around eight months it becomes much more interested in children than adults. Then it becomes interested in children of the same sex as itself, and finally it becomes most interested in itself. But how does the child recognise what is "like me"?' Again, imitation is the key.

In an experiment the infants are seated in front of two slides, one showing a little girl, and the other showing a little boy. Bower

Cross-dressing: *when infants are cross-dressed, boys in girls' clothes and vice versa, children can still correctly recognise their own sex by the movement, whereas adults are fooled.*

timed how long the infants looked at each slide, and found that the boys will look more at the slide of a little boy, and the girls prefer to look at the slide of the girl. Boy models were dressed in frilly dresses, and photographed holding a doll, girl models were dressed in dark-coloured dungarees, and pictured banging a drum. When shown pairs of slides like this, the infants wrongly identified what was 'like me', because they were using the cultural cues as the guide. The little boys seemed to look longer at the girls dressed as boys, and the girls looked more at the boys dressed as girls.

But this result changed totally once the infants were in movement. Film of the cross-dressed infants was substituted for slides. 'The infants were no longer fooled. Once they saw moving children, the boys looked more at the boys, even though dressed as girls. The girls looked more at girls, even though dressed as boys.' Clearly there was something about 'movement' which was more important than cultural cues for recognising what is similar or dissimilar to oneself.

'If movement is so critical, how can one analyse how a baby perceives movement? How can you give them a pure movement which doesn't have anything cultural – hair length, dresses, dolls, or anything else? It seemed an insoluble problem to provide a movement pattern with all other cues of gender or even "humanness" removed. But then I remembered a technique which Johansson had used in quite a different experiment, and thought that this could be adapted . . .'

Reflective tape is pinned on the child's joints, and the lights are dimmed, so all you can see is the movement of the joints. The child is then encouraged to run to and fro between toys, and will be filmed while playing this game. What appears on the film is a very abstract pattern of dots which reflect pure movement for each gender.

When adults see the resulting film, they can rarely spot the difference. But infants have no problem in identifying the gender of the babies who had modelled the display: twelve-month-old boy babies looked more at patterns generated by little boys, and the girls looked more at the pattern of dots generated by girl babies. 'These results seemed extraordinary because the infants were looking at patterns which were completely abstract, and yet they could recognise their own sex even better than when given full-scale colour film.'

When Bower and his colleagues analysed the film frame by frame it appeared there were subtle differences in the movement patterns. 'Some were to do with biology; girls' hips have a little more weight and they tend to swing more than the little boys' skinnier hips. Other differences were cultural: girls tended to take smaller steps, and bend from the knees, rather than from the hips, possibly because of wearing slightly more restrictive dresses.

'But the point is that these differences were very slight, undetectable by adults, and yet the infant could recognise what was like itself. Just as in the imitation experiment, they seemed to be aware of their own movement, their own "proprioception", and could map it onto something similar – even though they had never in their lives before seen a display like the one used.'

At last it seemed Bower had proof that infants can perceive and interpret purely abstract features of information, such as pure movement, rather than needing all the sensory cues – hair length, type of clothing, type of toy – to make a correct interpretation.

Everything was beginning to fit into place. The reaching and imitation experiments showed infants were certainly perceiving something – their world was not totally chaotic. The learning experiments had provided the vital clue by indicating that the child was not particularly preoccupied with the sensory event, the reinforcer, but more with establishing its own 'control' over it. This was borne out in the object concept work – again with the same result. The infant was not concerned with the colours, shapes, textures of the objects. It was the formal qualities – movement, position and place – which were influencing the child when figuring out the problems of objects.

'Then I thought these "formal" (rather than sensory) properties of stimulation were the kind of features which could be presented and interpreted by several senses. Consider, for example, the *movement* of the mother's breast to the infant. Movement might be sensed through smell or touch. *Symmetry* is another example of a formal property of stimulation. If straight ahead, a sound source produces exactly the same stimulation in each ear. If it is to the right, the right ear is stimulated earlier and more intensely than the left ear, and if to the left the opposite happens. Symmetry works equally well for detecting smells, vibration, or something visual.

'Like *movement* and *position*, *symmetry* of stimulation is independent of any sense – it is a formal property of stimulation. I thought maybe the child's perceptual world was keyed to perceive these formal properties, rather than respond to specific sensory details.' Bower needed to test this, and the experiment he devised has had considerable implications for treating handicapped children.

The Sonic Guide

'The experiment was very ambitious. Training infants to *transfer* perceptual information from sense to sense seemed almost impossible. What we needed was a device which could change formal properties that would normally be easily seen – symmetry, movement, place – into sounds. Once this was done the device could be used on sighted children in the dark, or on blind children to find out if they really could "see" through sound.' But what device could do this?

'I remembered echo-location devices that were used in the Second World War, and thought these could be taken as a model. The ideal would be a device which continuously irradiates the environment with ultrasound, and converts reflections from objects into audible sounds. I preferred ultrasound because it can generate echoes from smaller objects than audible sound.' After innumerable difficulties Bower and his colleagues eventually came up with the sonic guide.

This is worn as a headband by the child, and gives out an ultrasonic pulse. The pitch of the audible signal indicates the distance of the objects from which the echo came. High pitch means distant objects; low pitch, near ones. The amplitude of the signal codes for the size of the irradiated object (loud = large, soft = small). The texture of the object is given by the clarity of the signal. Since the guide is entirely man-made, humans have no evolutionary history for using the device. Bower was expecting slow, gradual learning to be necessary. So he was astounded by the results of the first session.

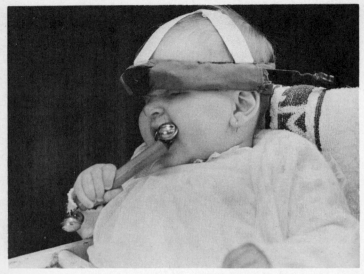

Sonic Guide: *in a unique experiment Bower designed the sonic guide and trained blind children to 'see' by using sound as a medium of perception.*

The child was a sixteen-week-old congenitally blind infant. A silent object was moved slowly to and from the infant's face. In the fourth presentation his eyes started to converge as the object approached, and diverged as the object moved away. In the seventh presentation he used his hands to reach out for the object. Then they tested him on objects moving to the right and the left. He tracked them with his head and eyes, and swiped at the objects.

His mother was sitting by, encouraging him. He slowly turned his head to remove her from the sound field, and then turned back to bring her in again. He did this several times, clearly with immense delight. It was almost as if for the first time he was playing peekaboo with his mother, and deriving terrific pleasure from the game. It was an extraordinary morning's work because the child seemed to interpret the abstract sound signals, and use them to perceive more about the world around him.

Bower has subsequently used the sonic guide on several congenitally blind infants of which the most remarkable was Vicki. She started using the guide when she was about seven months. At this stage she was learning to crawl, but she was frightened of moving far. After several sessions with the guide she became much freer. As her mother says, 'It taught her that there's more around her than she can actually touch. She knows wherever she walks she'll eventually come upon something solid . . .'

Bower considers, 'It's a terrifically brave thing for a blind child to take a step – after all, the child doesn't know if there is anything there. But now, at two years old, Vicki will walk up and down stairs, which is rare enough for a normal sighted child . . . the guide gives her a very complicated signal from the stairs, but she actually likes this complex input, and loves running up and down stairs. If the guide is removed, she has learned to stamp her own feet – sending out sound waves to get echoes back to orientate her. Her progress is slower, but still confident.'

Vicki, although blind, most certainly has a perceptual world. 'I think it's more like our visual world reduced to skeletal outlines . . . there is no colour in her world . . . in the normal course of development, a child whether blind or sighted will learn that sound is a property of objects. Doors slam, you can bang drums, cars make noises. This is to see sound as a property of objects, rather than as a medium of perception. In Vicki's case, she is using sound as a medium of perception because something which wouldn't normally make a sound, an open door, she can perceive because of the pattern of echoes provided by the guide. Equally, with a flight of steps, it would be very difficult for us to go up and down the stairs blindfold, but for Vicki this is easily done by interpreting the echoes.'

When Bower tried the guide on *older* children he found they couldn't benefit from the signals. Once a child has learned that sound is a property of objects, they seem to lose the ability to use it as a medium for perceiving objects, and the spaces between them. This has important implications for our understanding of perceptual development.

After many experiments using the sonic guide, Bower reached the conclusion that a new-born child is most sensitive to the formal properties of stimulation – such as symmetry, movement and position. What is more, the formal properties can indeed be transferred from sense to sense – visual information transferred to sound – and so on. Initially, it seems the senses are not specialised to pick up detailed sensory information – colour, shape, texture. During perceptual development the senses become 'educated' by experience.

'Our adult perceptual world is very sensory, full of colours, smells, sounds, and so on. But the new-born's world is not sensory, it is perceptual. The child picks up the formal characteristics associated with sensory experience, without picking up the sensory experiences themselves. For example, if a bunch of flowers is presented to us, we adults would see this as details of colour, texture, shape and smell. For the baby, these sensory qualities would be less important than the approach, the movement of the flowers towards him, which could be picked up through the eyes or nose. The change in stimulation produced by the approach of the object could be perceived through either sense.

'Likewise, when a child looks at a human being the child is initially picking up some quite abstract quality of humanity. It is not recognising each individual human being, it is picking up a very abstract formal characteristic, the basic outline common to all faces . . .'

'Now this is unlike the two previous philosophies. The nativist would say the child responds to colours, sounds and smells as we do. It can see the world in exactly the same way as adults. The empiricist would have the child in a "blooming, buzzing, confusion" with no order in the senses. But I think children are responding to the forms of stimulation, and the sense that gives the best form is the sense they will specialise in . . .'

The nearest we can get to understanding that world is to subject ourselves to a classic experiment in perception. Imagine three sensory events, a flash of light, a single sound, and a touch, each in a different place. What adults perceive is movement between the three locations. We do not see the movement, hear the movement, nor do we feel it. We 'perceive' it, an experience as close to pure perception as adults can attain, an experience probably like all the experiences of the new-born child. During development, a transition occurs from the child's very general perception, to a specific information coming through each educated sense.

'It is one of the paradoxes for developmental psychologists that the more we find out about the world of the child, the more we discover what we have lost. Perhaps the greatest loss is in the area of perception. Infants are much more open to the available information. They can perceive features which are meaningless to adults, such as, in Vicki's case, the sound pattern generated by the stairs or an open door. There is a pay-off for us of course. With our sophisticated senses we can use as little information as possible to get through the day. Perception is an effortless business . . . but perhaps we should be aware that there is a price to be paid for this: that there is more around us than our specialised senses can perceive.'

Dr Tom Gold FRS
Professor of Astronomy, Cornell University, New York

Tom Gold was born in Vienna in 1920, the son of a businessman. The family moved to Berlin in 1930, but when Hitler came to power in 1936 his father considered the political atmosphere too uncertain and began to look at how he could move the family to England. Tom continued his schooling in Switzerland and eventually joined his parents in England when he won a place at Trinity College, Cambridge, to study engineering in 1939.

World events then took a hold on his life. In the next few years he was interned as an alien, transported to Canada and then employed by the Admiralty to work on early radar theory. After the war he was to become famous as one of the exponents of the Steady State theory of the origin of the Universe. His work in proposing new and often provocative theories in astronomy and physics has continued ever since. The nature of collapsed neutron stars and what the surface of the Moon would be like for the astronauts to walk on are just two of these scientific stories.

In 1956 he left England, where he had been chief scientific assistant to the Astronomer Royal, to become Professor of Astronomy at Harvard University. Since 1959 he has been at Cornell University as Professor of Astronomy and Director of the Centre for Radiophysics and Space Research.

There's no Virtue in Timidity

Dr Tom Gold FRS

Paul Andersen

'I suppose my ambition was not directed towards any particular area. I was just going to do whatever interested me at the time. I was interested in some areas of biology, some areas of astronomy. I was deeply interested in science and I had read about these different areas and I was going to amble along, totally confident that if I touched any of these subjects it would be successful.'

Tom Gold is by nature someone who enjoys debate. He revels in the chance to puzzle over a piece of scientific theory and produce a fresh idea. His thinking will appear too opinionated to some scientists on occasion. For others the opportunity to discuss a new concept with him will be a source of stimulation. To a few he will be plain wrong.

However he may appear to others, he has always been fascinated with just asking questions, and providing new thoughts on how the Universe fits together. From his early schooldays he felt he knew how to achieve this. When at school in Switzerland he had had to learn Latin and English History for the Cambridge entrance examination. 'This was an interruption to my learning of the things that really interested me.' Once at Trinity College as an engineering student he soon realised what he wanted from science. 'Engineering didn't really interest me. I could not learn about concrete beams for ever and ever. I was interested in the pure scientific problems of physics and biology. I read a great deal about biology when I was supposed to be doing engineering. The other things I read were the fascinating books by Jeans and Eddington on the arguments within astronomy that were of considerable interest at that time.'

Sir James Jeans was one of the first great popularisers of science. During the 1930s, astronomy and the new discoveries of what seemed to be an infinite Universe of stars, nebulae and galaxies caught the imagination of both the scientists and the public. The issue of what were the origins of all these objects in space was constantly under discussion. Photographs using the

29

great telescopes of the day were revealing the size and distance of the nebulae from Earth. They showed how once you left the stars of our own Milky Way there was galaxy after galaxy each more distant from the Earth. The optical limit of these discoveries was about 250 million light years. Yet it seemed likely that the galaxies went beyond this great distance. These observations raised many questions about how the stars were formed and how the galaxies were created. But Tom Gold had to wait before he could join this scientific debate.

Before he had completed his first year at Cambridge he was arrested as an enemy alien. 'I think it was on 12 May, two days after the Germans invaded the Netherlands and Belgium. The police chief of the Cambridge area took it upon himself to intern all Austrian-born people. My parents, who were then in London, were all right but I was interned. It lasted nine months and was a pretty rough time. After being taken to a camp we were left to sleep on just a concrete floor. Then a few days later we were taken to Liverpool and shipped out to Canada. It was a dreadful time. I think there were eight hundred people in the cargo holds of the ship. As we left Liverpool harbour we heard that another ship of internees had just been sunk on the way to Australia. Everyone had been killed. So it was not the happiest of circumstances.'

However, there was one piece of good fortune for him on his journey. He met Hermann Bondi. 'It was the first evening of internment and he was the person I happened to sleep next to on the concrete floor. We became very good friends. He was already well known as an outstanding mathematics student, so after we had been in Canada a short while we started a sort of campus. There were a lot of intellectual people among us and we had a university where Bondi talked to me about physics, dynamics and so on. I learnt a great deal at that time, I must say.'

The irony of his position as an alien would be made that more pointed in the years to follow. After nine months the British government saw the error of its ways and brought all the Austrian internees back. Tom Gold returned to his studies at Cambridge. Bondi, who had finished his degree, was taken into the Admiralty signal establishment on his release. 'There we were, treated as enemy aliens for the best part of a year, and then we were released and almost immediately Bondi got into what was the most secret part of the Admiralty, designing radar. He was put into a section which was run by somebody by the name of Fred Hoyle. He got on very good terms with Fred Hoyle and suggested to him that I should join that same section. Although Hoyle didn't know me he very kindly exerted himself to have me join when I had finished my degree. Well, it took a few months for the security clearances but eventually I joined. Although none of us had any great experience in the field we learnt things very fast.'

This meeting of Bondi, Hoyle and Gold in the keen atmosphere of secret research was to forge a lasting relationship that would bring new theories on how the Universe was created. The three of them had taken accommodation in an old farmhouse close to an RAF bomber station. As the aircraft came lumbering home from their raids on occupied Europe they would dump any remaining bombs in a pit at the end of the runway as a safety precaution before landing. With the windows rattling to this occasional barrage, the three men would discuss cosmology.

'Hoyle was very insistent that in the evenings we talk about other things than radar, and in particular, astronomy. I had heard the conversation for months between Hoyle and Bondi, with Hoyle incessantly driving at the major questions of the time, asking, "Just explain to us what this observation of Hubble is all about, what does it mean?" Bondi would sit on the floor and solve the mathematical problems. He would sit cross-legged scribbling away with long equations and every now and then look up at us with some question and Hoyle would say, "Now, do this!" Bondi was a superb mathematician but he got so carried away that once I remember him asking, "Now tell me, at this point, do I multiply or divide by $10^{(49)}$?" '

Hubble's observation that the galaxies were moving away from each other led to the idea of the expanding Universe. But what did it expand from? In the 1940s the most popular view was a primordial Big Bang.

'Hubble had seen that the galaxies were moving apart from each other and of course that meant that one could extrapolate back in time and say that a certain time ago everything must have been very close together. But there were difficulties with this idea. It looked at the time as if the age of the Earth was older than the expansion time of the Universe, and therefore it would seem from that theory alone as if expansion from one point could not be true. You could not have the Earth with all its geology already in order and then have this monstrously tightly packed Universe all around it. So it seemed as if a different cosmological theory was needed from that point of view alone. On the other hand, Hubble had clearly seen that an expansion is taking place. We didn't doubt that. The question arose all the time. What is a better theory than the expansion from a point?'

The Steady State Theory

The questioning continued throughout the war years and on into 1946 when they were all back at Cambridge. 'Then one day I went along to Bondi in his room in Trinity – I remember this quite distinctly – and I said, "How would you like it if the Universe was in a steady state and if matter was being created as fast as it is moving apart, to make up for the moving apart all the time?" Bondi laughed a little and he said, "What do you mean, created from what?" I said, "Well, in the Big Bang what is matter created from? Suddenly a monstrous amount of matter appears from nowhere, so why should I not have a little bit created continuously all over the place?"

'And he said, "Well, yes, I suppose so. But there are so many constraints on a theory of cosmology like that, you know. Don't take yourself too seriously; we'll be able to shoot this down in short order." A few days later I brought it up again and said, "What's wrong with it? I have worked out approximately how much matter has to be created and it is an awfully small amount. It's only one hydrogen atom a year in a gigantic volume. You would never see it happening, so how could you tell?" Bondi seemed to take a little more kindly to it then and he said he would work out the mathematical consequences. He worked on the geometrical consequences of the idea of a steady state cosmology. I just insisted that the overriding rule was that any large area remained in the same configuration. The galaxies are moving apart and new ones would form from the newly created matter and they would drift away so that any region of space would always look the same on a statistical average.'

The Steady State Trio – Tom Gold (left), Hermann Bondi (centre) and Fred Hoyle at a conference in the 1950s.

When it was published in 1948 the Steady State theory put its authors at the centre of a furious debate. 'At first there was a period of complete incredulity on the part of the astronomers of the day. We were heavily ostracised by many people and within the Royal Astronomical Society we had a very hard time. We knew it was a shocking idea to suggest, but we had gone over everything very carefully including all the subsidiary arguments before we dared to announce it in public. You see it meant that one thought of infringing the conventionally believed laws of physics, namely that matter cannot be created out of nothing. But on the other hand when you consider what we really know about these laws, we were not infringing them. The rate at which this matter would have to appear is so slight that there would have been no way of directly observing it. We kept hammering away at the point that you have to suppose creation of one kind or another has happened. Why is it better to think of one big miracle rather than, as somebody else called it, thousands of little miracles? The laws of physics are all a miracle.'

At the time Tom Gold was employed at the world-renowned Cavendish Laboratory in Cambridge as a junior research worker on a project to build vacuum equipment for a new particle accelerator. He did not feel a great enthusiasm for this and had found that the zoology department had some more intriguing problems. At the same time as he was considering the idea of a new cosmology he spent time as a physicist working on the theory of how the human ear operates. But the publication of the Steady State theory was to catapult him from such relatively obscure science into a very public arena. The origin of the Universe was, and remains, a topic of intense interest. The steady state principle with its implicit notion of continuous creation attempted to bring as complete an understanding as possible to existing knowledge.

'The Steady State theory made a systematic study of what was otherwise merely a collection of facts. It made it systematic in saying it does or does not fit with this very simple viewpoint. And for that reason, if for no other, it was undoubtedly very valuable. It forced people to think out what the ongoing processes in the Universe would have to be. Could we begin to understand what was necessary if the stars were being constantly formed? And could we understand how the chemical elements which they possess are created out of some simple constituent like hydrogen in a continuing process?

'In the Big Bang it had been thought that all the elements could have been produced in that one gigantic moment of creation. But with the Steady State theory it became absolutely clear that there had to be some process of generating the distribution of the elements on a continual basis. If the stars and galaxies were being formed then somehow the variety of elements that we knew to exist on the stars had also to be made. And indeed Hoyle and others pursued this idea and it led to the wonderful discovery, perhaps one of the greatest this century, that indeed the elements are cooked up in the stars. Stars that we see and are familiar with.'

The Steady State theory made a lasting impact on astronomy and was referred to as the perfect cosmological solution during its heyday in the 1950s. It even prompted the biologist Francis Crick to ask himself what the perfect biological principle might be when he heard Tom Gold speaking about the idea. But as new observations were made by astronomers it became more difficult to fit them into this simple theory. Radio astronomy was rapidly becoming the source for extraordinary details of ever more distant galaxies and high-energy objects in our Universe. The discovery some years later of the microwave signal of heat radiation that could be extrapolated back to the Big Bang was for many scientists the final proof that Steady State was no longer tenable. But for Tom Gold it had always fulfilled a secondary purpose, of producing scientific debate. 'I think what it did for the thinking of the day was to expand the kind of thoughts that people were willing to have. Just the idea that the physical laws could be different to what had yet been noted, but without conflicting with any actual observations, was then carried into other areas.'

The Impact of Radio Astronomy

During the 1950s the great radio telescope at Jodrell Bank and the research being done at Cambridge had made Britain the centre of discovery in radio astronomy. 'Radio astronomy undoubtedly started as an outgrowth of the radar work during the war. Many people with great technical skills were available after the war and it was known from just the random pointing of radar antennae towards space that this research was worth pursuing. I remember myself, having no notion of this field, turning a receiver towards the Sun and noticing a great increase in the signal noise. At the time we did not know what it was caused by. But progress was very rapid and it soon became clear that we were seeing things that one could not in the first place see by optical means.'

It was clear that this was to be a major branch of science and the United States wanted to catch up on the British achievements. Tom Gold was invited to Harvard University in 1957 and two years

The giant radio telescope at Arecibo, Puerto Rico. Built in a natural hollow, the 1000-foot dish is the largest dish radio telescope in the world. By moving the antenna suspended above the dish, an image is brought into focus at the radio receivers. The pulsar in the Crab Nebula was discovered here.

later went to Cornell University to set up and direct a centre for radiophysics and space research. One of his ambitions had been to build an upward-looking antenna from a huge hole in the ground.

'I regarded that as the next step after Jodrell Bank. It would be a much larger instrument than Jodrell Bank, but one where the steerability was limited to the movement of the Earth. With the rotation of the Earth you get a certain slice of the sky that you can investigate. But with a much larger antenna you are able to investigate that part of the sky with a much more sensitive and efficient antenna.' This idea was to come to fruition in the great radio telescope at Arecibo in Puerto Rico. A natural bowl in the Earth's surface was turned into a 1000-foot-diameter dish antenna under the direction of his colleague Bill Gordon. It was operated as a part of the Cornell centre and would feature in many of the future discoveries in radio astronomy.

Determining what exactly these many and varied radio beacons in the Universe were was precisely the kind of problem Tom Gold enjoyed. The big radio sources were as much as 10,000 million light years away. 'Such enormously intense radio noise coming from different areas raised the question of what was really going on in these locations. What could have concentrated such a fierce amount of energy to produce these radio signals that could be received over such distances? It was a totally new set of phenomena in the Universe compared with what astronomers had previously seen. And we had no understanding of what processes were at work. When we first saw radio noise coming from the sky it was from the Sun. If you were to listen to it there was just a hissing sound. Eventually we began to recognise that the basis of all these emissions were highly energetic particles moving in a magnetic field.' Gold was to present new ideas on the role of magnetic fields in our solar system and in particular on the effect of solar flares and cosmic rays as they interacted with the Earth's magnetic field.

But the provocative explanation he gave for a new radio source was to be his next major challenge to orthodoxy. 'The discovery of the pulsars was announced in the spring of 1968, in February. I had a feeling that here was a wonderful puzzle. There were these extraordinary signals being received. What could be the astronomical object that gave rise to them? The announcement said that there were pulses of radio as quick as four pulses a second from one source – once a second from another source – with precisely regular timing from one pulse to the next. That of course was an enormous puzzle to everybody. What kind of an object could be doing that kind of pulsing? Various things were clear immediately.

'They must be very intense objects, because at any kind of distance at which stars are from us, the amount of energy that was coming out in these bursts must be enormous to reach over this distance. Then, secondly, they must be small because pulses that are only a small fraction of a second in duration can't have been radiated from a large volume of space. If a large area was responsible then the pulses would come at different times, because of the time it took for the light to travel across any great distance. This would have the effect of washing out any sharp pulses. It was clear that the intensity of the radiation coming out was just unbelievably great compared with anything that we had heard of before. So what was it? My view was immediately that this was the long-considered neutron star – that dense form of matter which had been discussed as a piece of theory but for which astronomers had thought they would never be able to find evidence.

'It had been known for quite a few years that ordinary stars like the Sun resist gravity or resist the infall of their matter towards their centre, as a result of the heat that they have inside. The enormous temperatures at the centre of a star mean that the individual atoms are rushing around and bumping into each other. This puffs up the star and holds all the matter apart. The source of this heat is the nuclear burning of the star's hydrogen and helium gases. Now heat, of course, gets lost to the outside and the fuel for this furnace eventually runs out. Once this happens the star must collapse. When you look at a star which has a mass ten times that of our Sun, which means it is a million times the mass of the Earth, then gravity is a very strong force. It is such that when a star that size cools down, it will collapse into an object that is a million million times denser than the Earth.

'One had thought that this was an interesting concept of the theoreticians that the matter in a star could form such an extremely dense object, a neutron star as we called it, but we had not thought how we might ever see one. But the two aspects that made it possible to detect the pulsars were the aspects that nobody had thought of in connection with a collapsed star. Namely, that when the star collapses to this high density, there are two things it will do in the extreme. First, it will spin up its rotation and produce an immensely powerful magnetic field. In the same way that a skater spins himself up by pulling the arms in, so as you take the mass of an ordinary star from far out and it collapses into this very dense package, it will whizz very fast. It can spin as much as a thousand times a second. Unimaginable to think that an object the size of the Sun could turn itself around a thousand times a second.

'The other thing that had been ignored was that the magnetic field of an ordinary star, very mild in strength, would become enormously strong in the collapse, so that one would end up with a fast spinning object with a very strong magnetic field sticking out of it. Now that can deliver energy to whatever molecules of gas there are in the surrounding space by whizzing it up. I found it easiest to think that just this whirling around of this immense magnetic field – our estimates were that it was a million million times stronger than the Earth's magnetic field – this whirling around at such high speed meant any charges or particles of gas would be speeded up to enormous velocities. And in these extreme conditions one can understand that very intense radiation would be produced.'

The Pulsar Controversy

With such a major observation as a pulsing beacon out there among the stars it was natural that the scientific community took a great deal of interest in discussing the implications. Popular reports of the pulsars had asked whether it could be a signal from outer space. Tom Gold took his explanation to the organisers of an international conference that was held in New York a few months after the announcement of the observation. They were no more willing to listen to his idea than that of little green men being the source. 'I asked for five minutes during this two-day conference to describe my notion of rotating neutron stars and why I thought this was the explanation for the pulsars. They thought this was such an absurd explanation that they did not grant me the five minutes.'

In a few months his theory would be accepted by everyone but, as with much of his work, it met with deep scepticism because it was at the time so revolutionary. Also Tom Gold now had a reputation for being something of an inconoclast. 'I think I see myself as being very independent. I don't take anything for granted but think through each problem afresh. If I read a textbook on some subject I am very critical all the time. In my mind I am saying, just tell me the bare facts, I don't care for your interpretation, I want to work it out for myself. Just to repeat the well-trodden path is not worthwhile, because to make progress one sometimes has to look at unconventional views to get a new interpretation and discover things.' At the time, the idea of neutron stars – and their even more esoteric counterpart, the black hole – were unknown concepts to many traditional astronomers. 'There was a controversy at the time. It was very difficult for many people to conceive that there could be things on the scale of whole stars that could collapse and pour out gigantic amounts of energy.

'I used to describe the idea for fun in terms of a cube of sugar. If you dropped a sugar cube's worth of neutron star material together with an ordinary sugar cube from the leaning tower of Pisa – as Galileo was supposed to have dropped different objects to see if they fall equally fast – these two cubes would fall almost exactly equally fast, except for the small effect of air resistance. But the difference would become obvious as soon as they hit the ground. The sugar cube would just lie in the grass but the neutron star cube would continue to fall right through the Earth, as if it wasn't there!' This extraordinary condition of matter – where a sugar cube's worth would weigh 1000 million tons – was to create real controversy among astronomers. It was difficult to conceive of matter being so compressed by the force of gravity that the atoms with their electrons are crushed into what is one giant nucleus, the electrons, which normally help matter to stay apart, having been crushed out of existence to leave mainly neutron particles jammed next to one another – the neutron star.

Nevertheless, confirmation of the theory was to come very soon once it was clear what to look for. 'When we thought it was rotating neutron stars that were making the pulsar signals, the next thing was to discuss where you would find more in the sky. Neutron stars we understood could most easily be set up as the imploding object of a great explosion in a star, a supernova, where a star runs out of fuel and part of the star collapses in whilst the rest is thrown outwards. Such a supernova will produce a brilliant bright light in the sky that lasts for a week or so. Now if neutron stars were one possible product of such stellar explosions we ought to look, we argued, in locations where supernovae had happened in the past in the hope of finding a pulsar there.'

Within a few months of the announcement of the rotating star hypothesis, a group of scientists in Australia led by Bernard Mills had found a pulsar. The difficulty was that their observation was not fully accepted as the site of a supernova which meant that doubts still existed about the theory. But Tom Gold did not have to look far for the final confirmation. His colleagues down at the great radio telescope in Puerto Rico were taking measurements on a very special object in the sky.

The Crab Nebula, some 6000 light years away from Earth. The first photograph of the irregular gas cloud was taken in 1899. A similar photograph taken today will show that the Crab Nebula is growing in size.

'The really great advance came when the observatory at Arecibo found the pulsar in the Crab Nebula, going at thirty times a second. This huge object in the sky was known to be the remains of a supernova explosion that had occurred in AD 1054. It had been a marvel to astronomers for many years and in particular they had questioned where the energy came from to produce the spectacular light it emitted. The puzzle of the Crab Nebula's energy source was then resolved. In fact I remember doing the calculation. Namely, what would have to be the power output from the Crab pulsar if it was to feed the whole of this shell of gas with enough energy to make it shine? I had predicted that the pulsars would be seen to very gradually slow down, because they are losing energy from their spin. It was a wonderful closure of this cycle of ideas to find that the Crab pulsar was losing energy from its spin at just the rate that was necessary to make the shell shine. The moment we'd got this far was in a way a new leaf in the explanation of events in the Universe. Now we had really seen that gravitational collapse to these very high densities is the power source to the high-energy phenomena.'

The Moon: A Dust-Covered Surface?

While he was working on the effects that strong magnetic fields had on the Universe another subject had attracted his attention – the Moon. It was to lead to a scientific controversy that became headline news. During the 1960s the steady exploration of space moved towards the goal of a lunar landing. Tom Gold had been looking at the surface of the Moon and its origins. He suggested that it must be dust covered. But how deep – an inch or a mile?

'I started to become interested in the Moon during the fifties. Initially it was a general interest in the photographs and trying to decide what could have been the cause of that distinctive surface. I came to the conclusion after a few years that the numerous craters were impact holes from large meteorites striking the planet, probably a common event in the life of the solar system. Also, most of these craters would have looked a great deal sharper when they were first made. So there must have been erosion of their surface edge for them to look the way they do now. Then I argued that if a lot of erosion had occurred I couldn't see how it could take place on any coarse pieces without wind and water. So I reasoned that the grains must be pretty finely divided since I could understand that some forces were sufficient to move tiny dust particles.'

During those early years of space flight the debate continued on what the surface of the Moon might be like. As the Russian Luna craft and the NASA Ranger missions sent back ever-improving pictures of the planet so the argument grew more intense. 'I was able to demonstrate with a colleague, Bruce Hapke at Cornell, that the reflection of sunlight from the Moon fitted precisely with a surface covered in a dark rock powder. I travelled to NASA with samples of such a powder, and said, "When you fly to the Moon this is what you will find on the surface. Here is a bottle of it, fake material, but this is what it will look like." Very few people believed me at the time. Some people's reply was that there might well be a tiny bit of dust. "About as thick as the dust on my piano," was one remark. My real fear was of dust blowing up from the rocket exhaust during the landing, and that it did. When the Surveyor craft landed it churned up about four inches of soft powder and people said, "Maybe it's five or six inches deep." Then eventually, when the astronauts drilled six feet down from the surface, they said, "Well, maybe it's ten feet deep."

A close-up photograph taken on the Moon's surface. The granular structure of the dry dusty material covering the planet can be distinguished. Apollo XI *made the first successful landing on the Moon in 1969 and brought back rock samples. Volcanic activity in the past is suggested by the appearance and content of some lunar samples. Today the Moon is a 'cold' planet, unchanged for millions of years.*

Man on the Moon. The variety of rock sizes and type is seen in this photograph from the Apollo mission. Rock samples from the highland regions were found on analysis to range from 3900 to 4200 million years in age. In contrast rock material from the lunar 'seas', the flat regions, have ages of 3200 to 3800 million years.

'NASA didn't go along with the dust theory at all. I had offered to set up a training facility for the astronauts to practise in a dusty environment to see if any of the equipment might go wrong. But they trained instead on lava terrain which was very hard. It happened that when they were on the Moon the life plugs on their suits did go wrong from dust clogging them.

'I think the idea for lava came about because scientists investigating the planet had the initial idea that similar geological processes took place to those on Earth. So when in the photographs they saw flat plains of a solid material, then they said it must be frozen lava, because that is the only thing we know that flows flat. And so the craters were the extinct sites of volcanoes.

'There was a very funny occasion when Fred Hoyle gave a talk on my behalf at the Royal Astronomical Society on the subject of the Moon's surface. He mentioned my discussion of meteor impacts as the cause of the craters and the then president of the society asked Fred how he could discuss the idea of meteors causing the craters when in his opinion any meteor hitting the Moon at speed would just bounce off. Some people laughed but

'. . . One that didn't bounce off . . .' The world's largest meteor crater in existence, the Baringer crater in northern Arizona, USA. It is about 185 metres deep and 1300 metres across.

not all. Years later I received a picture postcard of the great Baringer meteor crater in Arizona from Fred. On the back he had just written, "Here's one that didn't bounce off!"'

His idea for the origin of the Moon's surface was to become known around the world by specialists and the public alike. Largely because the notion of dust seemed an amusing alternative to green cheese, cartoons in newspapers showed future landings of spacecraft disappearing from sight. It was to show yet again how his ideas could produce furious debate. 'I emphasised that it was a rather crunchy material, that the dust would clog together and make a fairly stiff, cake-like substance. That indeed is what it is like. But people always confused the depth of deposit with the depth to which you would sink. This was one possibility, but not one that I took very seriously. I said I might have a little worry about it and that I would prefer to walk on a line like on a glacier. I was quite annoyed at times about it being said in the media, "Gold says there is a mile of dust and so everything will sink a mile out of sight." But reporters like to report things that are exciting and there was nothing I could do to stop them. And once it became the general belief, even scientists accosted me and said, "That's what you said, isn't it? Don't deny it."

'I think many people believe that I try and be deliberately perverse and think along lines that are different to what is normal. It's not true. I just try to think every problem through from the beginning. The urge to understand the world around me is what undoubtedly drives me. It is very rare for me just to relax. If I have nothing to do I find myself vigorously thinking. And I can do this for hours.'

The Earth: A Gas-Filled Planet?

The topic that has most recently occupied his mind is the origin of natural gas on Earth. Not unexpectedly his theory is radical and has brought strong condemnation from some geologists. 'What I am working on now is the origin of carbon on the planet and linked with that the outgassing of natural gas from the Earth. I am quite persuaded that natural gas is in large part derived from the deep interior of the Earth. This is important not only as a scientific discussion of the origins of the planet but also because of the practical considerations of finding new sources of energy.

'I am very keen now that one can solve the energy crises of the world by understanding how we can find the very large quantities of gas that I believe to be at reasonable depths. It is produced from the original carbon substance that exists from when the planet was formed out of carbon-rich meteoric material. This material, which is inside the Earth at depths of a few hundred kilometres, is constantly being cooked and methane gas released. Now, of course, this runs counter to the conventional view that oil, coal and gas all derive from biological material that has been pushed underground. What I am saying is that vastly more carbon has come to the surface of the Earth from inside than has been produced by the decay of plant material over the millennia.'

As with his earlier theories, the 'deep gas' hypothesis has brought Tom Gold into a long, and as yet unresolved, debate. Although the 'puzzles' have changed and some of his early ideas were incomplete answers he still pursues an independent line. 'I'm quite ready to brush aside what other people have done and to think again. This approach brought success in my earlier years, and has become established with me. It is the way in which I can proceed, in which I can make a contribution. Many other people can do very useful work in another way, I don't want to give the impression that my way is a universal recipe. But it takes all sorts to do science and it takes this outlook also. I am perfectly willing to put out new ideas and face the razzle, face the opposition. This deep gas theory has provoked a large amount of opposition. Perhaps there is one way in which I have aged because now I am much more careful to do my homework. Now, when I put out a new idea I have a reputation to defend, and I didn't when I was young.'

Professor Patrick D. Wall DM, FRCP
Director, Cerebral Functions Research Group,
University College, London

As a young medical student, Patrick Wall was concerned that although modern treatments of illness were usually quite effective, distressing symptoms such as pain were all too frequently ignored. Indeed, theoretically, the very question of what pain was had been forgotten over the centuries. The last new scientific model of pain was proposed in 1664 by Descartes. And his ideas survived for three hundred years, curiously intact in spite of their inapplicability to patients' suffering.

After completing his medical degree at Oxford University, Wall went to study in America, because 'this was the thing to do . . .' He worked for a while at Yale, and then moved to the University of Chicago. Here he met three scientists who were pioneers in the fields of neurophysiology and computers, McCulloch, Pitts and Lettvin. Together they failed to find evidence of existing theories of communication within the brain, and this laid the basis for seeking a new theoretical approach.

In the early fifties Wall was offered a post at the Massachusetts Institute of Technology, which was literally humming with new ideas and techniques. He met another associate professor, Ronald Melzack, and they began an exchange that eventually led to the publication of the Gate Control theory in 1965. The theory was to revolutionise our understanding of pain.

Wall returned to England in 1967 and continued his research at University College, London. He also founded the journal Pain *in the hope of bringing together clinical experience and scientific research. Although he has received many awards for his work, he feels the major reward is to be able to help patients and for this reason he regularly visits pain clinics in London to discuss cases. He has established a research centre in London and regularly collaborates with other groups of scientists and clinicians, particularly in Montreal, Jerusalem and Beirut.*

The Paradox of Pain
Professor Patrick D. Wall DM, FRCP

Deborah Cadbury

Patrick Wall's scientific career has always been rooted in clinical practice. Patients have provided the motivation for seeking out new ideas, and also been the ultimate test of them. Possibly because of this, he feels there really can be a serious conflict when a scientist faces a patient.

'The patient after all is reality. The scientist has in mind a model based on experiments or hypotheses. Then there is a process of fitting. Does this patient fit this model? Very frequently he doesn't and then you really face the conflict. Some scientists might be tempted to resolve it by neglecting part of the patient, ignoring some of the facts. Others might try to juggle with the facts, to persuade them to fit the model. But what I would try to do is to modify the model very honestly until it does seem to explain things . . . and then hopefully the ultimate test is to see if you can provide new therapies.' It was this approach which drew Patrick Wall into the puzzle of pain.

While studying medicine at Oxford, he came across patients with many different types of pain, from those caused by relatively minor injuries through to chronic debilitating pain. Yet quite apart from scientific theory, even conventional wisdom did not seem to fit some of these cases. It is, for example, widely believed that pain always results from injury, and that its severity is directly related to the extent of the physical damage. But many of Wall's patients did not bear out this simple relationship between pain and injury.

'There are circumstances which are terrifying and puzzling where there is severe pain and yet you can't discover anything wrong . . . we are unfortunately seeing many of these cases coming from motorbike accidents. Motorbike riders now wear helmets which do an excellent job of protecting the head, but leave the shoulders as the next thing to be hit and damaged . . .'

A network of nerves leave the spinal cord at the neck to supply the arms, but on impact these nerves can be totally ripped out of the cord and are impossible to replace. The patient has a paralysed arm which he cannot feel, and if touched there is no sensation. But what he can feel is a ghost or 'phantom' arm.

'The phantom doesn't exist but it feels more vividly real than the actual withered arm by his side . . . because of the phantom the patient will be absolutely convinced that there is intense pain in his missing or paralysed arm, although it lacks sensation. Now this is not madness, this is an error of machinery . . .'

For example, Barry Procter, a young man who had just such a nerve injury after a motorbike accident, says, 'About three weeks after the accident I was discharged from hospital – my arm was paralysed. Then I began to notice pain . . . a constant buzzing, stinging, crushing pain, a sort of burning sensation, and worse still I developed shooting pains – it's like bubbles exploding in your hands. You can't predict them, you can't concentrate, you can't even finish a sentence or hold things . . . it's strange that people can't see how bad the pain is . . . you expect them to be able to see my hand jumping about and pulsating, and of course they can't.'

But apart from cases like these of pain without injury, the reverse can also happen of no pain in spite of severe wounds. 'Almost everyone has experienced injuries which they only discovered later by accident. For example, when President Reagan was shot in 1981 he did not realise he had been hit. In the car driving away there was a discussion as to why he was feeling so sick . . . it was some time before the seriousness of his injury was recognised.'

In a now famous study which was undertaken during the Second World War, Beecher interviewed soldiers wounded in battle. To his amazement, when severely wounded men were carried from the battlefield, only one in three complained of sufficient pain to require morphine. Many even denied having pain from their extensive wounds, and expressed surprise that their injury did not hurt.

Innumerable incidents of this sort had been reported, and Wall and his colleagues wanted to clarify the facts. 'We went and interviewed 138 patients who were admitted to an emergency hospital with bad injuries, including fractures, dislocation, cuts and burns. Yet it turned out forty per cent of them had no pain at all at the time of the accident. All were fully aware of the seriousness of their injuries and the miserable consequences . . . one girl with her leg blown off said, "Who is going to marry me now?" Yet she was not in pain. There was evidently something about the circumstances which just didn't allow a flash of pain to be perceived for over a third of the patients.

'When President Reagan was shot in 1981 he did not realise he had been hit . . . it was some time before the seriousness of his injury was recognised.' His experience of injury without pain is not uncommon.

49

In the 1980 Derby, Henbit injured its right foreleg some several hundred yards before the finish. Yet the brave horse still went on to win the race, only afterwards showing signs of pain.

'It is tempting to explain bizarre situations like this – obvious injury with no pain – using words like shock. But when you think of it, what do you mean by shock? These people were not in shock in the sense of being unable to pay attention, unable to talk, unconscious or anything of that sort. Many of them were talking sensibly, fully aware of what had happened and the extent of their injury, and yet it did not hurt.' 'Shock' seemed to Wall a very inadequate description of what was occurring – and it certainly could not explain some other examples of injury without pain.

In some cultures there are rituals which would horrify a Western observer, and yet don't appear to cause any pain to the participants. In East Africa, for instance, people undergo an operation for chronic headaches where the scalp and underlying muscles are cut, exposing a large area of skull. The skull is then scraped by an expert while the patients sit calmly, quite secure in the expectation that this procedure will bring relief of their extreme pain. The patient does not seem to feel pain and yet is certainly not in shock. Nor are participants of religious or tribal initiation ceremonies, performed in many other cultures. These ceremonies appear agonising to us, but for the chosen celebrant it's quite the reverse: a state of exaltation.

Injury without pain is not only a human attribute. Animals can show the same facility. 'For example the horse Henbit, winning the 1980 Derby, fractured its right foreleg some three hundred yards before the end of the race, and yet ran absolutely perfectly, faster than the other horses, and only afterwards began to limp. Henbit was not acting like a clockwork mouse, it was responding to its training, its nature, the events of the moment, the excitement of the race. That excitement allows the animal to shift attention away from the injury . . . it is not at all a mechanical puppet being pulled along by strings. . . .' Only much later did the horse show its pain and agitation. In spite of the best veterinary care it raced only once again and came last.

The more Wall studied these anomalies, the more the puzzle increased. There was pain without injury, injury without pain, pain disproportional to injury, people unable to feel pain, cross-cultural differences. All these cases defied common sense, and as it turned out, they also defied the scientific theories.

Descartes' Theory of Pain

Any medical student in the fifties and sixties was literally soaked in Descartes' classical theory of pain and sensation, which had survived from the 1600s. 'This view was so deeply entrenched in

'Descartes' theory of pain as a straight-through pathway from the injury to the brain was so deeply entrenched in people's thinking that it has been presented to us as fact not theory.'

people's thinking that frequently it was presented as fact, not theory. It did, of course, have the advantage of being very simple.'

But for Wall at least, that was its only virtue, because it was somewhat limited in explaining the anomalies outlined above.

'Imagine an injury to the foot. Detecting nerve fibres will deliver the message about the injury to the spinal cord and then to the brain. The result is sensation. The person now becomes aware that his foot is in the fire and removes it to safety. The sensation of pain in this case has prevented a severe injury.'

For Wall this theory rested on two rather striking assumptions. 'The first is the idea of a straight-through channel from the skin to the brain with each pathway taking one message about one type of event. Descartes illuminated this idea by comparing pain to the bell-ringing mechanism in the church. A man pulls a rope at the bottom of the tower, and a bell rings in the belfry.' The psychological dimension of experience (bell ringing) is presumed to bear a one-to-one relationship with the physical dimension (pulling the rope).

'But you need only examine your own experience, or certainly examine other people's, to see there is something seriously wrong with this. What about the injured civilians who felt no pain? According to Descartes, once the injury occurs the fire-alarm system would go, and the pain would be perceived. But the patients were not first perceiving the pain and then cleverly suppressing it. The pain just didn't occur.'

Equally inexplicable were the people with phantom limb pain, or pain spreading unpredictably to other parts of their body. Here there is no injury, no pathology, so how could the fire-alarm system be triggering the pain? It seemed clear that there was not a one-to-one relationship between the psychological dimension of experience (the pain) and the physical dimension (the injury).

'Of course, some of these paradoxes had been known for centuries. But there was a common trick for explaining them.' This explanation resorted to the second assumption of the theory. This assumption, 'which Descartes was extremely insistent upon, was to see mind and body as two totally distinct entities . . . sensation was a two-stage process – first a body mechanism, and then the mind. This dualism is intuitively very appealing. When you and I have a pain, it feels as if there is an "event" which is somehow separated from "you", who are thinking about the event. Language enforces this double approach: "*I* have a *pain*" suggests that your "mind", "yourself", is quite separate from the trouble-some event, the "pain". Because we intuitively think in this sort of double system, it seems very reasonable to propose a model of this sort.' Furthermore, dualism provides a convenient explanation for the anomalies.

'Scientists would quite simply put the abnormality in the mind. It was believed that the mechanism, the fire-alarm system, worked, but the mind somehow mysteriously introduced these variables.' This 'trick' protected scientists for centuries from facing the real problems of the Descartes model.

In its twentieth-century form the basic assumptions were still intact, although there were refinements. It was thought, for example, that there were many types of nerve endings in the skin, each programmed to respond to a particular stimulus. Information was still relayed up a straight-through pathway into the spinal cord, and then there was thought to be a pain centre somewhere in the brain where the message was interpreted.

'But, of course, if you believe in the fire-alarm system then you would look experimentally for this sort of alarm, and having found fibres signalling the presence of injury people would not ask broader questions. Are there other factors involved? Do other signals intrude on the fire-alarm system? Scientists continued to design experiments which fitted the simple model because they only asked simple questions.'

The Massachusetts Institute of Technology

Wall, having finished his medical degree at Oxford, studied in America at Yale and Harvard, eventually reaching the Massachusetts Institute of Technology in Boston. 'Here in the 1950s there were very important discoveries being made. Shannon was working on information theory, Chomsky was working on speech, and breakthroughs were being made in electronics and theories of coding. But above all, people were dissatisfied with old ideas and there was questioning, constant questioning about methods of communication: in electronics, speech, or, in my case, the nervous system. How does one part of the nervous system communicate with the other? What are the rules? What are the codes? And of course there were a number of interesting analogies that we could turn to and these changed our way of thinking by making us ask wider questions and helping to break the classical mould.'

At the same time another quite different approach was suddenly made possible. The techniques of neurophysiology and neuroanatomy were developing and it became possible to examine the nervous system in more detail than ever before. Wall, at this stage, was working with a young Associate Professor called

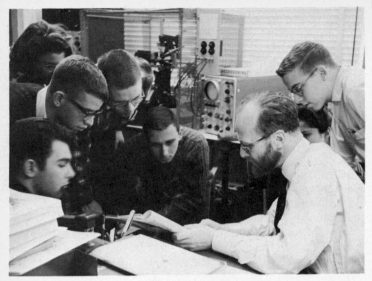

Professor Wall worked at MIT in the early 1960s. 'It was a very exciting atmosphere where people were dissatisfied with the old ideas and there was constant questioning . . .'

Ronald Melzack. 'We examined individual nerve fibres coming in from the periphery and there, so long as we only studied healthy nerve fibres, the Descartes model held. But as soon as we reached the central nervous system in the spinal cord the model collapsed. The real break came at that point.'

They found that injury messages coming in from peripheral nerve fibres were being passed on to specialised nerve cells in the spinal cord. These first receiving cells appeared to be influenced by other inputs which could modify the pain-producing message before it was transmitted further up the nervous system.

'The first influence we discovered was that other messages set off by innocuous events were coming in from the periphery and of course we all inevitably thought, what about all those funny things you do like rubbing, like scratching, like massage, like why you wave your hand about when you hurt yourself? We realised that even naturally, when faced with a small injury, one of the things you do is actually add more impulses. We looked for a reasonable explanation for this, and it turned out that these extra impulses tended to block the transmission of the injury-produced impulses.

'The second influence we found was that all those cells were under immensely powerful control from orders coming down from the brain. So, far from being a nice, reliable fire alarm, if you look at the first receiving cell in the central nervous system alone, the process was much more complicated.'

Wall and Melzack were very surprised by this finding. 'We had expected that at some stage the nervous system would become complex and controlled, but we did not expect that the message would become influenced as soon as the nerve impulses entered the spinal cord. This set in chain the endless process of going back and rethinking what you saw in a patient, or actually felt oneself, and then going back to the detailed model and trying to figure out what mechanisms might be involved. It was at least five years of very hard work. Quite apart from the technical problems of studying the nervous system in such detail, it was puzzling to see the classical model demolishing, and not knowing what to put in its place.'

The technical details of the nervous system were remarkable. 'To our astonishment we did not find specialised cells in the central nervous system each doing only one thing. Cells were evidently tuned into many different types of events. To make matters even more complicated, we found that when we added more than one stimulus at a time to a cell, the stimuli would interact. Some of them added to each other, causing excitations, and some of them subtracted, causing inhibitions. And this introduced us to the real puzzle, the real complexity.'

The Gate Control Theory

Wall and his colleagues eventually proposed the Gate Control theory in 1965. In very simplified form there are two important components in the spinal cord. Firstly there is the *substantia gelatinosa*, which consists of densely-packed cells extending the length of the spinal cord. These cells form part of the 'gate control' or threshold on incoming signals. They are influenced by messages coming in from the periphery, and by central controls, i.e. orders coming down from the brain.

The second part of the gate are the transmitting cells, known as T-cells. These are the first receiving cells of the central nervous system, but they are regulated by the *substantia gelatinosa* before passing on the message. The whole package is affected by the intensity of the stimulus, how different stimuli interact, excitations and inhibitions, the diameter of the nerve fibres between cells and, most important, the central controls from the brain. But if activity in the T-cells reaches a critical level then the message is fired up the central nervous system and pain will be perceived.

These physiological discoveries created problems for the Descartes model. This was partly because there was not a straight-through channel from the skin to the brain; impulses were changed as soon as they reached the spinal cord. But also mind and body were no longer separate. In the *substantia gelatinosa*, mental processes and incoming impulses act together to create sensation. The perceived sensation was no longer separate from the perceiver.

'We came to the conclusion that dualism really is a philosophical trap, and that in fact what you are thinking and what you are feeling are so intimately connected that it is actually not useful to separate mind and body in this sense. They really are acting as a unity.'

Quite apart from the Descartes model, other familiar notions were called into question. For instance the concept of a 'pain centre' in the brain was found to be rather inadequate to account for the complex sequence that leads to the perception of pain. They found that many parts of the brain were involved; the thalamus, the limbic system, the hypothalamus, the brain stem reticular formation, the parietal cortex and the frontal cortex were all implicated. The notion only makes sense if the whole brain is considered as a 'pain centre', which clearly wouldn't do.

Another popular misconception was that of variation in people's pain thresholds, which people use to account for the differences in pain experience. But Wall and his colleagues found that all people, regardless of sex, race or culture have a uniform 'sensation threshold' – the lowest stimulus intensity at which a sensation like touch, warmth, tingling, is first reported. The sensory apparatus is essentially similar in all people, in spite of the fact that people report those sensations differently.

One by one, both popular misconceptions and scientific theories were undermined by the new ideas. 'We knew this was going to be an intellectual crisis because we were attempting to replace a very simple straightforward theory with a much more complex one. That frequently generates antagonism, because it is much easier for people to hold onto the simple theory and continually park the exceptions on one side. We kept on pointing out that there were now more exceptions than rules, and that anyway, the detailed mechanism never fitted the rule.'

The whole experience was rather reminiscent of Kuhn's version of scientific breakthrough. 'If you can take a very complex subject and come out with a very simple statement, that is a winning and socially acceptable conclusion. If you take a socially acceptable simple idea and point out that it's too simple then you're in difficulty, and we were certainly in difficulty.

'The worst difficulties came from our scientific colleagues. "The Gate Control theory of pain: an unlikely hypothesis" was the title of one paper (Schmidt, 1972). Another scientist wrote, "I think therefore that one ought at this stage strongly to support Schmidt in his attempt to prevent the Gate Hypothesis from taking root in the field of neurology" (Iggo, 1972). Another writer added (Dykes, 1975), "In addition to its dubious veracity the theory is incomplete."

'The people on our side were the clinicians because they had been battling with the problem that the Descartes model and its descendants really didn't explain things, and they came more and more on our side when it turned out that this idea not only explained disease, but also provided new therapies which were a genuine benefit to patients.'

Implications of Gate Control

Until this time, the emphasis of treatment for chronic pain was on chemical or neurosurgical approaches. Both of these had their limitations. Chemically, ninety-nine per cent of these drugs come from only two families of compounds, the aspirins and the opiums. None of the available drugs affects pain alone so that as the dose rises and is repeated, unacceptable side-effects occur.

Surgery, too, had its limitations. Much ingenuity has gone into surgical techniques such as cutting selected peripheral nerves, or pathways in the central nervous system, and they can be very effective for short-term control. In the longer term, there can be problems with the pain recurring, or sometimes with unpleasant sensations appearing as a result of denervation.

But the Gate Control theory had a significant impact on treatment of pain, by broadening the conceptual framework within which the control of pain could be understood. 'The theory indicated that pain perception depended on two very important inputs, sensory input – other messages coming in from the periphery – and secondly psychological input.' It followed that if you could manipulate these two inputs, pain might be reduced.

'The first working test of the theory was electrical stimulation. We predicted that adding electric impulses should relieve pain in the same way as rubbing, stroking, massage, or adding any other sensory input.' Additional stimulation to peripheral nerves should help inhibit the T-cells which transmit the injury signals. Wall tried himself as a guinea-pig first. Electrodes were implanted on the skin and the current switched on. The sensation he felt was a buzzing, tingling feeling, which only became painful if the strength of stimulation was greatly increased. But when he tried this on patients with chronic pain, the result was remarkable. In many cases a brief period of stimulation, such as fifteen to twenty minutes, brought relief for many hours. Barry Procter showed a typical response.

He was given electrical stimulation using a portable device. Silicon electrodes were placed on his arm and connected to a pocket-sized, battery-operated stimulator, worn at the waist. The frequency and duration of the pulses were fixed, but he controlled the strength of the pulses himself until he felt a comfortable tingling in his arm. Barry reported, 'After having worn this for about twenty-four hours I got about sixty per cent relief from the pain . . . and actually it was a quite ecstatic feeling to be without the shooting pains, because you can't predict them . . . to know that when they came they weren't going to be half as severe . . . it was, as I say, ecstatic.'

Electrical stimulation has been used today on hundreds of thousands of patients, with machines made by more than forty different companies. The procedure is simple and free of side-effects and has come to be used as an initial treatment for many chronic pain syndromes.

For Wall this success was very rewarding. Developing a new theory 'involves a whole spectrum of pleasures, starting with the enormous kick you get the moment you first recognise something is new, something is wrong. There is pleasure in proving an existing dogma wrong . . . a much deeper pleasure, of course, in developing what seems to be a more coherent picture, especially if this can then be translated into therapies to help patients, who were after all the original motivation.'

But there was yet another landmark for the theory – its success in accounting for psychological aspects of pain. Recent studies have confirmed that the patient's ability to shift attention, his moods, attitudes, his interpretation of the injury, all exert a powerful influence on pain. 'Therapies such as cognitive training, and coping strategies descended from the air of witchcraft into something solid – if jelly-like – the *substantia gelatinosa* of the spinal cord.

'Let's take hypnosis as an example. This turns out to be a highly peculiar and unusual state. You realise what is happening, the patient is taking the word of somebody else. This is absolutely dependent on a definite relationship between one person and another, and it is in fact a very intellectual state, the patient is saying "I do not feel pain." If you examine the patient, he is showing all the signs of pain, and unfortunately, hypnosis frequently doesn't last. The patient forgets that other person and makes up his own mind about things.

'The mechanism of hypnosis is still debated. Some people argue it is a unique state of consciousness to which anyone can aspire, others claim that success really depends on the patient's personality, especially their compliance.'

There is less debate about the value of relaxation. This can produce striking physiological changes, decreased metabolism, lower blood pressure and respiration rate: all these can reduce the patient's anxiety and influence pain perception. Some pain clinics now also teach specific coping strategies, biofeedback conditioning techniques, stress training and so on. Many of these can aid pain relief but none seem to abolish pain entirely, and nor are they equally beneficial for everyone. The effect of the person's own character and will to help himself should not be underestimated.

For example, another patient, Mr Blackman, has suffered very severe pain for several years after being knocked down by a car. The nerves supplying his left arm were ripped out of the spinal cord on impact, leaving his arm paralysed. 'As a result the T-cells in the spinal cord which would normally receive sensory messages from his arm are no longer receiving messages. They have become more and more excitable, and now they are shouting all the time. To make matters more difficult some of the cells (in the *substantia gelatinosa*) that would normally regulate the T-cells are also damaged, making it even harder to turn off the false message.'

In spite of his severe pain, Mr Blackman has adopted a positive attitude to life, continuing with his work and coping as well as he can. He says, 'I hope against hope they will find something to stop the pain, but I think you've got to be philosophical about it . . . I can cope, I can get on all right. People help you in so many ways . . . you have to get on with life and not think about the pain.'

The chemical basis of character, and why some individuals cope with pain much better than others, is still largely unknown. 'Of course, in theory it is possible to get considerable changes in personality just by soaking the brain in one chemical – alcohol. But to understand pain-control mechanisms scientists need to know much more about specific chemical reactions.'

In 1975, there was a breakthrough. Scientists made 'a very exciting discovery, that you are making inside yourself opium-like compounds – narcotic compounds. And, of course, people naturally said, "Fine, this will be the explanation for these pain-control mechanisms that we have . . ." But progress has been slow.' These natural narcotics, enkephalin and endorphin, have been identified and located but it is far from clear whether they affect control mechanisms.

Wall has been tackling these problems by attempting to map the natural history of pain. 'The whole approach of both Descartes and the Gate Control theory was really attempting to handle the immediate consequence of injury and acute pain. But what is very apparent is that pain actually has a natural history; even a little cut is followed by a sensitive area . . . a spread of tenderness.' Chain reactions are set off in the brain in response to injury using a whole set of chemicals, peptides, molecules responsible for growth, and many others which still have to be identified.

'I think the Gate Control theory really does provide a framework in which mind and body are not separate – mental processes can directly affect physiology and vice versa. However, it's true that we are really quite a century away from understanding exactly how mental processes such as shifting attention can, chemically and neurophysiologically, affect pain.'

The Function of Pain

'Pain obviously has a function, and you can see what that function is by looking at that very rare type of person who is perfectly normal except that they never feel pain . . .' These people have to learn not to injure themselves. 'When you and I have minor injuries we are in a bit of pain and for the next few days we are on guard, we don't use that hand or leg . . . but these people don't do that and their joints can become very seriously diseased.' So pain not only teaches the avoidance of injury, it also aids recovery.

There is, however, pain for which the value is less clear. 'For example, I think in the case of a phantom limb that the system is going wrong, that really is an error . . . also someone with cancer or arthritis knows perfectly well what is happening, so why do they need to have the same pain message going on and on for weeks? I think maybe in these cases the pain is overdone. It is not useful, rather it's a demolishing aspect of the patients' disease. You can account for why this occurs in evolutionary terms. During evolution a set of priorities were built for the whole of behaviour, and pain has taken a very high priority, signalling "you're not well yet, take it easy . . ." and that is unfortunate for those in chronic pain.'

There is yet another kind of pain, mental pain or anguish, 'the sort of pain you feel with the death of a friend. There I think it's an analogy. You are acting as though you are injured . . . in the one case actual injury, and in the other the death of a friend . . . and the type of emotional reaction produced will have similarities.' The function of this sort of pain is very complex. 'We need to understand a great deal more about the emotional reaction and its similarities to other sorts of pain.'

But if there are some types of pain with no apparent physiological value – can we account for them in other terms, religious terms perhaps? 'There certainly are schools of thought, religious people, mystics, who would try to persuade you that pain is somehow character-building, ennobling. I do not accept that at all. My own line would be that now the individual and society should fight to reduce that suffering. I see nothing ennobling in suffering.'

Professor Abdus Salam FRS
Director, International Centre for
Theoretical Physics, Trieste

Abdus Salam was born in the country town of Jhang, Pakistan, in 1926. By the age of fourteen he had achieved the highest marks ever recorded in the entrance exams for the University of Lahore. He went to St John's College, Cambridge, where his exceptional ability was recognised with the title of 'wrangler' – the traditional Cambridge term for a first-class mathematician. He won a double first in physics and mathematics, and before he had completed his doctoral thesis he had published important work on quantum electrodynamics. He was set to become one of the great figures in the arcane world of particle physics.

His humble background was to make him a champion of the under-developed countries and he has used the international acclaim of his work to create a unique centre for scientific co-operation at Trieste in Italy. He shares his time between being its Director and that of Professor of Theoretical Physics at Imperial College, London.

In 1979 he shared the Nobel Prize with two other physicists and is proud to be the only Moslem scientist to receive this honour.

Behind Reality
Professor Abdus Salam FRS

Paul Andersen

'When I was at school in about 1936 I remember the teacher giving us a lecture on the basic forces in nature. He began with gravity. Of course we had all heard of gravity. Then he went on to say, "Electricity. Now there is a force called electricity, but it doesn't live in our town Jhang, it lives in the capital town of Lahore, a hundred miles to the east." He had just heard of the nuclear force and he said, "That only exists in Europe."'

This story of what it was like to be taught in an underdeveloped country is told with humour and excitement. For Abdus Salam, the days since have been spent sharing his enthusiasm between two great interests: physics and development in the Third World. In both he has become an international figure.

The 1930s, when Abdus Salam was still at school, was a period of rapid and sustained advance in physics. The discovery of radioactivity at the turn of the century by Madame Curie, and then later the theory of the nuclear atom proposed by Rutherford, had completely changed scientific thinking on what was considered to be the structure of nature. An atom was no longer an indivisible sphere but was made of a tiny nucleus, with electrons surrounding it. How nuclei or electrons interacted with one another was not clear at the time, but by 1946, when Abdus Salam went up to Cambridge University, some progress had been made.

'When I started research we believed that all matter in the Universe consisted of four discrete types – protons, neutrons, electrons and neutrinos – and that there were four fundamental forces between these four types of chunks of matter. Between the proton and the electron there was the electromagnetic force. The second force was the strong nuclear force, a force between a proton and a neutron. The third force, the weak nuclear force, was a force between pairs of protons and neutrons on the one hand and electrons and neutrinos on the other. And finally there was the force of gravity which is an attractive force between all these chunks of matter.'

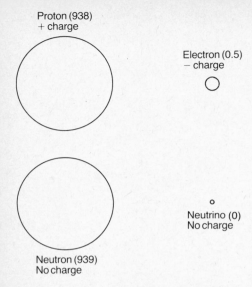

Proton (938)
+ charge

Electron (0.5)
− charge

Neutron (939)
No charge

Neutrino (0)
No charge

Relative masses of particles in brackets in mass energy units

'When I started research we believed that all matter in the Universe consisted of four discrete types – protons, neutrons, electrons and neutrinos.'

The discovery of these forces and particles had been turning points in modern science. Newton had been the first to observe and analyse the nature of the force of gravity. In the nineteenth century Faraday and Maxwell had described the nature of the electromagnetic force in their work on electricity. Then when Madame Curie made her discovery of radioactivity, what she had in fact been observing was the effects of the weak nuclear force within the atoms of radium. Rutherford's later explanation of the composition of the atom was to set the scene for understanding about the strong nuclear force that held the nucleus together.

It all seemed very tidy. 'We felt that the physics of the day had reached the end of the road. The Greeks had wanted to explain all the phenomena of nature through postulating four elements: fire, earth, air and water. We had substituted their elements with four fundamental entities: protons, neutrons, electrons and neutrinos.

'When we look at the world it's incredibly diverse. This diversity seems on the face of it difficult to describe in terms of so few principles. We believe, however, that all these diverse phenomena could be understood in terms of just those four fundamental objects and the four forces. The force of gravity is seen in the fact that we all remain on the Earth and that the planets move around one another. In our language this is a manifestation of the force of attraction between a proton and a neutron and an electron and a neutrino.

'All other phenomena on Earth itself are associated with the second force, the electromagnetic force – the expression of matter in its hardness, its softness and in its colour. It is incredible in its simplicity that all these diverse phenomena are a consequence of a force that exists between the proton and the electron.

'The third force, the strong nuclear force, is something that we are not so conscious of on earth. It is the force that keeps the protons and neutrons together. To see its operation in its purest form you have to go to the stars. The Sun is using this force to produce the vast amount of radiation which comes to us in the form of sunlight.

'Finally, there is the weak nuclear force which manifests itself most clearly through radioactivity. Through the operation of this force, the neutrons are being transformed into protons and electrons and neutrinos.' While the mathematics for such a picture is complex, the underlying notion of a few simple particles and their attendant forces being a complete description of the Universe is a startling scientific achievement.

A Unification of the Four Forces

But this image was not to satisfy the physicists for very long. Perhaps there was some way in which these conceptual quartets could be linked together. They might just be the expression of some yet more basic principle.

For example, one of the greatest achievements in scientific thinking in the twentieth century had been the linking of *mass* with *energy*. These two very different concepts were brought together through Einstein's genius in that renowned expression, $E = mc^2$. And there had been earlier examples – the example of unification of electricity and magnetism.

'At the beginning of the century these two were thought to be absolutely distinct forces – the electric force and the magnetic force. However, while they appear very different on the face of it, electricity and magnetism are basically the same force. This was proved by the work of Faraday and Ampère, who showed that if you take an electron that is stationary, then you can sense an electric force in the space around it. Once you begin to move that electron, you will get a manifestation of the magnetic force as well. The magnetic force is not a fundamental thing, but is connected with the electric force through the state of motion of the electron. The realisation that these two forces were of one fundamental origin led to the concept of the electromagnetic force. When I started research, one of the things which we began to look for was the possibility of a further unification between the four known forces.'

After his first degree at Cambridge University, Abdus Salam joined the Cavendish Laboratory where Rutherford had carried out his experiments on the structure of the atom. It was an outstanding laboratory for experimental work and a focus for physicists around the world.

As a research student, however, Abdus Salam found his temperament more suited to theoretical rather than practical problems. 'I had very little patience with experimental equipment. To be a good experimenter you must have patience towards things which are not always in your control. I think a theoretician has got to be patient, but that is with something of his own creation, his own constructs, his own stupidities. So after three months of experimental work at the Cavendish I just gave up. I went to my supervisor and said, "I'm sorry, I would like to turn back to theory."'

It was the right decision. In the following years his work in the field of quantum and particle physics was to achieve many breakthroughs in thinking. While the four fundamental particles were replaced by families of such particles with names like quarks and leptons, the principle of the four forces remained. For many years Einstein had attempted to find a theory that would bring two of these forces, the electromagnetic and gravity, into a unified theory. In his work *General Theory of Relativity*, published in 1915, he had shown that gravity was in fact the expression of the curved geometry of space and time. For the last years of his life Einstein had struggled to achieve this further simplification of nature's principles with a unification of gravity and the electromagnetic force. It was a quest that brought only failure.

Abdus Salam was to attempt the problem from a different perspective and succeed. 'Einstein's failure kept physicists away from the question of unification of the forces. Not many people were actively pursuing the idea since it was considered a dead end. We realised that Einstein had been singularly blind about the nuclear forces.

'We consciously chose to ignore gravity because we knew that

that was the hardest problem of all. It had beaten a man like Einstein. We started to look for a unification between the electromagnetic force and the weak nuclear force. On the face of it, these two forces are very, very different. You are trying to unite what is a long-range force with a short-range force. The electromagnetic force can be felt at almost any distance. If you put an electron on the table and if you have sensitive enough instruments, you can see the effect of it a hundred metres away, or even one kilometre away, if you wish.

'But not so with the nuclear forces. The nuclear force, and in particular the weak nuclear force, is very short range. The weak force manifests itself only if the proton and the neutron and the electron and neutrino which are participating are 10^{-16} centimetres close to each other. This is an unimaginably short distance, something we never come across in ordinary life. But to me as a physicist, when I speak of distances of 10^{-13} centimetres, the smallness is really irrelevant. My task is to go behind the reality of these short-range and the long-range forces and to search for the unity that may exist between them.

'To give an analogy of what we are trying to do, let us look at ice and water. They can co-exist at zero degrees centigrade, although they are very distinct with different properties. However, if you increase the temperature you find that they represent the same fundamental reality, the same fluid. Similarly, we thought that if you could conceive of a Universe which was very, very hot, something like 10^{16} degrees, unimaginably hot (the present temperature of the Universe which we live in is very low, around $-270°$ centigrade), then it was our contention that the weak nuclear force would exhibit the same long-range character as the electromagnetic force. You would then see the unification of these two forces perfectly clearly.

'To arrive at that sort of temperature, you have to go back into the early history of the Universe. At the time of the Big Bang, the Universe was presumably infinitely hot. And then it started to expand and as it did so it cooled down. When you come to the epoch of the order of 10^{-11} seconds after the Big Bang, you come to the stage where the low temperature allows the weak nuclear force for the first time to be distinct from the electromagnetic. That is the zero point of the ice and water example. If you are hotter than this "zero" (as you were in the early part of the Universe) then you would see no distinction between the two types of forces. This was our idea for the unification of the forces which of course was arrived at after twenty years of work.'

The Big Bang theory

One of the most striking developments in science over the past decade has been the linking of particle physics with cosmology. The search by physicists for a single theory that will describe the fundamental nature of all matter as we know it has led to an intriguing picture of the early Universe.

The predominant view among cosmologists is that the Universe began with a Big Bang which threw matter out in all directions, and that it has gone on expanding ever since. The first observation to suggest this was made by Edwin Hubble in the 1930s when he discovered that the galaxies were moving away from the Earth and each other. He had found that we inhabit an expanding Universe. An explanation to account for this was that the Universe began with a giant explosion – the Big Bang. However, it was not until the 1960s, when the existence of a microwave background radiation was discovered, that Big Bang theory was finally accepted. This radio signal corresponding to a temperature throughout the Universe of 3°K was the lingering remnant of heat from the initial explosion.

In the first moment of time, everything in the Universe was compressed into an unbelievably dense form. So crushed was matter that physicists have to start the clock of time some few moments after zero because the laws of nature will not extend to that point of infinite temperature and mass. It will be a few hundredths of a second later that the undifferentiated soup of matter and radiation begins to resemble the rapid collisions of particles in an accelerator. But here in the early Universe the temperature is at billions of degrees and particles are annihilated and formed in continuous collisions. Matter and radiation are in a constant flux. As this unimaginable fireball of energy expanded in size so it cooled – and has gone on cooling until now, when there is just a trace of heat, at 3°K.

It was the cooling of the Universe which brought the familiar matter of atoms and molecules into existence – after about one hundred thousand years the temperature had dropped sufficiently for the nuclei to combine with electrons. Physicists have been able to construct a table of time versus the size of the Universe and then create a model of the Big Bang which charts the appearance of the high-energy particles as they are found in the falling temperature of the Universe. Today the Universe is between ten and twenty billion years old and its temperature so low relative to the primordial soup that matter is organised into stars, galaxies and life – frozen into a state of existence.

	TIME	TEMPERATURE	SIZE
Big Bang	10^{-43}	10^{33} °K	10^{-4} cm
	10^{-37}	10^{28} °K	1 km
	10^{-11}	10^{16} °K	1 million km
Today	10^{18}	3 °K	10^{22} km

An Asymmetrical Universe and a New Particle

In this view then, the present world is full of interactions that are asymmetrical, but at the moment of creation, in the first nano-seconds of the Big Bang, all interactions were united in one universal force. As the Universe has cooled, so this symmetry has been broken to reveal the distinctive forces of gravity and the weak nuclear, the strong nuclear and the electromagnetic force. The difficulty has been in achieving a satisfactory mathematical formulation that would accurately describe both the symmetrical as well as the asymmetrical situation.

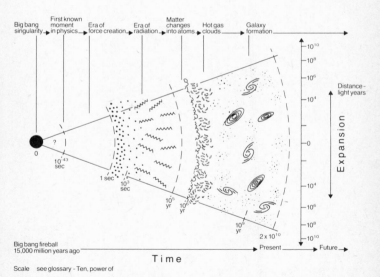

A view of the Big Bang explanation to the origin of the Universe. The unimaginable nature of matter in those early few moments of time is where the present known laws of physics stop.

In 1967 Abdus Salam was able, with Steven Weinberg, to provide a unified theory that became the paradigm for much future work. Although they had been working independently, their ideas made use of several important conclusions that had been reached during the previous years. One of these was the idea of spontaneously breaking symmetry. But how does symmetry break spontaneously?

'Suppose you have invited twelve people to a dinner party. They are all waiting to sit down at a large round table. Now if you don't know the rules, you could sit anywhere and take the side plate from your left or right. This is the symmetry situation. But once someone has made the first choice, everyone else has to follow suit. The symmetry of left-right is "spontaneously broken".'

The acceptance of the new theory of unification was slow in arriving. 'In 1967, when our work was completed, there was no notice taken of it at all. I remember lecturing in 1968 at an international conference in Sweden and a very eminent physicist responsible for preparing the conference summary did not even

The European Organisation for Nuclear Research (CERN) was founded near Geneva in 1954. The original site in Switzerland was doubled in size by the addition of land across the border (crossed-line) in France. The path of the underground proton synchrotron, SPS, 2.2km in diameter, is drawn on the photo.

consider the subject worth mentioning. So you can be ignored for the good reason that your ideas are not in the stream of things.'

However, the theory had made predictions that could be verified by experiment. The most revealing of these was that a new particle exists at extreme energies. To test this theory they had to convince the experimental physicists working on the great particle accelerators to build new equipment. To create, in principle, conditions that will be similar to those first few moments in the birth of the Universe.

'I have been describing how unification of the weak nuclear and electromagnetic force could occur in terms of the Big Bang and the temperature of the Universe. Now, of course I do not need this concept in terms of proving the theory because we are going to make that environment in the laboratory. If it occurs in the Universe, fine. If it did not, it would not worry us. We are looking for temperatures of the order of 10^{15} degrees and we can produce them in the particle accelerators. In the European laboratory of CERN, outside Geneva, a 6-kilometre-long track of magnets is used to accelerate particles to enormous velocities. Accelerating

Inside the underground tunnel of the CERN particle accelerator laboratory near Geneva. The particle beams are directed by deflecting magnets: the lines curving to the left carry protons into a storage ring while the right-hand beam is kept in a straight line.

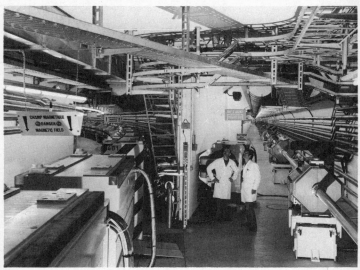

protons and antiprotons to these enormous energies is equivalent to giving us that environment of high temperature.'

In the late 1970s experiments were conducted at the Stanford Linear Accelerator Laboratory, in California, that confirmed one part of the necessary conclusions of the theory. But it was not until 1983 that final confirmation was obtained with the discovery that the predicted particles – the intermediate vector bosons – did exist. Called W^+, W^- and Z^0, these particles were seen for a few fleeting moments under the cosmic conditions of the CERN accelerator. But this temporary existence was enough to demonstrate that the unification theory was an accurate description of the fundamental nature of matter.

In an unusually bold decision, the 1979 Nobel Prize in Physics was awarded to Abdus Salam and two other theorists, Steven Weinberg and Sheldon L. Glashow, for their work on unification: four years before the confirmatory experiment at CERN. In the intervening years, the work had continued on unification theory and had developed in mathematical terms to show how the third unification with the strong nuclear force may be achieved. But the experimental proof of the third unification was yet further away.

'When we come to the unification of the strong nuclear force with the electromagnetic and the weak nuclear force it is to take the same analogy of ice and water; can we include steam? The transition temperature where these forces unite would be of the order of 10^{28} degrees Kelvin. But if you were going to make an accelerator which could have the type of energy available to produce that kind of environment, then it would need to be so large it would extend from the Earth to the edges of the galaxy.' However, this further unification allowed for an indirect experimental proof. The theory had predicted that the fundamental particle, the proton, would decay. But why?

'The proton and the neutron possess the strong force: the two make up one family of particles. The neutrino and the electron possess the weak force, another family. Now if you wish to believe that there is a unification between these two forces, then these two families have in some way to be part of one bigger family. And if they are from the same bigger family, then one member can substitute for another – the particles are interconvertible under suitable conditions. The implication of that is that eventually the protons (or the neutrons) could disappear and turn into anti-electrons or neutrinos.

'So far in physics, it had been assumed that the proton was a fundamentally stable particle and that it exists for ever. Indeed if it did not live a long time we would not be here. If the protons and neutrons disappear there is no nucleus, no atom and therefore no matter as we know it. That is why the existence of life was the first proof that the proton lives at least 10^{10} years. The time it has taken for the Universe to produce life.

'Our calculations, however, showed that actually the proton lives much longer. In fact only after 10^{30} years can the proton turn itself into an anti-electron. Or put another way, if we take ten tons of matter, any type of matter, and we look upon the protons contained inside it, we shall find in a year's inspection that one proton out of the ten tons of matter would disappear. This proton turns itself into an anti-electron plus photons. So the task of an experimental proof is to detect that one proton disappearing.'

As with Abdus Salam's other theoretical work, it would have to wait for the experimental physicists to be convinced enough to undertake the experiment. The major experiments in particle physics are planned years ahead and employ a great number of specialists. And often, with completely new ideas, the theorists have to wait for new equipment to be built. 'I remember there was a large conference in 1974 in London and I spent all of it trying to buttonhole people and persuade them to do this experiment. It was only when the other theory of the unification of electricity with the weak nuclear force was confirmed in 1978 that a stampede began to test this new theory in which the three forces were brought together.

'In 1980 a joint Indian-Japanese team started working in a disused mine in the Kolar gold-fields in southern India. There, 7000 feet below ground, they have this beautifully air-conditioned chamber with 150 tons of iron sheets placed inside. The reason for this depth was to find an environment where you are free from any background of stray events that may ape the results you are looking for. To catch a proton in the act of turning itself into an anti-electron you surround the material, in this case 150 tons of iron, with very sensitive photo multipliers that can detect the minute flashes that occur at the transition. With those 150 tons we expect the counters to click just two or three times in the whole year showing that a few protons have disappeared. Now two or three times is not enough statistically, you must have hundreds of such events before you can really say that the protons do decay. And if they do decay, then three forces will have been united into one single force.'

The decay of the proton could offer solutions to some existing problems. One of the puzzles of modern cosmology is the absence of galaxies with any significant amounts of antimatter. We can observe vast amounts of matter throughout the Universe, but what has happened to the antimatter that necessarily must have been in existence in equal amounts at the moment of creation? If there is an asymmetry or an unequal behaviour in the operation of the weak nuclear force between matter and antimatter, then anti-protons may decay faster leaving just protons. So while there may have been the same number of protons and antiprotons in the early Universe, as it expands over time and the antiprotons decay faster, you are left with a largely proton-filled Universe. But this decay must also mean that eventually everything will disappear. In 10^{30} years half the atoms will lose their protons; it will certainly be the end of life as we know it.

Although a number of laboratories began experiments they have yet to provide convincing evidence of proton decay. The Kolar gold-field experiments claim to have seen three events of proton decay. A group in Japan at Kamioka claims two events. A group working at Irvine, Michigan, and Brookhaven, Mississippi, with the largest sample of protons under view, has found no decay candidates. They claim that protons live at least as long as 10^{32} years. Thus proton decay for the moment is uncertain, but this may change. This is science, not dogma.

Science and the Future Generation of Physicists

'It is just not true that when someone like myself gets up and proposes a new theory that I expect I will be right. It may never happen. The proton may not decay. You may be as eminent as you wish, but the youngest member of your audience can get up and contradict you and perhaps be right.' It is this perhaps which adds to the excitement Abdus Salam feels about science. For him the challenge of providing new ideas and then putting them forward for others to analyse and test is a constant source of pleasure. He enjoys sharing this enthusiasm with his friends and family.

'I would like to interest my own children, as my father did. Regretfully, they do not listen to me. I tried to bring up my youngest daughter as a physicist. She did do physics at school, and I remember in 1973, when we worked out the theory of proton decay, telling her that I thought the proton was unstable. Well, she went to her A-level teacher telling her this was what her father said. The teacher said, "My dear girl, whatever nonsense your father teaches you at home, don't put it in the exam paper or you will fail." And she did fail. And then she took up literature.' He enjoys telling this story and although perhaps unable to galvanise his family into scientific endeavour, he has not failed with colleagues and students.

'My whole background from Pakistan was that of mathematics and theory, and I think the emphasis on symmetry is something which I have inherited from the culture of Islam. The belief in unity, in there being one simple cause for all the forces that we see, has a basis in my spiritual background.' A devout Moslem, Abdus Salam sees his scientific endeavours as entirely in keeping with the Koran's teaching to 'reflect on the phenomena of nature' and to 'satisfy the sense of wonder at creation'. This shows in his eagerness to engage others. He has worked tirelessly to bring science to the Third World, and to improve the chances for others who come from a background similar to his own.

'For the majority of people like myself there simply was no experimental physics. Experiments cost money, and there are no equipped laboratories. You never get around to doing any experiments and the result is, as it was for me, that you receive a training that is entirely theory. One very stark example of this was told to me by someone who had been visiting Bangladesh. There, one of the schoolteachers was lecturing to the students on a chemical experiment. He said, "Gentlemen, think of my finger as a test tube, and now I am pouring sulphuric acid into it," and he showed the movement of pouring the acid onto his finger. "And now I shall add some iron chips to it – see, this is sulphuric acid with iron chips in it." This is the situation of experimental work in many of the developing countries. I, fortunately, had the great example of my father who took a vast amount of interest in my school work.'

Abdus Salam also had a certain amount of luck. His success at school, in what was then the Punjab region of British India, would normally have led him into a civil service job. 'I was very fortunate to get a scholarship to go to Cambridge. The famous Indian civil service examinations had been suspended because of the war and there was a fund of money that had been collected by the Prime Minister of the Punjab. This money had been intended for use during the war, but there was some left and he created five scholarships for study abroad. It was 1946 and I managed to get a place in one of the boats that were full with British families who were leaving before Indian Independence. Of course, if I had not gone that year, in the following year there was the partition between India and Pakistan and the scholarships simply disappeared.'

In an effort to make education less of a chance affair for students from the developing countries, Abdus Salam has cam-

Professor Salam working with visiting physicists at the International Centre, Trieste. Over two thousand scientists from around the world come to spend time at the Centre each year – pursuing research topics or being taught by well-known specialists.

paigned for more international aid for educational training. Since the 1950s he has been an active voice in the United Nations as a member of the Advisory Committee on Science and Technology and the Foundation Committee for the UN University.

In 1964 he achieved his ambition with the creation of the International Centre for Theoretical Physics at Trieste. At a meeting of the International Atomic Energy Agency in 1960 he had proposed the setting-up of a centre where scientists from different countries, north and south, east and west, could meet and exchange ideas.

'I certainly feel a responsibility to bring to the notice of the people in power in the developed countries the importance of science and technology for developing countries. I believe that science transfer should precede technology transfer to the poorer countries. But this is often neglected in the aid we receive from the wealthy nations. They forget that unless you have a manpower that is highly proficient in the sciences, the transfer of technology will simply not take place. We set up the Centre at Trieste with the help of the Italian Government and United Nations agencies to enable scientists from developing countries to work at the highest levels of research.

'After I had studied at Cambridge, I had gone back to Lahore in 1951 and was teaching there at the university. But as a physicist, I was completely isolated. It was very difficult even to get the journals and keep in touch with my subject. I had to leave my country to remain a physicist. It is the lack of this contact with others that is the biggest curse of being a scientist in a developing country. You simply do not have the funds, the opportunities, which those from richer countries enjoy as a matter of course. There are not the communities of people thinking and working in the same fields. This is what we have tried to cure by bringing people together at the Centre.

'The Trieste Centre is trying to provide help so that a scientist can remain in his own country for the bulk of the time, but come to one of the Centre's workshops or research sessions for three months or so. There, he will meet the people in his subject, learn new ideas and be able to return charged with a mission to change the image of science and technology in his own country. The majority of the activity at the Centre is concerned with non-particle physics pursuits. We have begun a course where staff from CERN are providing a course in the use of microprocessors for scientists from all over the developing countries. This is the first such course being done anywhere in the world for these people.

'The most important point is that we in the developing countries have been sold by well-meaning, and perhaps not so well-meaning, people the idea that all we need is technology – borrowed ideas. Lord Blackett, my mentor at Imperial College, used to say, "There is a world supermarket of technology, go and buy it and take it home." That is just wrong. Technology simply does not take that way. You need to have in every country a core of people with discrimination at the least, and that is what we are hoping to provide at Trieste.'

In its first year, the Centre was host to 150 people. Today, over 2200 visitors from around the world spend time there. All this has meant a greater demand on Abdus Salam's energy and less time for his own research. Despite this, he still manages to pursue the theory of grand unification and to provoke thinking on how it is that matter fits together.

The Final Step

'The next step in this unification is the final step which Einstein wanted to take first. Einstein wanted to unite gravity with electromagnetism. We have replaced electromagnetism by the combined, electronuclear force. Can we now achieve the final step and unite this force with the gravitational force?

'Well, if we look at the events after the Big Bang, we believe that possibly the electronuclear force was indistinguishable from gravity when the Universe was 10^{-43} seconds old. There are two distinct ways of looking at this proposal and resolving the difficulties that exist in the mathematical theory.

'One way is to conceive of a Universe having eleven dimensions. This is a new idea. Instead of the four space-time dimensions which we appear to live in and which Einstein worked with, we try to conceive of an eleven-dimensional Universe existing before 10^{-43} seconds. Then around 10^{-43} seconds after the Big Bang there is a transition with seven of those dimensions being "compactified" into small sizes of the order of 10^{-33} centimetres, and four dimensions remaining with infinite ranges. We cannot discover the seven "compactified" dimensions by any direct means, but their indirect effect is what we see as the electronuclear charge. This is a very speculative view at this stage.

'A totally different idea is that space-time is indeed no more than four dimensions. But that when we go back to 10^{-43} seconds after the Big Bang, then at these very small distances of the order of 10^{-33} centimetres, we find a granularity in the structure of space and time. That granularity is like cheesiness, worm-holes, or little scoop cuts. And it is this cheesiness which persists to the present epoch as electronuclear charge. Now this idea also is highly speculative. We will need experimentation if we are to find a way that will determine which of these two points of view is correct. It need not be very elaborate experimental work. One suggestion is to look for the force of anti-gravity and if we discover such a force then indeed space-time does have seven extra dimensions compactified, as well as the four of space-time as Einstein conceived them.'

Fifty years later, Einstein's problem of bringing gravity into line with our understanding of the other forces of nature remains. To date, the theories of unification of the electromagnetic and nuclear forces are the closest description we have as to how nature behaves. It has enabled the cosmologists' view of the origin of the Universe to be understood in terms of the ultimate building blocks of matter. Our conception of the very beginning of time and space has been brought closer to our grasp and to experimental test. It remains now for the physicists to take us still further to the boundaries of what is reality.

Dr John H. Crook
Reader in Ethology, University of Bristol

John Crook was born in Southampton in 1930. For over three generations his family has operated a group of village grocery stores in Hampshire. As a schoolboy at Sherborne he was an avid bird-watcher. He then went to University College at Southampton, to study zoology – and spend much time down on Southampton Water watching the wildlife.

In 1958 he received his Ph.D from Jesus College, Cambridge, for his study of the social behaviour patterns in Weaver-birds. He travelled across Africa for this work and returned again when he took to examining the behaviour of primates. In 1963 he joined Bristol University to develop ethological research in the new psychology department. After a year spent at Stanford, California, as a visiting fellow at the Centre for Advanced Study in the Behavioural Sciences he returned to Bristol with a strong interest in Humanistic Psychology. As a result he established the Bristol Encounter Centre and later the Bristol Psychotherapy Association.

During the 1970s he made a number of expeditions to the remote region of Ladakh, on the Kashmir/China borders. A long-term interest in Zen teaching and Buddhism has persuaded him to attempt a synthesis of his behaviour studies with the development of human consciousness.

Programmed for Insight?
Dr John H. Crook

Paul Andersen

'I think there is always a worry about any scientific view which seems to suggest that human beings are automata. That free will does not exist. That we have no choice in our behaviour. If we are to understand the origins of human behaviour I would advocate a much more careful study of the way in which social psychology and biology interact. In this way it can be seen that our understanding of the flexibility of human behaviour does not contradict with our ideas of human biology and evolution. Both in terms of individual psychology and our social structures we are not confined by our biology.'

Since the middle of the nineteenth century when Darwin delivered his great work on natural selection and the theory of species evolution, the position of mankind as a member of the animal kingdom has been a subject for debate. Opposition to the idea of man as the result of primate evolution began with Bishop Wilberforce, and the argument has never fully disappeared. Despite the body of scientific evidence that has been produced to demonstrate the principles of evolutionary theory through practical examples among plants and animals, the theory has remained a contentious issue. In recent years the teaching of evolution as part of biology in American schools has drawn complaint and opposition from Christian fundamentalists. But for the scientist, the issue has been one of attempting to explain the myriad variety of nature by determining the precise role of genetics and how natural selection works.

The origins of human anatomy and physiology can now be demonstrated in fossil remains; but how mankind acquired the distinctive features of intelligent and conscious behaviour has always seemed beyond this scientific approach. A biological explanation for the development of the human mind has been missing, and although psychology and the social sciences have endeavoured to describe individual and cultural patterns of behaviour, they have failed to offer an evolutionary argument for human consciousness. John Crook believes that new ideas coming from the study of animal behaviour begin to show how this most complex of human characteristics may have evolved.

'The justification for looking at man from an evolutionary point of view stems, of course, from Darwin. His great work had shown that animals are physically adapted to their environment through natural selection. In competition with others of the same species, those individuals that could find food most effectively, avoid predators and survive, reproduce more successfully than others. This is the key point in the notion of the survival of the fittest. Now to a biologist this theory should apply equally to behaviour since, after all, this is simply anatomy in motion.

'The classic approach to the study of animal behaviour begins really with Konrad Lorenz who listed four questions that you had to ask to understand the behaviour of an animal. If you take the example of the male pigeon meeting a female it will go through a routine of bowing and cooing, to which the female may respond. The first question is to look at the causal mechanism in the brain. What physiological activity is associated with this pattern? Might there be hormonal changes associated with it? Next, we ask what function does it perform? With the cooing pigeon, the male is stimulating the female, so the behaviour has a sexual role. The third area is the evolutionary question. How did this pattern evolve over time? Finally, how does this particular behaviour develop in the lifetime of an individual? If the behaviour was a genetically determined, innate pattern, how does it get organised to produce the behaviour in the mature animal?

'Lorenz's traditional approach produced plenty of evidence that animals often have specific patterns of behaviour that are inherited from one generation to the next. These became known as *fixed action patterns* and ethologists have been largely concerned with their analysis. Initially this work did not extend to studying the social relations of animals.'

The 'Behaviourist' Approach

An alternative tradition to this work of zoologists was taken in psychology where instead of examining animals from an evolutionary perspective, their behaviour patterns were compared directly to human activity. The emphasis was on discovering how rules of behaviour could be learned by animals. Discoveries here could help in understanding human activity. The origins of the psychologists' approach lay in the philosophy of John Locke, who held that the human mind was a blank sheet and that everything it contains is a result of associations brought about through learning. The scientific study which took this view found expression in what became known as 'behaviourism'. Its leading exponent was John Watson, who in the early part of this century began to study animals in his laboratory in the United States.

He and his colleagues put rats inside mazes or boxes in an attempt to discover how complex behaviour patterns were acquired. Such experiments drew on the ideas of Pavlov who had shown that you can condition an animal to respond in predictable ways. If a hungry dog was shown food it would begin to salivate. This was a natural reflex action. If you put a rat in a box and wanted it to learn to press a lever every time it saw a light, this could be achieved by conditioning such a reflex by rewarding the rat's action with a little food each time. Eventually the rat's behaviour would become reflex, in that every time it saw the light it would press the lever.

Such laboratory observation and testing was concerned with establishing how animals learned to do certain things. The early 'behaviourists' hoped that they could develop laws of learning through extreme simplification in laboratory tests. The results were highly successful and during the 1930s a great volume of work was published. But problems arose in how to generalise from this to the much more complex patterns of behaviour of animals in their natural state, or indeed to human behaviour.

'Some of the most instructive learning experiments were done with rats running in mazes. A theorist called Hull developed an elaborate argument about how a rat learned to run through a maze to the goal box. The basic idea was that animals have *needs* such as the need for food or sex. These needs take the form of a *drive* that activates some part of the brain. In the case of food it could be the level of blood sugar that creates this. When the blood sugar is below a certain level this is picked up by some kind of sensor in the brain, and, in theory, the brain then generates a *drive* to go and look for food. So the rat begins running through the maze until it finds the goal box where there is the reward of food. As soon as this happens the *need* is reduced and the *drive* turned off. This is positive for the animal and so there is an association between the reward in the goal box and the path that led there. Perhaps the first time the rat ran through the maze it was quite slow, but over a number of experiments, the animal clearly learns to run the maze. The learning was brought about through reinforcement, as each successful attempt brought a reward. The principle then put forward by "behaviourism" was that animals have these basic *needs* and that learning comes about through reinforcement. This thinking went along for some time and indeed a considerable amount of work was published that interpreted human behaviour in this way.

'A very interesting series of experiments was conducted during the 1920s by Tolman and his co-workers. Rats were put into a maze which did not have a goal box. After being allowed to run freely around they were then taken out and a goal box put into the maze. This group of rats was then compared to another group which had no experience of the maze. Now, in theory, both groups should take about the same length of time and experience the same difficulty in finding the goal box. What actually happens is that the group which has run the maze previously does much better. In other words, they have learnt something about the maze without reinforcement. The phenomenon is known as *latent learning* because the animals appear to have learned something about the maze simply through observation. This raises many questions about how the actual exploration was being reinforced.

'The early theory was that the rats were learning the actual movements and building up sequences through rewarded action. If, however, they were learning without rewards something more complex is suggested; that they were actually creating a concept of the maze or, put another way, "a map in the head". Now as soon as you begin to talk in terms of maps in the head, this is something which a psychology focusing only on behaviour cannot deal with. So, as a result of experiments on behaviour, you have discovered something which is not simply behaviour but is something "mental" going on in the head. This then opened up research on the interior, cognitive processes that were involved. And with humans it is these cognitive, higher mental functions which are of course of the greatest interest.'

A Biologist's view of Learning Theory?

For the biologists, who were approaching the subject from an animal's instinctive patterns of behaviour, this knowledge was useful but difficult to interpret in terms of what may be going on in the wild. In particular, if the fixed action patterns of the pigeons' mating behaviour were inborn, what was the role of learning? However, if the genetic code is responsible for certain behaviour, it must also influence how this behaviour may alter as the animal develops. The feeding action of a bird, for instance, will alter as it grows from a chick to an adult. The behaviour may also be influenced by its habitat. If you put an animal in one environment the pattern of behaviour which develops may be modified from that in another environment. Before long it seemed inevitable that this division of animal behaviour into two sciences, one dealing with learning and the other concerned with innate behaviour, was due for change.

'Modern ethology has been concerned with an integration of these two views. When I went to Cambridge in the 1950s there was much discussion of how psychology and ethology could find a common ground. When we came to look at the complex social behaviour found among certain birds, or monkeys, or ourselves for that matter, neither genes nor learning alone were sufficient to explain such elaborate societies. My own interest was always on the social organisation and evolution of behaviour, particularly in bird populations. As a teenager I used to sit and watch the gulls on Southampton Water. It struck me then that the gull's day was organised into different patterns of movement – flocks would fly upriver at certain times and congregate in roosts in the evening. At high water, when the mudflats were not exposed, they would fly inland to feed. So there appeared to be a link between what the birds were doing and the ecology. Now the study of behaviour which Lorenz had pursued was quite different to this. He tended to look at animals in a kind of captivity. At his farm the animals were free to wander about but he would have close contact with them. I kept my distance from animals and observed them out there in nature.

'My own research began in the fifties studying Weaver-birds. The idea was to see what effect the environment might have on the social behaviour of closely related species. It was a really exciting study which took me to many different countries. I travelled across East and West Africa, India, the Seychelles and in all saw about one hundred species of Weaver. I would just stop wherever I found the birds, sit down and watch them. The kinds of things I was interested in were whether they lived in flocks or whether they lived in territories, what sort of food they ate and what their courtship behaviour was.

'In Senegal I studied the Quelea, a species of Weaver that lives in thorn-bush country on the edge of the Sahara. There you would find about five hundred nests in a tree that was only the size of a large room. The birds would come in and build these nests, so densely packed that each tree looks like a little haystack. The constant coming and going was overwhelming at first and it took many days to see that there was organised behaviour in what seemed like chaos. Although I had some vague idea of what I

Weaver-bird nests fill a tree in the East African bush. In the savannah lands the male birds construct a series of nests and attract one female after another.

wanted from this study, I had no idea really of the patterns that were hidden in the data I was collecting.

'The interpretation of the results was in some ways the most exciting part. I came back to Cambridge with piles and piles of notebooks from the expeditions. And I can remember to this day the quite extraordinary excitement as I was sitting there in the library drawing up tables of correlation and slowly the meaning of all the figures became apparent. It's not often in your research life that you have the thrill of seeing the meaning coming out of the page at you. It was so exciting I remember I used to walk up and down the Cambridge zoology library saying, "My God, it works, there's something here." The behaviour is often so very complex that you don't believe you found anything until it stands out like this.

'What was coming out of my observations was that the social structures of these different species were quite clearly a function

Nest of a Weaver-bird with the male working on building the elaborate structure.

of their ecology. The most interesting aspect was the mating behaviour, because some of these birds were monogamous and some were polygamous. Now with the Weavers it is the male which builds their distinctive nests. So one question was how many nests do they build and how many females can they get to come to these nests?

'The finding was that in the forest environment there was just one nest and the male would attract a female to it, and they would form a monogamous unit where both of them would rear the young. In the savannah, however, you had a situation in which the male birds would construct a series of nests and attract one female after another. So what could it be about the savannah and the forest that produced this rather radical change in the mating system? Well, the theory that came from this was that in the environments where you found monogamy, as in the forest, there was a much more constant supply of food. Conditions there vary relatively little over time. In the savannah, though, the situation was quite different.

'In the African savannah there is a monsoon season where the rains come and produce a tremendous burst of growth of grasses and insects. So there is a period when the food supply is grossly in surplus to the requirements of the birds which means that the female is capable of looking after the young on her own and doesn't really need the male. So that sets the male free to mate with other females.

'Now, of course, one of the cardinal principles of adaptation in evolution is that both sexes are trying to maximise the number of their offspring to push their genes into the next generation. A male can do this by adopting a strategy of having several nests and several partners. But he can't do that if there isn't sufficient food for the mother to rear the young by herself. So under those circumstances, polygamy is given up and the male has to participate in a monogamous relationship. This kind of discovery shifted the emphasis away from the study of fixed action patterns to the study of social interactions. Now we could see that these rather complicated features of social life were intimately connected with the ecology, such as the amount of food or the size of the population.'

Primate Behaviour

During the 1960s interest grew in the study of primate behaviour. Monkeys and apes are the closest relations to man and if ethology was to offer any evidence for the evolution of human behaviour, how monkey society became organised might give some clues.

'At about this time I was fortunate in getting an appointment at Bristol University with Professor Ronnie Hall. He was involved in the study of baboons in Africa and one of my reasons for moving to his department was to try and see if it was possible to look at monkey society in the same way as I had with Weaver-birds. Many of the research proposals at the time had as their prime motive the notion that we could understand humans better from looking at our relatives among the monkeys and apes. So, when we look at monkeys, we are trying to imagine the state of social life of our earliest ancestors. In describing how such primates develop their social behaviour we then infer the kind of biological changes that the protohominids must have gone through to become the human animal of today. No single factors are sufficient to explain the development of language or human culture but certain examples of complex behaviour may enable us to extrapolate towards human action.

'I was interested in what kind of mating system the Gelada baboon had and I travelled to the highlands of Ethiopia to observe the herds in the wild. At first, when you arrive in the field, all you can see is a great mass of animals milling around. It is just as chaotic at the centre of a Gelada herd as it is in a Weaver colony. What you are looking for are the interactions between individuals. Experienced monkey watchers can usually learn to identify individuals or, if the groups are too big, you have to list your animals by categories: one-year-olds, two-year-olds, males, females and so

A group of Gelada baboons. The larger male is the head of a party of females and young – the harem structure. A herd may contain ten or more such groups.

on. Then it is a matter of drawing up check lists to record what the individuals are doing or how they are interacting with one another. There might be two or three hundred baboons and the question is, how are they organised?

'What gradually transpired was that if I chose particular target animals to look at – particular males, for instance – and kept my eye on them for half an hour or so, I could see that when a male moved, a group of females who might be quite separate from him got up and moved with him. So this seemed to indicate that there was some kind of grouping within the herd, rather than a single hierarchy. And then you would get those marvellous occasions when a whole herd would be on the move across the hillside and I could see that they were bunched into parties; groups focused on one male, each with a party of females, in other words, a harem structure.

'Now, of course, out of that came some very interesting questions. How do young males acquire harems? Or how is the reproductive system transferred from one generation to the next? To answer these questions, study over a long period of time is required to follow the different generations, and a lot of this work was done by my colleague, Robin Dunbar. We discovered that there are two means by which a male Gelada could acquire a female following. One method is simply for the young male to associate regularly with a particular harem, and, because of this frequent association, the old male in charge of the group accepts his presence. Then, after a while, when the females are old enough, the two males split, each with some of the females.

'The other way was direct confrontation and attack. What was especially intriguing was that after these contests the old male was allowed to remain in the group and look after his own youngsters. The young male then does all the mating, but the two males remain in some sort of association. Now in lions and langurs, when similar fights occur, the incoming male kills all the babies, the reason being that if that male takes over a group of females biologically he wants to see his own offspring reproduced. So he wants to mate with the females and get his own line of babies under way. If the place is cluttered up with the previous male's young he can't do this. But in the Gelada this doesn't occur. Why could this be?

'Robin Dunbar noticed something very interesting. Occasionally, after two males have been fighting for what might be a couple of days, a third male comes in and goes off with all the females, the other two animals being too exhausted from their own conflict to defend the harem. So the association of two males could be a sort of bargain whereby they collaborate to resist a possible takeover by a third male. "I won't kill your babies if you help me defend this unit which I've just taken over. On the other hand you must allow me to do all the mating and you can look after your kids until they've grown up." It's a nice story and, of course, it needs a great deal more observation to check the theory. But good stories are also good hypotheses.

'Many examples of collaboration, even altruism, have been found among social groups of animals in contradiction to the strict Darwinian view of survival through competition. In the unlikely setting of a pride of lions we find highly collaborative behaviour between two males who jointly rule the group. Once it became clear that there were many cases of such behaviour it was obvious that any theory which could account for this would be highly significant in relation to human life, since one of the most obvious things about humanity is the way in which so many of our common endeavours involve some form of collaboration. And yet there is a fundamental paradox here.

'Darwin is arguing for the survival of the fittest, and it would seem that the fittest is he who looks after his own. Therefore where you get a case of animals helping one another, this would seem counter-intuitive. It shouldn't happen, animals should be thoroughly selfish, thoroughly nasty, maximising their own gain all the time. So how is it this doesn't happen? A theoretical suggestion was made in the fifties by the geneticist and entomologist William Hamilton. He published a very instructive paper which for the first time made sense of altruistic behaviour in Darwinian terms.

'His theory stressed that the important thing to remember was the number of genes which an individual passed on to the next generation. Obviously an animal can pass its genes on to the next generation directly through its offspring. But these genes are not unique to that animal; they also occur in its immediate relations by virtue of common descent. My sister has about half of the same genes as I do. I am quite closely related to her child, who also has genes in common with myself. Hamilton pointed out, therefore, that natural selection will probably act not just on my fitness to produce my own children but also on what he called *inclusiveness*; my fitness, plus fitness which accrues to me as a consequence of assisting a sister or other relative. In other words the genes which I put into the next generation are those of my own offspring plus those of my relatives whom I may have assisted. Immediately here we can see a Darwinian explanation for the evolution of altruism, since there may be many occasions when I would gain from helping my relatives. This idea has become known more recently as "kin selection". This discovery meant that one could begin to think of human partnering also in terms of kin selection.

'A further development was presented by Robert Trivers who in the early seventies put forward an analysis of another kind of altruism. He gave it the term *reciprocal altruism*, and, although it requires rather strict circumstances for its evolution, it explains how assistance can be given to a non-relative. Trivers argued that the selection process will favour altruistic behaviour where individuals provide a benefit to another greater than the cost to themselves. This can only develop in small groups where opportunities for many instances of "give and take" exist, and interactions are frequent. This is the kind of situation that occurs in highly social animals living in dense groups such as the apes and monkeys. In order for this reciprocation to develop there has to be some understanding among individuals of who is who. It couldn't happen in a huge anonymous crowd; it could only evolve in groups whose size was small enough to allow for intimate knowledge of one another, and where the circumstances for reciprocation were quite frequent.

'Trivers' theory was originally described before there was much evidence to support it. The interesting thing is that we now have some results from Packer, who studied the baboon *Papio anubis* in Tanzania, which seem to confirm the idea. He was able to demonstrate that in a competitive situation where one male wants to obtain a female from another male he calls up a friend to help him drive off the old male. What is exciting is that the reverse then happens quite predictably; that when the male who has been called upon as an assistant wants to do the same thing he calls up the male whom he helped previously. These encounters often involve a lengthy fight and the animals may incur some injury in offering assistance. But in spite of this the cost is less than the benefit of being able to reciprocate with another animal in order to achieve certain aims.'

The Emergence of Intelligence

While the evidence for reciprocal altruism needs further examples from behaviour studies in the field, the idea of co-operative behaviour is now firmly established in ethologists' thinking. The early concern with the genetically-determined, fixed patterns of behaviour has given way to an exploration of how the environment may influence forms of social life. The complexity of interrelationships between animals living in close groups is now the focus of interest. Members of such societies are clearly not robots acting out preordained programmes of behaviour but show signs of intelligence. Is there some connection between the emergence of such mental skills in higher animals like chimpanzees, dogs and humans and the development of social organisations? The environment has been seen to influence how members of a society of animals may behave towards one another. The emergence of intelligence or conscious patterns of behaviour is the next challenge for the biologist. Here, the separate threads of thinking in ethology and psychology begin to draw together.

'It is quite clear that when we look at animals whose social behaviour is as flexible and elaborate as baboons' and chimpanzees' we cannot explain their behaviour in terms of instinct alone. Clearly something else must be involved since innate behaviour can only change from one generation to the next by natural selection. An animal will only be able to adapt to environmental changes that are also quite slow. But suppose the animal is living in an environment which changes quite rapidly or in which it has to solve problems quickly. Then, evolution through selection of particular behaviour patterns will just not do the job of adaptation for you. In such circumstances some greater flexibility is needed and this can only come about through learning. There must be some additional ability to react to changing circumstances, a capacity to learn and to solve problems.

'A classic demonstration of this is seen in the chimpanzee that is put in a cage and the keeper suddenly has the idea of hanging the bananas from the top of the cage. How is the chimp going to get the bananas? They have always been on the floor before; it is an entirely novel situation. What the chimp does is sit back and look at it for a while. Now if the experimenter has put some boxes in the cage, after a while the chimp will pile those boxes up and climb up to the bananas. This probably depends on prior learning, for example, it may depend upon the fact that the chimp knows from previous trials that it can stack the boxes. But the insight is how to use that bit of learning to solve this particular problem of getting to the food. The Russians have developed a special experimental technique, the study of extrapolation. And in principle it's very simple. I saw it demonstrated in Moscow when I was there some years ago in a test of the wolf's ability to extrapolate from one situation to another.

'You have a panel in front of you and there is an aperture in this through which a bowl of food is seen. When I was there they

A classic demonstration of the chimpanzee's ability to react to its environment is the problem illustrated by a bunch of bananas put out of reach. Using available boxes the chimp builds a platform to overcome the problem.

brought in this great wolf and stood it in front of the panel. Suddenly the food bowl is moved to the left or right. The question is how quickly can the wolf extrapolate from where the food bowl was to where it has moved to. In the test the animal quickly moves its head in the direction suggested by the movement of the bowl. The wolf is sharp in its response but if you tried this test on a more humble mammal, such as a rabbit, it shows no response. In fact, it is possible to classify animals into those which can extrapolate easily, and those which cannot. So we have a very real and interesting question. What is it that causes some animals to have this ability and others not?

'If we look at this from the point of view of the animal's lifestyle we see that the rabbit has a rather simple pattern of life. It has a strategy for getting food, a strategy for finding a mate and a strategy for surviving in the context of predation. Ethologists have talked about these as evolutionarily stable strategies. That is to say they are strategies which have evolved through time and they are probably fixed. It is more than likely that they are anchored in the genes. But when you have an animal like the wolf where the problems of finding food are highly varied, a kind of fixed sequence of behaviour is insufficient. It needs to have an *open programme* so that it can build into this strategy things which it has learnt.

'Why should some species need to have a lot of information from the environment in order to make their strategies work well? The answer is, I think, quite simple. If we look at the most intelligent of mammals like hunting dogs or wolves, these animals are faced with prey which present themselves in innumerable different conditions and which can escape in many ways. So they have to learn the skills of hunting. Furthermore, they may have to learn to operate in a pack and collaborate in hunting, also to solve both hunting and social problems.

'There is a very nice story of Canadian observers studying wolves from an aeroplane. Flying around they watched a pack of wolves moving across the snow. In one instance they saw the pack divide into two groups. One party lay up behind a ridge; the other went around and overlooked a herd of caribou and ran down the hill, panicking the caribou which ran straight into the ambush of the other party of wolves. A great deal of experience and learning is required for such collaboration. It is therefore possible to see that in the case of the hunter, intelligence, insight and the capacity to learn are very important.

'When we look at the primates we do not often find species which are solely meat-eaters. It is not a prime characteristic of apes, so why are they so intelligent? One possible answer to this question lies in the complexity of the social relations in primates. The Gelada baboon has very involved relationships between individuals, and similar examples can be seen in chimp or gorilla societies. With all these interrelations between animals there must be some sense of who is who. An individual here is different from somebody over there. The different properties have therefore to be kept in mind by any individual in the group so that it can behave accordingly. If it is the big male who is aggressive then I know to keep my distance. If I want to ally myself with X, I need to know who X may already be friendly with.

'Intelligence and the learning capacity seem to arise especially from this complex social life, as well as from the need to hunt prey. Now, of course, our ancestors were both socially complex and also hunters. It is probably no accident that the increase in the size of brain seems to coincide with the gradual emergence of that type of behaviour in the early hominids.'

Contemporary ethology has now given a biological perspective to much human behaviour. But the unique human qualities of mind set us apart from all other animals. We have the capacity to experience our own thoughts and to pass these on through language and our culture. The development of language relies on the processes of the mind, not the least of which is a sophisticated memory. And we learn a language only because we have the capacity to do so. The study of these internal processes in evolutionary terms is now beginning and for John Crook this is the most enticing challenge.

'We can now explain a great deal about the reason why human beings are the sort of animal that they are. The social life we lead can be seen in terms of the evolutionary strategies while our culture and language come from being established within the open part of our strategies. From the arguments about altruism we can recognise the origins of collaborative behaviour and through our understanding of why some animals are more intelligent than others, we can begin to see what the sources for our abilities to reason and be intellectual might have been. So when we ask what man is, we can take a biologically-based perspective. A curious problem is that this still doesn't help you or I understand the nature of our own experience. It may explain what we are, but it doesn't explain who we are. It is here that we have to try and bring ethology and social psychology together.

Consciousness

'I have had an idea about this based on the work of Bob Trivers on reciprocal altruism. He pointed out that when you have two animals helping one another on the principle of returns of benefit, "you scratch my back and I'll scratch yours", there is always the possibility of cheating. I might not return the benefit or avoid doing so in some way. It is clearly going to be of significance to you to know whether I am going to cheat or not. How are you going to know? It must require some form of monitoring or observation of my behaviour to detect if I am sincere. We describe this capacity as empathy, so it could be the case that if I wish to know whether or not you are likely to cheat on me I need to empathise, to put myself in your position in some way and experience what your real feelings are. But in doing this there is obviously the danger that I may over-empathise with your position and lose connection with what it is that I am feeling about the situation. To compensate for this risk there needs to be a counteracting ability to distinguish between myself and another. This is certainly an ability that we are aware of having but can we imagine how our ancestors evolved it? Can we see a capacity for this in other animals?

'Well, there are some experiments by Gallup on self-recogniton in chimpanzees that bear on this. In these he observed the behaviour of chimps when faced with a mirror. In the first trials he put a little paint on the animal's nose and when the chimp saw itself in the mirror it tried to rub the mark from its nose, not from the mirror. This is taken as evidence that the chimp knows that the face it sees is "me", my face. This appears to be a high order of insight because monkeys don't seem to be able to do it, nor cats and dogs. But children can do it when they are very young. In other words the insight that that "thing" there is "me" is quite restricted in the animal kingdom. This ability to spot that one is the agent of one's action requires some form of evolved capacity.

'I have been arguing that in evolution the old biological strategies gradually develop open programmes within them which could be filled by learning. These segments of the animal's overall strategy of behaviour enabled species to develop patterns of action that were not just instinctive but which were flexible. In human evolution this led first to the creation of social groups showing co-operative behaviour towards close relatives and on to reciprocal behaviour within the group. The next step was the development of intelligence that enabled more complex interactions and with this arose the need for greater subtlety in dealing with individuals. The capacity to recognise self in a situation is the next great step. I would argue that the uniqueness of man is something to do with our capacity to experience oneself as an agent in the world: self-awareness.

'It may well be the case that chimpanzees have some knowledge of their role in the interaction within a social group, but it is very doubtful whether lacking language they can conceptualise it. Our possession of language allows us to conceptualise the notion that when I lift the teacup, it is "I" who is the agent of lifting it. The development of language for effective communication allows the inference to "I". If you ask which came first, language or consciousness, I would think that the two evolved together and that there are many refined stages in that evolution. The human baby seems to recognise from quite early on that certain of its actions in the world produce effects. By smiling as a baby I can produce a smile in my mother. Now as soon as I recognise that events in the world are sometimes a result of my own behaviour, then human intelligence is certainly capable of moving quickly to say "there is something here, an agent, there's a me".

'If this is what happens in the development of the human baby one must try to imagine what kind of process over an infinitely longer period of time was going on in the protohominids who were our ancestors. The social complexity of such groups would demand the passage of information about particular reciprocating action and partnering. With language, words and concepts about the environment, we are able to relate further with one another. We are able to exchange rules, values and techniques about what is appropriate. And this constitutes the conceptual, interior world of how to live, how to fulfil the biological strategies but using a world of knowledge. This is what is in the open programme. And perhaps the most important thing in that open programme is this notion of "myself" as an identity. The evolutionary process has allowed the individual to put together a set of ideals about "his" or "her" place in a particular society. The open programme is human culture itself.'

Dr Sydney Brenner
Director, Medical Research Council Laboratory
of Molecular Biology, Cambridge

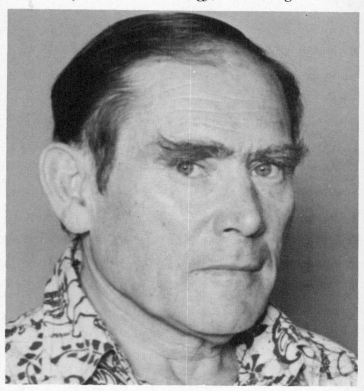

Sydney Brenner has an unusual background for someone who is now director of one of the leading scientific research institutes in the world, the MRC Laboratory of Molecular Biology, Cambridge. Although his mother was Russian and his father Lithuanian, he was brought up in South Africa, where his father worked as a cobbler. When he was fifteen he won a scholarship to the University of Witwatersrand in Johannesburg to study medicine. By the time he had completed a Master of Science as well, he could go no further in South Africa. He began looking for an academic post overseas.

In 1952 he arrived in England with a scholarship to study at Oxford University. While he was there, studying bacteria, new scientific developments were taking place in biochemistry and cell physiology which heralded the beginnings of molecular biology. Sanger discovered that proteins have a molecular structure. Watson and Crick discovered the structure of DNA.

The stage was now set for rapid development in molecular biology. Brenner and a small group of colleagues were right there in the footlights, and the discoveries they made are so remarkable that they have been likened by some to 'the Eighth Day of Creation'. Scarcely a hundred years after Mendel recognised there must be an 'inheritance factor', our understanding of genetics was put on a detailed molecular basis, paving the way for what has now become a vast new field of genetic engineering.

The scientist Peter Medawar once said, 'It is advisable to work on important problems that are soluble, because history does not know about those working on important problems which are insoluble!' But with characteristic disregard for any sort of accolade, Brenner has recently been tackling the most ambitious question of all. What more do we need to know in order for our understanding of biology to be complete? His research takes the form of 'gedanken', a thought experiment where he considers what we would need to know to build animals. It is an idea that may fill some with fear, others with admiration, but for Brenner it is simply an integral part of the 'main delight of doing science . . . the endless possibility it gives you for solving puzzles.'

The Entry of Molecular Biology

Dr Sydney Brenner

Deborah Cadbury

Sydney Brenner was brought up in a small town in South Africa called Germiston. Unlike his parents – who had little education – he displayed an enthusiastic delight in science from an early age.

'Ever since I was a small boy I was interested in living things and had a small laboratory in a garage where I didn't make explosives as most small boys did, but extracted pigments from petals. I was amazed to discover that I could get changes in colour with pH.'

Not surprisingly his progress through school was very rapid, and when he was fifteen he was ready to go to university. His family had little money but the local town council provided a bursary. So in 1942 Brenner went to study at the University of Witwatersrand in Johannesburg, making a daily journey by bicycle and train.

At this time careers in scientific research were very limited. Sydney Brenner already knew that the area that fascinated him lay somewhere between cell physiology and biochemistry, but no such science existed. 'I was strongly advised to read medicine because the only academic posts existed in medical schools. You see, in those days you only had three alternatives in biological sciences . . . you either became a school teacher with a BSc degree and taught botany and zoology in a school, or you went into agriculture, or you did science as part of medicine.' There was no possibility of a career as a biological research scientist.

'I think I must have been the world's worst medical student. I didn't like it very much and used to duck most of the lectures.' In spite of this he studied medicine for over four years. 'It was actually four and a half years because I failed my clinical medicine final examination by not diagnosing a patient as having diabetes. She had cleaned her teeth with a particular brand of toothpaste, and when I was told to smell her breath that was all I could smell. However, I went back for six months and finally passed.'

During his medical science studies, Brenner became increasingly interested in genetics. 'I continued doing science and started studying chromosomes. I think I was the first person in South Africa to study animal chromosomes . . . I knew they were the seat of inheritance – we've known that since 1895 – and that their prime constituent is a substance called chromatin, which somehow carried the characters of the organism, but we did not know *how*. I thought you could study this by looking at chromosome structure, and for two years I made a detailed analysis of the chromosomes of the little elephant shrew . . . and I got a Master of Science degree for that.'

During this time Brenner supported himself by working as a laboratory technician after hours. 'It was the war years and although South Africa was not directly affected by the war, journals didn't come and it was impossible to get chemicals. One of my jobs was to make amino acids for the nutrition work that was going on in the Anatomy Department. I made a huge amount of cysteine, and can remember visiting all the barber shops to collect hair and then hydrolysing it according to classical methods. I think I just had to depend on myself because there was nothing from the outside . . . it was a very difficult experience trying to do science in a provincial and isolated atmosphere.

'Nevertheless I was fortunate to belong to a privileged section of the community because I was white . . . but South Africa was off the beaten track and science is an international culture of metropolitan centres, and being in the network is terribly important.'

Brenner began to look for a place in the network. He knew that a department in Cambridge University specialised in his area of interest. 'So I wrote to Chibnall who was the Professor there . . . but I didn't get a reply and that was the end of that.' Fortunately he was soon awarded a Royal Commission Scholarship and a place at Oxford University to work for Sir Cyril Hinshelwood. He arrived in England at the age of twenty-four. With a medical degree and Master of Science he had gone as far as the South African university system could take him. Less than thirty years later he was to be Director of one of the leading scientific institutes in the world.

The Entry of Molecular Biology

At this stage molecular biology did not exist as a subject. 'The structure of the gene was still very opaque . . . we knew it had a function, that is, somehow it made proteins and enzymes, that it could be recombined in different ways, and that parts of a gene could be separated by crossing over. The strange thing was it could also mutate, and the altered gene could produce a completely different enzyme. People would draw little pictures and say, "When you have a gene that looks like a square then you make a good enzyme, then somehow you shake this up by mutation and the gene might look like a triangle and make another enzyme which may not be so good!" But the details of this seemed completely impenetrable.

'We really knew nothing about the structure of proteins, and we knew even less about the structure of genes . . . but, even so, we still had a base to start from. Although we did not know it at the time, the basic problems of molecular biology had already been defined; it was to discover the connection between the structure of genes and the structure of proteins. So all the great changes that started in 1952 and go on to 1953 provided the basis for the entry of molecular biology.'

The first was Sanger's proof that proteins have a chemical structure. Muscle, cartilage, hair, skin, hormones and enzymes – all these are proteins, the basic building blocks of living organisms. The key constituents of protein are just twenty different kinds of amino acid, of which some hundred to thousand are arranged in a precise sequence on each protein molecule.

The twenty key amino acids coded by the gene:

1 Glycine	2 Alanine
3 Valine	4 Leucine
5 Isoleucine	6 Serine
7 Threonine	8 Aspartic Acid
9 Glutamic Acid	10 Asparagine
11 Glutamine	12 Arginine
13 Lysine	14 Cysteine
15 Methionine	16 Phenylalanine
17 Tyrosine	18 Tryptophan
19 Proline	20 Histidine

Sanger identified the structure and sequence of amino acids in the insulin molecule, a protein which regulates blood sugar.

'One of the most striking memories of my life is going to a lecture given by Fred Sanger at Oxford in 1953, on how he determined the exact sequence of insulin. Sir Robert Robinson, a very great organic chemist, stood up in astonishment at the end and said, "Well, now we know that proteins have a chemical structure!" It's amazing to think that up until that work most chemists believed that proteins were a kind of statistical glob, just

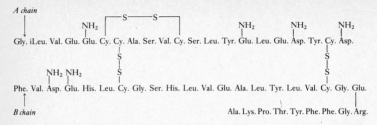

A chain

Gly. iLeu. Val. Glu. Glu. Cy. Cy. Ala. Ser. Val. Cy. Ser. Leu. Tyr. Glu. Leu. Glu. Asp. Tyr. Cy. Asp.

Phe. Val. Asp. Glu. His. Leu. Cy. Gly. Ser. His. Leu. Val. Glu. Ala. Leu. Tyr. Leu. Val. Cy. Gly. Glu.

B chain

Ala. Lys. Pro. Thr. Tyr. Phe. Phe. Gly. Arg.

In 1953 Fred Sanger determined the structure and exact sequence of amino acids in the insulin molecule. 'It was amazing to think that proteins actually had a precise chemical structure.'

amino acids lumped together like plastic. I think this was one of the cornerstones of the subject and I remember feeling tremendously impressed that the chemistry of these complicated molecules could actually be worked out.'

The race was now on to understand the structure of genetic material itself. It was known that the prime constituent of the chromatin in chromosomes was deoxyribonucleic acid, or DNA. But what was this DNA? Scientists in America and England were interested in the problem, and the race is a story of professional rivalry, secrecy, and occasional flashes of brilliance. As one scientist put it: DNA is like Midas gold; everybody who touches it goes mad!

But it was Watson and Crick who produced the answer and went on to win the Nobel Prize. On 25 April 1953 *Nature* published a letter in which they – with disarming understatement – proposed a structure for DNA. They suggested DNA consists of two phosphate-sugar helical chains, coiled round each other. The chains are held together by hydrogen bands between 'bases'. There are only four kinds of bases along the whole length of DNA, and they always pair in a specific way, adenine with thymine, guanine with cytosine. Watson and Crick modestly added, 'It had not escaped our notice that the specific pairing we have postulated immediately suggests a possible copying mechanism for genetic material.' And of course they were right.

Brenner went to Cambridge from Oxford to see their molecular model. 'When I saw the original model standing on a table in a room I would myself inhabit a few years later, everything became clear and obvious. But many people were not persuaded because they thought there had to be protein in the genes, or because they thought that unwinding the strands would be impossible. It took a

In 1953 Jim Watson and Francis Crick proposed a structure for DNA. For Brenner this was a turning point because it was possible to understand how genetic information was encoded in very precise chemical terms.

while to convert everybody . . . really to shake them out of the idea that simplicity cannot give rise to complexity.'

However, the discovery had an even greater significance. 'I think it changed the style of thinking. The revelation of the model and all that followed was that we could formulate a loose concept like "information" in very precise chemical terms. You could now talk about a sequence, and about sequence information.'

Brenner had a chance to talk to Francis Crick and Jim Watson at some length. 'We discussed how genes were connected to proteins. Of all the things that had emerged from the model the key problem had now become very clear indeed, and we called it the "coding problem": how was genetic information encoded in the gene?'

The Coding Problem

Sydney Brenner travelled in 1954 to America and then spent 1955 and most of 1956 in South Africa. At the end of 1956 he was given a post at the Medical Research Council's scientific laboratories in Cambridge, to help to initiate the genetic work. He shared an office with Crick and they would talk for hours about molecular biology. 'We knew DNA is a one-dimensional sequence of four components, the bases, and, when unfolded, proteins could be seen as another linear structure of twenty components, the amino acids. The question was . . . how do you go from the gene language to the protein language? The coding problem had one enormous attraction: it looked possible that you could crack it, solve it, without doing any work at all . . . we thought that there might be something in the sequence which would allow us to work out the code, and indeed Gamow tried this very early.'

George Gamow was a brilliant cosmologist who was renowned for his ideas on the origins of the Universe. Everything began in a 'Big Bang' millions of years ago when all of energy and matter exploded into being, and expanded gradually to our present Universe. His ideas have survived in modified form and still dominate cosmological thinking.

Gamow happened to be visiting a friend in Berkeley, California, when he heard about Watson and Crick's work. He took up the challenge and within a matter of weeks had worked out a scheme whereby DNA could directly order the sequences of amino acids in proteins. His scheme was such that the sequence of four bases could specify the amino-acid sequence, by amino acids locking directly into 'holes' in DNA.

Brenner was somewhat amused by this work. 'I mean, Gamow's idea was curious in that the model had no real physical represent-ation. One couldn't see a credible mechanism for the recognition specificity. I was interested not only in the theory of coding, but in models which led us to what was actually happening in the real world. I have always believed that, if you have a theory, first of all it should be logically correct, and contain no contradiction, and then you must define at least one plausible biological implementation of it.

'We all thought that Gamow's code would never work, but this would have to be proved and then we would need something to put in its place. We soon realised we might not be able to decipher the language of DNA by looking just at its internal structure, as Gamow had tried to do, but would have to decipher it by finding the Rosetta stone – that is, by finding the actual code.'

The first problem was how many bases correspond to one amino acid? Clearly, more than one base would correspond to an amino acid, because there are only four of the former, and twenty of the latter. Indeed more than two bases would be required, because if the bases rated in pairs that still only gives sixteen possibilities, which is not enough.

Bases	Amino Acids
1 AA	Glycine
2 CC	Valine
3 TT	Isoleucine
4 GG	Threonine
5 AC	Glutamic Acid
6 CA	Lysine
7 AT	Methionine
8 TA	Tyrosine
9 AG	Proline
10 GA	Alanine
11 CT	Leucine
12 TC	Serine
13 CG	Aspartic Acid
14 GC	Asparagine
15 TG	Arginine
16 GT	Cysteine
17 —	Phenylalanine
18 —	Tryptophan
19 —	Histidine
20 —	Glutamine

A two-letter base code still could not produce all the amino acids.

'So we thought the code was likely to be triplet, that is, three bases corresponding to one amino acid. Gamow's code was an overlapping triplet code, but I proved these codes were impossible. We were left with the idea that the DNA strands were read from one end, three bases at a time with no overlapping . . .

'Now at this time there was a considerable interest in chemical mutagenesis, making mutations in DNA using chemicals. I had been working on a specific type of mutation induced by proflavin, which was an acridine dye. There were many puzzling features about these mutations in that they always seemed to destroy the function of the protein. One day Francis and I were discussing this in the famous "Eagle" pub in Cambridge, and we began to wonder whether the acridines were causing additions and deletions in DNA rather than substitutes. This would destroy the meaning of the message, and thereby the function of the proteins made.'

Imagine a gene composed of the repeated triplet, CAT, CAT, CAT. Suppose the dye 'deleted' a base:

> Cytosine
> Adenine
> Thymine
> C
> A̶   *Deletion*
> T
> C
> A
> T

or 'added' a base as shown below:

> C
> A
> T
> *A*   *Addition*
> C
> A
> T

Brenner and Crick realised that this could be used to discover properties of the code. 'If you take the message CAT, CAT, CAT . . . and delete one of the bases, say, cytosine, then, beyond the deletion, the message is converted into gibberish – ATC, ATC.

> C̶   *First Deletion*
> ⌈A
> |T
> ⌊C
> ⌈A
> |T
> ⌊C
> ⌈A
> |T
> ⌊C

'If you delete yet another base, say, adenine, you get a second form of gibberish – TCA, TCA, TCA . . .

✂ ✂
✂ ✂   *Second Deletion*
⌐T
 C
⌐A
⌐T
 C
⌐A
⌐T
 C
⌐A

'But if you delete a third base, thymine, you convert back to the original message – CAT, CAT, CAT . . .

✂ ✂
✂ ✂
✂ ✂   *Third Deletion*
⌐C
 A
 T
⌐C
 A
 T
⌐C
 A
 T

'This is a simple summary of the outcome of a large number of experiments. It is an astounding result because it means if you put three similar mutants together, the message will come back to normal again. One mutant is no good, two are no good, but three is good again, then four is no good, and so on. The experiment to show that three mutants restore the correct phase of reading was done by Francis while I was in Paris doing another experiment . . . and it worked perfectly.

'By simple genetic experiments, we had proved that the size of the coding unit was three, i.e. it was a triplet code . . . that it was read from one end, with no overlapping . . . and that it was likely to be a highly degenerate code. But a name was needed for the coding unit.

'It happened that Seymour Benzer had invented a number of words to describe the components of the gene and, being a physicist by training, he always ended them with "on". The first word he invented was "cistron", which was the unit of the cis-trans genetic test, and this word has survived. Seymour also invented the word "muton" which was the unit of mutation, but this did not survive because it came out as "mouton" in French . . . there was even the suggestion of the "switch-on" as the unit of turning a gene. One day when we were joking about this in the lab, wondering what to call the element in DNA that corresponds to one amino acid, I said, more or less as a joke, "Let's call it a codon." That word has survived.'

The Messenger

Concurrent with this work on mutation, Brenner and Crick had been working on another problem. How did the encoded information in the gene translate physically into proteins? Was transfer direct? Was there some information intermediate like a messenger molecule?

'We knew there was an apparatus to make proteins in the cell. The amino acids just did not come and sit on the gene and then get zipped up, which is what Gamow postulated. But he could be forgiven because he was after all only a cosmologist. The best idea really was of an information intermediate . . .

'The machinery for synthesising amino acids in the cells is very elaborate. It was already known that small particles in the cell called ribosomes were somehow involved, and also that these ribosomes contained molecules of another kind of nucleic acid called ribonucleic acid or RNA . . . and it was reasonable to assume that these ribosomes in some way contained the working copy of the gene which was then the template on which the amino-acid sequence could be assembled. But how did the information get out of the DNA and into the ribosomes?'

Many of these problems were discussed by correspondence through an organisation that Gamow had founded called the 'RNA Tie Club'. The club's emblem was the RNA tie, which was embroidered with a green sugar-phosphate chain, and yellow bases. Membership was limited to twenty, one member for each of the amino acids – Brenner's acid was valine, and this was etched on his club tiepin. In spite of this almost boyish enthusiasm, most of the papers were actually written by Crick and Brenner who were toying with coding ideas for many years.

'Everything came together in a meeting which was held in my room at King's College in April 1960, where a number of us had collected to discuss these problems. The Paris group, Jacob and Monod, reported experiments showing that although the ribosomes at some stage contained the genetic information encoded in DNA, they could not be the information carriers themselves . . . so what was?

'At one moment I saw with blinding insight – it was just a moment of illumination – that there had to be *another* RNA, which was the messenger, carrying the information . . . and I knew how to prove it. It just clicked, and I remember very clearly that at one moment only Francis and I were talking to each other, and no one else was understanding . . . it was just as though everybody else had disappeared and we were alone.'

Of course Brenner still had to design an experiment that would test the idea: that would prove there was another RNA, a messenger, going from the DNA to the ribosomes.

'Later that very afternoon, I formulated the precise experiment. François Jacob was staying with me, and I outlined the idea to him. If you consider a bacterial cell with its own DNA, this DNA makes RNA, and the RNA is packaged into the cell ribosomes . . .

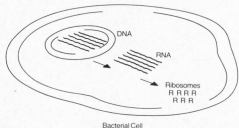

Bacterial Cell

'If a phage invades this bacterial cell, it injects its own phage DNA which makes phage RNA. The old idea would have it that the phage RNA molecules get packaged into *new* phage ribosomes, and that these make the phage proteins.

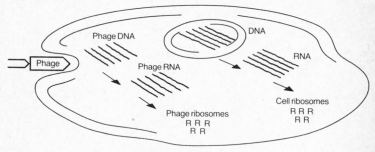

First Hypothesis:
Phage makes new ribosomes

'On the contrary, the messenger idea implied that this new phage RNA could act as a messenger for the phage DNA, and simply be added to the old cell ribosomes. The ribosomes were like tape-recorders, and the messenger RNA was a tape inserted into pre-existing tape recorders.

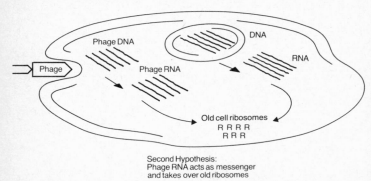

Second Hypothesis:
Phage RNA acts as messenger
and takes over old ribosomes

Brenner designed an experiment to test the existence and function of messenger RNA, by observing the behaviour of phage when it invades a bacterium.

'The two hypotheses could be clearly distinguished by finding out whether the phage RNA was in new ribosomes, or added to old ribosomes.

'François Jacob and I did this experiment together later that year because we both had planned to be at CalTech in June. We had three weeks to complete it. We worked like dogs but nothing would come right. The ribosomes kept falling apart – it was just a mess – and people around us began to say, "This is going to take a long time, you just can't do this so easily. You will need at least a year of work to find out all the conditions and so on . . ."' But of course they underestimated Brenner.

'One day in Malibu, as Jacob says "sur la plage", we had an idea. I suddenly leapt up and said, "Magnesium, more magnesium!" and we rushed back to the lab and shovelled the magnesium in. This stabilised the ribosomes so they didn't fall apart. It was quite funny, because it was the last chance experiment; if it didn't work we would then have to give up.

'I remember it was at the same time as Kennedy was being nominated for the Democratic Presidential election in 1960 . . . everybody else gathered around a television set to look at the final nomination ceremony, but François and I gathered around our

Geiger counter in our armchairs, and we sat and we waited for the results. The counts came out and they were very low . . . they stayed low . . . and then the peak came, and we shouted and cheered. And each time the counter went to the next sample, the peak rose and I remember us saying, "Enough, enough, now you must turn around and go down again," which it did . . .'

The results proved conclusively that the new phage RNA was indeed a messenger between the genetic material, the DNA of the invading phage, and the protein synthesising equipment of the host cell, the old ribosomes. 'It was a great experience, but then it took six more months of hard work in Cambridge to complete all the experiments . . .'

The picture that finally emerged for transferring genetic information into living organisms was remarkable. DNA remains in the nucleus, but the helix is opened, the two strands separate and can be copied precisely by RNA. This messenger moves out of the nucleus into the cell's cytoplasm. Here the ribosomes move down the RNA from one end to the other, reading off the triplet message and drawing together the right amino acid for each triplet. In this way a sequence of amino acids is built up, and the resulting chain folds into one protein molecule. The process was to be repeated with many different templates to make all the different proteins in an organism.

'I think that was probably the last of what I see as the grand experiments, where you can do things, so to speak, with no hands . . . and one of the things about the work we did at Cambridge was to set a very high value on ingenuity and what I would call "elegance", but elegance is a much devalued word in biology now.

'The elegance was in the coupling of a rather subtle theoretical analysis of the problem – something you could not see immediately – together with a very simple way of demonstrating it, simple almost to the point of being off-hand. We mostly worked with bacteria. Bacteria make holes in agar layers in petri dishes, that's how you count them, and you simply crossed them and scored "yes" or "no". The remarkable thing is that from the study of these simple observations you could deduce deep things about DNA coding at the molecular level. It was also a field where you could have an idea one night, go into the lab the next day, and by the end of the week you would have an answer . . . but these were absolutely unique situations, and unlikely to be repeated. It is quite a marvellous thing to have lived through those days when just a handful of people worked to make a new science.

'By 1961 the whole nature of the genetic code had been solved, much was known about the chemistry of protein synthesis, and we had got to this long-missing part of the framework, messenger RNA. One might well ask, as we did, was molecular biology over? Here is a subject that started in 1953 and finished in 1961 . . . many people really thought that.'

But not Brenner. He had turned to even more ambitious questions. In a sense these anticipate what might be the next paradigm shift. A mere eight years had been sufficient for molecular biologists to find a way of expressing 'inheritance' in precise chemical terms. Brenner wanted to go much further. Surely biological 'organisation' – how cells differentiate and become specialised – could also be understood in precise chemical terms, and would rest on a few key principles still to be discovered?

In 1983 Brenner remarked, perhaps slightly regretfully, 'In the thirty years since then, molecular biology has become a world-wide endeavour, with thousands of laboratories producing enormous catalogues of molecular components . . . but this kind of reductionist approach, reducing organisms to a kind of telephone directory, is *not* going to lead us to an explanation of living organisms. I still think there is something else to be discovered.' In the final section of this chapter, Brenner describes how he set down a different route searching for what might be required for us totally to understand living organisms, and complete the route from genes to behaviour.

The Promised Land

'By 1963 I was becoming interested, not in making molecules, but in making animals, since this is the final test of our understanding in biology. In a sense, true genetic engineering does not yet exist . . . you can't go and order a mythical beast from anybody. And if we take some of the mythical beasts that have been created in the imaginations of other people, like centaurs, and ask how we would design and build them, we can begin to see why genetic engineering does not yet exist as a practice.

'If you look at a centaur carefully, you will see it is a six-limbed animal, it has to have two sets of lungs, two sets of intestines and so on . . . there would be a number of mechanical problems in joining all these together. Let us even suppose we could deal with that. Our job in designing a centaur is not to do what the Ancient Greeks did – which can simply be called hopeful transplantation surgery – where you cut the top off a man and glue it onto the bottom of a horse. We have actually to design the genes that will make a centaur, and today we just wouldn't know how to go about designing those genes, or even to say what genes we would require.'

The issue is not simply one of understanding biological organisation – how, for instance, to place the horse's heart and the man's heart so that they function. It is much more fundamental. 'If you think in terms of how to build animals and explore the limitations, we can certainly build proteins, but organisms are much more than bags of proteins, and complex organisms like ourselves do not emerge from nothing in their final form. They undergo a process of embryological development.

'Every complex organism begins with an egg, and the egg divides, and goes on dividing, eventually generating a very complicated structure composed of many different kinds of cells, each doing something special . . . so the real problem about designing complex animals is how to go about programming the whole of embryological development.'

In 1963, with these ideas in mind, Brenner began a long search

If we could build mythological figures such as this centaur, Brenner considers our understanding of biology would be complete.

through the literature, looking for the ideal organism for the study of such problems. Eventually he chose a tiny worm, *Caenorhabditis elegans*, which normally lives in the soil. The aim was to observe every detail of the animal's development, to find out if there was a formula for growth and differentiation, just as Sanger had found proteins have a formula for their molecular structure. If such a principle could be uncovered, then it should be applicable to other animals.

'Evolution is a conservative process . . . once a good mechanism is created it tends to be incorporated and passed on. Whatever we found in the worm for controlling these developmental processes, we should be able to find in ourselves . . .' Together with a few younger colleagues he embarked upon an exhaustive structural analysis of this animal.

'We focused particularly on the nervous system because it displays all the questions that we wanted to work on. It has cells with different biochemistry, but more than that the cells are in different places and connect to each other – by long processes, often running the whole length of an animal. This raises special questions such as how do these processes find their way? How accurately is this done? And in what sense is this all represented in the genes?'

The work took years. But, together with collaborators John White and John Suston, 'We were able to deal with all the technical problems, and collect all the information. We built a wiring map of the complete nervous system, so we knew which cells are connected to which, and how and where they were joined, and we found that this little worm – which only contains about a thousand cells – has a defined structure, a cellular formula, which we could write down. The worm was remarkable because not only does each adult have a fixed structure, but every cell arises in the same way during development.'

They reached a point where they had mapped the cell lineage, the pathway for the production of each of those thousand cells. Never before had so much been known about any animal.

'I've often wondered whether the work on the worm has developed the way I hoped it might. The simple aspects of finding new techniques, getting the facts, have gone much as expected . . . but when I ask myself what would be equivalent in the worm to, say, the way we determined the triplet code, one possibility might have been the following: we'd have looked at a piece of the animal structure, discerned some odd feature, some extraordinary pattern . . . and from that we could have deduced the way the structure was created. And then we would have done one simple experiment to prove the principle. Alas, nothing like that has happened.

'One should not underestimate the nature of the problem that we are facing in this area of biology. The pessimist will say you have to understand everything; identify all the genes, find out what they all do, and how they work in the cell – so we would have to know an enormous amount about a worm in order to make one. But of course that denies the possibility of a single open door, through which we may enter the promised land, the breakthrough portal. Of course everybody is waiting or looking for this break-through portal and the pessimistic view is that it's not going to be there . . . there are simply lots and lots of foothills to climb before you get to the top of Everest, and you'll only discover then that you're at the top.'

However, needless to say, Brenner is not a pessimist. He analyses the problem, and tries to find out about the promised land by means of analogy.

'Our main difficulty is to find a language to talk about these matters. Think about a bacterial cell as a model of a complex system and first just consider its biochemistry. We have a cell with several thousand chemical reactions going on in the same tiny little space, a thousandth of a millimetre across. The reactions are going on simultaneously, so every twenty minutes the cell doubles in size, divides accurately, and repeats the process.

'Many people have asked, "Why doesn't the bacterial cell explode or shrink to nothing? How can you control four thousand chemical reactions in this space? Who is the master controller?" There have been searches for the master controller . . . but it has not yet been found, for the very good reason that there isn't one!'

If there is no master controller in a bacterial cell regulating chemistry, development, cell division, how could the cell be organised? Brenner suggests that 'anarchy' provides the best metaphor.

'If you look at what I call a "computational" model of a bacterial cell, it works through anarchic demons, with the strict boundary condition of capital punishment for greed. That's all. If one component gets too greedy then the whole system dies, and evolution must then minimise greed.

'Each chemical reaction is catalysed by an enzyme and each enzyme specified by a gene. There are several thousand different small molecules bouncing around in the cell and undergoing chemical transformations. How, one might ask, does any enzyme find the small molecule product of its predecessor? In the past people have thought what might be called the "assembly-line" model would be inevitable. That is, an enzyme takes its product and hands it on to the next one, which hands it on to the next, and so on . . . but it is nothing like that at all.

'Everything is thrown out into the solution and everything is banging against everything else . . . so it's more like a "broadcast" system. Chemicals are being broadcast from all centres, to all other centres . . . there are no physical addresses in a bacterium, no co-ordinates where you may find an enzyme. However, there are logical addresses because each enzyme has been built by evolution only to recognise the collision with the right substrate. All other molecules just bounce off and even although only a small percentage of collisions are the right ones, the collision frequency is so high that there are enough of them.

'A bacterium is actually wired up; but everything is wired to everything else, and a large number of the wires are ineffective. Only the important ones, where a molecule will bind to a protein or enzyme, work. All regulation is by local systems control. Each little sub-system is tooled to ignore everything else and only consider its own product . . . so there is nothing in a bacterium thinking about four thousand problems and trying to optimise this, because that would surely need a giant computer.'

One may well ask whether this image in a bacterial cell of organisation and development as a form of anarchy really applies to higher organisms. 'Of course, the interesting thing to ask is, what would there have to be in the development of complex organisms, if there *was* a master controller? Now the master controller – whatever it might be – would have to deliver instructions to, say, the big toe as it was developing, and say to the big toe, "Now start developing!" And the big toe would start to grow. However, in all systems where there is a hierarchy you have to report back to the master, so the big toe would have to tell the master, "I have stopped developing, what do I do now?"

'If you imagine this going on for the whole organism, what you soon find is that the master controller gets choked by its own messages, and spends most of its time coping with these, so there's no time left to do anything else. This is often called the administrative catastrophe . . . a lot of work is done but nothing comes out at the end because all that is happening are discussions on the priorities of what ought to be done. Apart from this argument, there are also difficulties in thinking of a logical locus for the master controller.

'So the picture that I have – and I agree that it's totally unsatisfactory – is that development should be seen as an "information retrieval" system. The genes are a library with a lot of useful information in them which evolution has collected. The organism is viewed as something which progresses through time, from one state to the next; its development is rather like turning the pages of a book . . . and when a cell divides, a page gets turned, and you can now read the information on the next page. All this is done by historical unfolding rather than by something that issues instructions, and sends signals, and has timers and so on. This may sound terribly unsatisfactory, but I think it is still the best way to approach these problems.

'This means I would not be looking too deeply for genetic control, because if there are too many genes that just do nothing but regulate other genes, then we're once more back to the administrative catastrophe . . . I don't think we'll find too deep a level of hierarchy if there is a hierarchy at all. The tendency of people to discuss development and regulation in hierarchical and command terms may reflect something about ourselves rather than about the animals we study.

'At the end of the day, you may well ask where all this is leading to. Let us suppose we have the complete structure of an animal. We have the complete cell lineage, and we have the exact formula and sequence of its DNA. Will we "understand" that animal? . . . and will we have an understanding that could be transferred to human beings, or centaurs, or any other animal?

'I think it will be a long time before we know the final answer to that question, and I hesitate to make any predictions. However, in the spirit of molecular biology, I must say that, in principle, if I had the gene script and enough information about the interpreters of the gene sequence . . . then I could understand how that animal is built. I say so because, in a very strong sense, that gene script *must* contain the complete description of the animal, and in that sense animals should be computable from their gene scripts alone, if you only know more about the interpreters. When we have all of that we can build centaurs, or worms, or anything that you please . . . and only then will genetic engineering have come of age.'

Dr Dan McKenzie FRS
Reader in Tectonics, University of Cambridge

Dan McKenzie was born in Cheltenham in 1942. After the war his family moved to London when his father took up a medical practice in Harley Street. He went to Westminster School and when the time came to consider a career, his physics master sent him on a visit to his old college, King's, Cambridge. Taken around to meet and talk with a number of the dons, he was offered a place; 'a staggering example of the old boy network', in his own words. But in the entrance exams he won his place with a state scholarship to read Natural Sciences.

After his BA at Cambridge, he completed a Ph.D in geophysics. Less than a year later he published work on the 'plate tectonics' theory: it was the start of a revolution in geological thinking.

In the years that followed he travelled from Cambridge around the world on field trips and visits to other research institutes. At twenty-five, he had become an international figure in geology. In 1976 he was elected to the Royal Society. Dan McKenzie lives in Cambridge with his wife and son.

The Day the Earth Moved
Dr Dan McKenzie FRS

Paul Andersen

'I think that the basic framework of plate tectonics that we put together at the end of the 1960s is not going to change at all. Our understanding of the evolution of the sea floor is now largely complete. However, I don't feel that the extension of this idea to the continents will carry anything like the same weight: we are still very uncertain about what precisely happens on the continents. But to take an analogy from something which is more familiar, Newtonian mechanics, when that was understood by Newton an entire area of scientific endeavour suddenly fell into place. The changes which Einstein produced in this field, for instance, have not altered the fact that if we want to know where a spacecraft is going when we launch it from the Earth we use Newtonian mechanics; we don't use relativistic mechanics. Now, in a much more humble way, the idea of plate tectonics is going to remain as the basic idea of how the planet behaves.'

At twenty-five, when just fresh from finishing his doctorate at Cambridge, Dan McKenzie helped bring about a revolution in geology that changed our view of the Earth. For the first time there appeared to be one theory that could account for earthquakes, volcanoes, mountain building and the drifting of whole continents. The study of the Earth's crust, tectonics, had remained largely unchanged for over a century. How the forces of the planet were exerted to create the mountains and landmasses had been left to mainly descriptive study without any clear ideas emerging on the nature of the underlying processes.

The notion of plate tectonics, in which the Earth's surface consists of about ten internally rigid 'plates' moving continuously relative to one another, was to provide a stunning theory on the nature of the Earth's architecture.

'I think plate tectonics has changed our whole attitude towards the evolution of the Earth because one now has a framework in which we can look at events. Once you realise that the plates are in motion and that their boundaries are the geological faults, such as

San Andreas fault in California – a meeting of two plates. The disastrous San Francisco earthquake of 1906 was the result of movement between the Pacific and the North American plates.

the San Andreas, then the existence of earthquakes in the region is perfectly clear. It can even give a rather primitive method of earthquake prediction. Those areas on the plate boundary where there hasn't been an earthquake for a long time are clearly at risk some time in the future. When we look at the subduction zones where one plate is diving under another, the crust melts and produces volcanoes. This has put a very different light on our understanding of the origins of igneous rocks. We now have some sort of model as to what occurs in these areas and can test the composition of the rocks at sites like Mount St Helens to see precisely what is happening.

'In a completely different direction it has changed our ideas about the way in which animals and plants are distributed across the planet. We can now make reconstructions of what the Earth looked like and see that, where certain animals or plants were in existence on a particular landmass, they remained with various pieces of that land as it separated. The marsupials in Australia, we believe, arrived there by walking across Antarctica, which then separated as a landmass to isolate them on the continent.'

How Early Enthusiasm was Crushed

For a scientist the opportunity of being present at a time of major change in a discipline's thinking is rare, and to be a part of that revolution when just beginning a career befalls few people. Dan McKenzie's choice of geology as a research subject had really come about after a false start in the field. At school he had discovered that to pursue his scholarship to King's College, Cambridge, he needed to start a new science subject in addition to the chemistry, physics and mathematics he would study at university. He was told to choose between physiology and geology. From the school library he took out all the books on both subjects.

'The physiology books were modern textbooks for medical students and were extremely dull. There were only two on geology: Lyell's *Principles of Geology* and Geikie's *The Ancient Volcanoes of Britain*. These I thought were marvellous and I went up full of enthusiasm for the whole subject. But when I got there I found that really rather little progress had been made since they were written. The enthusiasm which came through in Lyell's book seemed no longer to exist. It had become a study of minutiae and the big issues were really rather lost in this affair.

'Consequently, after a year I gave it up in favour of theoretical physics. I had always wanted to do research, so in my last year I started to look around rather carefully. I talked to a number of people whom I knew, including Fred Hoyle who thought I should do biophysics, and Maurice Hill who was sure I should do geophysics. Maurice was my director of studies and he and Drummond Matthews were marine geologists working at Madingley in the geophysics department. They were quite determined that I should be a geophysicist and they took a great deal of trouble to interest me in the subject. I went out to the labs with them and met Teddy Bullard who was the professor in the department. I must say it impressed me very much. It was known at that time as the best club in Cambridge, which is a very fair description of it still.

'There were about fifteen or twenty research students and perhaps six or seven staff. Everyone knew each other very well and did their work very effectively. But the notion that what people were working on would become the basis for a major change in the

Earth sciences was not at all clear to the people who were sitting around having tea at that time. I liked the atmosphere and so chose to do research there with Teddy Bullard as my supervisor.'

McKenzie began by working on the problems of seismic wave velocities in the Earth's mantle, putting to use the quantum mechanics he had studied in physics. From this work grew an interest in the way the material of the mantle moved and altered beneath the Earth's surface. In 1966 McKenzie finished his Ph.D at Cambridge and went to New York for a conference that NASA had organised on the history of the Earth's crust. The discussions which took place galvanised McKenzie's ideas on what he should do next. On the agenda was a subject that seemed reminiscent of the grand-scale geology of the nineteenth century. It dealt with the movement of the sea floor and how this might give some clue to the origin of the continents. What is more, it seemed to match up with some ideas which his tutor Teddy Bullard had expressed on the 'fit' of the continents.

The Victorian View of the World

'The ideas of continental drift really started with some rather wild speculations in the nineteenth century. In particular, a German meteorologist, Wegener, was impressed by the fit of the continents in the South Atlantic. He was a very imaginative guy and he took to this with almost evangelical enthusiasm. He pushed the idea of continental drift in every way so that any evidence which could be interpreted as horizontal movement of the continents was grist to his mill. He made very little attempt at finding out if the evidence was actually right or simply errors in observation. Geodetic measurements were made of Greenland and Canada which he found showed a rate of motion between North America and Canada of eleven metres a year, but these calculations were quickly found to be grossly in error.

'The mixture of what were some really good observations, such as the fit of the continents in the South Atlantic, with these bad measurements discredited the whole idea of continental drift. Scientists picked on the unsound parts and rather easily disproved them, and as usual forgot about the parts which they could not deal with. Few people then took the idea seriously and for the next fifty years nobody thought carefully about what would happen if the Earth really was mobile.'

This idea of the Earth as a fixed and rigid planet had received considerable support and there was an intimidation from within geology against any challenge to the idea. As Dan McKenzie had

found, much of geology was stuck with inherited views and concerned with classification of rocks rather than the discovery of an overall framework to the Earth's development. However, the introduction of geophysics with its emphasis on using physical and mathematical techniques was set to change that.

'The geophysicists certainly started off with very little interest in or time for the geologists. Geology had for a long time been dominated by some strongly held views on what the Earth was like

A view of the Earth's interior. Under the influence of the heat from the Earth's core the material of the mantle is believed to move as a fluid. It is this circulation of material that is thought to drive the plates on the surface of the planet.

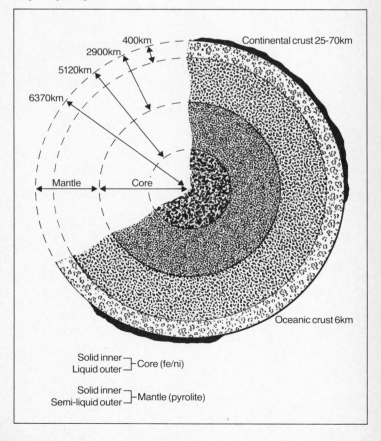

400km
2900km
5120km
6370km

Continental crust 25-70km

Mantle   Core

Oceanic crust 6km

Solid inner
Liquid outer ⎬ Core (fe/ni)

Solid inner
Semi-liquid outer ⎬ Mantle (pyrolite)

as a planet. In particular the idea that the Earth was basically solid had been argued for by some very influential figures. Sir Harold Jeffreys, for instance, who was an eminent mathematician and Professor of Astronomy, had also carried out a lot of work on seismology. From his and other seismologists' work it had been shown that the Earth was fundamentally a solid.

'In the nineteenth century people had thought that because lava came out of volcanoes there was some sort of liquid layer which went all round underneath the Earth's surface. The early results from seismology then very clearly disproved this notion: they indicated a solid Earth. But this was really a misunderstanding about the properties of matter. For we now know a great deal more about the behaviour of materials and in particular that at the high temperatures found within the Earth there can be a continuous flow of what are perfectly good solids.

'For geophysicists, the physical and mathematical techniques that we use are the new tools for looking at the Earth. The object of what we are trying to do is very like that of the geologist in the field with a hammer. But you cannot study what interested me with a hammer. To look at mountain building or the ocean floor you need seismology, satellite photographs and suchlike to tackle these problems which enables you to consider a great many more problems than were available to classical geology.'

New Science, New Ideas
The development of this new emphasis had come about in part as a result of the Second World War. Marine geology had been of importance to the British and United States Navies as they ranged back and forth across the Atlantic and Pacific Oceans. There was new echo-sounding equipment for the location of submarines, and the new atomic weapon had meant a renewed interest in the setting-up of seismic sensing equipment to measure the results of explosions. From within physics there was an increased understanding about the behaviour of materials and, with the arrival of computer processing during the 1960s, complex mathematical modelling of geological behaviour was now a practical proposition.

'I think the change in our views about continental drift began with the war. Up until then it was still disregarded by the establishment and for many years after the war the subject produced an extreme ferocity of argument among Earth scientists. However, by the time I was a graduate student in 1963, a number of people had begun to take a broader view; in particular Harry Hess at Princeton and Tuzo Wilson at Toronto.

'I remember that Harry Hess had been invited to give a talk to the undergraduate geological society at Cambridge in 1962 on sea-floor spreading. I was in the audience and I recall that Teddy Bullard introduced him as "Admiral Hess" which got things away to a good start since Hess had been an Admiral with the United States Navy during the war. What Hess had done was to put an echo-sounder on his convoy ship and take different routes each time he crossed the Pacific to the Far East in order to map the sea floor. After his success in bringing to light new information about the sea floor a lot more people in the subject became involved with research ships. The result was that over the intervening years we had begun to see what the bottom of the sea looked like, first of all just the topography and then with more intense sound sources we could actually look at the sediments beneath the sea.

'Several things gradually became clear from this work. One was that very little of the sea floor was older than perhaps a hundred million years. This became clear simply because people lowered instruments and took samples, and they all turned out to be young. We also learned that there were ridges running down the middle of the oceans largely devoid of sediment: and that the sediment increased in thickness as you moved away from them. Hess had a very good reception from everyone at the talk and Teddy Bullard was favourably inclined to the idea of sea floor spreading.'

The Mystery of the Magnetic Stripes

In addition to this work on the sea floor a quite different area of study was producing interesting results. Geologists had discovered that rocks were differently magnetised according to their age. Old rocks were found to have a magnetic field that was not the same as present-day material. It had been difficult to interpret these results, but when it was discovered that the sea floor contained similar variations in magnetic direction a second piece of the jigsaw was unwittingly revealed.

The magnetic stripe story began with two people, Mason and Raff. They had built a magnetometer which measured the main magnetic field of the Earth and could be towed behind a ship. They wanted to try this magnetometer out and eventually got permission to send it on a survey ship of the US Navy. The ship was actually making a classified study of the shape of the sea bottom off the North-West coast of America. So they were able to put the magnetometer over the side and record measurements as they sailed back and forth, with the result that they obtained a very good two-dimensional survey.

A magnetometer on board the deck of a survey ship. Towed underwater behind a ship it will record the strength of the magnetic field across the sea floor.

The striking thing that came from this was first of all that there were these magnetic anomalies, the stripes. When you looked at the magnetic readings drawn on a map of the sea floor there were lines of positive magnetic fields and lines of negative fields. This was published without any really satisfactory explanation as to how it could have arisen.

The difficulty with this work was that the bathymetry was classified and so we did not realise until long afterwards that there was actually a ridge in the middle of this survey.

The existence of ridges on the floor of both the Atlantic and Pacific was well known at this time. But this small region off the coast of Northern California and Oregon was not seismically very active and had not been identified as being close to a ridge. For this reason the penny didn't drop that there was a symmetry of these magnetic stripes about the axis of a ridge.

But it was this survey and the discovery of the magnetic stripes which gave Drummond Matthews and Fred Vine at Cambridge their idea. It had begun with a different survey in the Indian Ocean where they had surveyed an underwater volcano and found

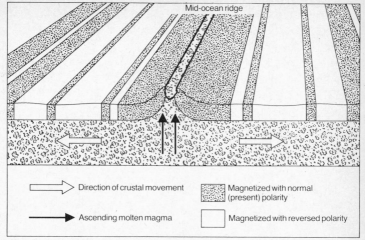

Sea floor spreading with the creation of 'magnetic stripes'. Geologists discovered that rocks were differently magnetised according to their age. As molten rock came to the surface and cooled so it took on the magnetic polarity of the epoch.

the magnetisation of the rock to be exactly opposite in direction to the present-day magnetic field.

Teddy Bullard at the lab had been working on the reversal of the Earth's main magnetic field for some years and so at tea one day when they were talking about the volcano he could say, 'Oh yes, the reversals of the main field, they've been known about for ages.' Once you realise that the main magnetic field of the Earth reverses not periodically but more or less at random then the changes in the volcanic rocks take on some added meaning. Their idea was that as volcanic rock is produced from the ocean ridges and meets the cold sea water it cools and takes on the magnetic field of the time. And so the stripes are a record of the whole history of the sea floor's movement.

'So by the time I began as a graduate student in 1963 a fair number of people in the subject were thinking very seriously about sea-floor spreading. We had a great number of visitors from abroad and it was Tuzo Wilson visiting from Canada who suggested the name "plates" for the large areas of sea floor that were moving apart at the ocean ridges. The idea that the continents had moved was gradually gaining favour again and much of the debate rested on the crucial evidence of the magnetic stripes.'

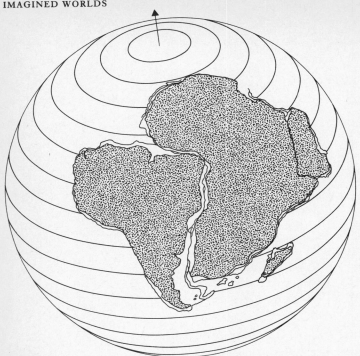

The fitting of the South American with the African continent. Although the idea was originally proposed in the nineteenth century, it was the advent of computers in the 1960s which made possible an accurate description of how it could take place.

Despite the evidence from the marine survey ships and their increasingly accurate sensing devices many people appeared to possess an emotional aversion to the theory of sea floor spreading. For many young research students it was more than their careers were worth to publish anything on the subject. While this often fierce argument took place among the establishment figures, Dan McKenzie was occupied with his own particular research problems for his Ph.D.

This work was on the behaviour of the mantle, in which he analysed the speed at which seismic waves travelled through this material beneath the Earth's crust to determine how dense and hot it was. And when, after its completion, he went on his first visit to an international conference, this expertise with the physical and mathematical systems came into focus with the work of his colleagues at Cambridge. The meeting in New York was the catalyst for the theory of 'plate tectonics'.

'I was working on something quite different but when this work on the magnetic stripes was presented with the interpretation of sea-floor spreading, it completely changed the thinking of a whole group of people, including myself. We all went away saying, "This is the new thing, this should dominate our research." Some time after that conference I was sitting in the library at Scripps Institute of Oceanography where I was working for a few months in 1967, and reading Teddy Bullard's paper on the fit of the continents. What he had done was to use a mathematical construction on the computer to fit the continents on either side of the South Atlantic together, i.e. Africa and South America.

'What he described was the rotation of South America about a pole towards Africa, the idea being that any rigid motion on a globe between two plates, in this case Africa and South America, can be represented by rotation about some axis. But it suddenly struck me that this could be of much more general importance because he could only make this fit if there was no deformation of the South American plate. Now exactly the same thing is shown by the magnetic anomalies. You would not get nice straight magnetic stripes if there were internal deformations within the plates. So this idea seemed to have a much more general application in describing the relative motion of the plates. What my colleague Bob Parker and I then did was to work on the idea that deformation was the important thing. At this time the seismic network was giving a worldwide map of earthquake locations. We suddenly realised that if the plates on the surface moved rigidly then the earthquakes must mark the boundaries between them.

'The key idea which gave rise to plate tectonics was that the regions away from these boundaries were rigid and moved with no internal deformation. This was something that was implicit in a lot of the earlier work but it was making it explicit which really allowed us to do all the work since.

'We could then divide the world up into a mosaic of plates by the earthquake locations we knew and, taking the plates as rigid, begin to see if there was some way to describe the motion between two plates as a simple rotation about an axis: in the same way as Teddy Bullard did for the South Atlantic. The area we chose to try this was the North Pacific. It's a particularly good place because there are really two plates involved, North America and the Pacific. And you can follow the relative motion where the two plates are separating to where they are coming together. We could then look to see if this motion agreed with a simple rotation for all round the North Pacific.

'The result was very striking for it worked extraordinarily well. Suddenly the geological world made sense. The familiar shapes of continents and oceans became irrelevant. What mattered were the shape of the plates. The new theory gave geology a framework which made us look at the plate boundaries because they held the key to everything. At the boundaries where plates are moving apart are spreading centres, where material from the Earth's hot mantle is rising up to form new ocean floor. There are also boundaries where plates come together called subduction zones. Here, one plate rides over another which sinks down into the mantle. That sinking plate melts to produce volcanoes. And then there are boundaries where one plate slides past another, as with the San Andreas fault in California.

'We could now divide the surface of the globe into a number of rigid caps with their boundaries marked by the lines of earthquakes. It was much simpler than most of geology. These caps, some of them very large like the Pacific cap which covers almost a third of the Earth's surface, move with respect to one another. And all earthquakes are produced by the relative motion between these spherical caps. The thickness of the caps is somewhere around one hundred kilometres, and underneath is material of the same composition but because it is hot, around 1300°C, it can flow slowly over geological time and accommodate the horizontal movements above. The world record for how fast they are moving is seen in the South-Eastern Pacific where the plates are separating at about twenty-five centimetres a year. The width of the boundary is less than two kilometres, so if this went through your back yard you'd certainly know about it.

'The sense of order which this brought to all the things which one knew about and had been taught was immense. There was then the excitement of seeing how far one could go with the story; whether one could go to just the right point with the ideas since it was clear that everybody was going to go through and spend the next five years sorting out which parts were right or wrong. The feeling at the time was a great sense of getting everything to fit together. Now, when I look back, I suppose it was just an incredibly lucky business to be at the right place at the right time.

The incidence of earthquake activity shown on this map of the world indicates the boundaries of the rigid plates that make up the Earth's surface.

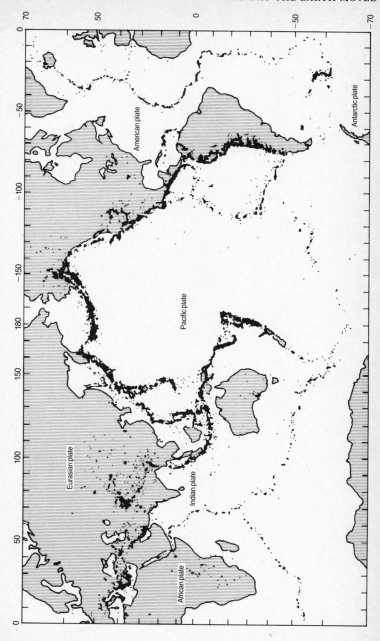

American plate

Antarctic plate

Pacific plate

Eurasian plate

Indian plate

African plate

'A lot of it was the fact the people who had really taught me how to do science had been thinking along such productive lines. They had got very close, but had not quite put the story together. When Bob Parker and I wrote what was the first paper on plate tectonics, neither of us were really known. But within a year we had become extremely well known by everyone in geology. That was enormous fun. We could go to conferences and take on the grand people in the subject and prove them to be wrong. You could really set about them and make them look foolish in front of an audience. There was a certain undergraduate delight in doing that.

'I must say that I did get known for doing this, and being particularly beastly. Then I guess I grew up and stopped taking such pleasure out of it and thought more about what I intended to do next in life. Because after all, you have one good idea at the age of twenty-five but are you going to have any more? For a number of people in the subject that was indeed the end of it and they have not been heard of since. I felt that would just be miserable.'

A Complete Theory

The first paper on plate tectonics was published in *Nature* in December 1967, just thirteen months after the New York conference which had stimulated this new thinking. That piece of work was the first of many by Dan McKenzie but remains his most famous. It rapidly became the new orthodoxy and provoked a range of worthwhile research topics over the ensuing years. Everything in geology could now be examined as to how well it fitted this all-embracing theory of the Earth's development. Plate tectonics, as a description of the mechanisms at work, was so complete that within a decade it was on the syllabus for every school geography class. For Dan McKenzie the years following publication were hectic but rewarding. He spent time working at the Scripps Institute of Oceanography in California, the California Institute of Technology and Cambridge University. While based at the Lamont-Doherty Geological Observatory in New York he spent a month exploring the Indian Ocean on board a survey ship. He came back with data that, once interpreted, would illustrate the geological evolution of that region. It also proved to him how well the theory worked in practice.

However, as Dan McKenzie readily acknowledged, the theory of plate tectonics lacked two essential items: there was no really good description of continental tectonics, and the underlying cause for the movement of the plates was not understood. So he set to work on both problems.

'The question was, where was it going to lead to? One thing that was not clear at the time was whether the idea would also work for the continents. If we look at the process of plate destruction, where one plate is going underneath another, this process depends on the sinking slab being denser than the hot material around. Now the continental rocks are lighter so they float with the result that when a continent drifts into one of these zones where plates are being destroyed – a subduction zone – continental material is too light and won't go down the hole. So the thing jams up. The processes that occur thereafter are quite complicated and we don't fully understand what happens. However, what appears to take place is that because the continental material will not go down the hole, either the spreading slows down or consumption starts somewhere else. The continent becomes stuck there and starts to be squeezed sideways and it's this which acts to form mountain ranges.

'I thought that the existing data on present-day deformation of the continents was really not very good, and that the right thing to do was simply to start from scratch. My idea was to use the methods which had been so successful in the oceans to carry out fieldwork where we could at earthquake locations. The area I chose extended from the Azores in the Atlantic, as far East as Iran. Such a large area was particularly important since one of the lessons of plate tectonics for me was the importance of studying an entire region and its surroundings.

'The most striking feature was the extreme complexity of the earthquake mechanisms. There was no simple story. The general framework of that region is that Africa is moving northwards with respect to Eurasia, so you would expect to find a shortening along the whole of that zone. In fact we found every variety of deformation and it has been the piecing together of what was really going on there which has occupied me for the ten years since plate tectonics was discovered.

'We have made a great deal of progress, and in areas like Iran it is a relatively simple picture. There, the plate boundary which is seismically active is not a sharp boundary but a wide belt that is shortening everywhere. When you go further west there are many more complications, with fragments being shot sideways. It seems to be one of the features of these continental collision zones that bits of the continent are expelled sideways: much as pips can be expelled from an orange if you pinch it. And some people like to call this orange-pip tectonics for that reason.

'Another feature of continental tectonics which turned out to be very important was the stretching of plates. Instead of the motion being taken up along a very narrow line along which the plates were created, as it is in the oceans, you get a zone where the plate is stretched. What happens is that you start off with a thick plate which is floating on a hot, soft mantle. As the plates start to separate they are suddenly stretched and thinned and hot material from below wells up to fill the gap.

'Then, when the extension of the plate stops, this hot material cools and the whole thing subsides to form a sedimentary basin such as the North Sea. The real test of this idea lies in the fact that there is only one variable: the amount by which the plate is stretched in the first place. From that you can calculate the changes in thickness of the continental crust and the heat flow with time in a basin. Such observations can then be used to test the idea, and in the North Sea it seems to offer a good explanation of events.

'I think that if it works as well in general as it has in the North Sea, this very simple idea is going to have very important economic consequences. Because it gives the subsidence history and also the temperature as a function of geological time, it is possible to calculate how rapidly organic rich material will change into oil. The oil companies have become very enthusiastic about this and have perhaps taken the idea too far too fast. It is not clear to me that all sedimentary basins were formed in this way and I feel we need some more thorough testing before it is widely used.'

What Drives the Plates?

'The question as to what drives the plates is really the major intellectual challenge left in tectonics. If we can account for all the features on the Earth with a simple model of rigid plates then clearly we are not going to be able to examine the dynamics of what happens underneath in the same way. It's all very well to make progress by splitting off the driving mechanism from the geometry of the motions but it's quite another matter then to try and make progress with the cause of those movements.

'We think the mechanism is some form of thermal convection, which is not actually saying a great deal. Thermal convection can take a whole variety of different forms: the weather systems are largely a form of thermal convection as is your kettle when you boil it. The plate motions themselves are clearly convective, because the sinking regions carry cold material into the Earth. The reason why we think that overall process is convective is simply that the amount of heat that the Earth is losing is more than sufficient to keep the movements going. We have had to go right back to first principles to study how fluids behave and to understand the types of things that can go on. In contrast to plate tectonics, where everyone has an idea of what will happen when you slide rigid blocks around, the behaviour of fluids is very much more complicated. What is needed now is a framework of understanding in which to think about mantle convection.

'Through the use of satellites we can now for the first time see the circulation of material underneath the plates. The really striking thing about this circulation in the mantle layer is that it seems to be quite irrespective of the plates above. Many people were surprised by this poor correlation, but I had long believed this would be the case. If you take the analogy of an iceberg floating in the sea, you can watch the iceberg's movement but this doesn't tell you in detail about the small-scale circulation that is going on beneath the iceberg. It is not reflected in the motion of the iceberg. The mantle situation is rather similar. The movements that we see going on underneath the plates are on a much smaller scale than the plates themselves.

'The question of how precisely we can describe these circulations of material within the mantle is difficult to say at the moment. We have been looking at meteorology for many centuries and have still not achieved numerical models that enable us to predict the weather. At present we will have to live with similar, uncertain mathematical models of the mantle circulation.'

This new challenge of the mantle convection story is not only complex but, as ever, the subject of scientific rivalry. If the material of the mantle does move as a fluid under the influence of heat from the Earth's core, how deep is that circulation? Is it restricted to the outer 700 kilometres of the planet or does it extend right down to the core itself, a depth of perhaps 3000 kilometres? Dan McKenzie is part of the group which believes in the restricted circulation – and for the moment the evidence seems in their favour. But being successful in science is not necessarily a matter of being on the winning side. Fresh ideas and original experiments are essential to break with past thinking and provoke new concepts about the world.

'There is no question that "plate tectonics" has become the new orthodoxy. But in an interesting way I'm not part of this orthodoxy, which, to a large extent, is a group of geologists who have used simple notions of the theory to understand the evolution of the continental rocks. I remain one of the doubters about their interpretations. But I think that the history of the Earth sciences has contained a number of people who have maintained doubts about the majority view. And I think that these are the people who are really the essential part of science. If there were a vote, their views would get completely squashed. But science is not a matter of democracy. It is not a matter of taking votes. There is something which is right and something which is not, and that's what in the end matters.'

Dr Walter Gilbert
Senior Fellow, Harvard University

Walter Gilbert was born in Boston, Massachusetts, in 1932. His family moved to Arlington, Virginia, in 1939 when his father, an economist, was invited to join a 'brains trust' that was a part of President Roosevelt's New Deal. He went to school in nearby Washington DC and was a serious but sometimes absent student. He often skipped his classes to go and read science books in the great Library of Congress near the Capitol. When he left it was with a string of awards and the highest marks possible in science, mathematics and English.

After studying physics at Harvard he went on, in 1954, to postgraduate studies at Cambridge University where he worked on mathematical problems in particle physics. One of his first scientific papers was published with his tutor at the time, Abdus Salam. He returned to Harvard where he became an assistant Professor of Physics. In 1964 he changed his scientific career with an appointment as Professor of Biophysics, then later Professor of Biochemistry. This move from elementary particle theory to molecular biology eventually led to a Nobel Prize in 1980. The discovery of how the genetic material DNA could be analysed in terms of its chemical make-up was one of the major events in the 1970s. The techniques which brought this about became known as 'bioengineering' – it was the beginning of an entirely new industry.

Wally Gilbert was one of the first to see the commercial possibilities of making radically different medical and industrial products and he founded Biogen in 1978. From 1981 to 1984 he was the chairman of this international company while remaining active in research.

The Serpent in the Garden
Dr Walter Gilbert

Paul Andersen

'When I began in molecular biology in 1960 we knew only the very simplest outlines of the genetic material. What entranced me with the subject was the idea that there was this material and it controlled everything in the living cell. How it did these things we had no real idea. We knew the structure of DNA since that had been discovered about seven years earlier. But we didn't know how this DNA made the proteins or what the controls were. In fact we didn't know what we call the genetic code – the exact connection between the structure of DNA and its constituent amino acids and the proteins of the cell. From our present viewpoint we then knew very, very little.'

The announcement of the double helix structure of DNA by Watson and Crick in 1953 had brought a revolution to biology. The discovery that the genetic material of inheritance, the nucleic acids of the living cell, deoxyribose nucleic acid, fitted together in a spiral form was a turning point. Now it was clear that its chemical composition could be fitted into a regular pattern with particular chemical groups, the bases, always occurring opposite one another in the two strands of the helix.

Order was brought to how information was passed from one generation to the next. When a cell divided, the double helix unwound along its length and a complementary copy was made of both strands to produce two exact copies of the DNA. One to remain in the cell, and the second to pass into the new cell as its genetic material. The linear nature of the chemical groups gave an understanding of where all the information necessary to make the many products found in a cell was stored. The science of molecular biology came alive with this revelation and for the following twenty years the discoveries of how 'life' worked were rapid and sustained.

'The critical aspect of the DNA structure is that one strand with a series of four different groups, the bases, matches up to a second strand in which complementary bases are aligned. The four bases,

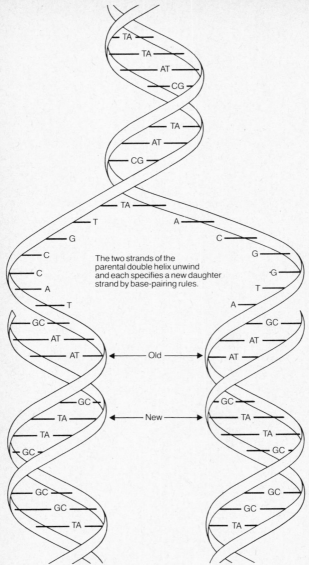

The two strands of the parental double helix unwind and each specifies a new daughter strand by base-pairing rules.

Guanine (G) always pairs with cytosine (C) while adenine (A) always pairs with thymine (T). Deoxyribonucleic acid, DNA, is a double helix spiral of base pairs.

adenine, guanine, cytosine and thymine, are commonly referred to by the letters A,G,C and T. Each base is so shaped chemically that only one base will lie across from it. So that thymine always lies across from adenine, and guanine always lies across from cytosine. These four letters can be used to write anything that is encompassed in the genetic information. And the connection between these four letters and what is finally done with that information is called the *genetic code*. Rather than writing out the entire structure of DNA, we can often just think of it as a chain in which there are a series of four letters written along its length. All of the chemical information in the DNA is hidden away in the order of those four chemical groups, A,G,C and T, that lie along it.

'A gene is some region along a DNA strand and in a bacterial cell the simple genes are about one thousand chemical links long. The entire bacterial cell makes up to three thousand different products, and so it has about three thousand different genes. That means it has a piece of DNA that is three million links long in something that is actually a few millimetres in length. It is as thin as any usual molecule which means it is only twenty angstrom across.

'In the human cell there are over two billion chemical links and if this was stretched out in one string it would be about six feet of DNA. In fact it is broken up into forty-six pieces, which are the individual chromosomes. The basic question is, how does this genetic material operate? The fact that DNA is inherited from one cell to another doesn't tell us anything about how the cell really functions. It tells us where the instructions are kept but not what those instructions are. We knew that a cell is primarily a protein factory in which these protein molecules can carry out a chemical reaction, or be a building block of muscle or hair tissue, or it might be the substance that gives colour to our eyes. Through an elaborate chemical machinery in the cell's cytoplasm the information from the genes is translated into something specific and unique for the cell. The existence of the particular protein molecule has been dictated by a sequence of bases along the DNA.'

Because DNA is located almost exclusively in the cell nucleus, whereas most protein manufacture occurs in the cytoplasm, some transfer of information has to take place from the nucleus into the outer cell area, the cytoplasm. By the 1960s the mechanism by which proteins were manufactured in the cell was confirmed as involving a messenger RNA – a single strand of nucleic acids. The DNA in the nucleus copies a part of its length onto a complementary strand of RNA which has very similar chemical groups. The position at which it starts to copy the DNA and where it stops is a complex part of the control mechanism that exists within the coding of the DNA. The single strand of RNA passes into the surrounding cytoplasm where it begins to copy its code into a string of amino acids – the protein. The sequence of chemical groups along the RNA act as a template for the protein, specific amino acids from the cytoplasm binding onto the RNA at specific sites. In this way, the protein is built up into a three-dimensional group of amino acids; in the sequence dictated by the messenger RNA.

How to Isolate a Gene

The discovery of how protein synthesis took place within the cell was a major step. This work had established that an average-size protein containing 400 amino acids required a section of DNA comprising about 1200 base pairs to code for it. The subject of much of this study in molecular biology was a single-celled bacterium *Escherichia coli* which is a common inhabitant of the human intestine.

The next challenge was to see how the control of the DNA in higher plants and animals took place. The biologist wanted to follow the activity of single genes to understand how fertilised eggs divide and differentiate into the highly specific cell types that make up body tissues and organs. The difficulty was that there was no way in which the DNA could be mapped and individual genes isolated. In the simple *E.coli* bacterium, mutant forms could be rapidly bred and genetic cross-breeding carried out to produce strains of the bacterium that would produce specific proteins. This was obviously not practical in the higher animals. What was needed was a way of isolating fragments of DNA that coded for particular proteins from the large chromosomes of animal cells. When Wally Gilbert chose to move from physics to molecular biology, unlocking the DNA molecules was his awesome task.

'In particle physics we were trying to discover exact details of the forces that make up the world by examining the fundamental particles of nature. What I found similar in molecular biology was the idea that a very general principle in physics gave one a means of understanding a whole range of effects. The sequence of DNA, with that order of chemical bases along it, is the most primitive object that we have in biology. All of the information that dictates the nature of the cell is carried in that structure. I became intri-

Dr Walter Gilbert in his office at Harvard University.

gued by the possibility that a general understanding of the life processes in terms of molecules might be useful in predicting a number of different things.

'In the sixties, our abilities as molecular biologists were solely those of an analytical scientist. We could take apart the cell and get particular pieces to function but we couldn't actually test our analysis in any critical way. The difference between this and a synthetic field like chemistry is that in chemistry you can test your ideas by making predictions and then put these ideas into practice by making something new. With the development of recombinant DNA techniques we can now test individual ideas about the cell by trying to put together a new molecule that would have some of the properties that a gene must have.

'In the middle seventies, one of the great advances was our development of very easy techniques to work out the sequences of very long stretches of DNA. The idea that I had with Alan Maxam in developing the chemical sequencing was a very simple one. We thought that maybe you could take a DNA molecule, just one strand, and measure the distance from one end of it and the position of any specific base, such as the guanine. But how do we actually measure the distance of something in a molecule which is an extremely threadlike object?

'First of all, we depend on having very large numbers of molecules of DNA, all copies of a specific molecule. A bacterium has a single molecule of DNA which we can reproduce thousands of times until we have test tubes that contain billions of copies. Next, we have to find some region of the DNA and cut out some chunk that might be 1000 or 10,000 links long. We are able to do this using restriction enzymes which recognise specific places along the DNA and cut it, like a little pair of scissors. The enzyme feels its way along the DNA and "sees" the chemical appearance of the outside of the molecule. When it finds a certain shape in the sequence which might be CC or GG it cuts the DNA at this point. With these chemical scissors we are then able to isolate a test tube full of just this length of DNA. The problem then is to work out the sequence along it. In the early seventies the only way was to work back from one end, nibbling back one chemical group at a time. So that the first might be an A, then a T and so on. But you couldn't learn much more than a few bases from this method.

'Our method was to label molecules using a radioactive element that was attached at one end of the piece of DNA. With this we are able to know the position of a molecule as the radioactive chemical decays. Then we break these molecules at, say, the guanine base rather than any of the others. We break the DNA not just at the first G site – if we did this we would have only molecules of a particular length – but at the first G, and the second G, and so on along the DNA. In this way we have a collection of molecules of differing lengths.

'This sequencing method depends on breaking only a few of the molecules at any particular site, about one in a thousand. At this stage we cannot see where the breaks have occurred; we just have a test tube of differing lengths of DNA. To separate these we use a process called electrophoresis in which we use an electric field to push these molecules through a jelly-like material. The jelly-like material blocks the motion of the molecules under the influence of an electric field and the small molecules move more easily than the larger ones. The result is that the small molecules move down to the bottom of the jelly-like sheet while the larger ones stay near the top. If we put a photographic film over this jelly-like sheet the decay of the radioactive marker exposes the film and leaves a dark band.

'Each of the dark bands gives us the position of a characteristic length of DNA. So if we use the same procedure for the position of the As, the Ts and the Cs we have the positions of all four bases. In fact with one single film you can estimate all the distances from one end to each of the bases. With this single film you can read off a pattern of bands and as your eye goes up the film you are essentially reading the pattern of letters or bases along a DNA sequence. In one go you can read from 100 to 500 positions along a strand of DNA. This is a total change from what we could do ten years ago. When Alan Maxam and I worked out one of the first pieces of DNA it took us two years to reveal 25 units along the DNA chain. Today one person can work out some 10,000 bases of DNA in a year. And the process is growing ever more rapid.'

At the same time as Wally Gilbert was developing his techniques at Harvard in 1977, Frederick Sanger at the MRC Laboratory in Cambridge had discovered a similar process for sequencing DNA. The ability to sequence exactly any given chain now meant it was a simple step to determine the amino-acid sequence of the protein specified by a region of DNA. The secrets of how the genes functioned could now be examined. Such a breakthrough, happening in two separate research establishments, was unusual, but not unique.

'It was both an example of serendipity and how basic research functions, in that we did not predict a year before that we would devise a sequencing method. We were working in a totally different direction and I suppose we had the insight to see the relevance of a technique for a more generalised use. We were looking at how a control protein identifies a particular region of DNA in a bacterium. A control protein picks out one gene among the several thousand in the DNA. We knew the protein bound to the DNA, and we had actually worked out the sequence along the DNA that it bound to. But we didn't know how the protein touched the DNA. Our experiments were devised to find out which bases the protein came into contact with on the DNA. The way we did this was to use the chemical properties of DNA to break it at a certain base. We made use also of the fact that if the protein was bound to the DNA it would block that breakage at that point. This simple idea led us to think how we could recognise where the breakage point is. And we did that by measuring the distance between the end of a DNA molecule and the breakage.

'The recognition of serendipity is a good thing. In some ways science becomes poised for discoveries. At the time we were working, Fred Sanger and his co-workers in England produced a sequencing method based on some of the same ideas and other quite different ones. Both emerged at the same time, and had either one been five years later it would not have been of interest. As it was they arrived together and gave the world the techniques that were needed to work out the structure of DNA rapidly.'

Bioengineering

Three years later, Wally Gilbert shared the 1980 Nobel Prize for Chemistry with Fred Sanger and Paul Berg. By this time the techniques which had been discovered had brought a new word into the vocabulary – bioengineering. In 1973, Herbert Boyer, Stanley Cohen and their co-workers had devised simple test-tube procedures to produce recombinant DNA molecules. Using these, microbiologists were able to move simple pieces of DNA from one micro-organism to another. Within the scientific community the issue arose as to whether these simple procedures might pose a potential threat. Could some of the new genetic combinations produce virulent forms of disease that were man-made natural disasters?

At scientific meetings in 1973, the social implications of recombinant DNA work were discussed. Within a very short while this scientific deliberation was headline news. The idea of scientists being able to tamper with the design of nature brought public fears that a Pandora's box had been opened that would bring appalling results. Paul Berg, who had pioneered a great deal of this work, convened a meeting in Asilomar, California, in 1973 that brought all those working in the area together. The aim was to assess the hazards of manipulating DNA in the laboratory and to see if guidelines for safe working were needed. The outcome was to fuel a public debate and bring government attention to the scientists' work over the ensuing months. Wally Gilbert's work was in just this area at that time.

'Up until the sequencing methods were discovered, the only DNA we could look at were the small plasmids – those small pieces of DNA that occur within bacteria separate from the chromosome itself. All the work in terms of the control of genes had been done in bacteria because they were much simpler to look at than the DNA of animal cells which are almost a thousand times more complicated. But in the middle seventies the recombinant techniques came in which allowed us to analyse the genes of animal cells.

'The recombinant DNA techniques enable us to remove a piece of DNA from the human cell and place it into a bacterium. As that bacterial cell grows we produce very many copies of that DNA. This means we can examine that particular piece of DNA in great detail. This ability to reproduce a specific piece of DNA underlies the current advances throughout biology. One of the things we try to achieve is to isolate a specific gene. We take all the DNA from a human cell and break it with an enzyme into about a million pieces. Thus we can have a large number of copies of just one fragment of DNA which we then insert into a small circle of DNA that we isolate from a bacterium. These plasmids have between 3000 and 5000 links of DNA material while the fragment may have anything from 100 to 10,000 links along its length. With an enzyme we are able to cut into the plasmid and open up the circle of DNA. Now we take these broken circles of DNA with the human DNA fragments and, with an enzyme, fuse the two together. This new circle of DNA can then be put into a bacterium by mixing it in a culture with the bacterium. The bacterial wall is made weak by treatment with a chemical and as a result some of the bacteria then take up these circles of DNA.

'The process works because one bacterium takes up one DNA molecule and grows into a colony containing from one million to 100 million daughters. Generally this DNA molecule has some ability to produce a specific product, a protein for example, which gives the bacterium a particular way of growing. It may endow the bacterium with an ability to resist an antibiotic so that only that bacterium will grow into a colony on the glass dish. Once we have that colony we can grow that particular bacterium as much as we like. We are able to examine the DNA molecule, work out its total sequence and structure. We can understand that gene.

'I remember a particular part of the recombinant DNA development work where I was involved with the discovery that we could take any DNA fragments and stick them together. We could take a fragment, add it to another, cut a piece, add a third and work out the entire structure. That ability enabled us effectively to "switch on" any gene to order. I remember the days of wild excitement that I went through when that idea first emerged. It is one of the reasons for doing science, when you have that high excitement of finding that specific ideas work out.

A Puzzle within the Genes

'In the 1978–79 period we discovered with these methods that the genes in our bodies have a quite different structure from that found in bacteria. The genes in bacteria are simple continuous regions along the DNA with a start and a stop point. A messenger RNA copy of that region is made that translates its entire length into protein which then folds up on itself and does something in

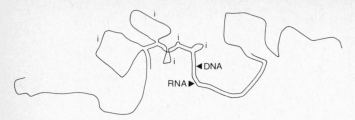

The DNA strand is being copied into a messenger RNA strand that will then activate protein synthesis in the cell. The RNA will be the template for the protein's structure.

the cell. When we looked at a gene from a human cell it is much longer, sometimes ten times the length. But not all of that DNA codes for the final protein. Only certain regions along its length are translated into the protein.

'There were non-coding sequences of the DNA, which, when the RNA molecule was copied inside the nucleus, looped into a hairpin shape. These we called *introns*. The information from the DNA came from perhaps three or more separate regions along the DNA strand, which we denote as *exons*. This *exon-intron* structure of a gene, where the information is carried in regions along the DNA, separated by long regions that do not appear in the final translation into a protein, explained a number of things about the functioning of our genes. It also showed us why the body has over ten times the amount of DNA expected.

'But it also left us with something of a puzzle. Why is one gene expressed in terms of three regions along the DNA whose information will then be tied together? And why should another gene be expressed in terms of ten or fifty little regions along the DNA whose information is finally tied together to make a single protein? So far the explanation which I feel most happy with, although it is something I and other scientists are still arguing over, is that it is to do with the way in which our genes have evolved. Each of the separate elements, the *exons*, represent a little piece of the protein that has been used in some other gene in the past. What we see when we examine a specific gene from the DNA of our bodies is the set of fragments that the gene was made of, hundreds of millions of years ago, as it was assembled out of the fragments of information that correspond with fragments of protein put together to make the final protein.

'I think the first reaction in discovering that genes in animal

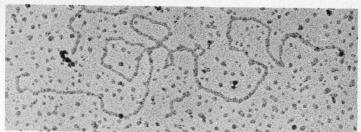

The thread-like molecule of a single strand of DNA (deoxyribonucleic acid).

cells were discontinuous was a tremendous surprise. We had thought we understood the basic rules by which genes functioned from looking at bacteria. At the moment there is great curiosity at what the underlying reason might be for this. If the structure is broken up in a way that represents the evolutionary nature of a gene then each new gene we look at tells us something of how its function has arisen. The biologist has always recognised that the crucial element in an enzyme was only a few amino acids that originally catalysed a chemical reaction. The rest of the complicated structure of these proteins was added step by step over evolutionary time. Exactly how this came about we had no clear view until now. The *intron-exon* structure of genes gives us a view of what the pieces are that evolution has put together to make the final genes.

'This gives us a very different picture of evolution. In our bodies the structure of the genes is split while in the bacteria it is continuous. We are used to thinking of evolution as proceeding from the primitive organisms, like bacteria, up through to the higher animals. Now we can look upon evolution the other way round where the genes in our bodies look like the original biochemical structures. In this picture the bacteria do not look like our ancestors but like our offspring. They are the polished remnants of a long evolutionary history in which they have learned to breed faster and faster, compared to the cells in our body, and have lost all of that extra DNA.

'It's an interesting philosophical argument that scientists have got into. This break-up of the gene in the DNA is a consequence of not only the past act of evolution, but of evolution still progressing. If your prejudice is that man is the highest form of creature to be made, then you will look at the genes in our body and ask, "Why haven't these genes reached a state of perfection?"'

While this intriguing discussion came to occupy a greater part of the experimental work in molecular biology, the social implications of bioengineering became headline news. In 1974 newspapers in Europe and the United States reported fears that drug-resistant strains of mutant germs could bring new diseases. The British government set up a working party on the Experimental Manipulation of the Genetic Composition of Micro-organisms under Lord Ashby. For all scientists working in the field, this public examination and scrutiny created a very unusual working environment. It also exposed them to a debate for which they were unprepared.

'When the recombinant DNA techniques were first suggested in the early 1970s, a certain amount of concern was expressed within the scientific community. This worry was based on a set of questions about whether or not moving a piece of DNA from a human cell to a bacterium would give the bacterium unusual or possibly dangerous properties. That discussion among a few scientists then led to a general call for a moratorium on all research involving the moving of DNA from animal cells to bacteria. The debate among us turned on what safeguards we should use in case there were any problems with the experiments, and to ensure safety.

'From the scientist's point of view this was a sensible way of going about it. The thinking was that if we agreed on the conditions necessary to build a safe laboratory, we could continue the research and ensure no hazard was being exposed. We didn't realise that if we built a safe laboratory and started doing research in it the general public would look at this and say, "My God, those must be terribly dangerous things, otherwise you wouldn't need those safeguards." We fell into that trap.

'Many themes came together in the recombinant DNA discussion that we had in the United States. In this country one of these themes is a fear of germs, bacteria. There is the sense that in some way the bacteria around us are out to get us at all costs. Another element of the debate turns on a fear of technology. The recombinant DNA technology in biology was seen as akin to the physics of the nuclear energy programme and the bomb. To a certain extent this was encouraged by the biologists. There was a curious form of illusion among those who began working in this area of recombinant DNA that said, "Stop us, we're doing something important and you can tell it's important because it's dangerous." It was a macho impulse to say, "Here, you can see I'm really doing an important experiment because if those bacteria got

some arguments have been based on general political theories which have nothing to do with the science. There has been the issue of the commercialisation of science. Over the years public money has been used to develop the basic research which is now moving out of the laboratories into an applied area. We're moving molecular biology into an industrial framework. Is the public being ripped off by this? I don't think so. I think in fact that this is exactly the desired outcome of that public expenditure over a thirty-year period. The underlying role of this public money is to create new knowledge that will eventually turn into new industries.

'We have moved from a period in which we could only look at bacteria and take them apart either by mutation or crudely knocking out particular properties, to a period in which we can take a bacterium and add to it a specific product. This gives us the ability to take an abstract science and actually make it function in the world. This is one of the things I find extraordinarily exciting now.'

Professor Roger Penrose FRS
Rouse Ball Professor of Mathematics,
University of Oxford

Roger Penrose was born into a family of intellectual athletes, with members accomplished in either scientific or artistic fields. His uncle, Sir Roland, acquired a considerable reputation as a surrealist painter, and later founded the Institute of Contemporary Arts. Lionel, his father, was a famous geneticist who loved the tricks and wizardry of numbers and passed on his enthusiasm to his sons. Roger Penrose's older brother, Oliver, is also a professor of mathematics, and his younger brother, Jonathan, has won the British Chess Championships no less than ten times.

Lionel Penrose brought his family to London after the war, and Roger Penrose went to study at University College. Eventually he reached St John's College, Cambridge, to do postgraduate research in mathematics. Here he attended lecture courses given by two very distinguished physicists: Paul Dirac, a leading figure in the revolution in quantum mechanics, and Hermann Bondi, who was dealing with mathematical problems in the Theory of Relativity.

Inspired by such brilliant tuition, Penrose soon found himself tackling fundamental questions of how mathematical geometry related to physics. He reached a point where he was contemplating nothing less than a reformulation of Einstein's ideas in a different geometric framework. The eventual result was 'twistor theory' – a completely new mathematical description of the Universe.

From 1964 to 1973 he was at Birkbeck College, firstly as a Reader and then in 1967 he was appointed a Professor of Applied Mathematics. It was during this period that he gained two prestigious awards, the Heinemann Prize and the Adams Prize, and also became an FRS.

In 1973 Penrose was offered a post at Oxford University as Rouse Ball Professor of Mathematics. Here he and his students have embarked on a lifelong research programme to explore the possibilities of twistor space, and their work has attracted considerable interest among mathematicians throughout the world.

Beyond Space-Time
Professor Roger Penrose FRS

Deborah Cadbury

For most of us the idea of 'space' conjures up images of star wars, shuttle flights, even journeys to far-flung planets in outer space. But to a mathematician such as Penrose the idea of 'space' conjures up a quite different, and much more abstract, journey.

'In mathematics we often go beyond three-dimensional or even four-dimensional space, to eight, ten, a hundred or an infinite number of dimensions . . . these spaces are invented basically in order to understand, to get a better feeling for problems and puzzles . . . my own personal interest has often been in spaces which have an important relevance to the physical world, and deal with the space in which we live.'

But to Penrose even this is not straightforward. Apart from the three-dimensional 'void' of our immediate senses, there is space inside simple, everyday, *solid* objects. As he explains, 'Imagine that we are travelling inside, let us say, an oak table. What we encounter first are the wood fibres, then the cells, and eventually atoms . . . and if we carry on inside, we find that the atoms themselves are made up of very tiny little particles – protons – separated by great volumes of empty space . . . and if we imagine for a moment that each proton is the size of a tiny ball-bearing, we find that the average distance between protons is more than the distance between the furthest walls of the Royal Albert Hall . . . so that means even a seemingly solid oak table is composed almost entirely of empty space.'

Sir Arthur Eddington, when remarking on this phenomenon, referred to his 'two writing tables'. One is the common-sense solid object familiar to sight and touch. The other is 'a scientific table, composed ultimately of mathematical entities like the solutions of differential equations, yet infinitely more reliable for describing detailed behaviour'.

This intrigued Penrose because it pointed to a shortcoming in physics. 'Although for many centuries physicists have tried to understand the solid matter of which things like tables are composed, there has been comparatively little attention paid to the nature of the space itself . . . that's been thought of as mainly the province of mathematicians and philosophers. But I've always felt that to understand properly what is going on in nature, one needs a much deeper understanding of the structure of space . . .'

In contemplating such problems while a pure mathematics research student and Junior Fellow at Cambridge, he was stimulated to learn more about physics by his contemporary, the physicist Dennis Sciama, which led him to new insights.

Penrose found himself comfortably straddling two subjects – maths and physics – from a perspective which pointed to curious paradoxes that would not be evident to someone tutored only in one. The first paradox arose when comparing the mathematician's view of space with the geometric framework underlying all physics. Penrose noticed that although both subjects purported to derive their rules from nature, both used fundamentally different geometrics in order to do this.

The Divergence of Physical and Mathematical Geometry

The Greeks were the first to produce a clear mathematical theory of space. They developed a very precise geometry based on straight lines, circles, ellipses, parabolas and many other kinds of shapes. For Penrose, this was an intellectual landmark. 'In a way it was the first physical theory, an extraordinarily accurate description of the spatial world. They encompassed a great deal of information in some simple axioms and theorems describing fundamental truths about circles, triangles, squares and so on . . . there's something very appealing in this kind of thing . . .' The construction of Euclidean geometry was simplicity itself: the basic ingredients were *points* in three-dimensional space – the dimensions of height, longitude and latitude. Everything could be constructed from points.

Centuries later, when the physics of motion was started through the work of Galileo and Newton, they based their ideas on the Euclidean view. 'In their theories of dynamics, which could describe a whole range of things from how individual particles behave to the elliptical orbits of whole planets round the Sun . . . the basic ingredient of matter was now the pointlike particle, which moved in a three-dimensional space. So there was a very close correspondence between the physics and the geometry. The point either played a role as the basic ingredient of the geometry, or as the basic ingredient of matter – the "point particle".'

But all this changed with Einstein. Early on in this century he presented his Theory of Relativity. This was to overturn the physicists' view of how geometry related to the structure of matter, and the way matter behaved. The geometric framework underlying maths and physics had diverged subtly.

As Penrose explains, 'The main difference was that instead of having a three-dimensional space, in Einstein's relativity theory you actually need a four-dimensional space. Time had to be treated as an additional dimension, as well as the three spatial dimensions.' Although at the time the ideas of relativity seemed extraordinary, from its rules Einstein derived fundamentally important properties, such as:

$$E = mc^2$$

Whole new areas of physics opened up. The equation above, for example, which equates 'energy' to 'matter', was a crucial factor in the release of atomic energy.

'But the implication of all this was that the physical point particle no longer corresponded to a point in the geometry ... Suppose you imagine that a square (a) is the whole of three-dimensional space yesterday, and square (b) is the whole of three-dimensional space today, and another (c) represents tomorrow ... In effect we have a dimension "time" going up the page, and the whole page represents four-dimensional space-time. Now imagine a particle "o" in this space-time. It persists, of course, over time so it would need to be presented in each square, a,b,c. Now to describe the entire history of that particle you need a whole succession of points joining together the particle of yesterday, today and tomorrow ... making a one-dimensional curve.

'So in space-time, a particle is no longer represented by a "point" but by a "line".' And if particles have become 'lines' in space-time, what about 'points'? 'A point is an event which has no continuation in time, it just blips for an instant in one square, say (a), and no longer represents a particle ...'

When quantum mechanics started, and Heisenberg introduced 'The Uncertainty Principle' in the 1920s, the discrepancy between maths and physics was made even greater. 'This was because the particle was not even localised in space any more. It was spread out, having wave characteristics and particle characteristics ... one can't even think of the quantum-mechanical particle as being a one-dimensional object, it's smeared out over space-time ...'

For Penrose this discrepancy was a matter of some concern. 'From the time when I was a research fellow ... it worried me that

In space-time a particle is no longer represented by a point, but by a line.

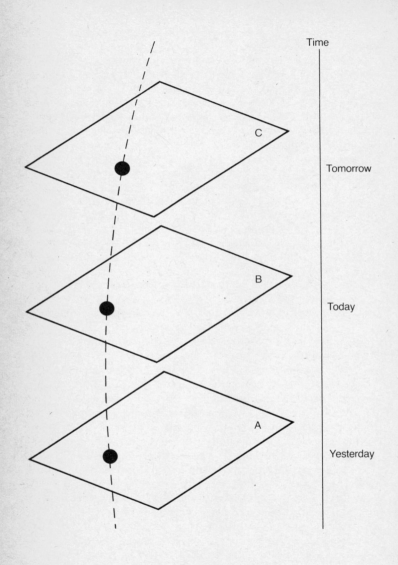

Point /Particle/line

the basic objects, the points in geometry, were not really like the basic physical objects, the particles. It seemed to me that they should be, if both maths and physics were describing the truth about nature. But I never really found anyone who was troubled by this in the same way as I was . . . and that surprised me too. I think seeing the problem this way was an important element in my own further thinking in these areas.'

Spaces where Physical Theory breaks down

Penrose soon came across a second anomaly, and it was his work on this that established his reputation quite early on in his academic career. In the sixties it was becoming evident that there were serious problems with existing physical theory. General relativity predicts extreme distortions of space and time during two kinds of 'singular events' in the history of the Universe. The first of these 'singular events' or 'singularities' occurred at the very beginning when matter was created.

'According to present ideas, everything began about 10,000 million years ago, when the whole Universe seems to have been concentrated effectively into a tiny point. We need a description of this "point" but it is impossible to calculate because densities and space-time curvatures become infinite here . . . there's just no way to describe the actual state of affairs at the Big Bang in terms of known physics . . .'

There is a second kind of extreme distortion of space and time, where rather than the expansion of matter from infinite densities, the reverse occurs in the collapse of massive stars. When they come to the end of their evolution they collapse inwards to form what's known as a black hole. 'Here the gravity becomes so powerful that it will counteract any of the forces between particles and crush the whole thing to such an extent that the density just goes up and up and up . . . beyond even that extraordinarily high value one finds inside an atomic nucleus, a singularity is reached at the centre.' At this point the theory of space-time itself gives up, very much as it does at the origin of the Universe.

'When I started to think about these problems, I rapidly became intrigued by black holes, partly because at that time there was quite a lot of doubt about whether they actually existed. The first serious scientific work about black holes was done by Oppenheimer and his students. This was the same Oppenheimer who later worked on the atomic bomb. He predicted the collapse of a star right down to a minute size, where it reaches a point of infinite density – a singularity. But to make any progress at all in his

calculations he had to assume all stars were exactly symmetrical
. . . and the collapse would be exactly symmetrical inwards.

'I think people didn't feel convinced by his argument because,
after all, if you imagine matter falling symmetrically directly
inwards towards the centre point, then it's not so surprising that at
that central point you would derive infinite densities.

'But suppose there was a bit of irregularity in the collapse – and
it's true you would get large densities – then the different parts of
the matter would miss each other and could come swirling round
and come whooshing out again. And so you might not necessarily
get a singularity . . .'

Penrose was keen to establish whether these extreme distortions of space and time really did occur in nature. 'I was able to
look at this problem from a different point of view. Previously,
people had made a lot of assumptions and done complicated
calculations . . . but I had been doing work of a rather general
qualitative geometric kind for a quite different purpose in relativity . . . and suddenly I saw a way of applying my techniques to the
black hole problem without needing to make any assumption
about symmetry . . .' Penrose was able to provide an elegant
mathematical proof that the singularities predicted from Oppenheimer's work did exist, irrespective of symmetry.

Penrose published his proof in 1965 and became something of a
celebrity in the field, invited to give lectures in various universities
and conferences. The real achievement, though, was rather more
personal: a step forward in his thinking. 'As a result of this I
became quite sure that inside the black hole one definitely needed
some new kind of physical description of what was happening. We
needed a new physical geometry which could handle extreme
"singular" distortions of space and time in a precise way.

'So I had really been concerned about two kinds of problem . . .
first the divergence between physics and maths at a fundamental
geometric level; second the problems within existing physics in
describing certain extreme kinds of space-time. But I had also
been nagged by a third problem which to me was even more
important than the other two . . . and that had to do with the kind
of number that one uses in the description of physics.'

Imaginary Numbers in a Real World
The idea of a real number seems a very precise description of
nature. You can calculate everything from the number of people in
a room, to the distance of the furthest star. Even the negative

numbers come in useful for describing some things such as a bank balance or dates in the past.

-5 -4 -3 -2 -1 0 1 2 3 4 5

But Penrose considers, 'There's nothing particularly special about what we call "real" numbers; in fact they're surprisingly limited. It's true that you can do things like adding, multiplying, subtracting, dividing quite happily ... but there are other operations that you often find you need to do, such as taking a square root. If you want the square root of 1 that's fine, it's either 1 or -1, but suppose you want the square root of a negative number like -1. The answer is not represented by any real number. For example, 1 multiplied by itself does not equal -1. Well, you might say that -1 doesn't have a square root, but mathematicians are not happy with that. They often prefer to invent things if they don't seem to exist originally – at least it may seem like inventing, but the significant "inventions" are more like discoveries. So from the mathematical point of view it turns out to be helpful to introduce other kinds of numbers, which we call "imaginary numbers". Suppose we invent a number – which I'll call "i" – and let that represent a square root of -1.

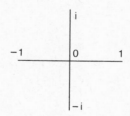

'The rule is that if we multiply "i" by itself, we get -1. Now that by itself doesn't do much for us but if you can represent the whole plane with these numbers built up from "i". Imaginary numbers can be any size from, say, 0.0001 to 1,000,000i. They can even be negative like -10i. These imaginaries can be "added" to real numbers to fill out an entire plane (see overleaf).

'And, having done that, you find this whole two-dimensional picture can give you the square root of not just -1 but any number you please. It's one of these miracles that are not infrequently encountered in mathematics. You start off trying to solve one problem then the answer solves a whole lot of other problems that you had no idea could be solved in this way.'

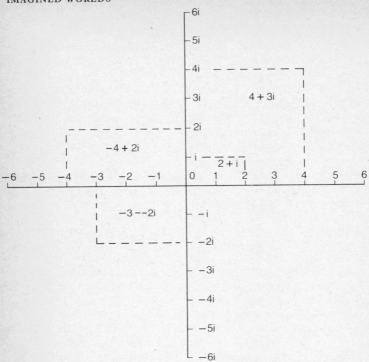

This combination of imaginary numbers with real numbers makes up what are aptly named 'complex numbers' which are governed by their own highly controlled and logical rules.

'Complex numbers were introduced originally as a convenience – if you like, for tricks in solving equations. They were also useful for solving problems in physics, although they had never seemed to apply in a fundamental way to the "real" world of classical physics. But when quantum mechanics was introduced in order to describe molecular or atomic phenomena, it was found that one needed to base the whole understanding on these complex numbers.' This was necessary to account for the way particles were sometimes wave-like, and sometimes particle-like. Complex numbers with their two-dimensional structure gave the best description.

'Now it was always very personally puzzling to me that you seemed to need these two *different* kinds of number entering in a very basic way into these two areas of physics. To solve the intricate details of behaviour inside the atom you needed complex numbers, and yet for things on a much larger scale to describe space and time you needed real numbers.'

Penrose's discomfort with existing physical theory stemmed from his belief about physics. 'It seemed to me that physics ought to be a much more unified kind of structure . . . that one ought really to be using the same kind of number to describe physics on all scales. I suppose it also goes back to the feeling of the rock-solid dependability of mathematics . . . the more we can make our physics rest on a coherent mathematical scheme the safer we are in our understanding. I don't think this discrepancy bothered most physicists as much as it did me because they tend to feel maths is something just to be useful occasionally, and I don't think it worried pure mathematicians so much because they're not basically interested in physical problems.

'I think it's when you're looking at both that you begin to see how odd it is that these two distinct number systems are needed. And between the two it is the complex numbers, rather than the real numbers, that have the kind of power and elegance that seem best suited to govern the structure of the physical world.' Penrose was starting to contemplate nothing less than a reformulation of all of physics, using complex numbers.

In 1963 he went to the University of Texas to take up a temporary teaching position. 'But these three problems just kept coming back . . . the divergence between mathematical and physical geometry . . . the singularities which pointed to a fundamental weakness in physical theory, and finally, even more important, the way number is used in physics. I was puzzling over all these and was trying to find a different way – a completely different way – of looking at the description of space-time, so that I could build up physics on a radically new basis . . .

'I think it was when I was coming back from a weekend holiday in Texas that suddenly an idea came to me, and this led me to a reformulation of physical geometry which made sense of the turmoil of different ideas that had been milling around in my head. It was really a new way of looking at space-time structure in which I was trying to change the basic physical ideas of points and dimensions. I realised that the role of the space-time point could be completely taken over by a different object: something that I now refer to as a "twistor".'

Twistor Theory
The diagram gives some idea of the geometry of a twistor. It's made up of circles which all link each other in a specific way and

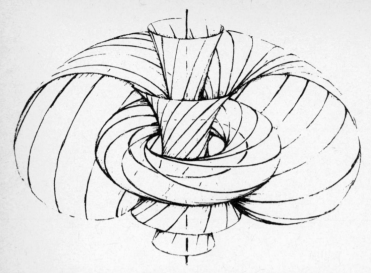

This geometry represents a 'point in twistor space'. These twistor points are the fundamental building blocks in the Universe, from which Penrose hopes all theories of matter and space can be derived.

lie on a family of different tori. The whole complicated shape represents some very precise mathematics expressed in complex numbers. The twistor is to be understood as the basic ingredient – or 'point' – in a new space: twistor space.

'This space is not three-dimensional like ordinary space . . . it's six-dimensional. And the dimensions can be expressed in terms of the degrees of freedom of the twistor . . . First of all you can turn it around its axis in two directions, that's two degrees of freedom . . . or you can move it forwards and backwards and from side to side, that's four dimensions . . . or you can move it along the direction of the axis, and finally you can make it bigger or smaller . . . that's a total of six dimensions.

'Now this six-dimensional space – this "twistor space" – is to be viewed as more fundamental than the three dimensions of our familiar space, or even than the four dimensions of the physicist's space-time. Here in the new twistor space, the different dimensions refer to properties of a particle travelling with the speed of light, its motion in space, its energy and spin.'

The concept of the twistor 'point' has to be understood in relation to this spatial description as it develops with time.

'Suppose that the three spatial dimensions of our previous picture are flattened into one plane . . . time is the vertical axis, so each plane represents a different time . . . Now, as the twistor moves from plane to plane, it is really the *entire* picture that represents one *single* point in twistor space.

'This is unlike the previous way in which the concept of "point" had been viewed in physical geometry. What we mean by "point" has changed . . . it is not like the old Greek concept of a point, which is localised just in spatial geometry . . . nor is it like a point in space-time which is something with only a momentary existence. Here the twistor point can be used to represent the entire history of an object – say a photon – as it moves along at the speed of light.'

Penrose saw these points as the fundamental entities of the Universe, the building blocks from which all theories of matter and space could be derived. 'This was a very exciting time for me, although the work turned out to be very difficult . . . the way in which the geometry fitted together had many unexpected features that really spurred us on. Eventually the theory went a long way towards resolving the three puzzles that had troubled me before.'

Twistors and the Three Paradoxes
'Consider first my philosophical worry that the "points" underlying physical geometry seemed to have diverged from the "particles" with Einstein's space-time . . . well, here the basic element of the geometry – the twistor – can represent the basic qualities that a particle can have, such as energy, momentum and spin . . .' Mathematically a twistor is not quite identical to either particles or points in space-time, it lies somewhere in between both concepts. In some ways it is more like a 'fuzzy' particle, which brings it closer to the quantum-mechanical view of the wave-particle.

In addition to the geometry of twistors representing properties of particles, twistor space can also be used to construct the points of space-time. 'It turns out that a "line" in twistor space corresponds to a single point in space-time and this means that, in principle, everything around us can be reformulated into the twistor framework . . . from the particles that make up objects, to the photons that permeate space, even to the structure of space-time itself. In fact, it's one of these minor miracles that this worked out so well and that really encouraged us to carry on . . .'

Penrose soon had another success. 'One of the most extraordinary things was the way twistor theory fitted in with Maxwell's theory. Maxwell was one of the very great physicists comparable with Galileo, Newton and Einstein.' His major contribution was the system of equations that govern electromagnetism and light. 'But his equations also describe the structure of everyday things, like the solid oak table I mentioned. Now how on earth do you get something that is solid when it is mostly composed of empty space? It's because of the electromagnetic forces that permeate the spaces between the particles making it seem solid . . . if you want to understand the structure of most things you have to understand Maxwell's theory.

'So I'd been working, struggling to try to get Maxwell's theory into twistor theory in some reasonable way. In principle you can always translate things into the twistor scheme, but with Maxwell's equations it seemed, at first sight, to be an awful mess. But one day, by looking at things differently, and incorporating a certain type of mathematical "trick", I found that it suddenly became incredibly simple . . . I saw how to explain all these complicated equations in terms of just one simple little function. The solutions of Maxwell's equations came out automatically, without one needing to solve any equations at all – it was very impressive to me that such a thing was possible . . .'

Penrose was also able to incorporate many of Einstein's ideas into the twistor view. Take for example Einstein's general theory of relativity, which describes gravity. According to this theory, gravity is created by the curvature of space-time. 'The problem was that then space-time becomes warped . . . I tried to translate that into the twistor view, and for a long time it seemed impossible. How can you ever translate something like that into twistors? The maths seemed very difficult.'

Penrose made the same assumption, that gravity is caused by mass generating curvature in space-time. 'However, I used twistor space instead of space-time, and I found I could translate Einstein's equations into twistors. At least it seems that we're about halfway to a complete solution. It's something we're still very much working on, and on the whole it looks promising.'

His aim is nothing less than to use curvature in six-dimensional twistor space to account not only for Maxwell's electromagnetism and Einstein's gravity, but also all the nuclear forces. 'So the theory really seems to have dealt quite well with the first puzzle about the divergence of mathematics and physical geometry. We've translated large chunks of physics, both subatomic and macroscopic phenomena, into twistor ideas but the theory also offers scope for dealing with the second puzzle – the distortions in space and time where physical theory breaks down, such as in black holes and the early Universe . . .'

When densities and curvatures reach infinity at certain space-time points, it is impossible to calculate physical conditions. 'But because in twistor theory we aren't taking points as the basic ingredients but twistors, there are certain ways around such difficulties. So we hope we have a plausible way of tackling problems of this nature, which had previously seemed insurmountable . . .' Penrose and his research team have a rough method of approach but twistor theory still has a long way to go before it can describe detailed conditions at a singularity.

'Perhaps the most important thing to me was that twistor theory deals with my third aesthetic concern about the normal use of complex numbers at the quantum level in physics, yet not for anything on a larger scale . . .' Twistors are built up completely of complex numbers, which means that physics can use the same kind of number on all levels to describe the structure of the Universe. The six dimensions of twistor space are described by just *three* complex numbers.

From a mathematical point of view this is a key achievement. 'Certain things in mathematics have much more intrinsic elegance than other things and complex numbers have much more of this than the real numbers have . . . it's much more satisfying if one can base one's physics on those parts of mathematics which have this power and elegance than on parts for which this is less true . . .'

Penrose has been working on twistor theory for about twenty years. It is now an established branch of mathematics, with twistor theorists, some of whom have been Penrose's students, in departments in various parts of the world. In spite of this, Penrose feels that progress has been slow at times. 'The way I feel about the programme as a whole is a combination of optimism and frustration . . . there have been long periods where nothing has seemed to happen . . . some parts of the theory are mathematically very difficult, there's no doubt about that.

'On the other hand, there have been these moments when things have worked out suddenly much better than one would have expected and these sorts of "miracles", if you like, really make the thing come to life . . .'

A Mathematician's Style of Thinking

Do all mathematicians think alike, ruled by number in a logical and calculating way? Not according to Penrose. 'I think it was one of the great surprises to me when I first went to university as an undergraduate . . . I was rather expecting to find that all these people specialising in mathematics would just think as I do, and

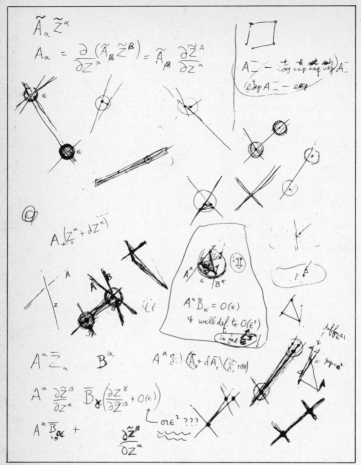

'My notebooks look like a lot of doodles,' Penrose confesses. *'There is an intermediate stage of thinking about things which is a very visual one for me.'*

instead I found more different ways of thinking than I'd ever encountered before . . .

'In my own case, a lot of mathematical thinking is done with visual images, much more than seems to be usual among mathematicians. Aesthetic criteria are very important in mathematics, though usually these are not directly visual ones.'

Penrose's view of mathematics as an art form is borne out by his notebooks which are filled with drawings vaguely reminiscent of Leonardo da Vinci. 'Yes, it's true, my notebooks look like a lot of doodles,' he confesses, 'but these diagrams all represent something very concrete to me, even though they're things which would often be very difficult to express in terms of equations and so on. Once I've got the idea of what I'm trying to do, then finally I can represent it in a way which would be acceptable to other people . . . but there is this intermediate stage of thinking about things which is often a very visual one for me.'

His delight in puzzling over geometric shapes and algebraic tricks is not just restricted to reformulating Einstein. 'Often I toy with ideas just for fun. This is a puzzle I designed which for me shows how maths can create its own beauty . . .

'Here you start with just two different interlocking shapes in two-dimensional space, but as you fit them together the pattern never repeats itself because of the careful design of the pieces.

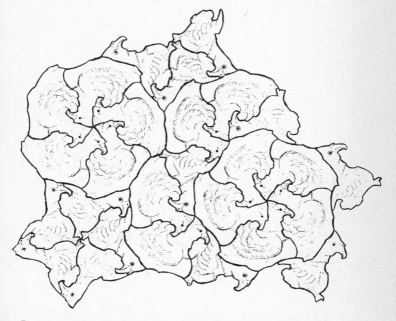

Penrose used mathematics to generate puzzles and designs. 'Here you start with two different interlocking shapes, but as you fit them together the pattern never repeats itself because of the design of the pieces.'

The complete pattern is generated by the mathematics ... you start with just simple shapes and the maths unexpectedly takes over and can produce an infinite but highly controlled variety of shape and pattern.

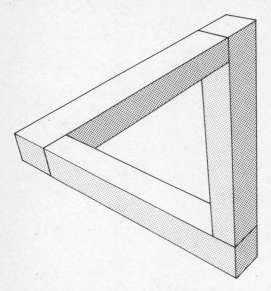

Penrose designed the 'Impossible Triangle'. Although each part seems consistent, the whole triangle is clearly inconsistent.

'If you get the design right for the basic ingredients, then the mathematics does the rest. So it's rather like twistor theory, where the twistors in a sense fit together to produce an infinite variety of physical structures and the space around them.'

Penrosian shapes and puzzles have been used by a tiling company and even by artists. In the 'Endless Staircase', the mathematical design is such that you can keep on climbing and never get to the top. This was adapted by Escher for his famous lithograph, 'Waterfall'. The water tumbles down the fall, and works its way around, apparently on a level, but suddenly, mysteriously, you find you're at the top as though the water has been flowing uphill. The essential feature about this is if you look at any small portion of the picture it is a perfectly consistent representation of something that could exist in space ... but if you look at the picture as a whole it does not make sense to us, although no part in itself is wrong. It

Escher's famous lithograph 'Waterfall'. This was based on a Penrosian mathematical design.

turns out that this kind of idea also plays a fundamental role in twistor theory.

Apart from the love of puzzles and beauty there is another quality which Penrose values in mathematical thinking. 'It's really essential, and it's something that one builds up with experience, that one should often be able to intuit results before you know for sure whether they are right or not. One can make a clear distinction between good intuition and prejudice . . . because you can finally check up and see whether the intuitive thoughts that you've had are right or not. If it is just prejudice, then you come unstuck because finally you would see that the proof does not hang together. Over the years the remarkable correspondence of twistor theory with physics has strengthened my views that mathematical intuition and elegance is really a very good guide, not just to do the maths itself, but also to truth in physics.'

Penrose does, however, regret one aspect of the twistor theory: that it has not yet proved to be directly useful to physicists. This keeps him continually struggling. 'The theory is not very strong on predictions I'm afraid. We play around with it and have good fun trying to rephrase things in different ways, coming up with some nice bits of mathematics and hoping that it's going to produce some deep insights. We would love to have predictions . . . like anyone else we would like to be able to say, look, we predict a new particle with such and such a mass, and go and look for it . . . and, lo and behold, there it is. That would be wonderful but we're not at that stage . . .'

Even though this hope always seems to lie tantalisingly just round the next corner, Penrose would not give up. 'For some strange reason even in my most depressed moods about the subject, and sometimes I have them, I don't feel the whole thing has been barking up the wrong tree. I feel there's enough in the mathematics . . . in the many surprising relations between the mathematics and the physics which have come to light, to ensure that at least we have something which is here to stay.

'You see, when you take Maxwell's equations and find that there is this other remarkably simple way of looking at them using twistors you ask, why should this be? If Maxwell's equations were just any old equations then that way of reformulating things so simply just wouldn't have been there, unless it was an amazing fluke . . .

'So really the theory has changed my view of nature, finding new instances of such a close unity between the real world and the mathematics. In a sense what appears to be physical reality all around us is deceptive . . . in my view, the deeper reality is actually the underlying abstract mathematics.'

Glossary

Ten, power of. To cope with the enormous range of scales, from the minute distances of the basic particles through to the distances of remote galaxies, physicists employ a convenient system of shorthand of multiplying by ten.

10^8 denotes that 10 is multiplied by 10 eight times, or means 100,000,000. It is commonly referred to as ten to the power of eight. A minus figure indicates that the power equals the number *divided* by that many multiplied tens, i.e. 10^{-8} denotes that 10 is divided by 10 eight times.

Angstrom, (Å), a unit of length, 10^{-10} metre or one ten millionth of a millimetre.

Bacteriophage/Phage, a virus which can only infect a bacteria, and which reproduces its genetic material inside that bacteria.

Bathymetry, measurement of depth, especially of the sea.

DNA or deoxyribonucleic acid. The fundamental genetic material in the nucleus of all cells, acting as the carrier of genetic information.

Electron, an elementary particle that is a constituent of all atoms and bears a negative charge.

Galaxy, a giant star system that is normally elliptical or spiral in structure. Each galaxy contains about 10^{11} stars. The Sun is just one of the stars in our own galaxy, the Milky Way. The Milky Way is 10^5 light years across and is millions of light years from its closest neighbour galaxy.

Hypothalmus, part of the forebrain containing nerve cells believed to control the sympathetic and parasympathetic nervous systems. Responsible for the regulation of vital processes such as the metabolism of fat, carbohydrate and water, sleep, body temperature and genital functions.

Kelvin, a unit of temperature. A temperature in Kelvin is equal to the temperature in Celcius (centigrade) plus 273.15°C. The units of interval in °K are equal to the units of interval in °C.

Lepton, a collective name for a class of elementary particles. Electrons, neutrinos and muons are leptons.

Light year, a unit of distance equal to the distance travelled by light in one year. It equals 5.8785×10^{12} miles.

Limbic system, area of the mid brain activated during motivated behaviour and emotional arousal.

Magnetometer, an instrument for measuring the strength of a magnetic field.

Nanosecond, one thousand millionth of a second, 10^{-9} seconds.

Nebula, a luminous area in space where a galaxy has formed or the constituent dust and gas clouds are coming together to form new stars.

Neutrino, an elementary particle that has zero mass and therefore to obey the laws of relativity must always travel at the speed of light.

Neutron, an elementary particle that is found in the nucleus of an atom. It has zero electric charge. Outside of the nucleus a neutron will decay into a proton, an electron and a neutrino.

Neutron star, is formed in a supernova explosion. The remains of the star collapse under gravity into such a dense state that matter is crushed to create an object that is only a few kilometres across but with the mass of a planet.

Pulsars, stars which emit regular pulses of radio energy. This pulsing signal is believed to come from a spinning neutron star.

Quantum mechanics, a mathematical theory that deals with physical phenomena on the very small scale, e.g. movement of electrons within the atom.

Quark theory, postulates that all elementary particles with the exception of leptons, *q.v.*, are made up from four quark particles. These elementary building blocks are hypothetical and have not been identified experimentally. They have been given the names *up*, *down*, *strange* and *charm* to identify them.

Ribosomes, particles in the cytoplasm of living cells which serve as the site for protein synthesis.

RNA or ribonucleic acid, found in the cytoplasm and nucleus of cells. The genetic information encoded in DNA is first of all copied into RNA before protein synthesis can occur.

Seismology, the study of earthquake phenomena.

Singularity, a, this is the point at which the known laws of physics break down. In a Black Hole matter is so condensed that nothing can escape, not even light, under the immense force of gravity. For the Earth to become a Black Hole it would need to be compressed to an object less than 3mm in size. At the centre of a Black Hole matter is destroyed in a singularity, a region where space and time wrap around in an infinite curve.

Supernova, at the end of a star's natural life the hydrogen fuel burns out and in a gigantic explosion – the supernova – the star collapses under its own gravitational field. This collapsed star is known as a White Dwarf, and if conditions are suitable it will continue to condense the remaining matter into a neutron star, *q.v.*